C000134930

ANDREW JOHNSTON

Primnoire

WARPWORDRESS
PUBLISHING

The manuscript, PRIMNOIRE, is dedicated to all on the autistic spectrum.

Contents

Acknowledgement

I would like to acknowledge Beverly L. Anderson. The opportunity to submit to Warrioress Publishing came up in a conversation with Beverly. And for that conversation, I am most grateful as it is the one conversation that will stay with me for all time.

Note to Readers

Trigger Warnings

Violence, blood, and some sexual content. Swearing.

Chapter One

⟨decorative flourish⟩

"We need to leave, Cole," Anna said, drawing up her hood, hiding the burns consuming half her face, "Grandfather will beg that I campaign if we're not quick."

She slipped, tucked, and buckled Cole's lengthy saddle strap, giving the storm bison a rub between his long silver hooked horns. She tapped two fingers to the pouch at her hip. The vial of deer lure sloshed inside. Anna applied the storm bison's bridle, hoping at such an early hour Williamton's people were asleep. It soothed her to walk under the waking sun with only the wind to upset the quiet morning.

Straw crunched as they left the dry-stone stable through a tall, aged set of doors. The final remnants of rain clouds manifested from Cole's nostrils and drifted out of them. Clumps of soggy straw clung to Anna's calf-length boots. She scratched behind the storm bison's ear. Cole nuzzled her cheek with his wet black nose.

She stifled a giggle at how cold it was against her cheek.

Anna looked up, narrowing her eye at the highest point of her home. The doors to her grandfather's balcony were shut, and the window beside it closed. *He hasn't woken yet,* Anna yawned, rolling her shoulders. Her lord grandfather had kept her up late, and all over Lamparien politics again. His passion for it was admirable, his care for others was truly boundless, but of late, with the need for a new prime or primnoire coming, his rants were growing repetitive.

She took in the homes beyond her own. Some homes were old and run down, built when her family founded Lampara and made its laws. The Brighton's had even secured binding trade agreements with each country bordering Lampara. She brushed a fly off her shoulder, putting aside history for the hunt ahead.

Anna and the storm bison passed a stretch of stables lining the length of her home's grounds. Banners swayed from the servant's quarters above, bearing her family sigil of a silver eight-pointed star on a field of red. Faint clattering and chatter came from the closest quarters. Its chimney bellowed smoke, reminding Anna to break her fast before leaving town.

Her eye rested upon the town's outer wall looming over the courtyard. Anna ran her fingers over the pale bear brooch pinning a flowing green cloak about her neck. She prayed the snow of last night hadn't melted. In recent years she'd found other means of tracking game, but two working eyes would have helped. The burnt skin sealing shut her right eye felt like rough leather.

The courtyard gate was shut, and she was certain the guard hadn't been changed. Anna stopped Cole for a moment giving the strap of her quiver a tug. It hung worn and frayed from Cole's saddle horn. The black falcon feather fletching of its arrows hissed across her fingers. She requested the fletching of red goose a week earlier, but her grandfather had forgotten to order their crafting. He lacked the patience for hunting she possessed and wasn't one for nature unless duty demanded it. And with her great passion for hunting growing with time he refused to deny Anna her happiness. Anna swallowed, rubbing her brow, giving her bow a firm tug, finding it secure.

The gate was barred with long thick boards across heavy iron hooks. Snoring whispered between the gate's narrow bars. Anna giggled. *Grandfather will have them scrubbing pots.* Strain ran across her face making it taut like fabric over a honey jar as she slid each board out. Dirt hissed and tiny stones popped as she dragged one board and then the second off to the side.

Peering up one last time to her grandfather's balcony, she saw a chambermaid open its doors then spin about and disappear. Anna eased the gates wide open, the dew of morning glistening across the grass beyond them. Cole's hind leg raised for her to mount him. She pressed a boot to it, mounting him like they practiced. The old storm bison, she thought, was the finest friend she had ever made. She kissed her pale bear brooch and asked the goddess it served for a smooth and peaceful day.

* * *

The mountain's narrow path always felt like a balancing act. Cole hugged the mountain side with his mass as they made slow progress from the forest encircling it. The day had been long, longer from Anna dragging her largest deer yet. She groaned, lifting her arms. They felt like jelly as she rested them, firming her grip on the reins. Her kill hung end to end over her old friend's thickly muscled shoulders and dark silver hump. She caught the waning sunlight against her cheeks, cursing for being out so late. With her hometown of Williamton hidden beyond the light, a scowl crossed her lips for the deer's cunning. Grass hissed underfoot once they reached the mountain's bottom.

There was a sudden slowing once the ground leveled off. Anna leaned past her kill, to find her friend panting. Her lips curled into a frown. Cole let out a low groan, his clouds thinning, sending spirits of rain.

"Come on, old friend," she said, rubbing his side. "You're too brave and swift to stop now."

She urged Cole to the trail they used before. His pace increased, and clouds thickened with her encouragement. Lightning clapped in the distance, jarring her from her bent position before she could draw in the scent of wet grass. Rain drops from Cole's clouds tapped the grass as the sound of lightning faded. The coming night no longer bothered Anna. Her nerves smoothed.

Trees not yet ready for winter clung to their leaves, giving some shade. Scurrying rabbits broke the near quiet, wind shifted the branches. A light, almost relaxed feeling resonated when she'd return from a hunt, like rolling in fresh snow. Anna wished she could bring the wood's sounds home.

Anna smiled, running her fingers over the thick winter fur of her kill. She hoped if the servants cooked it well, her lord grandfather may join her on a hunt. She licked her lips, already tasting the tenderness of the deer.

She pictured him upon his esant, in riding cloak, flying low with the wind upon the swift bird, and no word of what troubled Lampara on his lips. Sharing time with him in the woods mattered more to her than who governed. No lecture on a prime's ten-year governance or them proving worthy of being in charge for so long.

The main path was in sight, all the snow of last night gone, leaving behind damp smells and darkened leaves. She was still at a distance from Williamton. The town had renamed itself, honoring her grandfather after he saved her from the dragon. *I had wanted it for more than just a mount.* Anna grimaced and then reflected on Cole's silver hooked horns. Storm Bisons held near boundless energy in their youth, but when she purchased Cole, he already had been ancient in her mind. A smile crossed her lips. A dragon wasn't kind like a storm bison anyway. Dropping her hand to Cole's reins, she gripped them fiercely then snapped them. They made it to a good speed as the wind bathed her cheeks and carried Cole's storm clouds into the—

Flames tore through Williamton's rooftops. Anna yanked at Cole's reins, dirt churning, racing until they came to a stop. Fear gripped her throat to see the towering smoke grow thicker and higher with each second. The wheat field before her filled her nostrils with a raw, earthy scent, tainted by smoke. The small quiet town beyond the field had been her home since the age of fifteen, keeping her safe with its high walls and thick gates. It was an oasis for travelers amongst the legions of forest making up Lampara's Greethumb region.

Dark clouds drifted northward at great speed, lashing out with lightning bolts. Pouring out of the north gate at great speed was a man upon a mass of black. Trailing behind him like a tail were men in evergreen and scarlet armor.

Anna jabbed her muddied boot into Cole's side. The

old storm bison bolted onward. She narrowed her gaze, clenching teeth, finding they possessed too much a lead to follow. Anna pinned back her long shimmering black hair with a thin metal stake. The riders grew clearer with the speed of Cole's powerful legs. Their leader rode a black storm bison and whoever he was, only great wealth could grant someone a beast that rare. *Crack*. Lightning struck beside him. Anna gasped but the man crouched, jabbing his heel into the bison's side.

She shook her head at the thought of how aroused a black storm bison would have to be to create lightning. Toward the distant woods ahead of the riders there was no other storm bison. Without a source of motivation Anna wasn't sure how the black storm bison created its lightning.

Cries of pain filled her ears as she neared the west gate, but the town's thick wall should have made that impossible. Anna's senses heightened when she drew near danger or became stressed. She released a breath, hoping this time what drove her mad may be of use. *For once.*

There were no guards manning the west gate's towers. Anna moved on with the cries fading from her ears. She urged Cole to the north gate where the riders made their hasty exit. The gates themselves were branded by names of past citizens in copper. It kept the memory of those dead or moved on alive. She rested a hand to her chest, remembering her parents' names on the south gate. *I wish I'd have known them.*

The height and smooth surface of the town's walls made the north gate hard to spot. Anna licked her lips, hesitating where part of her lips had healed shut. Drawing in a breath, the town was like a barrel full of kindling, its home of wood and dry-stone. Another scream struck her ears, as if someone was being chased. She reached for her quiver, counting its arrows, eyeing the way ahead for the north gate. *30.* Anna held on to hope the group of armored soldiers had left and that her hearing had just deceived her.

She passed through the north gate, smoke consuming it like a foggy narrow gorge. It teased her nostrils as she swiped at its unrelenting gray. Flames stretched out ahead of her, torturing homes and shops the deeper she went. The trading post groaned from her left, its weakened timbers cracked and bent.

"Grandfather," Anna called. Footsteps answered, clopping swiftly and close. A man clutching scrolls to his chest burst forth from the smoke. The trading post released a final creak, crashing in a heap. "Norman? Where is Lord William Brighton?"

Norman spun with his hair a mess and ash on his cheeks. Amongst the chaos around them, he bowed to her, an ink bottle slipped from his pocket, smashing amongst the dirt. His lips trembled as he stood erect.

"He's guiding people out of the south gate, Lady Anna."

Relief filled her belly like cool water. Amongst the smoke, Norman Tilt, accountant to Williamton, bowed again. She secured Cole's reins around the horn of his saddle and slid down from his back. Her cloak caught on his thick gray coat, crackling with static.

"Thank you for this news," she said. Her heart quickened at his finely tailored red doublet. He looked upon her, blue eyes redden by the smoke. "Take Cole to where grandfather has led the others. Do you know why those riders came?"

Norman stuffed his scrolls in a saddlebag, straining to pull himself up. The blacksmith's forge belched out a great blast of flame, loosening his grip. Anna flinched as he clamored for balance. Anna held Cole close, his bleating boomed within her ears. She stroked his head, feeling the storm bison's clouds rush over her cheeks. Cole stomped in place. Norman hugged against his mass, gaging at the deer's open belly over the bison's shoulders. The storm bison's clouds grew enormously and released a torrent of rain. The droplets quenched flames lingering across the collapsed trading post.

* * *

"I don't know why they came," said Norman, swallowing hard, readying Cole's reins, "but I do know how we can save Williamton"

"Are you certain?" Anna said, remembering the accountant's struggle to mount Cole. "Maybe you should leave by the south gate and—"

Snap went the storm bison's reins. Anna leapt back, stumbling close to the blacksmith's shop. Its heat and flames jarred her memory, adding haste to her steps. Anna collapsed to one knee, gasping, her fear of fire consumed her. Great canals of sweat ran down her back. She peered over her shoulder, finding her cloak was on fire. She ripped its pale bear brooch off, holding tight the white stoned guardian. She staggered to her feet, clasping the broach close to her chest. At a distance rain pattered upon the road, striking homes. Below the rising nimbus clouds, Norman sent Cole down a narrow alley.

The sky filled swiftly with clouds sending rain over what burned. An inn nearby Anna wished had seen more business this past autumn began to burn. Visitors of her grandfather had stayed there, but in recent weeks the inn began housing fewer and fewer guests. Smoke billowed from the roof and lower levels. She moved closer, hearing no commotion from its windows. The smoke jabbed at her eye, stinging it before a sold sign tore away from under the building's timber awning. Wind sent it spinning into flames, devouring it in seconds.

Clouds gathered over the inn, their rain falling with great force. The inn's flames hissed, vanishing, the roof like a marble of black and brown. She sucked in a breath, wishing Gwen Mindal had kept the town's oldest residence. *Perhaps, whoever she sold it to will not want it now.* Eyed the structure once again and then drew in her lip.

She grew weary of Cole. His breathing had become more rampant once reaching Williamton. Her kill had evaded them over rough terrain and was still tied over her friend's back. She pressed the broach to her chest, whispering a prayer to Simdorn for her friend. She stuffed the guardian away and turned her head west over town.

"I must find where those screams came from before it's too late."

Chapter Two

A damp and muddy path stretched out behind Norman. Ahead of him, lit by the remaining sunlight, revealed Williamton's two main roads. He had been coming from the east end of town where the fires began an hour earlier. His heart pounded almost in rhythm with Cole's heavy panting. Gray swirling clouds blasted from the storm bison's thick black nostrils. The ground before Norman churned, mud sucking at Cole's hooves as they road onward. Norman chewed his lip; rain drops raced down his brow. A grinding pain filled his chest and flicked Cole's reins. *Damn my cowardice.* The moment had been there, he should have told her. Norman eyed carts blackened, collapsed, and burning. Anna would never forgive him for his silence. He had heard what wasn't meant for his ears. *Damn myself for being caught,* he thought, swiping as a scroll slipped from a saddlebag.

Clenching his teeth, Norman wished that the scoundrel with his long thick chin whiskers had refused his lordship.

He wished he would have returned later for the scrolls. As the sun sank, and his way grew darker, there was no use traipsing back to the past. There was no use wallowing in regret.

Norman pressed his legs tight to Cole's sides. He yanked at the saddle horn as his buttocks slid to the gray fur behind. The saddle was far narrower than a horses, and from where he used to live, a corbraswift's dome saddle required no use of balance. He'd never ridden a storm bison until today.

A rush of bile filled his throat, catching sight of crusted blood from where the deer had been gutted. The deer flopped up and down on Cole's back. Blood leapt from its belly, tapping, and running down the storm bison's horns. He sent the storm bison east where the flames roared and grew worse. The house Norman had long lived within rested at the neighborhood's center. His heart felt lighter to know Samuel had been guarding the south gate before the fires began. Samuel had taken him in and taught him to do things in measurements as an accountant would a man's savings. Norman cracked Cole's reins keeping to covering quadrants of the town.

A bad taste formed again in his mouth of bacon and milk he realized had been sour too late. Norman spat and rummaged through Anna's saddlebags for a knife to remove the deer. Norman felt the leather of a hilt and withdrew his hand, ignoring the loud gurgle of his stomach. *I will not cut loose what Anna worked hard for.* He re-buttoned the bags, snapping the storm bison's reins, turning him west.

Clouds swirled and gathered as he passed homes and shops. Some were engulfed in flame, others crashed and boomed as if the rain had given a final nudge. Norman flicked Cole's reins, turning up every alley. Women and children slipped past them narrowing things, slowing him and the storm bison. Screams rang out as people scrambled from doorways. "Hurry everyone," he urged. "Head for the south gate."

Shutters crashed open as man barreled through it. He scrambled to his feet and vanished amongst the smoke.

Norman pulled up on Cole's reins slowly. The poor beast was panting harder than ever, his clouds combusted before they could rise. They'd made it to the town's center. Rain battled with the roar of flames for supremacy. Williamton was gray in places with roofs up and strong, while others were black, collapsed, churning up great plumes of smoke. Toward the north, west and south rain clouds drifted and gathered, releasing thick droplets. The wind shifted the storms ever so. Norman held on to hope that was just a brief breeze, for clouds of a storm bison were easily carried. Another breeze rustled his hair as he climbed off Cole, slipping the beast's long black reins down with him.

At a distance people gathered beyond the south gate, huddled close to the woods. Amongst them Lord William Brighton sat upon his esant in a leather tunic and flowing cloak. A long sword hung from his back, its silver pommel shaped as an eight-pointed star. He raised his thick eyebrows at Norman. The years hadn't been kind to his lordship. Where once he sat tall with his red whiskered beard cut short, now he hunched, with bushy, prickly chin hairs.

"Norman Tilt." His lordship jerked his esant's reins. The long swift bird strutted up next to Norman, running its thin tongue across its sharp hooked beak. "Why are you in possession of my granddaughter's mount? And where the hell is she?"

Norman bowed to Lord William as he watched his lordship

13

survey the town. His lordship's esant possessed fierce glowing eyes. The feathers of its head were crimson and jetted back like talons tipped in black. Lord William narrowed his gaze on Norman, turning up his nose, grimacing.

"Lady Anna is still within the town's walls, my lord," said Norman.

Lord William raised an eyebrow, his lips trembled for a moment, retreating to a solid, firm line. His lordship huffed, snapping the esant's wide decorative red reins. Norman yanked Cole forward. They stumbled out of the lord's way as the esant squawked, its razor tipped talons gathered into a sprint, tearing dirt and grass.

"Remain with Cole and the townsfolk," Lord William called over his shoulder. "I will find her."

"What will you tell her of—"

Norman fell silent as Lord William took to the air. He pressed the storm bison's reins to his back and clamped his mouth. Amongst the townsfolk mounted men in scarlet plated armor and evergreen chain mail surveyed the people. Upon their breastplates a badge rested, one of an eight-pointed star of house Brighton within the jaws of Lampara's country sigil of a silver horse shaded in black. The horse seemed to clamp down hard upon the star. One word would have placed him in trouble with both Lord Brighton and the prime.

Cole huffed, easing down, dropping with a thud. Norman knelt beside him, eyeing Williamton. Flames vanished with the winds and speed of Lord William's esant. The bird was barely a blur to his eyes, and then, all at once the bird vanished.

"I hope he is honest with her," Norman stroked a dark gray furry patch on Cole's immense face, removing his scrolls. The storm bison dozed, blurry eyed, "as I should have been. She deserves as much for coming home to such terror."

Chapter Three

⁓⚬⚬⁓

Sweat poured down her cheeks, the west half of town a burning orange and black. Encroaching behind Anna, her storm bison's clouds stretched and manifested, over taking her steps. The air filled with rain, meeting the coming darkness as dampness reached her nostrils. She stopped short to the west gate, panting, running a fist across her brow. With the coming storm clouds Anna's hopes rose, soon the flames hissed and vanished. Faint cries caught her attention. She scanned every home, focusing hard through cracking of foundation stones and the downpour of… Her eye widened, catching sight of where the cries had come from. Anna dashed with all her speed, the screams growing louder.

Sweat blurred her vision as a mother and child raced out onto the street. Their home crashed, reaching out with a tongue of flames. Clouds overshadowed it, rain ripped at the timbers and quieted the flames. She pressed a hand to her pale bear broach nestled in a pouch on her belt. *Thank you, Simdorn, for sparing them.* Pounding snatched at her senses as she turned to find the goddess's temple before her. At its very peak Simdorn stood atop its bell tower, strangled by a serpent-like streak of blackening smoke. The goddess, wreathed in blackness, had long red locks, her face smooth and ageless within the open jaws of a bear. About her slender figure white robes hung, draping just short of the bell below Simdorn herself.

Anna's heart went into a sprint. The temple's diamond framed windows glowed a flaring yellow. The entrance between the pale bear statues supporting a crescent moon were chained shut. Anna searched for her knife, trembling, exhaling to center herself. Never had she picked a lock like some thief in her grandfather's books, but it was worth a try. *Dammit!* The knife was far off in Cole's saddlebags.

Pounding rattled the temple's doors, overshadowed by the pleas of priests. A thin shadow ran across her sight. Anna slipped the long, thin stake from her hair as she dashed to the temple. Her hair tumbled within the folds of her hood. Heat ran over the dark brown of her hunting leathers as she snatched the lock.

"I'm here," Anna said.

"Please free us," said a priestess amongst the roaring flames. Her voice was shrill and weak among the priests that pounded and bellowed for help. "Men came for her as we worshiped, but we refused to give her up. They set fire to Simdorn's house."

Anna wanted to ask more but stuck the stake into the lock. *What madness is it to set a town ablaze for one person?* The stake was thin and sturdy, navigating the lock with precision the more she tightened her grip. Anna twisted and pushed, her teeth clenched, the lock clicking and tapping. Her grip lessened, every finger taking a turn on the lock's metal. She composed words to reassure the goddess's servants, but nothing came of her efforts. Such madness of the chains sealing shut the temple doors was a ritual begun three days previous when Simdorn's priests wished for unbothered prayer. *Should I learn who they protect, this man will owe them his life.*

Heavy humming shattered the din of flames and caving roofs. The light from the sun went dark for seconds, then reappeared as shapes passed overhead. Anna wiped her sweat and tears away. The cries tormenting her senses went silent. She dropped both lock and stake. A long painful groan sounded from the temple roof. A rush of wind erased flames upon nearby homes, throwing back her hood. Hope rekindled in her chest. The sound of crowing came from the only bird she knew to be so swift. The esant's talons touchdown, snapping stones, dust filling the air as it settled upon the road. It was longer than two carriages. Its wings hummed, settling as her grandfather slipped from its back.

"Why did you not leave with Norman, Anna?" he roared. His esant flashed its crimson head, blinking its bright glaring eyes with lightning speed. Her grandfather brushed her aside. "Out of the way. I have lost the damnable key."

She pressed herself against the hind leg of a pale bear guardian. Lord William drew his sword, raised his brow to the crescent moon and whispered a swift prayer. *"Forgive an old lord's foolishness. Grant me strength in the days ahead, oh goddess."* He drew in a deep breath and faced the chains sealing the temple. Anna shook her head to regain focus. Lord William swung and severed the chains. Sparks hit and hissed against the temple's brick work as he drew back his sword. Anna eyed the crescent moon, thanking Simdorn for sending her—

"Why do you stand there, granddaughter?" he said, pointing his sword at the chains. "Help me in freeing Simdorn's servants."

The screams rose again but Lord William quieted them with assurance, speaking of their plight being over soon. Anna tugged at the chains, bracing against the stinging heat. The core of her palms radiated pain swiftly through her muscles. Her grandfather helped remove the first layer from the long brass door handles. He pulled swiftly, both hands retreated then grasped again for another chain link. It seemed his reflexes hadn't been lessened since she was a child. Even bent by age, his height nearly doubled her own as he switched places along the chains with her.

Anna untwisted the final chain then gave her grandfather a nod. He yanked it free, spreading his cloak wide, resembling a nutsnatcher's fleshy wings. They yanked open the temple doors, stumbling behind the pale bears. Shouts lead a stampede of priests in robes blacker than the smoke inside the temple. A crack and snap sent Anna trailing at the cloak tales of her lord grandfather. The temple folded in on itself, coughing up a wave of ash that consumed the white marble of Simdorn's guardians.

"Go swiftly to the south gate, Priests of Simdorn." Her grandfather turned back to her. His bushy gray eyebrows knitted together. His steel blue eyes narrowed. "Where have you been all this day? And why was Cole with Norman Tilt?"

"I… Norman rode upon Cole to put out the flames with—"

Crash. Across the way a home collapsed. Anna fell silent before she eyed the esant.

19

"Can we leave and find them?" Anna bit her lip. "Please."

Fear crept down her spin, teaming with the heat and the slow darkening of the day. Lord William looked down his nose at her. He sighed, sheathing his long sword.

"Let's go then, I can guess where you have been by the blood on your boot."

Anna eyed the collapsed temple once they both climbed upon the esant's back. The priestess's words troubled her mind. Her grandfather tugged at the esant's thick red reins, emblazoned with their family's sigil, the silver eight-pointed star. The esant took off at a sprint, wind whipped her hair and hood back. Anna wrapped her arms tight about Lord William's waist as the town blurred. The esant lashed out its wings, launching them into the air. She felt weightless for a moment, clouds brushing against her cheeks, the sun resembling a ripe fruit in the distance. Her happiness returned, storing away all she had seen. It fled at the dash of ash upon her grandfather's face.

"We are away from the flames I know remain a fear of yours, sweet girl," he said.

Lord William's words were tampered down by the heavy rain. All the town was under gray, swirling clouds, narrow openings through them fueled her worry. Anna bit her lip. Cole was nowhere to be found. She wrapped her arms tighter about her grandfather's waist. He grunted, patting her hand then strengthened his grip on the esant's reins. Her eye searched every alley. A horse rushed east, making her believe it Cole for a moment by its gray fur. Her mind raced to whether Norman had driven the old storm bison too hard. She swallowed and refused to believe her worst fears.

"I must ask you something," Anna said.

The esant banked right until its wing beats brought them over an open field beyond the south gate. She strained for a sign of Cole or Norman but again found neither.

"A priestess said the riders wanted a girl," said Anna, "but none of them gave her up."

Lord William slouched. His posture resembled a fishhook. His face was unreadable by the relentless wind in her eye.

"They were here for you."

Anna gasped.

"Why?"

The rain slowly subsided as her fear quickened, chilling her like a winter breeze. She couldn't remember ever doing anything wrong. At least nothing that would drive someone to set Williamton ablaze.

"Three months remain until a new prime, and primnoire will earn governorship of Lampara. Prime Luther has done more ill than good since coming to power again." Lord William grinned. A crowd appeared at the forest's edge. "He has two sons of his own campaigning." He grumbled, snapping the esant's reins. "The lads must desire to remove any rival to the position. You are trained well enough, and our family name inspires—"

Anna rested her hand to his shoulder and squeezed it.

"I know where your words go," she said. "I... I can't do it alone... I can't live up to the Brighton name."

"You can, Anna." said Lord William. His voice heightened; worry removed its usual depth as he began their descent. "Our family founded this country and can save it." he sighed. "I'm sorry. We have spoken of this on many occasion. I know what the dragon did to your face has robbed you of the courage to see the world beyond the woods. But I know you have

21

strength, Anna. You need only put it into a good cause."

Her lips trembled. She shook her head of the memory, grabbing at her hood to hide within it but the wind was in full grip of it.

"I made my choices that day, Grandfather, and I will forever regret them," said Anna. Tears ran over her lips, bitter like the elixir her grandfather's physician provided when her burns grew too painful. "The woods are the only world I wish to know. And though you want me to continue our family's legacy my answer remains… No."

Her grandfather let out a low hum, returning focus to flying. His silence left no place for her thoughts to find comfort. She gasped and pointed. A smile stretched across her face, catching sight of Norman knelt beside Cole. And from what Anna could see the storm bison was asleep. The grass grew brighter and greener, closer. The esant grabbed at the ground and caution vanished from her mind. Anna leapt onto the ground.

"Cole! Norman!" Anna cried. Her legs begged to give way before she tucked and rolled up in seconds. "Thank the goddess you both are safe."

Anna embraced Norman, his doublet a darker shade of red than earlier. His short chestnut hair a soggy mess like the scrolls under his arms.

"I pushed him for as long as I could," said Norman, turning to the deep labored breaths of the storm bison. "But he needs rest and I'm unable to remove the deer."

The esant cawed, followed by her grandfather's low angered breaths. The conversation of campaigning wasn't over. Anna felt guilt heave itself onto her shoulders but shrugged it off. She caught sight of the saddlebag her knife was in. She unbuttoned it, slipped free her knife, and cut the rope. Her shoulder went numb before the second rope brushed her fingers.

"Anna Brighton!" her grandfather said, pulling her around to face him. "The priests of our fair goddess knew where you would be. They … protected you."

He squeezed her shoulder so tight Anna dropped to her knees.

"Will you make such a sacrifice a waste?" he growled, releasing her. "I require an answer."

Anna rubbed the pain from her shoulder, rising to her feet. Williamton's people were out of earshot, which raised her spirits. Any misstep would go unheard but there was still Norman.

"I cannot do it alone, Grandfather." Her face tensed with rage. Her hold on the knife tightened. "I… I cannot thank you enough for your lessons, Grandfather, but I am far too damaged. No one wants a primnoire like me."

Turning the knife in her hand she cut the second rope. The deer's fur hissed against Cole's, thudding upon the ground. She stuffed the robes in a saddlebag, grabbed her kill by its brow tines and dragged. Sweat met their smoothness, slipping, the points dug into her palms. She was a hunter, one with ties to Lampara's first governing family. But after coming of age at fifteen and the poor choice of a dragon. To have authority, a role in her people's lives… It was all for another Anna whose senses didn't drive her mad under pressure. *And no one will follow a woman who is incomplete.*

"I'll campaign at your side, Lady Anna," said Norman, his tone firm with confidence. "I've learned much about Lampara as an accountant."

Dryness tormented Anna's throat. Her lips fumbled with one another, itching to thank Norman. She shuddered, resting a hand to her face. Lord William grasped the accountant's shoulders with his gnarled, tested hands and uttered what words finally came to Anna's mind.

"You're not a fighter, Tilt, and that is a key requirement of a prime," said Lord William. "Though I must thank you for your courage on this day. Williamton would be gone without it."

"I'll learn to fight, and Lampara's finances will always be balanced." Norman looked at her. His eyes were reddened from the smoke, yet they were soft. Anna could only return his gaze with apprehension. "I can be of great help to you, my lady."

"I appreciate your offer, Norman," Anna said, "but leading Lampara isn't where a burned woman belongs."

Anna focused on the town for a moment. The forest's tall pines peaked over its walls and between its homes. Echoes of the black storm bison's lightning met her ears. She caught sight of its clouds, though the evening sky soon made them invisible.

"This deer was to convince you to take up hunting, Grandfather." Anna dragged it before him, rising, strain fleeing down her back. "Give it to our people if you find its meat not to your liking."

She pulled a small handful of berries from a pouch on her belt, dropping to one knee beside Cole. Neither man said a word as the storm bison ate. Cole gobbled the berries. He licked his lips and rubbed his wet nose against her cheek. She smiled. Her friend stood upright as Anna climbed atop him. She sought to ride north to town, but pressure closed fast upon her ankle. Anna looked to find her grandfather, brow furrowed and knuckles white about her ankle.

"You had best reconsider your actions," he said, pointing beyond to the priests draped in their heavy, layered robes. "They will not forget your unwillingness to repay their silence. I shall not forget."

Her heart retreated into the depths of her stomach. Lord William narrowed his eyes, reminding her of their discussion within the sky. She formed her lips into a solid line, releasing a firm breath.

"I have considered my actions, Grandfather."

He released her foot, folding his arms.

"And?"

"I'll do what I am best at. I'll go on a hunt."

Chapter Four

Anna shut her eye tight against the chilling northern breeze, countered by the heat of quieted flames. She feigned a smile. Being half blind had at least one use. It kept hidden much of the destruction tormenting her heart. Her eye lost sight when the healing went wrong, forcing the eyelid shut forever. Her grandfather's physician offered to perform surgery but at such a time everything scared her. Night was upon Williamton. The fading embers of the west half of town prevented total darkness. Cole's clouds were gone from the sky. The air was musty and doused with the scent of mud and burnt debris.

She patted her friend's massive hump, his breaths labored and deep. Faint remnants of her kill's blood met her nose, crusted beyond her hand in thin streaks across the storm bison's fur. He lengthened his strides, ignoring his fatigue, keeping the drive within him going. She rubbed his side admiring him for it, peering up at her hometown.

Anna sucked in a breath, there was no use ignoring what

damage her quarry left behind. Homes deep enough into neighborhoods stood tall, their roofs solid and peaked. But the ones meeting Williamton's two main roads were collapsed and blackened. Their timber roofs lay in heaps, protruding from dry-stone windows. Voices breathed out from alleys of those venturing to salvage what could be. A tear ran down her cheek as they waved, then went about salvaging what remained of their lives. She waved, hoping to reassure them and herself, swallowing her sadness.

"Neither grandfather nor Norman must have mentioned my refusal," she said, keeping her voice low. "Williamton would expect me to campaign after aiding the priests."

Carts littered the road home, smoking or collapsed inward. Hoof prints crossed from one part of the town to another. Norman had covered much ground. And though his offer was tempting, his ability to ride unquestionable, Anna found accepting it too much to handle. She opened a saddle bag and tied her hair back with a length of cord.

Anna kept Cole at a slow pace, avoiding an assortment of deep muddy patches toward the north gate. Faint echoes of the black storm bison's lightning met her ears. She drew her gaze to the woods its rider sent it to. The reasoning for its rider and soldiers was clear, but setting the town ablaze with its lightning made no sense. *Especially with no lady bison to entice it.*

Once beyond the north gate Anna took in Williamton once more, aiding everyone in rebuilding crossed her mind, but it would have to wait. *Will you make such a sacrifice a waste?* Anna shook her head. Coin was needed to travel and gain support throughout Lampara.

"And grandfather would give it to me without question."

She focused on the south gate. Darkness kept it hidden except for the torches upon either watchtower.

She tugged at her bow, counting the arrows in her quiver. Anna slouched in her saddle and rubbed her brow of more sweat. Her grandfather may have trained her to wield a sword, throw a knife and strike true with an arrow but to kill a man was different. Anna put a heel to Cole's side, sending him into a trot. Storm clouds raced over his cheeks, the task ahead encompassing her mind. They needed to move faster but to delay the death to come felt right. *I'm a hunter, not a soldier.* Her attention fell to Cole's struggle to keep pace. Delaying what needed to be done by allowing her friend rest felt right, except under the circumstances impossible.

"You'll have a long rest, Cole." She patted his side. "I promise."

Will you make such a sacrifice a waste? She ground her teeth. Her grandfather's words churned over and over in her mind, but it did not mean they needed heeding.

"I will find those soldiers." Drawing her hood over her head tight, raindrops tapped its surface. "And if I am able, I'll stop them from telling Luther's sons I am alive."

Anna snapped Cole's reins and felt his immense legs propel them up a steep grassy hill. He blazed through bushes, crushing roots and small stones. Williamton was gone in moments as all her focus went to listening. Once she had come to a field, the thought of killing a man sent a flash of heat over her cheeks. *It must be done.* Tugging at the point of her hood she prayed to Simdorn for a swift end to this adventure and a return to a quiet life.

* * *

The lightning had long since fallen silent, and her nervousness slowed from a jabbing to a prickle. Anna sniffed, the scent of charred meat ebbing in her direction. It meant the riders were close, relaxed, and she hoped in a mood to make a deal to leave her hometown alone. Rain droplets clung to her hood as she narrowed her focus. A faint chuckle forced Anna to slow Cole several feet before a clearing. There was a divide at its center too wide for the old storm bison at her side to overcome. Anna rested a hand to Cole's shoulder and sighed. Their hunt was over, and she didn't want him hurt.

She spotted a tiny flicker of orange and red through the crack of a downed tree. She slipped off Cole's back, removing her bow and quiver. The strap of her quiver held tightly to her person. Her bow's string twanged as she strung it.

She crept to the divide's edge, jagged rocks littering it down to a muddy bottom. Anna leaned back, gripping her bow firmly. Twigs snapped and bushes rustled. What star and moon light escaping the clouds highlighted a man stumbling toward her. Nocking and drawing, she trained her eye on him. He was within such easy range he might as well have been standing still. Plated armor protected only his legs. The soldier wore a yellow tunic with brown laces on its collar. Over his heart within a spade shaped badge was a black badger. His head was shaven but for a tuft of red hair down the middle of his scalp. He froze in place; a twitch in his upper lip rustled his long thick chin whiskers.

"Who the fuck are you?" He belched, hovering a hand over a bollocks knife at his hip. "Can't I piss in peace?" His eyes grew to the size of apples. "Lower that thing before I call my men."

Strain ran up Anna's arm, pinching her shoulder. The

fletching chafed against her cheek with her eye narrowed down the arrow's shaft. Anna adjusted until the arrow met between his eyes.

"You tried to burn down Lord William's town," she said. "Why is his granddaughter a threat to Prime Luther's sons?"

The soldier drew in his lower lip and bit it, his hand danced slowly over the knife.

"Lady Anna is of age," said the soldier, "and by law our prime can't govern a third time. Those boys need all the help they can get."

Two lights rose from the distant fire, meandering toward them. Anna brought her attention back to the soldier, swallowing. Every muscle strained to keep her bow drawn.

"You best hurry girl," he said. "My men travel in pairs like good little soldiers."

"Let us," she said. "Let us strike a bargain."

"Oi." A deep voice bellowed from the trees. "Where you at, Lord Barden?"

"What do you have in mind?" Lord Barden smirked. "Hurry up now."

Her arms shook in sync, being anchored for so long had never been something Anna was used to. Being alive may keep all she cared for in danger, but if she could persuade this stranger to leave, there might be hope. Shouts and stomps of the smirking lord's men banged at her ears. She shook it off.

"What if I convince her not to campaign?" said Anna. "And you can tell the prime that she is dead."

Lord Barden lunged. Anna released. Flesh and clothing tore releasing blood from the lord's shoulder as his blade hissed overhead. Anna rolled to her feet, dashing for the woods. The lord whistled. It pierced the air and rattled her senses. Twenty men at most burst forth into the moon light with torches in hand. Their stallions flooded the tree line as the thunder of hoof strikes kicked up dirt.

"You won't make it far girl." Lord Barden groaned. "And we'll be paying the town another visit."

Nocking another arrow, Anna squinted through shadow and moonlight. Horse after horse leapt the gap as she sank deep into the overgrowth. She darted behind a thick pine, sweat enveloping her cheeks. Her every breath fled for a safer quarter. She glared at her bow. Anna thought back to her grandfather's rants, what these men wished upon her violated campaign law.

Yells and hoof strikes drew closer. An immense wall of storm clouds charged toward Anna. Dark marble-shaped eyes gave way to Cole's snout. Fear for her friend warred within her. She drew back a heavy breath with her bowstring, released, then took off at a sprint.

Thump. The arrow cut through a horse's neck, toppling it. Its rider cried, crushed, the torch within his hand snuffed out. Anna sent another arrow between the steel mouth shield and arrowhead helmet of another. Men shrieked like frightened nutsnachters, drawing swords, turning every which way.

Sharpness ran up her arm as she released a fifth arrow. Her wrist guard hurtled into the brush as pain lanced through her arm. Anna cursed through gritted teeth. She wanted to rub where it hurt, to hide once again. But with her senses in torment, and Cole drawing near, she cracked another arrow to her bow.

The storm bison brushed against her back, then raised his leg. Anna climbed upon her friend, hanging her quiver over his saddle horn. Anna sent Cole into an arc around the men, leaning low, releasing more arrows. Upon finger count ten arrows remained. The soldiers gathered their wits and followed, wielding torches and swords in combined rage.

The clouds parted and, in her rush to conserve arrows, silence fell. Anna pulled up on Cole's reins, reached, but found she must have removed her hood earlier. Her lips parted to draw in breath, but it left before touching her tongue. The men remained rooted like the towering sentinels behind them, looking to one another, pointing and laughing. Resting a hand to her cheek, all of it struck her emotions so hard tears fled her eye, growing in number. She fumbled to find another arrow. The laughter stole her courage and blinded every thought. Anna grew dizzy upon her friend's back, strength fled from her muscles like a pair of frightened doves. Footsteps followed labored breaths until Lord Barden stood amongst his men.

"What's all this?" He clutched his arm like it was ready to fall from his body. "Surround this girl this instant you…"

"Go ahead, my lord," said Anna, begging deep down for the clouds to cover the moon and hide her in darkness. "Have your laugh before carrying out your orders."

The lord's lips remained a solid, unwavering line. He snarled then barked an order for silence. Her bow arm fell to her side, strength to hold on fleeing with her courage. The weapon felt as if it had tripled in weight. Cole huffed and snorted at the men the closer they came. There was no way to hide anymore. She could see within their eyes a boundless humor even with their cruelty silenced. *I must escape for Grandfather.* Anna drew Cole back, his mass striking an immense oak as he snarled at the closest man.

"I know who you are now." The lord called his men to halt.

"If not for your hood earlier, I'd have remembered you," Lord Barden pulled a tiny chain from under his tunic. A pendant dangled from his blood tipped fingers. It was a "W" encircled by a ring of storm bison, esants, horses, and dragons, "I once worked for the Wayne Trading company. I… I sold you that dragon."

A cold sweat poured down her brow like a smashed egg against a rock. The once well-mannered man who had accepted her grandfather's coin, commanded his men to put away their swords. Anna rubbed away tears to find confusion in the eyes of men once captivated by the humor in her disfigurement.

"Are … you going to finish what the dragon started?" she said.

Lord Barden rested the pendant against his chest then clasped his wound once more. Silence built upon itself as a breeze toyed with his chin whiskers. Cole remained restless, stomping in place, eyeing the lord's red and green ranks.

"No," Barden waved. Soldier after soldier began the short jaunt back to their camp. Their slow departure put Anna's mind at ease. "I won't be. The prime's brats can win on their own."

"But my lord." said a soldier with thick eyebrows. "We have orders. You'll lose your title and…"

"Damn my title." Lord Barden barked. "I have done enough to this poor girl."

Every tense muscle loosened; the misery cleared from her mind, but the thick eyebrowed man continued to protest. Her breaths flew in quick successions from the anger in his eyes.

"Enough," said Lord Barden. "I got the title only because my former prime father died."

"Thank you, my lord," said Anna, bowing. "But I am not campaigning."

Lord Barden gave her a sour look. He untied a pouch from his belt and tossed it to her. It slipped from her fingers, the draw string catching on her thumb.

"That's for what we did to your grandfather's town."

"I thank you for this, but if the prime is willing to break campaign law for someone like me, then what of the others wishing to govern?"

"Prime Luther would have whole armies to contend with. Last I saw Williamton had enough blokes to guard their name gates. And only one peasant lord has put his neck out. A lot of folks support him. He's become somethin' of a legend with his bow."

Anna secured the heavy purse within one of Cole's saddle-bags. She ran a hand over Cole's heaving hump. He hummed and grunted, settling, his nimbus's ran over the grass like a morning mist. The thought of another archer intrigued her, but her anger for the lord's actions took precedence.

"You should not have threatened Williamton with destruction," she said, making a fist. "I am no threat to anyone. I did not enter my name."

"Well, some other bloke entered it in the final calling."

Thud. Her bow struck dirt.

"Who answered the final calling in place of me?"

"Your … grandfather."

Chapter Five

⟨꙯⟩

There was no greater darkness than the sleeping black storm bison. Streaks of lightning danced over its nostrils, overshadowing the crackle of the campfire. Anna ran her fingers slowly through the mount's well-groomed fur. Lord Barden spoke of Roland being the last black storm bison to have been bred successfully in one hundred years. That even before Lampariens began breeding for such rare a beast, few roamed the country. Anna met his gaze, her fascination vanished. Her lips formed a solid hard line. A deep caverning of disappointment opened in Anna's chest to see the storm bison like any other mount.

"I must return home," she said, narrowing her gaze. "You have not redeemed yourself with me. And my grandfather has much to answer for his deception."

"You be right in your words," said Lord Barden. "I don't think your grandfather, or I deserve any forgiving. I'm near the end by my guess." He tore free his sleeve to find his wound had stopped bleeding. "Once I return to the capital with news that you're still breathing, it'll be the ax for me."

Anna hesitated a moment. Regret lowered the lord's ginger eyebrows as he pressed thumb and forefinger to his brow.

"I thank you for allowing me to see Roland," her eye fell to her feet, "for sparing my life, but I mustn't remain with anyone willing to harm a town."

"I don't blame you, my lady," said Lord Barden. His chin sunk into his chest. "I deserve what's coming and can't hide since I'm too well known in Cillnar."

Anna turned back to find that amongst tents, feeding horses, and a low burning fire, all eyes were upon them. The man with thick eyebrows muttered something to the others, kicking up laughter like embers escaping a dropped log. *Bastards.* She drew away from Roland and shouldered her bow, to leave for the divide.

"You thinkin about campaigning with a target on your back?" said Lord Barden. "By now, it's too late to back out."

"No," she peered over her shoulder, shrouding her pity with a scowl, "there must be a way to relinquish my place in the running." Anna pulled up her hood. It felt like a shield against the soldiers' amusement. "I can't govern Lampara alone. No one wishes for a broken primnoire to govern them either."

"We need one who won't drain the country's coffers faster than they're filled. By my guess, you're wanting answers more than anything."

Anna nodded. And her grandfather must know how to end the struggle of campaigning before it gained strength. With such a secret kept from her combined with Williamton's suffering, the desperation in her heart was unbearable. *He must answer to the town too,* she thought, *His decision cost them greatly.*

"I thank you again for sparing my life," said Anna. "If you wish redemption, confess to Simdorn and turn yourself into someone not aligned with the prime's sons."

Lord Barden's face darkened for a moment as he untied Roland's reins from a tree beside them.

"Those folk will be hard to find. But," he spat, giving her a worried look, "you're right. At least allow Roland the honor of helping you across the crevice."

Anna shook her head, tempted by the offer, wanting to ride such a rare beast, but deep down she hadn't forgiven his lordship enough to take the offer. The black storm bison gave a disgruntled huff, sending crackles of lightning clouds from his nostrils. Anna made her way down to the crevice, taking off at a sprint. Twigs crunched and grass squashed under her footsteps. She leapt, keeping her eye straight as she waved her arms.

Her boots found purchase, thudding against the beaten dirt as she kept her feet going. She turned back to the tree line, to the faint flicker of the soldiers' fire. Relief poured down her chest to be free of their rudeness. She had never experienced anything like it before, and they had been less than willing to spare a horse for her to cross the crevice earlier. Anna pushed through the overgrowth to find Cole dozing, heavy eyed. A large puddle stretched out from his nostrils. He rose at the sound of her footsteps, bleating as she stroked his back. Emerging from the woods Roland followed his master out into the clearing.

"I want to redeem myself with you, Lady Anna," said Lord Barden. "I know a way to fix those burns of yours."

Anna mounted Cole. She sat up straight with the moon light revealing a softness to his lordship's green eyes.

"I have tried physicians."

"No," he chuckled. "Those quacks are useless. I'm talking about a wizard."

Anna grimaced, picturing an old face of mist, glowing eyes, and black robes containing secrets.

"Grandfather says wizards always take more than they give."

Lord Barden scoffed, pulling at his auburn chin whiskers.

"Why bother trusting what he says?"

"I have no way to find one," she said, contemplating it until finally understanding where he was leading her. "And I am uncertain whether I can trust you either, despite your wish to mend things. My wish to remain out of Lamparien affairs still stands."

With a snap, Cole turned about at great speed, sending them both deep into the dark woods. Anna peered back at the lord with his missing sleeve. A stiff breeze tugged at her hood. The lord's hand leapt to his bear arm from the breeze's chill. She shivered for a moment, sympathy for the lord tugging at her heart. To accept his offer was more tempting than anything in the world. Temptation though was one of many sins Simdorn frowned upon.

It wasn't just her grandfather who had warned her about wizards. Townsfolk older than even Lord William himself spoke of how wizards played on your wants. That no coin was demanded with their services, but if your words were not measured, a great price would come of it. A price out matching the worth of a man's conscience.

Anna secured her bow and quiver, ducking low from a collection of branches. As she eased into Cole's gait, she thought back on her actions. She saw blood run from the bodies of those she killed. Every emotion sank to the depths of her being to find she had brought these men down. She hoped to avoid killing, even when in the presence of Lord Barden for the first time. There were more arrows in the sword master's quarters should more men be sent to kill her. But if her grandfather repaired his wrong doings, more killing wouldn't come to pass. Snapping Cole's reins, he turned his head and bleated. Anna rubbed his side and offered a berry from a pouch on her hip to apologize. She wanted to trust in Lord Barden's regret, yet an eagerness for a possible change of mind plagued her thoughts. The eagerness clawed like a bear once on her heels a year back. Its immense paws had almost left her back a bloody mess if not for Cole catching wind of her screams.

"I'll see you have rest, Cole," she said, bending low, whispering in his ear, "before I confront grandfather."

She envisioned what to say to him, wondering now if with his secretiveness had her grandfather lied about her parents. Lord William once told her they died fleeing a band of robbers when Anna was a babe. That some young milk maid found Anna shortly after her parents were murdered. After seven years, when her grandfather became lord over Williamton, the truth became not of two robbed innocents but of casualties in a battle too brief for history to record. *Can I trust him anymore?* She sighed.

Anna came to the river she had rested at hours previous. She slid down from Cole's back and led him to drink. Pulling off her gloves she splashed water on her face. Cole's deluge ceased while he drank, a faint mist glided across the water as he lapped and gulped. The water sent a chill up her arms and into her chest. It reminded Anna of the coming winter, her favorite year phase, when game was easiest to track. Running

39

her hands down her face the cool water didn't soothe. *The battle was probably a lie.* Anna bound her hands into fists, dropped to her knees and brooded, sinking into the depths of her hood. However, many miles remaining until home, her grandfather owed her more than a removal from politics.

Dirt clung to her knees; water sloshed from Cole's lapping. Lord Barden's wish to make amends dwelled in her mind's eye. *His intentions are noble, but I still do not trust him.* Pulling her gloves on water trickled over the tight sleeves of her leathers. They clung to her arms like a shiny layer of skin. Anna took Cole's reins, leading him into the river, its waters halting at her hips. Rain tapped at the river's surface, urging her to move faster. It made Anna fear the coming chill before illness of throat and nose. Water sloshed and splashed against Cole's shoulders as they waded to the southern shore. The sky thundered before ground was within reach. Down the river, much of the stars and moon disappeared as another boom released, but with no lightning.

"Stop," A deep voice roared. "In the name of Prime Luther."

Anna turned to find the eleven remaining of Lord Barden's men. Swords hissed from their scabbards as every man lined the shore. The thick eyebrowed soldier unfastened his mouth shield. He sneered through yellowed teeth.

"What have you done with Lord Barden?" said Anna, urging Cole until they made it to shore. "He gave direct orders to stand down, and leave me—"

"We don't listen to those who betray our prime." He snapped his mouth shield closed with a *click*. "After her, men."

Anna climbed upon Cole, cursed at herself for unstringing her bow. It was wedged in its place across her saddlebags. Dirt kicked up, roots snapped, and the ground disappeared along with her legs as nimbus's rose in great sprints from Cole's nostrils. Heavy rain filled the air until trudging from the river fell mute. Shouts reached her ears, scrapping like a knife against bone as her nerves mounted.

Faint flames dotted the woods behind her, and soon, the old storm bison was panting heavily. Anna half wished to hide them both, but only trees and thickets provided any source of cover. She gasped. A hand clamped down on her arm. A torch flooded her vision with heat and light, piercing eyes under a sharp helmet. Her friend bleated and roared as another soldier seized him by the horn.

Anna yanked and punched, shaking her hand from striking the man's breastplate. He chuckled, then cried out, dropping his torch, and clawing at his face. Her fingers released the arrow's thin shaft. She spun, snatched the falling torch, and struck the other soldier. He released Cole as embers shattered and poured into his eyes. Anna grabbed and flicked her friend's rein as the gaining soldiers gathered speed.

Nine soldiers remained to plague her, waving their swords, cutting through raindrops. Their torches struggled from the wet onslaught. Light weaved through legions of trees until Anna found the steep hills leading home. Beyond them her heart leapt to see Williamton again, lit by flames not bent on destruction. She searched for the trail, grinned, then steered Cole toward it. Rocks gave way, the trail wide enough to hold them, but slick and runny from the thick rainfall. Anna pulled Cole's reins, urging the immense storm bison to hug the steep bramble hillside. Trees reached overhead, arcing like a set of ribs.

"Stop," called the thick eyebrowed soldier. "You are marked for execution."

Anna turned back, found her knife, and threw. It scraped a soldier's helmet then skipped into the rough. She kept forward, every breath a struggle, the trees were beginning to spin. Cole stumbled over a root, regained his balance, and huffed in exhaustion. Anna pressed her boot into his side, but her oldest and only friend was spent. Seizing every ounce of pride, she slowed them before reaching flatter terrain.

"You made the right choice, my lady." Removing his mouth shield, the thick eyebrowed man dismounted with sword in hand. "Now get off that beast."

Cole tugged at his reins, snorted, and charged but Anna slipped off him. The storm bison huffed, maneuvering his great mass like a shield, her bow within reach and quiver dangling.

"Move your beast woman," one man called. "Or we'll cut him down."

"Please leave him be," she said, shielding Cole with herself. "He only wishes to protect me."

Her head rang with pain as if being struck. Every noise enhanced from the strain of the soldiers pressing in. Anna clenched her teeth and eyed her bow, the men growing ever closer. Their plated armor evergreen upon its surface, and their chain mail a scarlet color. The country's sigil presented firmly on their breastplate.

This could not be her end, death on the run. She wanted it to be at an old age when life no longer granted her strength to hunt. A time when she could walk amongst the trees and truly listen to the sounds without worry for time. By then her grandfather would be long gone, and though her trust in him had been corrupted, a care for him remained deep and ingrained.

Lightning struck so close she covered her ears as screams rang out. She peered over the startled men to find two charred and splayed across the ground. Some men ran to their side, finding them dead, their horses dashed for the woods. Another crack went off throwing several more from their mounts. The men rose in time with a third strike, and then a fourth came but closer this time. Anna placed herself between them and Cole, her fear splitting her heart like an ax to a log.

"Leave her be you, gits," Lord Barden exploded from the woods. He thrusted and jabbed, yanking free his sword from a man's throat. "I won't allow harm to her."

Roland rammed into a soldier, forcing the man's sword free, summoning a scream and crunch as the black storm bison trampled him. The other soldiers charged but backed off as the black storm bison blew thunder clouds from his nostrils. Anna swallowed her fears, removed, and strung her bow. She drew and aimed for the thick eyebrowed soldier. He made for the hill's steep side, clawing at the overgrowth.

"That one's yours, my lady," said Lord Barden, cutting a sway across a man's throat.

The arrow flew shattering raindrops, ignoring wind, striking the soldier in his back. Anna let her arm drop, meeting Lord Barden's gaze.

"Thank you, my lord." said Anna. "I owe you twice for saving my life."

"You owe me nothing," he said. "I'm the one in debt, my lady. And I know where we gotta go to repay it."

"And where shall you find a wizard?"

She slung the bow across her back, mounting Cole as she heard the lord swallow. It was as if he were afraid but when their eyes met, he showed only courage.

"South to the mountains where they've been banished to."

Chapter Six

The rain stopped tapping against her hood, cool droplets clung to its fringe. Roland's lightning diminished from the sky, replaced by the howling winds Anna welcomed over all other noise. His lordship's last words robbed her of any of her own. A field of bushes and narrow tree trunks kept Williamton's northern gate at a distance. It was closed and men paced back and forth within its towers on either side. She was thankful for the darkness keeping the outlaw lord hidden. Swallowing her nervousness, the words finally came to her.

"You didn't command the dragon to breathe its flame," she said, tugging her hood point at a stiff breeze. "I was the one foolish enough to seek to please a few lord's sons."

Her mood grew dark like the fur of the lord's storm bison. He bit his lip and spat, holding strong to his silence while stroking his beard.

"I was desperate for coin," he said. "Had I not, the Wayne family would have smeared my father's name. I guess I done that myself, burning your hometown and all."

She clasped his shoulder. The bison's beneath them were in a conversation of their own, bleating and snorting nearly in sync. Anna relaxed her shoulders, releasing a pent-up breath. She found her anger for the lord melted slowly. *He should turn himself in.* The moonlight highlighted the wrinkles of his face, the slouch in his posture. She shook her head, deciding something she hoped not to regret.

"Your guilt warms my heart, my lord," she said, firming her grip on his shoulder. "I shall ask my grandfather to pardon you after he removes my name from the final calling."

Lord Barden looked up at her, rubbing sweat from his brow and cheeks.

"Good luck," he snorted. "We didn't quite get along last I saw him."

"He is a man whom the law is second to Simdorn," said Anna. "Will you be OK before I return?"

Lord Barden chuckled, hugging his stomach as if what she said were a joke.

"I ride a living fire starter. Remember?"

Anna failed to find humor in his words, realizing the meaning behind them a moment later. Roland, though gentle toward her and his master, possessed great potential for danger. She smiled back at his lordship to make it appear as if she understood. Pressing her heel into Cole's side she headed for Williamton. The darkness disguised its lingering smoke, but the smell remained. Once within earshot of the towers a guard leaned over and gaped.

"She's back!" he called over to the other tower. "Lady Anna has returned!"

"Open the gate," said the other guard, calling over his

shoulder. "Your lord grandfather will be pleased, my lady."

Rumbling ran down the gate's surface, rattling its names of metal. They eased back foot by foot, the gap forming wide enough as Anna flicked the bison's reins. She gave them a slight jerk, hastening their pace. She firmed her grip, releasing a whine from their leather. Anna made her way right, the smithy's shop like a gaping black wound. At the edge of its ruin, through all the ash and fallen timbers, the smithy's anvil lay on its side. She smiled, finding a small sense of hope. Her spirits rose from it, knowing someone could start again.

As she drew closer home, lantern light flickered on windowsills. The lights marking houses fortunate enough to survive Barden's attack. She peered up to her home ahead. It was made of chiseled granite blocks like Lampara's capital, each cut and smoothed to precision. Thick oaks stripped of bark and branches formed the roofing of different sections. Calm took her in its arms for a moment to be home again. Banners hung from every window with her family sigil gracing them. The lowest window belonged to the study. Light streamed faintly through its diamond window panes. Anna dismounted and led Cole around to the grounds at the house's back.

With a three-finger salute to their dome helmets, her grandfather's guards opened the gate. Ahead, torches highlighted the stable entrance, the doors opened with straw crossing under the entryway. And as she entered, the straw crunched and hissed under her boots. She unsaddled Cole, realizing had Lord William spoken of their conversation to anyone, a prepared stable was unlikely. Anna sighed, watching her friend settle in his stall. She closed its door, thankful for a moment.

* * *

Tension ran up into her chest with each minute she gathered what to say. Light crept from under the study door as Anna raised her fist. Anna brought it close to the door, its oak old and knotted in places. Her grandfather had to know of some way to pull out of campaigning. Although she wondered if he could stomach the embarrassment of doing it. Withdrawing was not unheard of for Lampariens wanting to govern. Anna bit her lip, daring to believe Lord Barden was wrong, that it wasn't too late.

She hoped to bring up the subject of pardoning him, and that the result wouldn't lead to his banishment. Anna clenched her teeth, the burns on her face tensed. She knocked.

"Enter."

Anna eased the door open, prolonging the moment, loosening the tension in her… She gasped, slamming shut her lips. Her kill's antlers rested on the mantelpiece, polished, illuminated by the fire below, twelve points and all. Upon the small table beside her grandfather's chair a plate was slick with grease. Within its center, like an island, was a small piece of meat. Anna turned to face the bookshelves, every breath fleeing from her lips. Her grandfather peered over his shoulder, smiled, and slid a book back in its place.

"My obvious guess is you were successful," he said, strolling toward her. He embraced her like she had been gone a month. "I'm glad you are safe." He kissed her brow. "I have decided with our town's recent tragedy to no longer push my interests on you. I shall instead embrace yours," he smiled, parting for his chair. "Seems much more productive."

"But?" Dryness enveloped her throat with his willingness

48

for change. "What of the prime's sons? What of another attack? More of the prime's men may come for me."

Lord William sat weaving his fingers together, pressing his brow to his knuckles.

"I must confess something to you, sweet girl. I—"

"You entered my name in the final calling," said Anna, the anger too strong to contain any longer. "You risked everyone's life over a responsibility I possessed no desire to take on."

"How was I to guess Prime Luther would risk breaking campaign law to benefit his sons?" he said, raising an eyebrow. "And how do you know I entered your name?"

He rose leaning against the mantelpiece. The fire highlighted the whiskers on his stiffened chin. His cloak puddled against the floor.

"I was successful. Enough so that Prime Luther will not know that I still draw breath." Anna yanked down her hood, pointing to her face. "And I shall say this one final time. No one wants to look upon their primnoire and not see beauty. I am not strong enough to govern over anyone. We must find a way to withdraw—"

"You were strong enough to take on nearly twenty men." Lord William pointed to her bow, strung across her chest. "And those men cared more for avoiding death than for the face of who was bringing it. I'm glad you left no one alive. But, I know of no way to withdraw your name."

"I did … leave one man alive" Anna sighed. "I ask you to deliver justice upon him instead of what Prime Luther may do for his failure."

"And who is this man? Where is he?" Lord William snapped. "How do you know if he hasn't already sent word for reinforcements?"

Anna turned away from him to a shelf packed with scrolls. *I had not thought of... No, he wouldn't.* Her breath blasted from her nostrils like an enraged storm bison. Lord Barden saved her life and twice for that matter. Anna saw no reason for betrayal in him, yet she was never best at reading people. She shook her head, remembering the lord's offer, his wish to mend the burns upon her face. Telling her grandfather this may alter the twist of disappointment in his eyes.

"His name is Lord Barden," she said, facing her grandfather. "He is the one who sold me—"

"I know who he is," Lord William roared. "He is the reason I cannot convince you to campaign" He took her hands into his own. He held them firmly, releasing the deepest of sighs. "I knew I could not trust him."

"What...? What do you mean, grandfather?"

"He didn't tell you." Lord William withdrew from her, eyeing the fire's glow. Her fears compounded with his silence. "Lord Barden came to our town with the intention you already know." He shuddered. "But I offered him coin to spare you, and to remember what happened with the dragon. And most importantly, I asked him to help me bring you to your senses."

Her heart was in free fall, remembering the pouch at her hip. Its contents swaying Lord Barden to arson, yet why use such an extreme. Anna felt her knees buckle. Two thousand people lived within the walls of Williamton, and her grandfather was prepared to risk them all for a world she knew wouldn't accept her.

"You're both mad. You won't help me," she said, wiping her eye of tears. "You love me but will not help me. You'd risk innocent lives so I may do what? The farthest I travel daily is to the borders of your lands. It has been five years since last, I have seen the capital."

Lord William dropped his chin. His neck bulged from his stiff high collar. The hunting leathers he wore were worn and brown. Its gauntlets covered the tops of his hands in an arrowhead shape, embroidered with the family sigil. He buried himself within the depths of his cloak. His heavy brow sunk, smoothing the wrinkles above.

"There is much at stake. You were my only chance of stopping what's coming." he said, swallowing and looking her straight in the eye. "I cannot govern a third time by law. You were Lampara's last hope, and I could not convince you. You may stay the night, but before sunrise I best not see you in this house."

Anna backed away, bumping against the open door. She clasped a hand over her lips as her mind ran through a thicket of thoughts. His words cut deeper than thorns within a brier patch. Lampara was foreign to her besides what woods had become like a second home to her. Even with Lord Barden's wish to make amends, it was apparent why she still needed to have anger for him. And yet there was enough regret within him that he felt like her only ally.

"I will be off to bed then." She eyed the antlers, the lone piece of meat on its plate. "I would beg you to use what influence you possess and free me of campaigning… But I guess I will have to withdraw myself, since I am no longer a part of this family."

"You most certainly are not. You have thrown all I have given you—"

She slammed the door, cutting short his words. Marching to her chambers, Anna cared not to hear another word from him again. Lord William had put her in an obligated position, and with it, set all she knew a blaze. She dashed up a set of spiraling stairs, meeting a long hall lined with braziers and littered with rushes. The rushes' scent tormented her senses, and the more she dwelled on his words, the worse the smell became. The rushes crunched underfoot. She made it to the hall's end and flung open her door.

Upon her bed lay two quivers of a fine, black leather, filled, to her surprise, with arrows containing fletching crafted from red goose feathers. She reached out as her anger for Lord William stretched and bent her fingers. Running her fingers over the fletching, it was soft and smooth, cut close to pierce the wind. She removed an arrow, laid it against her bow and drew. The balance was unquestionable, like no arrow was present, and the fletching kissed her cheek. Replacing the arrow, Anna reasserted herself to the present. A final answer was needed, and she reasoned before dawn's light to have it.

* * *

Emily passed her at the crest of the steps, nodding, putting broom to stone to remove old rushes. "I wish you'd listen to me like you did as a child, my lady," said Emily. "Your grandfather is a reasonable man."

Anna peered beyond the darkness of her hood. "If he were reasonable, then Williamton would not be in ruin."

The chambermaid rested her hand on Anna's, giving it a light squeeze. Within the pit of her stomach Anna felt as though her grandfather had changed. Why send her away for not sharing in his wants? He had taught her all she knew, so why had he not given her lessons in governing? Anna possessed no idea how to improve the life of another.

"Grandfather is too eager to change what he believes is wrong," she mumbled, withdrawing her hand. "I know I can fight if needed but if more is required of me, I'm... I'm no leader."

Emily nodded, pressing broom to stone. "Good luck, Anna."

Anna took each step two at a time, a pang of guilt pained her chest to see Emily sad. She meandered to the study, knowing it was the week's sixth day where her grandfather was going to be. Easing the door of his study open, he sat slumped in his chair asleep. The hunting leathers upon his person like a crinkled leaf. To wake him to say her goodbyes would have been proper. A good enough reason to ease the ache of her heart. but her anger thundered too loudly. She rested the pouch on the mantle between her kill's antlers. Twelve points in total graced the deer's head. The deer possessed a swiftness Cole was just barely able to match.

The arrows of both quivers rattled. She paused before the door. Anna peered over her shoulder to see if it had broken the rhythmic pattern of Lord William's snoring. He shifted slightly, crossing his feet. The heels of his boots dug into the old bear rug. A tear readied itself in her eye. Deep within the aged bones of her grandfather was a man with good intention. But somehow such good intentions found a misguided reason. She pressed her hand to the boiled leather of her fresh hunting garb, said a small prayer for his good health to Simdorn.

Out across the grounds Cole's barn sat, its lanterns still a flame. Beyond it an immense aviary housed her lord grandfather's esant. It had a cage-like structure to itself. The servants had tried housing it with chickens, but they were eaten before midday. She opened the barn doors and breathed in the wet straw. It smoothed her senses as she applied Cole's saddle and stroked his fury head. He licked her hand. His eyes captured her reflection, soft and heavy browed as if he knew this was a time for change. She mounted him after securing her quivers to his saddle horn. Their arrows were like flames erupting from his back. The butts of both quivers hung close to his shoulders.

Along her way, stable boys, the smithy, and her grandfather's personal guard gathered with lit lanterns in hand like a collective of lightning bugs. Anna cast her gaze up to Lord William's balcony, finding its doors closed. She unbuttoned the high collar of her tunic, exhaling. It felt as if the next few steps Cole took were the hardest. But he followed her lead always, except this time, there was no certainty of where it may end.

"Lady Anna."

Anna turned to the servant's quarters. Emily held heavy, folded furs close to her chest, taking off at a sprint, her skirt hem tucked into a sleeve. The guards eased the gate open to the vacant alley beyond. They buried their chins against their chests, one wiped a tear from his cheek. Emily made it to her side, panting, holding in both hands a long black cloak. It matched the black leathers of Anna's hunting garb. She had promised not to wear another cloak. Fire claimed the green one. She hesitated, slowly accepting Emily's gift. The old chamber maid folded her hands, bowing.

"Wherever may you go," Emily said, meeting Anna's gaze, "winter will follow soon."

The cloak was lined with nelka fur found only in Lampara's mountain-covered south. Rutoe tradesmen preserved and worshiped the immense feline after banishment to the south.

They halted the trade of its fur, slowing the near extinction of the red and green streaked beast. Anna let go a small smile and unfolded the cloak. It was heavier than her old one of silk and bear skins. *If anyone but Emily had given it to me...,* She swallowed the lump forming in her throat, wiping a tear upon her cheek, *keeping my promise would have been easier.* Emily bowed, brushing back her long, graying brown hair. As the gate fully opened the air grew cold. Before Cole's silver hooked horns pierced through to the alley, the guards bowed their heads. She turned back to everyone. Their faces brightly shown within the light of their lanterns.

"I cannot promise a return," she said. Her voice grew soft and clear. It drew out comfort from what she could see, yet she was unable to feel it herself. "But I put all of you in danger the longer I remain here."

There was silence amongst them all, even Emily, who leaned on her husband's shoulder. The master of arms held Emily close as she smiled a small smile. Anna flicked Cole's reins, filling the gate with his swirling clouds. They glazed over the fresh morning dew. Anna swung the cloak over her shoulders. To bid them all farewell pained her too much. She shut her eye and whispered a prayer Emily taught her long ago.

"Whether parted or together," she said. The gates whined and clattered shut. "By war or treacherous storms, every deed and smile from you has been sewn into my heart. May Simdorn send her pale bears to guide your remaining days steps, and the moon for which the goddess governs from never allow you to live in darkness."

After passing several neighborhoods along the town's main road the north gate was in sight. Fresh guards climbed ladders leading up to either guard tower. The sky was growing lighter. Crisp, cool wind raced through town, summoning creaks from shutters and hanging signs. She drew the cloak close about her shoulders, deciding to be firm with her fear. *I will tread with care next time,* she thought as footsteps came from far to her left. Anna gave Cole's reins a jerk. She didn't want to say goodbye to another person she cared for.

"Lady Anna."

Her heart stopped. Every finger strained until she found herself pulling up on Cole's reins.

"Norman," she whispered.

He was bundled in a coat matching the leather from his doublet of yesterday. She had checked last night if his scrolls were still in Cole's saddlebags, but they were gone. Norman stroked Cole's head. The storm bison rubbed his wet nose against the accountant's cheek.

"Did you forget a scroll, Norman?"

"Oh, no, my lady," he said, smiling. "I received word from my father when he returned home that you were with us again. I thought you might be parting for one of your early hunts. I wanted to speak with you about a matter."

Anna gulped. "I'm keeping to what I said yesterday."

"I understand," His face grew dark despite the growing light of morning. She worried her grandfather may have changed his mind and decided to do far worse than banish her. But Norman wouldn't be sent for that. "I saw something that no one was meant to witness."

"And what was it you saw?"

"Whilst you were gone, I had been at your home balancing Lord William's accountants. His lordship and a man with thick chin whiskers entered the study."

Anna peered over to the north gate. Its doors were shut; both guards had finished their climb and conversed with their comrades. A shudder ran through her as she faced Norman. Her guesses on what he may say next compounded.

"I was asked to leave," Norman continued, "Before I had made it to the steps, I remembered I forgot to give his lordship my report. The study door was open slightly when I returned. There were whispers beyond it of your name being—"

"Grandfather entered my name in the final calling, Norman." Anna interrupted. "And he asked the man you speak of to set Williamton ablaze with his black storm bison."

Norman raised an eyebrow, tilting his head.

"Whoever the man was he must have confessed this to you before you killed him. Your grandfather did ask the man to burn Williamton. He was given coin and some bottled substance. I believe it aided in creating the lightning."

Anna nodded. Her heart quickened as she folded her hand into a fist. Norman's words held more use had he said them yesterday. She knew of the bribe, but again why if Barden regretted selling her the dragon, did he not just leave. *His regret is a lie.*

"Why did you not tell me this before, Norman?"

Norman turned from her, tucking his chin against his chest.

"I was discovered before the man took on the task." His breath caught in his throat as he met her eye again. "I was forced to remain silent, or see my father killed. I ... know now I should have stayed away from business not my own."

Anna explained what she had learned since leaving yesterday, adding that whatever danger remained for his father, Samuel, that Norman's secret was safe. With a shudder down her chest, she cleared her throat, and finished with her grandfather telling her to leave town.

"I now go to the capital to remove myself from campaigning."

"But Lady Anna," Norman gasped. "The rules have changed on withdrawals."

"What are they?"

A chill ran down her spine as the wind failed to carry her heavy cloak. Norman rubbed his hands together before summoning up his words.

"Word came by cheefox months previous of public shaming deemed too childish for those wishing to withdraw from campaigning." Norman's lips trembled as he rubbed his fingers more. He drew in a breath finally and stiffened his chin, though his eyes were downcast. "Anyone who withdrawals, peasant or noble, must fight in the arena and win. If you lose, campaigning is your best choice, and should you refuse, you face..."

"Norman," Anna cried. "Please tell me what will happen."

"You face execution for cowardice."

Chapter Seven

E very feeling went numb after Norman's last words. Anna swung her leg over Cole and slid down until her boots thudded against dirt. Any strength she possessed before had abandoned her, every muscle gave way, dropping her to her knees. The dirt coated her fingers as she clenched them into fists. Norman knelt beside her, every word from his lips mute to her ears. She blamed herself for ignoring many of Lord William's rants about changes to Lampara. What else was different about the country so many of its people wished to govern?

"I have two choices, Norman," she said, licking her lips, tasting sweat. "I must either take on what I feel is impossible or fight to remain alive."

His hand rested on her shoulder. Voices rose from distant houses as her senses began to buzz so loud in her ears that her head hurt.

"I believe in you, my lady." He gave her shoulder a squeeze. "I know your choice will return your life to what it was. Let me go with you, and see it done."

She swallowed her fears for a moment, rose, and pulled down her hood.

"You know I have no home to go back to," she said, mounting Cole. Norman's eyes seemed to dim from her words. "I will go and fight because I am able. I've heard of someone who is campaigning. This man has skill with a bow and might be able to do what I cannot."

"Who is he?"

"I don't know," she said, "but there is someone I know who does."

* * *

Lord Barden was not where she had left him. Once they were well beyond the gate, and through a series of bushes and brambles, the outlaw lord emerged. He held the reins of a horse belonging to one of his men. The Lamparian country sigil emblazoned upon its saddles center, faded, and worn by use. Snow fell slowly in heavy flakes, their cold bringing no calm to Anna's frustration. She turned over in her mind what she recently learned. Piecing each part together bristled her growing curiosity. Before a question could be uttered, Norman dropped his hands from her waist and slid off Cole.

"Why does this man still live, Lady Anna?"

"Oh, bother," said Lord Barden. "What's the pretty boy doing here?"

"He is my friend, my lord." Anna rode up close to Lord Barden. The cut upon his arm showed slow signs of healing. "I was spared by him, Norman." She gave the accountant an assuring nod. Her senses went into a fit once focused again on Lord Barden. "I must still know why you set Williamton ablaze despite knowing me. What made my grandfather's coin worth such suffering?"

"You can stop calling me lord," Barden said, slipping a tiny bottle from a pouch on his belt. "Urine of a lady storm bison." Barden handed it to her. "My house name is Barden, but I feel my birth name, Nathan, is what I deserve now." Nathan gave the morning sky a glance. He sighed. "I do regret my recent misdeeds. Can you find your way to forgive a blockhead like me?"

Every muscle in Anna's face tightened with anger. It felt as though someone wearing an iron glove had punched her in the stomach. She had been taught since fifteen by Simdorn's priests about strength in forgiveness. The difference came when laws were broken, but deep down she couldn't fight her pity for him. She turned to Norman, a man she knew to be the wisest in her life.

"I'm lost to what I must do, Norman." Anna pressed a hand against her head, raking her hair for answers. "You were caught overhearing what you were not meant to. What made Nathen burn our town? Why did he take my grandfather's coin?"

"It doesn't matter now, my … lady." Norman stammered. "The town is safe, and you can—"

"Answer me!" Anna said. "You must know."

Anna brought Cole around until the storm bison sensed her frustration and charged Norman. She pulled tight on his reins releasing a wall of rain clouds. As it cleared, the accountant stood rooted to the ground, shaking, He pressed his hands together, eyes wide.

"His lordship … took your grandfather's money because,"

he said, "I'm not permitted within Lamparien borders. Lord William bribed him not to report my existence." Norman pointed to Nathan. "He aroused his beast with the storm bison urine to bring down its lightning. He did it not for the reason you know, but to leave evidence that his mission succeeded."

"That is a mad solution" Anna said, sneering at Nathan. "And what warrants you not being allowed to live where you were born, Norman?"

"He ain't what he seems, Lady Anna," said Nathan, folding his arms. "That one there likely with messed trousers at this point ain't human. Look."

Anna faced Norman again, finding a face of green. He had high cheekbones, and a well-defined jawline. His ears were pointed at the tops and lobes like thorns. His hair flowed down to his shoulders in a shimmering black like her own. Norman's skin became a darker green as he took a step back from Cole's huffing fury. He gritted his teeth as they sharpened to intricate points.

"I can no longer hide, Lady Anna." Norman met her eye, raising a hand. Flames formed over it in a flash. "I am a rutoe of the ignited clan. We are gifted with fire, and by my speech, I did long ago live like any other Lamparien."

"Do you go by something else beyond, Norman?" said Anna.

Anna clenched her teeth, failing to calm Cole as he growled at Norman. The rutoe slowly extinguished his hand, snowflakes hissed within its flames. She was unsure if he shook from nervousness or the growing cold of the morning.

"Norman is easier than the name I chose for myself." Norman focused on his feet for a moment. Anna let the tension ease from her jaw, finding his relief refreshing. "I am thankful you came when you did. Cole's storms were Williamton's best—"

"Let's go, Norman."

Anna urged Cole up beside him, finding the storm bison had sensed her trust in the accountant. Norman mounted Cole grunting from the saddle's narrow seat. Anna felt a deep warmth in his hands once they rested on her hips. For a moment, her heart danced in her chest to have him so close.

"Lady Anna, please!" Nathan cried. "I want to redeem mi-self."

She craned her neck back to him, the fur around her collar hid her face up to its nose.

"You would have been of greater help by refusing Prime Luther."

Nathan Barden glared at Anna for a moment, spat, and then covered himself in a cloak from Roland's saddlebags. He pressed his heel into Roland's side to join her.

"Do you even know the way to Cillnar?" said Nathan, thrusting his hood over his head. "I can at least guide you. I'll leave after that."

Anna met his eye, pulling over her hood as the wind blasted against her cheek. The cold usually soothed her, but this time it just reddened her cheeks and forced a shiver across her skin.

"You're right," she said. "Allow Norman the horse with whatever its saddlebags provide."

"Oh, you're kind like your granddad said, my lady," said Nathan. "I will find you a wizard mi-self once you head home."

She pulled up on Cole's reins as Nathan stopped to hand the

horse over to Norman. Looking at Nathan, it was difficult to remain angry. The man was persistent, more so than anyone she had ever met. Anna pulled her cloak closer around her shoulders and checked to see if all was in place and led them west. Nathan and Norman didn't speak amongst one another, which allowed her to focus. One had been where he should not have, and the other she found to be mad, unpredictable, but most of all her only way to be complete.

* * *

It was in the shadow of a tall stone pillar, gray in color, and branded with a chiseled Brighton sigil that Anna's ability to lead ended. Several pillars of the same size towered left and right at great distances marking the border of her grandfather's lands. Beyond Nathan Barden and his men only tradesmen entered them. The outlaw lord slipped a flask from his boot and downed some of its contents before offering some to her. Anna waved it away, asking which direction would take them swiftly to the capital.

"We can head straight as we 'ave been," he said, wiping his lips. "Or wait since we pressed on day and night."

She found herself in the webs of a coming yawn with the sun setting far east of them. Norman was on her right in line with her blind eye. He remained still in his wrinkled wet clothes and hadn't searched his saddlebags for a cloak. Anna looked him up and down, and realized his ability with fire must keep him warm.

"Can we stop for a rest, Lady Anna?" said Norman. "Cole appears to need it."

Cole had begun slowing before reaching the end of her

grandfather's lands. With the change of weather Cole's rains turned into snow. The added flakes slowed his steps and forced a weight on his breathing. If he were younger, Anna guessed, the journey and change in his storms would have been easier to manage.

"Let's take shelter under that tree," she said, pointing to a thick pine. "I thank you, Norman. My eagerness to reach the capital has pushed all of you too hard."

"You've got the right thinking," said Nathan. "Let's get some—"

"I was speaking of Cole and Norman." Anna snapped.

Anna dismounted, leading Cole to the tree, its green leaves and long branches held the weight of snow, leaving the ground around its roots grassy. She needed Nathan's guidance for the journey but finding complete forgiveness for Williamton remained distant. Norman joined her as she wrapped Cole's reins about the tree's trunk. His face spoke of disappointment, perhaps for how harsh she just was, but he had to understand.

"You did not start the fire." she whispered, watching Nathan find another tree for Roland. "I must keep control of him if I can. He might be of use later."

"You're right," said Norman, eyeing her burns. "Though I can't help feeling sorry for him. He saved me with his greed in a way. And if I'm not mistaken you are beginning to sound like a primn—"

She shot him a fierce glance from the shade of her hood. Norman raised his hands up in surrender.

"I'll get us some wood," Nathan said, crunching snow underfoot after securing Roland. "I'll be back in a snap."

Norman sat against the tree, drawing out a stone from

under his bottom. Anna removed her hood, replacing it with the one from her cloak. It was as if her anger was a dark untraveled road. Anna had not until recent events felt much anger. Frustration for her grandfather's bickering of politics and mortification by her encounter with the dragon five years previous, but anger was something only witnessed until now.

"I am grateful to be here, to be of help," said Norman. "You are angered by my assumption, I know, but can an agreement be found for your use of strategy?"

Anna found no answer for him at first. Outside of his recent words churning eagerness in her heart, a reason to be authoritative was necessary. She wanted to be complete again. Nathan knew how to give that to her. It felt wrong to use him, but his guilt felt far more real than she thought.

"I can find some forgiveness for Nathan." she sighed; stroking Cole's brow as tiny clouds wafted from his nostrils. "I still feel anger for Williamton, yet my heart tells me he is truly sorry."

"I must agree with your conclusion," said Norman, meeting her gaze with uncertainty. "Do you still intend to use him to find a wizard after winning your way out of campaigning?"

Anna folded her arms. She sat next to him against the tree.

"Yes," she said finally. "And I will forgive him and discard my doubts."

Norman nodded, "I must beg forgiveness then. Despite taking coin to keep silent I find his willingness to send me south offensive."

"I understand," she rested a hand upon his own. "How did grandfather know you were rutoe?"

"He is the one lord who provides work for rutoe."

Anna leaned against the tree for a moment, sweat trickled

down her cheeks from the cloak's warmth.

"I'm satisfied then," she said, finding his heat was the source of her sweating. "What must I know before we reach the capital?"

Norman let out a breath, meeting her gaze. He explained what was required of her to remove oneself from campaigning. A duel with everyone no longer willing to seek the role of leadership like herself. Anna gulped, refusing to guess the number of Lamparians who entered their name. Many lords and peasants were relations of previous primes, and it was tradition for their offspring to campaign.

"You will not be fighting them to the death," Norman continued. "But if you lose, we both know campaigning is your only choice."

Anna bit her lip, studying the grass poking from snow. She shook off the thought of execution knowing how one proceeded.

"I mustn't lose then," she said, looking up at Norman. Anna weaved a lock of hair behind her ear. "I thank you for your knowledge." She licked her lips, hesitating where the burns began. "You were always the wisest one in our class."

Norman's cheeks went a light shade of green.

"I must be fair in telling you," he said, "when we were both only fifteen, I realized—"

She rested a hand on his lap, finding her heart in some sort of race. The snow falling about them slowed with each moment passing. Anna removed her hood, still slightly hesitant, fumbling with the strange feelings swirling within her.

"You were always beyond all of us." Anna smiled. "Your fa… I mean Samuel told me he wished he had coin to send you—"

"I consider him like a father," said Norman. "He's a good man."

They both fell silent. Conversations of the past or present melted away as she could feel Norman guiding himself to within a breath of a kiss. She drew him slowly into an embrace, finding Norman far sturdier than his slender figure suggested. He pressed his lips to her own. They were smooth unlike her cracked and chapped ones.

Snap!

Anna cocked her head left, doing so more from half blindness than fear. Nathan emerged from the brush, poorly disguising a smirk on his lips. *He was watching.* She ignored the burning within her chest. Nathan rested the wood wrapped under his arm beside Roland. He removed the storm bison's saddle and placed it on a fallen tree.

"My guess is pretty boy stays and I go?"

"This 'pretty boy,' never had a lord's resources for education," Norman brushed wet grass from his legs, rising. "And can still weave words better than you."

Nathan stormed toward Norman. Anna stepped between them as Norman puffed up his boney chest, flashing his pointed teeth. "I need both of you for what's ahead," she said. "Stand down!"

Both man and rutoe pressed at her hands as she splayed every finger like strands of a web. Norman nodded, backing off as the snowfall slowly stopped. She eyed Nathan who had retreated without her notice. Nathan snatched her hand and rested a soft, flaky heel of bread in it.

"Here! Eat up, my lady," Nathan said. "You've got the real fight ahead."

She raised the bread to her lips, hesitant at first, wondering if she should remain awake tonight. Anna ripped it in two and handed half to Norman. He nibbled at it, keeping his diamond shaped eyes upon Nathan. They were redder than the sun's remnants weaving themselves through the forest's canopies.

"I've forgiven you, Nathan," Anna said. "You and Norman call a truce."

The crickets answered her first.

"Samuel said, an accountant's conflict is with numbers not men," said Norman. "I will accept a truce."

Anna smiled. Sometimes when Norman spoke it was like listening to scripture sent from the goddess herself.

"I've bigger worries than some illegal blockhead like him." Nathan spat. "Get to eating. We've got us a month's ride before winter takes hold, and we freeze."

Chapter Eight

Rising above the thousands of homes beyond the city walls stood swirling towers supporting oval structures. Cillnar possessed clean cut brickwork, flags whipping at the wind at intervals across its wall. It was less like the ancient city of Anna's memory and more like a monument to Prime Luther and his primnoire. A crescent moon arch of smooth granite balanced its ends atop the heads of snarling white marble bears at its gates. The bears' front paws were raised to defend the thick black wood doors between them. The wall encircling Cillnar held not just guard towers, but likenesses of both governors back-to-back in robes and flowing dress. Neither statue was a plain stone, but of the same scarlet and evergreen the soldiers under Nathan's command wore. The governing couple's term was near the end of its twenty years, and like Nathan said, the country's coffers stood no chance of remaining full.

The capital was also far larger than when Anna first saw it at fifteen. She pulled gently up on Cole's reins, Norman and Nathan slowing until aligned with her. Neither had tried to settle their differences, keeping to a silent truce. Norman had returned to the face she knew growing up, with curly chestnut hair and eyes the color of a mountain's stream. The way Norman truly looked impressed her more somehow, like it was a form of honesty shown instead of told. There was familiarness to it she couldn't place, an old dream that felt more like a distant memory.

"I haven't been this far west since I was a child," said Norman, his voice high, filled with joy in its pitch. "Prime Luther has been busy."

Nathan grumbled, "More like he allowed his coin gobbling primnoire to turn the city into a circus."

"I rather like it, Nathan," said Anna, smiling. "It was plain and crowded before."

"It's no less crowded," Nathan checked his person then surveyed their surroundings. "You'll need to surrender your weapons at the entrance."

Nathan pointed to a sign resting just atop a bush. It read, *'No weapon may pass. Confrontation comes with no sharp edge in Cillnar. Violation of such decree will be met with punishment.'* Anna returned her eye to the capital, recalling the city's layout Nathan had spoken of last week. A lump formed in her throat to leave the former lord behind. It was necessary should Nathan be recognized and questioned about her, but that didn't remove the guilt of leaving him alone.

"Do you know what the punishment is?" Anna asked.

Nathan stroked his thick chin whiskers and sighed.

"An eye for being dim enough to sneak weapons in."

Anna gulped, refusing to imagine what complete blindness was like. Her right eye knew darkness too well thanks to the burns over it, blotting light through its lid. The snow was well over Cole's hooves, tossed about from tracks of past travelers. His storm clouds filled the hoof marks with fresh snow, some of it turning to ice.

"What will you do while I seek removal from campaigning?"

Nathan took a nip from his flask and wiped his lips on the flesh of his sleeveless arm.

"There's a town some miles north of here called Natlendton," he said. "They serve a fine brew, and nutsnatcher races run from the morning until midnight. Head that way when you've won."

She watched him raise an eyebrow at Norman. The former lord sent his black storm bison into a gallop down a road overgrown and neglected. Anna rested a hand to her chest, finding some comfort from his confidence. They went down a slight hill until the road leveled out once more. The ground had frozen over the wagon tracks to and from the capital's distant doors.

"I don't understand that man, Lady Anna," said Norman.

"He has guilt for my past, Norman." Anna pulled her hood forward until only the tip of her chin met sunlight. "I'm uncertain of my chances, but whatever happens I know he will be there for me."

Norman pursed his lips.

"That fills pages for itself, but I don't see how someone can be both a scoundrel and a man of his word at once."

Anna found no answer for Norman's riddle. She was more familiar with the men of Williamton than those of the outside world. Perhaps small-town men were easier to read than those from cities and distant lands. Anna and Norman eased to a halt within a sprint's distance of the city gates. Men in green plated armor and thick red underclothing asked for them to part with their weapons. She sighed, removing her full quivers, and with tension she failed to hide, handed her bow over. The bow was a gift from a traveler she met at fifteen. The traveler showed apprehension and a hint of fear when first seeing her face but noticed Anna's eye upon his bow. He advised her to wax the string routinely to prevent weather damage. The guard received it, running his fingers over the wood, resting it carefully within a small shack. She smiled a small smile, finding her bow was beside another, well treated and clean like her own. *He cares for his bow like I do mine.*

"Does the young lad require a search, or will he surrender his weapons willingly?" said one guard.

Norman rummaged through his horse's saddlebags for weapons, or what else could have belonged to the dead soldier who once owned the horse. Leather flapped against the horse's sides until Norman's eyes widened with delight at a quill and several rolls of parchment.

"Just don't be poking anyone at a 'slap and stroke,' establishment." The guard chuckled at the quill's sharp copper point.

The second guard raced to a bell beside the shack, rang it, and waited. Its dinging rattled Anna's senses. She clenched her teeth, bracing when a distant bell answered back. She let out a frustrated breath as the doors eased open, both far thicker and slower than those of her hometown. They rode through as the sky grew gray with clouds. Snow fell with heavier flakes, more deliberate once both Norman and she were through, placing the city under a winter assault. Cole bleated at a storm bison pulling a wagon piled high with hay.

Anna was uncertain if he was more excited for the hay or the sight of another of his kind.

To her right she heard a faint growling and found a store holding in its windows wooden cages. A cheefox resided within each, the bars leaving streaks of shade across the face of some curled up comfortably in sleep. The awake cheefoxes played a game of some kind with their fluffy spotted tails. Above them hung a sign claiming the store possessed the fastest cheefoxes in western Lampara. The slender dog-like creatures with their short round ears and long narrow muzzle were large enough to carry packages of great weight. Anna felt a burst of passion in her chest, wishing she were a child again, riding one of these creatures of messages, racing through an open field with the sun at her back.

They continued down streets of cobbled stone. Anna recited the directions Nathan had given under her breath, leading Norman up long stretches of store fronts. Droppings of near every kind dotted the streets, some fresh, but Anna had grown used to such smells from Cole's barn. She heard Norman swallow his vomit and caught him draping his tunic over his nose.

They passed allies of dirt, walled on either side by buildings with bricks too old and numerous to count. One ally was occupied by a man lying motionless outside a side door to a pub. A strong smell like that of piss drifted from him, but the odor was shadowed by decay. Anna gasped, urging Cole with her heel at his side. The man's face was sunken, and rats nibbled his fingers. He was half buried in slush, shoeless, falling snow covering exposed flesh. Anna pulled both her hoods tighter over her face until she rounded a corner.

Her heart slowed its dashing beat as they passed a crowd

surrounding a man on a large barrel marked Wine of a Northern Vintage. The lettering was old and faded unlike the bright face of the man.

"Have you lads and ladies heard of the archer, Lord Arthur?" he bellowed with hands spread wide. "It's said he fought for our prime when the rutoe rebelled. Our prime and his lordship beat those monsters back good."

Norman stopped his horse and scowled, but Anna jerked him back by the collar.

"He insults my people," Norman whispered.

"I'm sorry for it," said Anna, "but I don't want the crowd harming you should you act."

Both were at least ten heads back from the man on his barrel as a tale of battle sent whispers throughout the crowd. Norman eyed her, a faint red surfacing in his irises. The red slowly died.

"You're right," he sighed.

"His lordship is said to have even released three arrows at once," said the man from his barrel. "He struck true all three to the chest of a rutoe viciously on the heels of our Prime Luther."

"Let's go, Norman," Anna patted his shoulder. "I wish not to have you hear any more."

They continued until the man's words faded into the distance. Anna half hoped some tragedy might befall the archer, finding the man's tales brutal. To think in such a way was a sin against Simdorn, but for Norman's sake she allowed herself to go against the goddess.

Noon's sun broke through the clouds after some time. A bell rang in the distance, deep and commanding. Anna ignored its chimes as she spotted an age eaten sign directing her and

Norman left for the arena. A line of carriages narrowed their way until a bridge led Anna and Norman over a wide frozen moat. Anna's eye grew wide as her lips parted.

Beyond the bridge were walls stacked one upon another. They towered a mile each with the lowest bricks made of an aged, cracked granite. Thick oak supports surrounded its base. The ground showed signs of sinking around them. From what Anna guessed, the arena was of little concern to the primnoire. Each added level possessed no polish to its stone. Poles ringing its top bore torn and weathered flags. An archway held firmly by two iron supports marked the main entrance.

In an illustration Anna once saw, the entrance had been manned by two pale bear statues at odds with one another, symbolizing Lamparians battling for power. Above both bears Simdorn herself held a medallion of gold and finished oak for the victor. She knew from her grandfather's rants this was the place which held the tournament to decide who was to be Lampara's governor. The medallion was missing from the goddess's hands.

The bears lay on their stomachs, no longer locked in combat, but their long claws of iron were paw deep in snow and dirt. Under them burned lit braziers with guards huddled around them, shivering, clutching spears to their chest. A man exited from under the left paw with the grace of a bird.

"Welcome to the Proving," the man said, raising a hand to the arena, bundled in white furs familiar to Anna. "I'm Simon Sanderson. Are you both here to fight your way out of campaigning?"

The man's breath came and went in faint bursts, a hint of mint raced from it. Black piercing talons of an esant button

76

the brown leather of his coat. Around the fringe of his collar fur puffed against his cheeks like fresh cotton. Anna's eye widened. *He wears fur from a ... storm bison.* She bit her tongue.

"I'm here to do so," she said, watching her tone. "The man beside me is my companion."

Simon pressed two fingers to his chin and then offered them with a welcome gesture.

"You, my lady, are just in luck. There remain only five left of the twenty-four to fight. Those who won exemption from this year's campaigning joined the spectators. The men and women destined to possibly govern Lampara have gone to earn the people's favor."

Norman rested a hand to her shoulder and whispered. "You will be fine, Anna."

He must have sensed her nervousness. So much of what she experienced since entering Cillnar was new to her. Anna bristled at the thought of people judging her from on high, and in great numbers at that.

"Where must I prepare for my fight?"

"I'll show you," Simon said, casting his hand to a tall pair of doors. They were aged, splintered in places, and distant from the guardians. "You, my lady, have evened out the remaining competition. You'll have an opportunity to fight until only two remain, and trust my words, all of them are more than desperate at this point."

What do you—"

"Time is of the direst now," Simon wagged a finger. "Follow me through the entrance if you will," he eyed Cole with a hint of interest, "and without the storm bison."

"But Cole is my—"

"It's wet enough from snow and blood within the Proving.

77

He will be fine with your companion I trust."

Anna huffed, steam belting from her lips like a flustered dragon. She dismounted, embracing Cole, his clouds adding weight to her hood with their snow. Anna hesitated for a moment, then handed his reins to Norman. Cole licked her cheek, washing away her disappointment.

"Take care of him, Norman." She frowned. "He's the closest friend I have."

Norman took the reins with a look on his face she didn't understand. "Good luck, Lady Anna."

She crossed between the bears through snow littered with hundreds of boot prints. Anna wanted Cole to be with her like he had against Nathan's men, thinking too that she would be permitted a mount as she dueled in the arena. Each step felt heavy, soon the darkness of the arena's entrance enveloped her. Distant burning braziers kept away complete darkness, but their light was not enough to see clearly. After some time, Simon turned right down a damp, musty hall. She drew back her hood, finding the darkness enough to allow a break from hiding her face.

"Did I hear that handsome lad call you, Lady Anna?" Simon said.

"Yes, my lord," said Anna, sucking in a breath, wiping sweat beads from her eye. "I am Lady Anna Brighton, granddaughter to Lord William Brighton."

"Fascinating!" Simon chuckled. "I'd never expect a withdrawal from a descendant of the first prime. I fail to understand the humor in it."

"My apologies."

Simon spun on his heels before Anna could shield her face, but then she remembered the darkness.

"I laugh, my lady, because it has been ages since Brighton's have shown interest in Lamparien affairs. Why retreat into silence again after all this time?"

Anna sensed the humor in Simon's last words. She clenched her teeth, readied to take a step forward yet found herself uncertain as to how he had wounded her feelings. Never had she embraced her family's past, and until recently, only wanted to have her life remain the same. Calm and away from the responsibilities of governing and having the country see her face. Anna made a fist, releasing her pent-up breath.

"My name was entered without my consent," she said, calmly. "I've not the knowledge or will to govern."

Simon clicked his tongue. His boots hissed against the straw littered over the brick at their feet. Anna continued to follow him. The mint from his breath grew distant with his steps.

"And yet like the others you possess a strong enough will to fight your way out of responsibility," said Simon. Grimness firmed his words as his pace increased. "I believe our prime made a poor choice in sanctioning these fights."

"How so, my lord?"

"Because, my lady," Simon peered back. "Public shaming is far more deserving of those not caring for their country."

Chapter Nine

The air was growing colder. Snow fell once more as the wind took hold of it, covering Cole's massive hump and legs, giving the old storm bison some of his youthful white back. The bison shook it off, groaning and huffing. Norman noticed the slowness in his movements as he did. They both needed shelter with there being no certainty of when Anna may resurface from the Proving. Norman decided they'd return when morning came, knowing Anna would scour the capital. *He is her closest friend.* He sighed, snow nipping and biting at his cheek. He couldn't feel the cold, but Anna's final word made him wish he did. Norman wrapped the horse and bison's reins about his hand, wishing he meant as much to her as Cole did. She had spent nearly all her time with the storm bison. Even riding him to their lessons at Simdorn's temple.

He led Cole and the horse over the bridge, their thick hooves clopping against the bridge's stonework. Norman moved a few paces ahead. The carriages narrowed the street so much that there was just enough room for them to fit. There were no horses tied to any of them. It sank his hopes of any inn having available stables.

He turned back toward the Proving peering between his horse and Cole. Deep within his heart Norman hoped Anna would succeed. But from Simon's words and what he knew himself of the rule changes for withdrawal from campaigning, Anna didn't possess the same desperation. Norman saw in her the strength of a warrior, one brave and swift like those of his clan in the south. He half wondered if Lord William had a rutoe train her as a child.

Norman shook his head, leading Cole and his horse up the street they had taken to find the arena. The buildings on either side reached high enough to blot out the great height possessed by the Proving. He said nothing of it to Anna before, but as the arena came into view, he had mistaken it for a mountain. Norman's thoughts drifted back to when they had reunited outside Williamton's southern gate. There was a fear behind the face Anna displayed, one that enhanced her words of not being fit to govern. And yet when she found him amongst the smoke, his arms overwhelmed with scrolls, she had given swift instruction on finding safety. *She truly doesn't believe in herself,* he thought. *Not in the way I or her grandfather do.* He kept onward after tying his horse's reins to Cole's saddle horn.

The street was paved with cobblestone, snow crunched in places it hadn't melted. Norman chose this direction to avoid the other which possessed brothels. He remembered a fine inn not far away. Cole huffed behind him. The horse was quiet in comparison, which by Norman's guess had been bred to be calm even in a fight. He hoped the inn possessed room for them both.

Reaching the inn, a sign above it read, *Restful Travels.* The door had a knocker shaped like a man sound asleep. He used it. And within minutes of the noise a woman opened the door. Warmth filled his nostrils woven with the scent of roasted duck.

"I'd like a room for the night, my lady," said Norman.

The woman was at least two heads shorter than him. And that wasn't counting the finely made brown, curly wig reaching a foot high. Faint gray hairs sprouted from where her wig met her ears.

"A room for a handsome man like yourself is no problem." She pulled her flower petal collar tight to her spotty neck as a stiff breeze swayed the sign above. "Will you be in need of lodgings for the mounts behind you?"

"Oh, yes."

Norman stepped aside as the woman squinted, raising a monocle ringed in gold to her left eye.

"The horse will do nicely in my stable around back," she said, letting the monocle drop from her eye. It dangled by a black thread pinned to her chest. "The storm bison will have to be settled elsewhere."

"I must keep him where I go," said Norman. "The storm bison belongs to a … dear friend of mine."

"I see." The old woman razed her monocle back up to her eye. "You're determined to honor your friend. I honor coin. And those rain makers cost nearly as much as an esant to house."

Norman frowned. His shoulders sank, remaining unmoved by the cold.

"I'll be on my way then," he said. "Your honesty is most appreciated."

He led Cole and the horse away, passing nearly a whole house. A crunching mixed with heavy panting chased his light footsteps.

"You might give Leo's a look-see."

Norman turned back to the old woman as she held firm her wig against the wind.

"Does he feel the same about my friend's mount, my lady?" said Norman.

"Yes. And he is more vocal about such things than me. But I know he tends to reward those who help him." she winked.

Norman grinned, running his fingers through his hair.

"I shall give him a try," said Norman, waving to the old woman.

The afternoon was traipsing along at a steady pace. Winters in Lampara tended to hasten the day's welcoming light. It took a short time to find *Leo's.* Several of the carriages trailing toward the Proving remained, lessening his confidence of room being available. *I must try none the less.* Cole had a strong will when required of him, but his age hindered it. Norman knew the cold wasn't an added factor. But the frequent travel was, for Cole was used to the lands belonging to Lord Brighton.

Norman eyed the sub-line below the tavern owner's name. *Poke and Tickle? What shall Anna think of me?* he thought, tying off Cole's reins to a ring by a window just below the sign. Formed into the window's purple panes was a woman half exposed, eyeing a bearded man on a bed sporting an erection. Norman rolled his eyes and raised a clenched fist to the door. Light flickered through the small diamond shaped panes of the window. A clopping filled the long empty street. Doubling and tripling in pitch until a patrol of ten men with arrow shaped helmets and steel mouth shields thundered by. Their capes were of a fine silk, stitched with the silver horse shaded in black of Lampara's governing house. Norman released a breath as he allowed his fist to fall slack. It was wise not to bring Nathan. For though the man was a scoundrel, the outlaw lord was seeking what Anna called redemption. Something he never expected from a man who thought Norman's people didn't belong.

The door creaked slightly as he entered, deciding mention of a storm bison in words was better than his previous action. Heat ran over his face from twin hearths, wide and many bricked, rising like massive supports to the tavern's open beer hall. Men sat at full moon tables; their laps kept warm by women possessing long auburn hair. Flowery perfumes combined with an overuse of eye makeup made him wish to keep a distance. These women had their 'talents,' as he once heard them called. *I do not wish to know what they are.*

For himself, Norman wasn't sure what he could offer Leo. There was too great a risk in using his flames to remove unruly patrons. And changing form may further heighten the city's distaste for rutoe. It pained him to admit such a thing, but the humans of Lampara had embraced the bigotry of their leader.

"What 'ill it be, young lad?"

Norman looked up to a man possessing a cleft upper lip below a full head of short curly hair. He went up to the bar, resting his hands on its aged, chipped surface.

"I need a place to stay for the night," Norman said, refusing to bite his lip. "I have mounts in need of shelter too."

"Well first thing, lad. They call me Leo. What be your name? I run a friendly whore house." Leo chuckled.

"Norman Tilt," he said, noticing the sign above the dozens of bottles behind Leo. "I will require only one room. I have tied outside a horse and—"

Leo raised his hand, peering past Norman to the window.

"It hasn't been foggy in Cillnar for months." Leo folded his arms. "If you be thinking I'm gonna house a storm bison, then you best have a wagon stocked with straw."

Norman eyed him curiously for a moment. It dawned on him, remembering what Cole's rains had done to the straw of Williamton's neighborhoods. He had only wished to remove the flames tormenting the town.

"Is there some way I can convince you otherwise?" said Norman, stemming a rush of anger at the bottom line of the sign. *Quiet One, 2,000.* Leo was using rutoe women to earn coin in a way unbecoming of his people. "I'm proficient at numbers for my profession is accounting."

"A copper counter, eh?" said Leo, returning his focus back to Norman. "Well, if you can," he heaved a ledger large enough to crush him onto the bar. Papers protruded from its sides like the fan feathers of a turkey, "sort this mess out then I might allow a storm bison this one time."

A deep throbbing doubt swelled in Norman's chest. He fought for focus to keep himself from reverting to his rutoe form as he took in the ledger. Leo licked his upper lip, cracking his knuckles after edging the ledger toward Norman. Norman slipped his hand into the deep pocket of his coat, finding the quill and ink bottle. *I must try. For though Anna considers Cole more a friend than I, my care for her remains.* He rested the quill upon the bar, untwisting the ink lid.

"Let's get started."

Leo grinned. "Good luck, lad. I'll have my boy, gather your mounts to be settled."

Norman opened the ledger as Leo snapped his fingers. The door creaked open then slammed shut once Norman began removing the loose papers between the ledger's pages. He settled on a stool topped in sheep's wool. There was a faint scent of cinnamon making its way through the heavy cigar and hearth smoke. A creaking came from his right as he poured over the pages. Leo's handwriting was to Norman's surprise finer than the barkeep's appearance let on.

Hands long and slender, sporting gloves missing the fingertips rested on the bar. A faint rattle familiar to him sent Norman's attention to a hooded figure.

Curled blond hair streamed down the woman's chest as she drew back her hood. Norman noticed the sharpness of her green eyes, and the youth in her face placing her a few years short of his friend. As she ordered her drink the dimness of the room made her gray leathers and arrow fletching like a shadow upon her slender figure.

"Admiring my arrows?" she said. "Or do you think I'm a part of Leo's talented selection?"

Norman shook his head as the archer winked at a woman resting at the bottom of a set of stairs. The woman smiled, aiming her thumb to the rooms above. The archer raised her drink then whispered something he faintly heard. *"Allow me to finish this first."*

"No. It's just you remind me of someone. I'll return to my task," said Norman, regaining his composure.

The woman took a sip of her drink. A red wine with a fine bouquet by its aroma.

"Is she an archer with good aim like me?" the woman said. "If so, I welcome her to campaign at my side so great change can be made for Lampara. It sorely needs it."

There was great need for change by what he had witnessed of late. Straw was far cheaper before his father's farmhand job was taken from him. The rutoe were seen with better eyes before Norman was brought to Williamton. And now assassinations were being done, breaking campaign law forbidding the tightening of competition.

"My friend wishes to withdraw from campaigning," he said.

"I see," The woman scoffed. Her eyes widened at the state of Leo's accounting ledger. "I suppose that is your storm bison outside. Leo was always willing to exchange a favor for another." She offered her hand. "I'm Emilia."

"Norman."

They shook hands before Norman drew out the last loose page from the ledger.

"What business may I ask brings you to the capital, Emilia?"

Emilia sloshed her wine in its glass, drawing in its scent.

"Tell me more of your friend," she said. "Why would she enter her name only to withdraw it?"

"She has her reasons," said Norman, resting his hands upon his lap, "And I am here to support her in what way I can."

Emilia chuckled, finishing her wine. "A man of numbers possesses a great mind too, right? Why not convince her to change her mind?"

Norman repressed a gulp, shuffling papers until all were upright and tidied.

"She is stubborn," he said. "If I were born a quiet one, convincing her to reconsider would be easier."

"I agree." Emilia rested her glass on the bar, pulling a

handkerchief from within her sleeve and dabbing her lips. "But I hear it's painful to have a quiet one in your head."

"What do you suggest? I see what you do, and I know my friend has potential."

Norman began searching for where his mind was going, making marks in the ledger, and totaling where he could. He'd not intended to change Anna's mind, but Emilia was right in every regard.

"Potential is good. I'd convince her of its existence."

"You have convinced me to try," said Norman, catching sight of the waiting woman. She tapped her foot on the step. "Our conversation is making your friend impatient."

Emilia peered over her shoulder, parting her arrows to one side. She turned back with a slight smile on her thin lips.

"My wife, actually. We stay at Leo's when we wish to be away from the norm of our lives."

Norman rested his quill on the ledger, retreating from the thoughts circling his mind like water a funnel.

"Where I'm from the norm is built on old ways."

"That sounds a tad boring," said Emilia, "if you don't mind me saying."

"I miss it sometimes. But work wasn't limited to certain folk as it is now."

Emilia rested a hand over his own, slipping off the stool to the hardwood floor.

"I hope to make work plentiful again in Lampara."

She made her way toward the steps, taking her wife's hand in her own. Norman admired the smile on their faces as Emilia met his gaze.

"Be without worry, Norman Tilt," she said, "you won't be hated for much longer."

Chapter Nine

Norman gasped. *How? How does she know?*

Chapter Ten

Anna discovered there were less people within the arena than she expected. She set foot on what Simon called the champion's platform. Others occupied parts of its lower levels, but her interest was trapped by the vastness of the Proving. A door lay below at its center, large enough to swallow Williamton. Straight ahead what looked like an immense spit loomed above the door, with ropes hanging limp at either end, high enough to align with the champion's platform. The ropes were wet from more than snow by how dark they were. Those who had won their way out of campaigning sat scattered across the arena. The wealthiest sat in colorful pavilions set against the steep incline of the seats. They aligned with a viewing box of white marble and pristine wood columns. Simon told her it was the primnoire's last gift to her prime before her recent death. Anna rested her focus upon the dust glazed stone at her feet. Her heart sank at first but with all she had seen it was hard to remain so. She turned upon Simon, seeing no point in the primnoire's immense spending.

"My lady can wait here if she wishes," said Simon, a bit out of breath from the stairs both had climbed. "Mingle with the other Unwilling as they've been titled," his voice went to a whisper. "Although I don't recommend the one behind us."

The man's garb was unlike any she had seen whether in Cillnar or back home. He wore a helmet in the shape of a disk that shaded his eyes with a small dome at the center, fitting snug to his head. His beard was close cropped and from his lips hung a thin unlit cigar. Upon his shoulders were evergreen plated armor, shaped like the leaves of a spade tree and his boots possessed stars that tinged when he moved. Anna's eye shot to his belt, unlike those upon the rest of the platform, there were identical knives on either hip. A third less ornate one peaked out from his boot.

"How is he permitted weapons, but I not my bow?" Anna hissed.

Simon motioned back to the man with his thumb, retracting it like a frightened turtle into its shell. "Ordermen are not ones to be separated from anything sharp."

Anna glanced over her shoulder for a split second to find the man leaning against the railing. She had never seen an orderman. He crossed his arms, sighing like he had been on the platform for some time. Simon let out a deep shuddering breath, then regained his composure. The arena rumbled. A crackling followed until the ropes below went taut. Clouds emerged from the doors as they separated. Passing through the rising storm clouds came a field of grass fenced in by tall posts wrapped in a black chain linked net. Anna shuddered. Drifting down from the ropes an almost unified bleating came to her ears. *Storm bison's.* By her count there must have been hundreds raising the platform she would fight upon.

"Why does the Proving torment storm bison's like this?"

Anna grabbed Simon by the collar. He gasped, shielding himself with his long well-kept fingers.

"I ... don't choose what beasts keep the Proving in motion, my lady," he said. "If I did possess such a choice, dragons, to me, are far better suited. I believe by the burns on your lips and chin you would agree."

She released him, gripping the smooth wood railing about the platform. Every sense was on fire as she drummed her fingertips. Her grandfather told her Cole had come from Cillnar by the Wayne trading company, and that the old storm bison was once a farmer's way of bringing goods to market. The storm bison's tasked with raising the field of green were white beyond that of a cloud, their hooked horns a shining black.

Anna stirred restlessly on the platform as two of the remaining unwilling made their way to the Proving's center. She squeezed the railing tighter as if turning her knuckles white might do the impossible and free the storm bison's far below.

Both Unwilling were upon the field, small to her eye, but the shortest one's gold armor glinted in the cascading light. The other wore armor of silver, rendering him nearly invisible as he stepped within the sun's brightness. They made her wish she had kept the money given to her by Nathan. Wearing only hunting leathers made her feel vulnerable for they were of better use against thorns than swords.

"You planning to win your way out of this, girl?"

Anna spun to find the man with his disk helmet staring at her. There was a sharpness in his steel blue eyes like she was a target for his knives.

"Yes," Anna said, abruptly. "I want to win and go back to my quiet life."

What life? she thought. *I've no home or coin to purchase one.*

"I doubt you've got what it takes," said the orderman. "The desperate tend to fight harder than most."

He removed his helmet, revealing hair slick with sweat and black like his tunic. The stranger brushed snow off his helmet and replaced it on his head.

"Am I not also desperate like the others?" said Anna, firming her tone. "I do not wish to campaign. I'm no leader."

The orderman raised a burning coal with the tip of his knife, lit his cigar, and then flicked the coal into the brazier beside him. Anna blinked.

"Your focus is already off balance thanks to your love for those rain makers." The orderman drew in a long drag of his cigar, removing it from his chapped lips. "And to answer your question, 'my lady', I've more to lose than peace and quiet." He appraised his cigar for a moment before placing it between his lips. "You see. No orderman like me takes pleasure in protecting a prime who don't give two shits about his people. The boy's and I didn't want assassination on our conscience, so we played a round of 'outpace the cheefox,' and well, my horse threw a shoe."

"But why do you come here if replacing Prime Luther was your intent? Sir?"

"My name is of no concern unless you become primnoire," the orderman said, a hiss in his voice like a serpent poised to strike. "I've got to win this before I'm found out and stripped of my disk helmet."

Anna turned away from him, unsettled by the man's demeanor. She knew her reason for being here mattered, and that it was for the best.

A gong rang out from above them, rattling her teeth with its deep thrumming. Cheers from those seated below followed it. The Unwilling clashed with one another, slow in their steps somehow. Every sword blow echoed like a knife dropped against brick in an opposing room. Anna admired their determination, tapping her fingers on the railing in her excitement.

"Duels were once fought on mount," said Simon. "They used spears with a pitch to divide the opposing champions. It appears these two are most determined."

The movements of both Unwilling grew clearer, the traveling clouds removing sunlight, turning their armor to a darker silver and gold. And in an instant the fight ended with a cry, weak, but tragic to her ears. A chill ran up Anna's spine as the man in gold seized his arm. His opponent knocked his sword from his grasp. The sword tumbled across the ground as his knees buckled, falling to the lush grass. The man in gold armor cast up his arm in surrender. The gong reverberated once more, and a faint creak below it drew her attention.

A woman wearing a flowing dress of green and red emerged. Her hair was bound back tight with a small pale bear pin. It made Anna reach for the broach in the pock against her belt. It was made of wood instead of the bright white stone the woman's bear looked to be crafted from.

"Would Ronald of Flood Street and Lady Anna Brighton make their way to the Proving's center," said the woman, in a voice sweet and clear.

On Anna's blind side footsteps clicked up the steps to her section of the platform. She faced Ronald, finding like herself, the young man wore no armor. He was shorter than her yet there was strength in his shoulders and calluses gave his fingers an almost protected look. Anna gasped. His face was burned too, but on the opposing side. His eye was unsealed unlike her own. He gave her a look she had never received from a man. It was lustful and his tongue moistened his lips like he saw Anna as some meal. She shivered, following him and Simon under the balcony where the woman stood poised, hands folded. Words wisped from the woman's painted lips. Anna couldn't hear them, but their movement was clear. *Watch that one!*

* * *

The familiar hiss of grass against her boots put Anna's mind at ease. Ronald entered from the opposite end of the arena. His sword's dull side rested upon his shoulder like its weight was familiar to him, while the sharp edge caught fresh light from the mid-afternoon sun. Anna had seen a similar sword when last in Cillnar. It was cast as one solid piece with a screeching eagle made of gold for a pommel and a hilt bound in brown leather. She held its twin, both aged well, except the eagle pommel of hers was vigilant and calm. Anna forced her struggle behind a blank face, finding the sword came up to her shoulder in its length. She had never learned the purpose behind both swords, but she knew that neither were for open battle nor the performance of execution.

"Are you ready, love?" said Ronald. "How's bout I beat you and then we leave for a go under the sheets?"

Anna dried heaved.

"What? Am I too crispy for ya?" He chuckled. "OK! How

about you call it quits, and when I win the tournament in two months, I'll have a wizard make mi self pretty for ya?"

"I'd rather," Anna swallowed her reemerging bacon, scraping her teeth against her tongue. "Bathe in horse shit."

Ronald readied his sword with a wide grin exposing his rotten, broken teeth.

"I guess we'll see who ends up on top then."

Anna raised her sword as Ronald charged. His arms remained steady, unlike her own, as he swung at her side. She sped forward with the sword's weight carrying her momentum. Her blade chimed against his as she held it firmly. Every thought focused on what he said earlier. Anna cried out, her leg collapsing and twisting. She released her sword, rolling on the ground, rubbing out the pain. Laughter from the seats beyond crashed upon her like a wave. The Proving wasn't filled, but the amusement made Anna's ears ring. She gulped at the sound of hastening footsteps.

"I can rub your leg for you," said Ronald, towering over her. "And by the look of you, I'm not the only one in need of patching up."

She climbed to her feet, ignoring the sun's heat beating against her cheek as the laughter carried on. Time for shame and dwelling on her past stalled as she realized something. The crowd knew Ronald and favored him despite his burns. His wielding of the dueling sword was skilled. *He's done this many times before.* She picked up her sword, charged, and he caught her strike near the crossbar of his sword. Compulsion demanded she hide her face, but Ronald's pride-sharpened smile jabbed at her like a needle stitching an open wound.

It pulled at her mind with every blow she gave, and everyone she blocked, of what may give Ronald more glory than he deserved. If she lost to him, earning Lamparien favor remained ahead before the tournament. And if she won, those in the crowd cheering for him might still follow Ronald regardless. Anna collapsed on her back, feeling the dull edge of Ronald's sword knock her legs out from under her. The crowd laughed again. She groaned as a cramping gripped her leg muscles. She clenched her teeth, dug the sword's tip into the grass and rose.

"You look tough, love," said Ronald, grasping his sword's hilt with both hands. "But looks don't make the fighter."

Ronald swung downward, seconds split in two, the sharp edge aligned with her shoulder. Anna spun the sword in the dirt and heaved with all her strength. Ronald cried out as spittle lashed from his lips. A crack sounded from his side as he collapsed. She dropped the sword and stumbled, righting herself. Anna clutched her arm for a moment, thankful he'd not succeeded, or it would be gone like her right eye. She found herself agreeing with Simon about public shaming instead of what she had just experienced. Ronald gasped and heaved, raising his hand with great unease. Another idea came to her, one that gave logic to having the Unwilling fight their way out of it, but it was something she wanted to confirm with Norman.

"Guess I better learn to block, huh, love?"

The gong rang out to signal the fight's end. Anna's nerves eased to a simmer. Those spread throughout the arena were silent, as if the man on his side were dead instead of injured.

"You fought well." Anna said, a bitterness on her tongue. A shuffle against grass made her turn to find men running to Ronald carrying a stretch of fabric held taut by two wood poles. "By Simdorn's grace," she swallowed, forcing what needed to be said. "I hope I didn't wound you to a great degree."

She backed from him, slow in pace as she made to leave. To refuse Simdorn's teachings of forgiveness was tempting for Ronald had been foul in behavior, but she wasn't about to go against her beliefs. The men helped Ronald, careful, yet not enough. He clutched his side, further wrinkling the boiled leather where her blow had impacted.

"Guess you'll find out when I'm in charge. I'll be making sure you know it."

Anna bit her lip hoping for the first time for someone to fail. Ronald winked at her, drawing a line across his throat with a finger.

"I think making you suffer will be me first act as prime."

"You will not have the chance," Anna barked. "There are others better to lead, and I shall win my way out of campaigning."

"Keep thinking so, love," said Ronald. "You got someone special up on that platform left to fight."

It dawned on her, dropping her courage to the depths of her belly. *The orderman.*

* * *

Tension slowly left her chest knowing Ronald was gone. It was no comfort that now he was to possibly become prime, or that many who watched their fight left with him afterwards. But what robbed her of complete relief was the orderman. She knew little about him except that he protected the prime, was swift in his movements, and worst of all feared. There was time permitted before her next fight to refresh. Anna stripped down to her bare skin and rested her hunting leathers and cloak upon a bench. Her feet clapped against old, cracked tile toward an immense steaming bath. A chamber maiden took her clothes, eyeing her burns, withdrawing her lip. She promised to provide whatever Anna needed. Anna sighed once the woman's footsteps faded away.

It wasn't until beyond her grandfather's lands that such fear had truly shown itself. Anna placed one foot into the bath, seethed at its heat, then placed the other in. *Grandfather was right,* she thought, *about Williamton.*

The bath was large enough for several women to wash within. Braziers stood like glowing sentries along the walls. A shaft of light touched the bath's center from a stained-glass window to her left.

Anna applied soap to the washcloth, scrubbing away a month's worth of filth, turning over the next fight in her mind. Simon said a former prime's grandson would fight the orderman first. She remembered him upon the champion's platform, a man servant at his side. The boy was rail thin with red locks. He wore pitted armor that hung heavy upon him, its gauntlets large enough to house a hedgehog.

She drew in the water's heat, watching wisps of steam rise from it. Anna rested a washcloth to her face. Despite her burns being long since free of pain, there was something special about having a cloth against them. A soft slow breath eased from her lips. It was as if she felt complete, and all that remained was for sight to return to her eye.

"Congratulations upon your victory, my lady."

Anna gasped, spun, pressing herself to the side of the bath. She sank neck deep, searching for where the voice came from.

"My apologies for startling you, Lady Anna." There was a

clopping of heels before a figure loomed above. The blond of her hair turned to gold from the window's light. "I'm Evelyn Wayne, our prime's mistress of duels and debates. I'm pleased you bested the street rat."

Anna crossed her arms, pressing them to her chest. She kept the woman's family name at bay, uncertain if it belonged to the owners of...

"But he will campaign with many to support him," Anna said, then wondered. "How can someone like him be—?"

"Loved by so many?" Evelyn interrupted. "He plays to the interests of the people. Lampariens were far more understanding and civilized twenty years ago. Some still are but life changes, and often from bad times outweighing the good."

Anna moved to the steps to find her hunting leathers were still gone. In their place new ones of an emerald color.

"I'll have your cloak returned to you, Lady Anna," said Evelyn. "The garb you came to Cillnar in will be so too if my gift doesn't—"

"No," said Anna, excitement swirling in her voice. "I'm most grateful for your gift."

"Good."

Evelyn sat on the bench, pressing her legs together. The mistress of duels and debates possessed high cheekbones. Her eyes nearly matched the gift resting beside her.

"True," Evelyn continued. "The scum has a head start on many who've gone off to win the hearts of the people. I can tell you though, Prime Luther's sons won't allow victory for Ronald."

Anna stepped from the bath taking a towel near the top step. Evelyn had an admiration in her eyes Anna was uncertain of.

"Why do you look at me as you do?" Anna asked, drying off and then wrapping the towel around her chest.

"'Tis nothing," said Evelyn. "You remind me of my daughter. There is a spirit about both of you Simdorn gives to few."

Anna smiled. A jolt went off in her head of something she neglected.

"A man came with others to kill me before I traveled to Cillnar. He spared me yet said before doing so that Prime Luther had sent him."

Evelyn gasped.

"Why would our prime send soldiers to kill you? He knows campaign law. His sons possess far too much support and coin to warrant such law breaking."

Anna bit her lip, pondering as she wrung out her hair if there was cause to tell Evelyn more. It was irrelevant to mention her grandfather or the method he used to spark reason for Anna being in Cillnar. She dressed in the new leathers to further stall the wish to share more with the mistress of duels and debates.

"My logic was the same as yours," said Anna, finding the leathers snug but with good reason. "I thank you again for your gift. There is fur lining from how it feels."

"Simdorn's high priest say winter will be longer this year." Evelyn smiled. "You'll notice the metal sown within it too."

Anna patted her shoulders and stomach to find thin yet heavy plating.

"I must ask despite my acceptance of your gift. Why give it?"

"Let's not further drift from the previous topic." Evelyn stood, folding her hands. "Once the sun has set the next fight will commence, making time short. If what you've learned is true, the Council of Affairs must be called. I can send word before your next fight."

"Can the council find the truth before then?"

Evelyn raised an eyebrow, placing a hand on Anna's cheek.

"You have my daughter's impatience too, Lady Anna. Investigations aren't as swift as an esant in flight."

"But I'd rather avoid another fight," Anna snapped, backing away. "This is all grandfather's fault. He entered my name and now I'm involved in affairs not my own."

"Affairs not your own?" Evelyn grabbed Anna's shoulder, the fur and plating gave a shield against the woman's strength. "There is much at stake if campaign law is being broken. Do you not care for Lampara if one of the prime's sons win?"

"I..."

"They're popular in appearance only. Neither have a mind about them for governing."

Evelyn stormed off to the door beyond the bench. Anna meant to follow but froze once Evelyn faced her.

"Lady Anna, there is much that has happened since Luther became our prime. Traditions have been broken, and the council cannot mend them without the prime's approval. I play by the rules for my daughter's well-being."

"How can the council bring Prime Luther or his sons to justice if this is true?

Evelyn narrowed her eyes to slits, opening the door.

"The council can enforce laws and safe-guard traditions while being both protectors and advisors to the prime. Why do you not know this?"

"I was never good at remembering history."

"You had best improve your memory."

"Why?"

"Because" Evelyn swung open the door, passed the maiden, and then faced Anna again. "Prime Harry Brighton shaped our laws."

Chapter Eleven

There was no purpose at present to hide her face. Both the hood of her new hunting leathers and the one from her cloak hung limp and empty down her back. All Unwilling and city folk not gone with Ronald knew her face. Her worry compounded more for Evelyn. The mistress of duels and debates had sent word to the council. She learned this through Simon as both looked down from the champions platform.

"Where is she now, my lord?"

"Above us as is her duty, Lady Anna," said Simon. "If I were you, or anyone for that matter, I'd give the council's most respected member time alone."

"I must give my apologies before the gong is rung."

Simon chuckled. "My guess is you wish to avoid campaigning more than anyone."

"What does Evelyn have to do with it?"

Simon Sanderson leaned against the railing as great braziers were lit at the rim of the Proving. The flames were immense, robbing the stars above of their brightness. Those upon the posts holding taut the net of the arena's center flickered to life as the Orderman and noble's son moved out onto the grass.

"Were you to strike already raw nerves with her," Simon said, "your life would end faster than the duel before us."

Anna raised an eyebrow; a laugh bubbled in her throat and then went flat from the concern in Simon's eyes.

"She doesn't appear a skilled fighter to me, my lord."

"Anna. She isn't just someone in charge of overseeing fights such as these. She's an orderman."

Anna stepped back from the railing, wanting to curl into a ball and hide within her hoods.

"But what about the man down…?"

"He's one tier below her. Deadly. But nowhere close to her level of skill."

Every sense pounded at her skull as Anna failed to calm herself. Simon moved to her in one swift motion, placing his hands upon her shoulders.

"You best leave her be," he said, offering an encouraging smile. "Focus on the fight below us and learn if you can."

Anna swallowed her panic, jumping within her own skin as the gong rang out across the expanse of the Proving. Both Unwilling stood their ground at first, the former prime's grandson took two steps back. His fear fueled Anna's as he applied his mouth shield. She grasped at her neck, forgetting again the absence of her pale bear brooch. When she looked up again the Orderman struggled against his opponent. He held his sword near parallel to his chest. The boy's sword soared downward, colliding with the crossbar of the Orderman's sword. They pushed off one another with the Orderman holding his weapon steady, but the boy in his cumbersome armor found his blade dug deep in the grass.

The former prime's grandson slumped over like a rag, panting, then throwing up his fists. Anna leaned hard on the railing, whispering every prayer of confidence she had learned within Simdorn's temple during Monday assembly. One for strength. One for willingness. And finally, one for believing in one's abilities. She drew in a breath to find the Orderman matched the boy fist to fist. The boy swung but like an angered serpent the Orderman delivered a blow, sending the noble's son flat on his back.

Anna set free her breath, knowing at least her prayers kept the noble's son confident. Yet the strength and speed the Orderman possessed made her realize the fight ahead was going to take more than her faith.

* * *

An abundance of relief washed over Anna's chest to know her fight would begin at high noon tomorrow. She made her way out of the Proving with both hoods over her head, doubting word had spread of her to the city. From the pale bear statue to her right a hint of meat, seasoned and charred, reached her nostrils. Fresh snow fell in sheets with the wind pressing against her face and lifting her cloak like a curtain before an open window.

She paused once beyond the bears, their cracks and fading detail coated in fresh snow. Fear crept down her spine. For a moment, she'd forgotten how to breathe, eyeing the grounds before the bridge. Cole and Norman were gone. Anna dashed to where the smell had come from. Guards huddled around a fire, a spit across dripped grease from the chicken it held. She skidded to a halt, feeling the full heat of the fire on her face.

"Have you seen where the man and storm bison went?"

One guard looked up with a sliver of meat between his teeth. He gobbled it up like a dog, grease smearing all over his lips.

"We ain't responsible for who leaves this dump, my lady." He rested his plate against the ground. "They've probably gone somewhere you can't freeze your coin purse off."

"Which way have they gone?" Anna said, eyeing the man strangely. She spotted tracks from the Proving, but snow was so tossed about that finding Cole's prints was impossible.

"The hell if I know." the guard said, thrusting his thumb back to the arena. "We protect the Proving, not rope pullers and pretty boys. Now run along."

Anna grumbled, pulling her hoods tight from a blast of cold air. She gave the Proving a good look before crossing the bridge. Temptation mounted the further she went to leave Cillnar and the Orderman fight behind. The calming bath of earlier hadn't eased the ache in her muscles from the first fight. If she did return to the Proving, was faith in her abilities enough to defeat the Orderman? It unnerved Anna to upset Lady Evelyn, and it seemed returning to the arena was the only way to apologize. She shook her head as she traipsed down the street. Many of the carriages were gone revealing shuttered windows with a faint glow seeping from some.

Above, an argument broke out and then a window cracked open. Anna leapt out of the way as a steaming brown liquid streamed upon a snow drift. A warm surge ran up her throat, lapping at her tongue. She sprinted, the stench like rotten cabbage. It was worse than storm bison dung. She swallowed, feeling her eye water.

Ahead, laughter rang out from on her blind side. A creaking came from a sign over its ajar entrance. *Leo's Poke and Tickle Tavern*

A bleating came from a wooden gate beyond and around the corner from the tavern. Anna's eye widened with her lips curling into a smile. She broke into a sprint, grabbed the gate, and heaved herself over it to face a wall of clouds. They drifted between the tavern and a bakery. The snow below robbed her of balance. Anna slid, swaying her arms. Snow caved under foot forcing her to her knees. Something wet lathered her face with affection, but she knew it to be one thing and one thing only.

"Cole!"

She embraced the storm bison, relief overpowering her. Anna rose with her friend's massive gray head in her arms, catching the whinny of horses beyond his bulk.

"Where's Norman?"

Cole's black marble eyes darted to a door where light flickered from a black lantern. Anna gave him another tight squeeze then checked the door, finding it locked. A moment later, the tavern sign creaked above. Dread filled her chest as she slipped inside, pushing the door shut to a wave of noise that jabbed at her senses like thorns from a bush. Anna thought this must have been the place the city guard mentioned. Norman was too civil for a place like this yet since learning he was a rutoe, new questions had surfaced. How could he wield fire and change form? There was little she knew of his people, and Anna half wondered if that was what he meant by not being allowed in Lampara. *He is kind.*

There's no reason for anyone to fear him. Anna made her way to a long bar with stools topped in sheep wool. Drinking was not her way, nor was it that of any true follower of Simdorn.

"Sir," Anna said. The scrawny curly haired man behind the bar peered over his shoulder. "Where might a man named Norman be? He came here with a storm bison."

The man draped a stained rag over his shoulder then wiped his hands on his equally stained apron. He squinted at her despite both being within an arm's reach.

"I don't recall the lad's name but am not too pleased with his mount soiling the stable. He'd better be a one-night stay, cause he's costing me coin."

Anna dug her fingers into the leather of her gloves. It wasn't Cole's fault, and yet it was never her burden to bear the cost of straw in his stable.

"He's a friend of mine and I can assure you his stay will be brief."

The man smiled giving a hint of a gold tooth from his cleft upper lip.

"Good to know," he said, resting his hands against the bar. "What will you be having?"

"Water."

"We've haven't any for drinking unless you're eager to share with the horses."

A chorus of chuckles made its way from the end of the bar. Anna's throat was dry. She guessed he was joking but wasn't certain the laughter was approval of it or not.

"I shall pass on a drink then," she swallowed. "Have you any memory of where my friend went in your establishment?"

Another round of laughs stirred up as the man behind the bar folded his arms.

"I feel high and mighty enough to campaign if my whore house is nice enough to be called an establishment."

A woman came from a door directly behind the man. Anna averted her gaze from the woman's round breasts, long flowing black hair, and alluring green eyes. The woman embraced the bartender from behind with a smile, revealing her pointed teeth. Anna focused her attention on the smooth wood gracing the bar's surface.

"Meet my leading money maker," said the bartender. "Rutoe have the prettiest women in Lampara." The woman kissed his cheek. "This one doesn't make a peep, otherwise good-bye the block."

Creaking came from Anna's blind side beyond a cluster of tables where men had begun singing an old tune. It was of Simdorn upon her quest for land. Anna's eye brightened, softening as Norman peered over the railing, scanning the patrons below. The men were upon a verse of how the goddess had found herself in a fog with fish as her only sustenance. Anna, like other Lampariens never found a taste for fish, allowing the scaled creature to be at peace should the goddess travel the seas or venture up Lampara's rivers to the lake, Crisuldon.

Anna made for the stairs, resting a hand to Norman's shoulder, telling him she had found Cole not far from where they stood. He removed his gaze from her, hinting at what Anna thought might be disappointment, but for what reason she couldn't tell. They climbed the stairs to a door cracked open at its top. A fire snapped and popped in a hearth near the window.

"Why leave the Proving, Norman?" Anna said, splaying her fingers over the fire to warm them. "And how are we paying for a room when—?"

"When we have no coin," Norman said, resting in a leather-bound chair. Gray plumes of stuffing puffed out around the top. "I saw that Cole required rest and we knew not when you'd be back. I offered my accounting services in exchange for a room. There's only one bed unfortunately."

She saw the bed was sunk and thread bare in places, its sheets were wrinkled, and a blanket folded at the end was frayed and moth eaten. Anna tightened her stance, thinking of that moment with Norman in the woods.

"I will be fighting at noon tomorrow," she swallowed, keeping her gaze upon the bed. She drew in a breath. "It will be against an Orderman."

Norman gasped. His eyes went wide enough to capture her worry like a butterfly net.

"You will…? I wish I could say you'll win. But ordermen are said to be legends even before bestowed with their steel disk helmets. Anna. Ordermen are protectors of whomever governs Lampara. Their training comes from century old lessons."

Anna removed her hoods, dropping down on the bed, raking her hair. She clasped her face in both hands. *Legends!* she thought. Laughter and song breath its noise through the floorboards. Legend was something she believed was just a word to draw attention to characters in a book. *Is it the same for Evelyn? And why have such legends not reached my ears before?*

"Is there no other way to avoid campaigning, Norman?"

Norman sighed. "There is one way, yet if you even tried, such a thing may lead to imprisonment if unsuccessful."

There was no need to ask what he meant; the beginnings

of sadness showed itself from the tremble of his lips. Anna rose, moving to him with a speed an esant would pale at. She held him close, feeling his nervous breaths against her chest.

"I will keep faith in Simdorn, Norman," she said. "Death by the hand of myself will never be my road out of my problems."

He rose from where he sat, peaking just above her eye level. His breath slowed to a crawl. Anna bristled at first as Norman kissed her forehead, but it tossed aside her worries for tomorrow. She returned his affection with the kiss she had been saving since last they parted. He drew in a breath through his nostrils as Anna loosened the string of her cloak. She took a step over it after it piled like snow drift at her ankles. Both made their way slowly to the bed as kiss overlapped kiss.

She had only felt such passion abound in her chest before with another. He was the one Anna believed would ask her to wed him before she rode the dragon. Pushing past old memories Anna felt Norman's chest, absent from its coat and tunic. It was smooth and barren of hair unlike the smithy's during summer months. She slipped out of her new hunting leathers, resting flat on her back as Norman began. Every motion snatched the breaths from her chest as she pressed him deeper with her heels. It drew out excitement from her like an eager soldier at the beginning of a battle.

Anna pressed his face to her chest, finding the noise downstairs overcome by the crackle of the hearth's flames and the hiss of straw in the bed's mattress. She pressed him deep with her arms, a hint of chill wisped from the window to her clenched toes. A shiver raced to her chest as her nipples hardened from Norman's movements. And with a final thrust the cold became a faint memory to the warm swelling within her. Norman rested beside her as they searched for breath amongst one another.

"I waited long for us to do this," said Norman. "If Simdorn doesn't favor you tomorrow we could both—"

She sat up erect, pressing her feet to the cold dusty floorboards.

"Leave now," she said, knowing exactly where his words were leading. "Count more coin for the bar keep, Norman."

"Why?"

The nerve of him. she thought, snatching, and pressing the blanket to her chest. Norman possessed no reason to imagine her failing. She thought of the man with his disk helmet, the sureness of him believing she didn't have what it took to win. Anna shot Norman a hard look, the man, the rutoe beside her puzzled even now by her frustrations.

"Because Norman Tilt, you know why we're here. I cannot and will not lose tomorrow. Now out!"

Chapter Twelve

The sun was near its highest point over the Proving, but during a Lamparian winter its heat seldom possessed enough strength to melt ice. Anna stood with her ankles swallowed by snow and her calf length boots damp from heavy flakes. The dueling sword in her hand was heavier somehow, as if her anger at Norman added strain to her aching muscles. Much of the pain in her back as she stood strong against the wind came from her bed. Norman sat amongst the crowd at the raised rows behind her, begging with eyes barely containing their rutoe red glow.

Her mind lingered on Cole as high noon approached. The storm bison remained outside the Proving, tied to the claw of one of the fallen pale bears. Anna was told by the barkeep no more straw would be lost to her best friend's breathing. It seemed something so basic as straw had become precious like gold.

She held back a sigh as the Orderman made his way onto the field. The sun's rays struck his helmet for a moment before making a retreat. He rested the dueling sword with its calm eagle pommel on his shoulder. Anna kept her sword ready, strain sending tremors up her arms.

The gong rang out.

Anna charged the Orderman, winding up to strike. He knocked her sword away then punched Anna in the temple. She released her sword as he swayed out of her way, watching her stumble with a grimness in his eyes. He yanked and Anna fell flat against the snow, crunching ice, sending tremors of pain up her back.

Shaking her head, Anna undid her cloak and shoved both hands into the depths of her hood. Snow crunched as she realized only her fist could defend her, but knuckle fights weren't her favorite. They lacked the distance given with sword or bow. She wheeled back as he came at her with his sword poised to strike. Anna grabbed her sword, heaved it up in time for blade to scrape against blade. Anna clenched her teeth so hard a slight whine came from her jaw. The Orderman snarled, forcing Anna to blink as she kicked his leg. He fell to one knee, drew back his blade, swung it and cracked Anna in the knee.

Pain surged like a fire gaining strength. The strike sent strain into her throat. She gagged and crawled away as the crowd jeered and called for her to yield. Every rushing sense coursing through her head made her wish to oblige them, but that meant greater dangers ahead. She placed weight on her foot, wincing when upright once more.

"You're beaten, girl," said the Orderman, getting back to his feet. "You don't want me to make you a cripple."

Anna eyed her sword. Its enraged eagle was only an arm's reach away. The scent of wet grass rolled in her nostrils, blood

115

lingered on her tongue. Temptation to lung for it snatched her every breath away. She concentrated on him, battling back the ringing in her ears. The crowd called out again, but their voices sounded muffled.

"I won't yield when I must campaign alone. Not when I've neither the skill nor coin to lead."

The Orderman chuckled. He raised his sword, resting the dull edge against his shoulder.

"Your confidence lies in an open grave, my lady. You want someone to bury you but desire a way out to open grass as well."

Every muscle ached as the air grew crisp enough to start a nosebleed. Anna shifted in her stance, finding herself in almost agreement with the orderman. She did wish to hide from the world. It was so much different than the town she grew up in. And with her drive to win her way out of her grandfather's foolishness, open grass was like freedom to her. By Simdorn's teachings open grass meant possibilities with so many blades of green reaching straight for the sky.

Rushing for her sword the Orderman grimaced, sprinting with his sword held high. Anna heaved the dueling sword up in time to catch the razor-sharp edge of his. He pressed, the stench of his cigar hailed from his breath, irritating her nostrils. Locking the crossbar of her sword with his Anna ripped it from his grip, losing her own with his resistance. Her eye followed the two blades but fell shut at a quick massive blow.

* * *

The room was near pitch black except for candles on either

side of the bed. They gave faint hints to the high ceilings and rushes filled the air with their scent. The stands supporting each tall candle were of brass, guiding each tiny flame upward like a spiraling staircase. Anna eased her head from the pillow, a blanket of dizziness wrapped itself about her eyes and mind.

At a distance sat a slim figure with his elbows pressed to his knees, folding his hands in prayer as he let out a low sigh. *Norman?* Anna thought, propping herself up with both elbows. He looked up at her after some time.

"Lady Anna," he smiled.

Her lips teetered on the edge of anger and relief as he moved to her bedside, dropping to one knee. His hair was a mess, brightened by the candlelight. Even alone Norman held to his human form. Anna suddenly wished he wouldn't, finding herself almost ashamed of her anger toward him. A lump formed in her throat before her lips had time to form a word. Her previous feelings about campaigning made ..., she gasped.

"I ... lost."

"Yes," said Norman. "Yes, you did, my lady. I'm sorry."

Anna shook with soreness and worry, collapsing against her pillow. Her last effort for victory had been something she taught herself. It was meant to both amaze and alarm before she'd done the same as the Orderman had her. Anna rested a hand to her blindside, shuddered, but then found herself lost.

"Where are we?"

"You're safe within my husband's home."

Emerging from the distant darkness, Evelyn's heels clicked against polished tile, hissing as they met the furs surrounding the bed. She wore a breastplate of gold, shaped to her figure with a sigil of two 'V's' fused to form a 'W' between her breasts. Below them, shaped from a green stone, were the same animals that graced Nathan's medallion. *Wayne.* Anna guessed. A dress of yellow silk flowed from the base of the mistress's breastplate. Within Evelyn's arms were the hunting leathers Anna wore from the Proving. She hadn't noticed soft night silks upon her person. They were light, unlike any she had worn as a child.

"I thank you for taking care of us, Lady Evelyn." Anna bit her lip. "Yet you seemed angry with me before my last fight."

"I possessed disappointment, not anger for you," said Evelyn. "Your family began it all. Choosing to make laws against governing by authoritarianism and dictatorships. Many like me have fought to keep it this way." Evelyn cleared her throat. "I've news from the investigation. We have learned—"

A door appeared to Anna's left, its light from the hall stretching across the room. *Click.* Anna gulped, firming her face like battle was to commence. *Click.* The door closed and soon within the candlelight stood the Orderman from the Proving.

"What do you want?" said Anna.

"Ease that temper, my lady," said the orderman. "And go back to sulking over your mistress, kid."

The Orderman turned, revealing Norman with a clay pitcher raised above his head. Norman's ears were pointed, and teeth were clenched. The red eyes of his rutoe form flared and then settled resembling dying embers. Anna gave him a nod. Norman slipped back to her side, morphing into human form once more.

"Leave us be, sir. And go back to the ordermen," said Anna, pushing herself up to feel less like a rabbit trapped in its hole. "I must now do what I know I can—"

"Please, cease your self-doubt," Evelyn interrupted. "It will get you killed long before your two months have expired."

"That isn't enough time to earn favor with anyone." Anna hissed. "I'm a nobody one to Lampara. A—"

"Again, with this poor me song and dance," said the Orderman. "You're someone now, my lady. Word is being spread about you campaigning. You'll be worse than a nobody if you don't survive the tournament."

Anna fell silent. She'd forgotten about the tournament. She folded her arms, pressing them to her chest. Everyone kept their gaze fixed on her. The Orderman slipped a cigar from his breast pocket, sheathing it slowly after the sharp look Evelyn sent him. Norman's lips moved to say something, but he looked to the others instead.

"What is it, Norman?" said Anna.

He backed from the bed, stopping in mid stride before his chair. "What if we search for the man, Lord, ugh, our friend Nathan spoke of?"

Her eye widened slightly with a faint smile crossing her lips. It could work and she would not be alone during the tournament. This mysterious man sounded strong and by Nathan's vague description clever. And yet, she sighed, neither Nathan nor any of them knew where this man might be.

"Who do you speak of?" Evelyn asked. "Time is swift and if he can campaign with you my men will find him."

"We do not know his name or where to find him," Anna said. "I know he isn't someone in the sights of Prime Luther. His prime-ship wants me dead."

"Wait." the Orderman barked. "That old man's breaking campaign law for those pretty boys?"

Evelyn turned to him, crinkling her nose, raising an eyebrow. "An investigation is underway, Phillip. You and I may be protectors to our prime, but I fear he seeks to be in control indefinitely."

"What do you mean?" Norman said, at Anna's side again.

"It means Prime Luther has found a way to govern beyond the law's limits," said Evelyn. "He needs only to stay alive, and with his cunning anything is possible."

"He wishes to be a dictator while using his son as a vassal." Anna gasped. "He would be his father's mouthpiece."

"In some twisted way. Yes," Evelyn said, flashing a grin. "So, what shall you do, Lady Brighton? Allow our prime to keep his hold on us all, or campaign and become our next primnoire?"

Anna released a deep sigh. Life beyond what she had grown up knowing was desperate and cruel. The capital couldn't trust Lampara's people to be armed with blades or bows. Dead men lie in alleys unattended, rotting amongst the living. What was in abundance for someone like her grandfather was in short supply for others. It reminded her of the crudeness in Leo and the guard protecting the Proving. But what churned her stomach most was the treatment of storm bison's. A creature she knew from scripture once prized for their strength and kindness.

"I will find a wizard and become Lampara's Primnoire."

* * *

The red goose fletching hissed across Anna's palm as she inspected her arrows. Slinging her quiver over her shoulder, smoke met her nose from the leather straps. Evelyn had given them food, water, and other supplies, even arranging for Anna's bow to be returned. The sun was at its early light giving a darker shade to their white shafts. Letting the final one drop back into her quiver, Anna and Norman made for Natlendton. Anna halted them just outside the city entrance, asking Norman if he remembered what direction the town was but the young accountant shook his head. She looked down from Cole at the guard beside her.

"Do you know which way my companion and I should travel to Natlendton?"

The guard looked up at her with a raised eyebrow then spat at Cole's hooves.

"You're pulling my ear aren't you, love?"

Anna leaned back a bit, keeping her face plain, ignoring the huge boil above the man's brow.

"It's my first time this far west." Anna said, half lying, wishing five years hadn't separated her from last traveling Lampara. "I am Lady Anna Brighton. I'm in need of direction to find a friend while campaigning to be Primnoire."

To use her family name as a way to snatch respect from another left Anna uneasy. Although, in Williamton everyone knew who she was, which made such a gesture pointless. The guard clapped his hands together and blew into them, rubbing both to remove the red forming from the cold in his fingertips.

"Head north toward them trees." He pointed to his left with a shaky finger. "Now be off with you. I don't spend my breath on rain riders like you."

"Come, Norman," Anna said, giving Cole's reins a flick. "We won't keep these men from freezing."

Norman chuckled, following her as a strong wind sent the guard's teeth into a chatter. Anna pulled both her hoods tighter to her face. *If I become primnoire such despising of storm bison's will be forbidden.* She gulped after the thought. What she never wanted was becoming more personal to her by the day. From the harshness of the city to distaste for the one creature she believed was the best in all the world.

They went north after receiving the rude directions facing a forest doused in white. Hints of green could be seen in the distance, and before long, the pine caressed Anna's senses from those trees reaching to greet her and Norman. Being with nature once more released her from the stone and mud confines of the capital. She thought of what Nathan had said of the town of Natlendton, reminded of the swiftness of nutsnatchers. Once when eighteen she saw two during what the master of arms called mating season. Both leapt from branch to branch performing twists and spins, the male with a dark streak of brown down its back. The female a light brown with tiny white spots.

Anna smiled as Cole's clouds released sleet in place of rain. The cold weather possessed power over a storm bison's clouds like it did the ones of the sky. She reached, gathering a handful of flakes and drank some before they froze. The snowflakes were light and soft like Cole's fur.

She remained quiet as they maneuvered through the overgrowth. The anger at Norman from the other night slowly subsided in pace with the snowfall. Anna could not help but want to forgive him. Norman never wavered from his loyalty, always helpful and though nervous at times, he wanted to see her happy.

"I'm sorry for growing angry with you, Norman."

Norman brushed snow from the top of his saddle horn. "I care for you. The affection we shared was something I longed to do. I believed you had grown to fully trust me."

There was a sadness in his words that melted the chill forming in Anna's chest. To weep felt right yet she wanted to remain strong for him somehow. She found herself caring for him more than when she had at sixteen, admiring only his appearance then.

"I...," she said, pulling up slowly on Cole's reins. "I trust you. I always have. And now that I see what has become of our country, I know someone must change it."

His eyes brightened to a swirling, yellowish red. The ends of his ears formed into points as his skin returned to its original dark green.

"Does this mean you wish for me to campaign at your side?"

"If campaign law permits an entry so late." she said. A warmth filled her to see him happy. "But I do wish to find Nathan first."

Norman parted his lips but then closed them. She knew he understood the fear still warden over her confidence.

"Understood, my lady."

"You may call me Anna."

He smiled. The wind played with the treetops releasing a light dusting over them. They went on for some time with Anna keeping low. Cole's size gave her one disadvantage in the woods, but with time she had learned to avoid shallow branches by mere instinct. Early mornings remaining light met them before entering a clearing. The clearing was short, meeting a frozen lake in the formation of a horse's tail. Toward the tails tip a stone bridge linked a road to an ocean of homes tipped with chimneys and surrounded by a wall of disheveled bricks. Gray smoke drifted from chimneys upon the tallest homes. Atop the wall shielding the dry, aged homes, wood spikes shot up like unkempt hair.

Anna and Norman followed the shoreline to the bridge. The wall protecting Natlendton gave little footing for a horse and storm bison. The air grew warmer by a few degrees as they neared the bridge, but Anna's nose ran from holding still the tears of earlier. Her heart was light now, still burdened, but lighter knowing she wasn't alone. She slipped her hand within her first hood, feeling the burns upon her cheek. *If he can accept me, then why cannot others? Why do I still wish to seek a wizard?* Anna swallowed, aligning her eye with the cracked stone of an arched sign at the start of the bridge. *Natlendton*, the sign read and, below in twisted writing it said. *Where Your Coin Finds a Happy Home.* She crinkled her nose at such odd words, wanting to ask Norman what they meant, but if she was going to win favor with the people, learning on her own was needed.

The town entrance was shut and manned by not men but by two pale bears of Simdorn. The goddess stood between both, shielded by their paws. Neither statue was of stone as Anna believed they should, but of worm-and-age-eaten wood. Anna slid from Cole's back, giving him a good rub behind the ear. She pushed open the doors. They creaked in response to her efforts. They were smooth, made of an older wood than the pale bears. The street beyond was deserted except for a gray tabby cat licking its paw at the street's center.

"The town appears abandoned, Anna," Norman said.

"The cold might be keeping everyone inside," she said, mounting Cole. "Winter has only just begun by the pure white of the snow. A month from now it will grow colder and hold hostage the sun in early evening."

"I see," Norman panned his vision as they came to a choice

of streets. "Which way do you believe Nathan has gone?"

"I'm uncertain, since he was easier to track by Roland's lightning."

They decide to head where wagons shallow with straw and piled with blanketed fruit formed a caravan down a narrow muddy street. A rush of icy wind scattered some of the straw strewn across it. Two men came from an alley, leaning against one another, sharing a bottle made of clear blue glass.

"Look what wandered into town, Paulberd," said the man squeezing the bottle by its neck.

"An ignited one and a storm bison," said Paulberd, letting off a fart. "Oh. Pardons, me lady. It came from the cellar, not the attic this time."

Anna gave the man a puzzled look, but then made the connection.

"Have either of you seen a black storm bison and a man with blond chin whiskers?"

The man in charge of the bottle downed its remaining contents, burping loud enough to send the cat sprinting from its spot.

"Pardon me self, m' lady. The last I saw another storm bison was at Liza's."

He pointed past them to a street beyond the town's center. Its homes leaned toward one another with open shutters. The gloom of it gave Anna a feeling she didn't like.

"My thanks, Paulberd," she said. "We will be off now."

Paulberd snatched the empty bottle, raising it to her. "Don't let Slick Street frighten ya, m' lady. The last bum snatcher was strung up by his acorns. We tolerate only thieves here."

Anna left the two men with Norman trailing her. His horse snorted as she snapped Cole's reins so hard it left the storm bison peering up at her as he dashed across cobblestones. She had never heard talk such as this. Anna felt a tug at her cloak, but she believed it was the wind. She crouched low until her eye peaked above Cole's hump. The homes and boarded up shops narrowed. In the distance there remained no place left to run.

Cole had far outpaced Norman's horse. It was as though the whole time she believed someone was about to reach out and snatch her from his back.

"Anna." Norman called, trotting up to her. His horse panted as he dismounted. "Are you alright?"

"I … was unfamiliar with what he said. The look in his eyes, as if he were this bum snatcher himself."

Norman sighed, resting a hand upon his horse's head, stroking its mane.

"Lampara has changed," said Norman. "Or it may have always been this way and neither of us knew it."

Anna sniffed back the urge to allow her nerves to overcome her. Every bit of it teetered on the tip of a needle. A warmth ran over her, but Norman was out of arm's reach. She removed her hoods, yet the warmth died only a little. She found the anger and fear from before had lessened. Creaking came from above like the murmurs of a waking bat.

A sign hung half rotted and eaten by age. Neither of them was certain it was Liza's until finding upon the door below a notice written on yellowed paper and stained by something fresh and fowl. Anna slid off Cole's back, tying both him and Norman's horse to a crossbar upon a post below the tavern's window. The window was dusty, but it held beauty against the storm of decay the town was in. Its diamond shaped panes were small, purple, with gold roses at the center.

Norman opened the door for Anna, bracing himself for what may come. Nothing. And then a lady, hunched and bundled up to her cheeks came to the door.

"Are you here for the nutsnatcher races?" she said, peering up at Norman. "They've been outlawed since the prime's last visit." The old woman spotted Anna, smiling a smile of browning teeth. "I'm sorry to disappoint, m' lady."

Anna wished to ask what became of the races, especially the nutsnatchers themselves, but time was short.

"We are searching for a friend," she said. "He has blond chin whiskers and rides a black storm bison."

The old woman's face sank into the nest of scarves about her neck.

"Poor lad. He kept weeping about a Lady Anna."

Norman raised his hand to announce her, but Anna cut him off.

"I'm Lady Anna."

The old woman brushed past Norman, taking Anna's hand gently in her own.

"He's been taken to the chop block."

Anna gasped.

"What for?" Norman said, eyes flaring. "Anna is here with us. No death came from—"

Anna shot him a look, but then realized her hoods had been down. She bit her lip, finding no repulsion had risen from the old lady.

"Why?" Anna said. "Why do you not recoil with me like this?"

"I live in a place far worse than those burns upon your face, Lady Anna. Your friend got himself drunk and spilled his guts to me. Sad thing is soldiers a table away congratulated him on serving some cause. I heard that part before they went to arrest him."

"Why arrest him at all?" Anna said. "I wasn't…"

"I'm sorry for not stopping them, m' lady," said the old woman. "Those soldiers made it seem to all me customers that your friend ordered the dragon to kill you, but your friend was so drunk he couldn't bring himself to protest."

Anna patted the old woman's hand, untied Cole. Cole raised his leg, clouds drifted from his nose to the shuttered windows above.

"Come Norman! We must save him. Where will they be executing him?"

The old woman pointed down the street, instructing them to head opposite the town's entrance until finding the head of a bear with its mouth open wide. Anna recalled her grandfather finding execution unjust before Williamton had been named after him.

Anna took off ahead of Norman, leaving the old woman in the midst of a storm. Norman mounted his horse, catching up to her this time. His horse and garb wet from the trail of Cole's clouds.

"How will we save Nathan, Anna?" he said, his face returning to human form. The green replaced by pinkish flesh and the black of his hair lightened to brown. "We may be outnumbered."

She turned to him, wishing for some reason to do what he could. To alter her appearance to her old unburnt self despite what the old woman had said. *Why can I not accept myself as others have?* Anna shook her head and thought about Norman's concerns, pulling up both her hoods.

"I must consider too people know I am campaigning," she

said. "It will not do well to harm soldiers of Lampara."

"You are right, Anna," said Norman. "But I fear now that may be impossible."

Chapter Thirteen

~~~

They turned right, cobblestones clicking and clacking under Cole's hoof strikes. Anna's quivers across her back, and her bow hung ready from Cole's saddle horn. She hoped words may prevail over the use of violence. Whatever was meant by "cause," must have meant removing competition for the prime's sons. She ran her fingers down the string of her bow to heighten her courage. A bend came in the street toward the sound of gathering voices. Pulling lightly on Cole's reins, Anna led Norman down an alley, stopping before a door. The alley ended at the town's outer wall. She needed time to think of what words may save Nathan. She slid off Cole's back, grabbed her bow and handed his reins to Norman.

"Why have we stopped?" said Norman, dismounting. "We may already be too late."

"We aren't," said Anna, realizing what was missing. A sound that would come to them when they reached Natlendton. "The temple's bell hasn't rung. A bell would have rung at the capital."

"You know more of history than you claim credit for." Norman smiled. "What do bells have in relation to execution?"

"A bell signals a man has been punished for his crime," Anna said, blushing at his admiration. "My grandfather outlawed execution in Williamton. He believed through banishment a man deprived of all he knew could be punished justly. The bell was removed from the town's temple when I was sixteen."

"A bell is rung at a Simdorn temple once a man is executed?"

"Yes. The goddess is a believer of cruel justice, and a bell signals its completion."

Anna turned up a narrow alley, finding reason in her grandfather's defiance of Simdorn's ways. There was much she knew of forgiveness, prayer, and remembrance of promises, but to take a life for great crimes seemed to counter those teachings. Perhaps, she thought, the goddess had her limits for the misdeeds of mankind like anyone else.

Her shoulders reached building to building the further she went. Every nerve raised the hairs upon her neck as she slung her bow across her back. At a distance upon a platform of aged brick Nathan stood slouched and quivering. One man in armor of the capital guard restrained him. Anna stopped short of the crowd, her heart pounding. The bear's head was like the one from home, opened mouthed and pointing to the sky. The bell announced an ultimate sin had been committed, and an axe was Simdorn's hand passing final judgment.

"This man shall be made infamous," said the judge, dressed in dark green robes. "Murder is the highest sin to dishonor of our goddess." He pushed Nathan face first into the bear's open mouth. "May Simdorn's guardian bear Isbran hold steady your neck, Nathan Barden. May you receive punishment with pride and dignity."

Anna pushed through the crowd, receiving curses along the way. She raised her hands once at the edge of the platform.

"This man is innocent," she said, climbing up until eye to eye with the green robed judge. "I am who you believe has been murdered."

Her fingers tensed, every nerve at the boiling point as the crowd demanded explanation. Many had only wrappings of cloth to warm their feet, others, garbed in a mishmash of coats. Nathan winched as he looked up. The bear's teeth left cuts up the sides of his neck, each sending streams of blood down into a funnel below his throat.

"Anna. You found me." Nathan swallowed. "I guess you won yourself out of the mess of campaigning."

She knelt before him, resting her hand on his cheek. It was wet and cold. The hairs of his chin whiskers were dark as if he'd been dunked in water.

"I failed, Nathan." Her throat filled with emotion. Every beat of her heart made it hurt to admit it. "I must campaign. And there is corruption above it all."

Fingers pinched deep into her shoulder as her hoods shaded her from a flash of light.

"Did I hear right or am I both deaf and daft?" said the judge.

Anna yanked herself free of his grip, the heels of her boots tasting the platform's edge.

"You heard right, my lord." Anna huffed. "I am Lady Anna Brighton."

"Can you confirm this, Barden?" The judge kicked Nathan in the ribs. "Be quick because if I don't remove your fat head soon." The judge pointed to the angered crowd. "They will."

Shouts boomed from the crowd. Each demanding for Anna

to move, and the axe to fall. Her mind felt as if it may split.

"She is who she claims," Nathan grunted. "Now, get me up. I'm still a lord no matter what the prime says."

Anna swallowed her nerves, yearning to relieve the pain in Nathan's eyes.

"I know of your cause against me," Anna said, lowering her voice to a whisper. "I'm to be killed to ease campaigning for our prime's sons."

The judge took a step back, his face reddening with rage as he clasped the green gem medallion around his neck. He leaned in close, raising a finger displaying the green bear ring of his station.

"We'll let him go but," He eyed the crowd. Soldiers on horseback came in from the main street, "you come with us. A life for a life, my lady, or I'll gut him here and now."

The judge drew a bollocks knife from his belt. It had a thin, triangular blade with two orbs above a long brown leather hilt. Anna looked at Nathan, with his hands bound behind his back. Nathan straightened his neck, easing out of the bear's mouth, but dropped into a coughing fit.

"I will go with you," said Anna. "But I must see that Nathan is tended to first."

The judge gave the chain of his medallion a tug then nodded.

"Fair enough," he said. "Lampara's lawmen are above all else merciful."

Anna went to one knee, the soldiers aiding her with Nathan. The crowd protested and questioned as Nathan went into another coughing fit. The bear's teeth scraped against skin, widening, and teasing his existing cuts. Once they had him up, Anna guided Nathan back to the narrow alley she had come from. Norman emerged in his human form, concern aging the youth in his face. Anna slipped an arrow from her quiver, severing Nathan's bonds. Anna smiled to see both her friends safe. A thin shadow raced down Norman's face.

"Anna!"

She jerked back, dropped the arrow, and collapsed to the ground. A horse whinnied as the crowd parted behind her like grass from a fleeing rabbit. The rope pressed her arms hard to her sides as the horseman dragged her through the streets.

"Norman!" she screamed. "Help!"

Anna twisted and turned as the horse increased speed. Her arrows rattled in their quivers and her bow's string pressed deep into her neck. A change came over the crowd as if the anger of before was nonexistent. Some chased after the soldier dragging her through the streets. They were met by more soldiers on horseback. Anna could feel her cloak tugging and tearing as its hood slipped from her head. The hood of her hunting leathers yanked at her scalp. She struck her boots against the ground to find no purchase, wanting to scream, fear blurring the townsfolk chasing after her.

A loud tear ripped the dangling half of her cloak as it caught under her boots. Soldiers followed on either side with no emotion upon their faces. A rush of heat raced overhead as a lashing tongue of flames flashed across her face. The rope went limp. She reached up with both hands and seized the rope, turning to find a wave of storm clouds filling the street, flashing orange and red in places. Screams rang out as she maneuvered herself free.

Anna made it to her feet as a face emerged from the clouds. At first, she thought Nathan had recovered somehow, but at such a speed it was impossible. The face was high above her, wet with snowflakes and blurred by clouds. She waded through the storm blanketing the street in snow, flames flashed away from her summoning ungodly screams. Something wet touched her cheek and by the heavy breathing beyond it she knew it was Cole. Anna embraced him then looked up; her jaw dropped to see Norman. His face was still human, brown in hair and absent of green in face. He gave her a nod before pressing on.

Readying her bow, she burst forth from Cole's storms, sliding across the snow, an arrow nocked. Her heart brightened in spirit to see Norman showing his bravery again as she released the arrow. Three soldiers charged her, towering upon their horses, the wetness of the snow bringing a shine to the metal of their helmets. She released three red goose feathered arrows, striking two men in the chest and pierced the eye of a third. Shouts came from her blind side, but no clop of horse hooves joined them. Another roar of flames flashed out the corner of her eye. Soldiers leapt from their horses into the snow, failing to put themselves out, the metal rings of their chain mail glowing red hot. The screams were loud and shrill, yet Anna refused to allow it to get to her. She had heard the screams of men before when Nathan was her enemy, and though it sent her senses into a race, it was live or see Prime Luther rule long into the decades.

Footsteps grew in pitch behind her. Anna drew an arrow, pulling back as she spun about, but didn't release.

"Where is my mother?" The little boy had a cut above his brow, grasping a wooden sword. "Are you going to kill me?"

Anna eased her arm until the arrow and her bow were both in one hand. She knelt with hood shading all but her chin.

"I aim for the soldiers young one. Let's—"

"Got you," said a voice, followed by arms tight about her shoulders. "We'll 'ave you out of the prime's way in no time."

The little boy screamed as the man pulled Anna back. Anna waved her hand at the child as he raised his sword, and then a woman came, kneeling and embracing the boy.

"Let Lady Anna go," the woman cried. "You're breaking campaign law. She's in the running."

"Oh, is she?" said the soldier. "Well, she's gonna find out she crossed the wrong folk."

Anna twisted and turned, thrusting her head back, but the man was too quick. They were within the alley she had left Cole and Norman earlier. Its darkness outmatched the midday sun, a rotting smell she hadn't noticed made her gag. Anna thrusted her head back again, striking true. The man's grip loosened a bit, removing the press of chain mail against her arms.

"Lucky shot, rich girl," he said. "Try that again. I dare you."

A sharp pinch went through her leathers and bit her side. Anna seethed. Never had she felt the sting of a blade. It dug deeper as she forced her screams down deep. The woman with her son dashed to the beginnings of the alley, calling for her release. Anna kept her footing yet as the blade dug, her knees grew weak. *I can't give in. What about Cole? Nathan? What about ... Norman?* She slammed the heel of her boot into his ankle. The man let off a yelp, losing his hold on the blade. Anna grabbed his wrist and slid out the blade as she thrust her head back, cracking him on the cheek.

Collapsing to her knees, Anna pressed her hand to her side, seeing the blade had been dropped. Her head throbbed as she stood and grabbed the blade. The man drew his sword, raising it high, charging like a bull angered by the fresh brand from his master. Anna lunged then spun, thrusting the blade into the man's gut, collapsing on her side. The man dropped, letting out a shuddering breath before his face struck the ground.

The woman entered the alley with her son at her side. She dropped to her knees and turned Anna over.

"That monster wounded you. I'll go and fetch help." She rested a hand on Anna's shoulder. Anna winced, finding every breath, every movement pained.

The woman hoisted her son into her arms, headed out of the alley as a shadow blotted out what light could be seen.

"Anna."

The shadow shrunk in moments. The voice it belonged to was deep and quick, but Anna welcomed it. "Nathan?" she said. Her voice wet and weak. "I am glad to of helped."

"Same for myself," he said. His breathing was no longer labored, faint streaks of red ran down his neck. "You're bleeding."

"A woman has gone for help. Has... Has the fight ended?"

"Yes," Nathan sighed. "But one of them got away."

Anna pressed her hand to her side. Her fingers slick with blood as she realized what was to come was her fault.

"I've doomed Natlendton," she coughed. "The prime will punish its people for helping—

"He won't do a bloody thing," said Nathan. "Now rest. I hear someone coming,"

The alley grew darker, filling with clouds and snow. Anna felt herself being raised with hands strong, but gentle as a familiar hump accepted her head. *Cole.* She grew tired. Her sight played tricks on her as the sun streamed against her face. The homes towering to either side blurred and stretched.

Anna breathed easy knowing at least she had saved her friend from the sharpness of unneeded justice.

Chapter Fourteen

Nathan held her arms to her chest. Where the blade had pierced her side, Anna's shirt was raised. The man's strike had slipped between the armor plating. A stranger held her legs down as Anna forced herself to remain calm. The hot poker would seal the wound and halt her bleeding, but to feel intense heat against her skin again was an unbearable reminder of her past. Light filled the barn they were in. Cole's clouds drifted out its immense doors from a stall beside it. She placed all her focus on the outside, the rising clouds and falling snow.

Hissss

Anna screamed. Her lips lashed open as her pain rose in vocal pitch. It felt as if she had shaken the aged rafters of the barn. Nathan and the stranger released her, clasping their ears. The poker clanged against brick, its tip like a fading star. She drew in a deep breath clenching her teeth.

"You have yourself some powerful lungs," said Nathan, releasing his ears from the grip of his hands. "You're lucky that, bastard didn't nick anything important, but you did bleed quite a bit."

A faint crackling and popping came from a stall near the barn entrance.

"Roland," she smiled. "I'm glad he is well."

"And the old boy is glad you're OK too."

She searched the barn, finding some straw wet from Cole's clouds. Nathan stood with a feeding bag in hand and opened Roland's stall. Cole's creaked open.

"Norman!" Anna grinned.

He held a bucket with a reddened rag slung over its rim. Her eye was more on his smile, the long black hair shaping his face. She sat up to receive a bow from the man who had held her feet down. His bow was low as if she was already a primnoire without needing to win his support.

"Your heroics have brightened the town's spirits, my lady," he said, standing up straight, folding hand over hand atop a ragged old tunic. "Natlendton has agreed to back you as our potential primnoire."

"But... I've brought the prime's anger upon you."

"I said he won't try anything," said Nathan, wiping his hands on his sides, wincing as he rolled his shoulders. "A whole town knows he's breaking campaign law now."

"He will know of what happened," Norman said, kneeling beside Anna. "A man escaped from the fight."

Anna gulped. She knew of the man escaping, dreading the possibility of Prime Luther sending assassins after her next. A series of worries raced through her head like papsa fish up a river during spring. Her worries spawned asking if she should continue searching for a wizard or travel from town to town like other campaigners. Soldiers and wild game she could handle, trained killers, possibly deadlier than an orderman were another story. She searched the barn, finding her bow and quivers behind Norman on a long bench.

"I feel I must still head south." She rested her gaze on the man. "I'm honored for your support. I ask you go and prepare Natlendton in case my worries about our prime come true."

The man bowed again, heading toward the door then paused.

"I'm unsure what lies south, m' lady, but my barn welcomes you and your storm bison any time."

Anna smiled, supporting herself with one hand so she may bid him farewell with the other. He bowed and turned, heading to a home near the barn's entrance. A child emerged from its open door, leaping into the man's arms, whispering something. The man turned to her with a smile, urging his child forward.

"And who are you?" Anna said. The child entered the barn slowly, halting just below the beginning of a hay loft. "I'm Anna Brighton of … Williamton."

The child took two steps back, eyeing Cole whose silver hooked horns caught the fading daylight. She was uncertain if it was the hitch in her words or … him seeing the burns on her chin that caused his uncertainty.

"He wants to see your storm bison, m' lady," his father called from the house.

She forced a smile, but it sent the child another step back. His lips trembled. His eyes shot over to Cole, then upon her once more.

"You may see him," said Anna, pulling her hood further over her face until only the steam of her breath showed. "Cole loves children."

He took a step toward the stall, looked at Cole and then at her as if she were a dragon guarding its master's castle. Anna offered her hand to him, but the boy shrieked, taking off for his father. She clamored to her feet, gasped, then dropped, finding she still needed rest. Anna found sympathy in Nathan and Norman's faces as she eased back against a hay bale.

"We head south," she said. "I do not wish to frighten anyone again."

* * *

Nathan and Norman moved at a steady pace behind her. Roland's electric like breathing cracking and popping amongst the howl of the wind. Anna pulled her cloak tight about her shoulders, its tail end mended by the little boy's mother. She peered back to Nathan, his saddlebags packed. The town had given them bread and cheese for their journey. Anna drew up her cloak's hood, keeping her eye on the bridge as they passed under the sign. Her heart remained thankful for Natlendton's support, but she could not accept the feast offered to her last night. The thought of other children finding her frightening was too much to bear.

The air had grown so cold it bit at the tip of her chin. Snow was replaced by icy rain with Cole's storm clouds following the sky's lead. She ran her fingers through the fur atop his hump to relieve the distress of her experience yesterday. It didn't erase the look on the boy's face from her mind, but as if sensing her misery Cole let out an immense blast of clouds from his nostrils. The clouds blanketed the frozen river below the bridge. She smiled, giving his reins a light jerk to hasten their trek towards the woods.

"I can understand now, Anna." Norman put a hand to her shoulder. His reach was challenged by his horse being smaller than Cole. "I don't know the rutoe lands in the south well, but my home city may be a place a wizard will venture."

She rested her own hand over his, the movement jabbed at her side, which was tender from the wound. Neither Norman nor Nathan had spoken since the barn yesterday. Anna was relieved they hadn't, for she needed the quiet time.

"I thank both of you for joining me on this campaign," she said. "For understanding my unease with the burns on my face."

Nathan gave a firm squeeze of his reins and nodded. "And I owe you more now for saving my life."

He loosened his grip and smiled. The black storm bison snorted, breaking up the gray of the day with tiny yellow lightning bolts.

"I would say what debt you feel exists has already been repaid, Nathan."

Nathan shuddered as if about to weep, though he blamed it on the cold. The woods brought a darkness to his face the deeper they journeyed into them. Heading south would take weeks, Anna guessed. She urged the others to increase their speed and cut down on time. Wind grabbed at her hoods as Nathan led them south. Each of them agreed to follow his direction. Nathan, once being with the Wayne trading company, had brought him all over Lampara. The Wayne's were one of the oldest families, employing lords and peasants from and beyond the country's borders.

After reaching a clearing, Anna saw it was mid-morning and had them give the storm bison's and Norman's horse a rest. She slid off Cole's back with slight unease, biting her lip once her feet hit the ground. Anna pressed a hand to her side, then told Nathan and Norman she'd fetch wood for a fire.

Light snow crunched with ice under her feet, her thoughts on all she had experienced since leaving Williamton. She found herself suited for a fight if needed, and able to place others above herself, yet she longed for the solitude of hunting. The child's face made her wish to remain hidden away from the looming threat of a dictatorship. With Prime Luther willing to break campaign law to see his rule continue there seemed no turning back.

The responsibility of gaining more favor from Lamparians may only take good deeds, yet deep down it didn't feel enough. There may be people from Williamton at the tournament to come, and she half wondered if they had learned what happened at the Proving. From what she recalled of her grandfather's ranting, Williamton had no potential primnoire they liked since her great grandmother governed. *Will they do so now?* Anna pushed a strand of hair out of her eye. She gathered stick after stick until her mind fell upon Nathan. *Should I win, will they demand I bring justice upon my friend?*

She took her time heading back to the others, treasuring the feeling of being around nature again. There wasn't much snow on the ground. Roots divided the ground where patches of grass lay covered in films of ice. The air was damp and bitter as she drew in a breath. Setting down the sticks upon a fallen log, Anna went to one knee, shutting her eye. An overpowering wave of nerves crashed upon her shoulders. Her head perked up, eye opening.

"None of what I have faced would have existed if not for Grandfather."

Anger compounded in her chest as she rose to her feet.

The pain from her wound dull in comparison. She knew she wasn't alone. Norman would campaign at her side despite not entering his name. And that Nathan, like Norman, had made up for his misdeeds. None of them would have been in this position had her grandfather allowed her to live out her life of solitude. Anna balled her fists, the leather of her gloves whining for relief from her rage. The wish to retreat into prayer came and went. It would have been for strength except now it felt as if she could split a boulder with her fist. She exhaled and gathered up the sticks.

A flash of flame sent her stumbling back before reaching the others. Cole and Roland bleated, filling the air with clouds and faint flashes of light.

"She's one of us," Nathan roared through the chaos, a whoosh from that of a sword following it. "I've made girls scream like that cus they love—"

"You are foul," said Norman.

Anna gathered herself up, discarding the arm full of sticks, pushing through the clouds until the sun revealed Nathan at Roland's side and Norman feet from him clenching a fistful of flames.

"What is the meaning of this?" said Anna. "We haven't the time for you both being at odds again."

Norman swirled his hand, dousing its flames.

"You're a rutoe, Anna," Norman moved to take her hand, but she backed away, "And the scream you released within the barn proves it."

Anna laughed, slapping him on the chest. "Your scream may be just as loud if you had a…"

Norman raised an eyebrow. She frowned, remembering how the barn's rafters shook.

"It means nothing," she said. "Cuts and bruises I can manage, it's burns," she pointed to her face, "that causes me the most pain."

Norman's eyes fell to the grass piercing the snow. Nathan's sword hissed back into its sheath as he cleared his throat. "And I's telling him that even men wounded bad from a fight can make you feel all is collapsing. It's called pain."

Anna thought back to the pain of her wound being sealed over. How her throat vibrated as if in rhythm with her emotions. She had no memory of such a thing happening when the dragon threw her from its saddle and breathed its fire. Her grandfather had released an arrow at its neck, stopping it from finishing her. It was by seeing the arrow in the dragon's neck that made a bow the only weapon she trusted.

"I must side with Nathan on this, Norman."

Norman looked up with a flicker of yellow in his red eyes. He sighed.

"It may have been my worry for you confusing my judgment," he said. "I know not what made me think you were a quiet one. Quiet One's cannot utter words without destruction to whatever stands in their way. You clearly have not that issue, or you would be an outcast like me."

Anna took his hand.

"Your worry for me brings me comfort." She kissed his cheek. "I worry for you too."

Norman embraced her. Anna felt her anger of earlier drain away.

"Let's make camp," she said, smiling. "On the morrow you can point us in what direction your home city lies."

Chapter Fifteen

⚜

The snow was high enough to bury oneself in, crusting both Roland and Cole's chin whiskers. Two weeks passed like the crack of a whip to a team of horses and the only scent upon the air was pine. Anna shared her saddle with Norman, his warmth soothing about her waist. His horse had taken a misstep. It still pained her to end the steed's suffering. It was different with a horse versus a deer or other game, and with the oats running low she had to choose between a wounded horse or the storm bison's. A storm bison's winter fur and plow-like hooves managed snow and ice better, being originally from the mounts where snow remained like a bad memory.

They crossed with caution into the lands belonging to the Kardans, an old house whose time governing spanned three generations over a divided sixty years. Norman had begun telling Anna of Lampara's great houses after they passed a tall pylon. At its top, engraved within its limestone, was a snarling dragon. It possessed horns that stretched back from its head to the sky. It was plated unlike most sigil markers in what looked to Anna like solid gold. She kept watch for motion amongst the brush, asking Nathan to do the same.

"We're near the center of Lampara," he said, riding on ahead with a hand firm to his sword. "The Kardan's rival Wayne's in coin. It's said their gold keeps Lampara safe."

"And from what I'm told," said Norman, "this will be the first year no Kardan shall be campaigning. Nathan is right. Without Lord Kardan's wealth our country would face invasion. Being that coin pays soldier wages and all."

Anna gulped. Invasion was a word she rarely heard and was taught to fear. She knew of countries beyond Lampara's borders, ones her grandfather told her of during his rants. The countries of Hausara, Pepnar, and Cocnam, said to be well-armed and jealous of Lampara. She pulled the point of her green hood forward and refocused on where they were going.

A great flapping came from overhead. It was familiar to her, raising every sense to full alert. Anna gave Cole a nudge at his side with her heel, catching up with Nathan and Roland. The black storm bison moved at a greater pace than Cole, the faint lightning from its nostrils melting a path through the snow while Cole's clouds created more of it.

"That sounded like an esant, Norman," she said, receiving a nod from Nathan.

"I've never seen one other than Lord William's." Norman peered toward the sky. "Could other great houses have their own, Nathan?"

Nathan pulled up Roland's reins with a faint snap. Anna aligned with him as another flap came and went in a flash. The hairs upon the back of her neck stood on end. She readied her bow, nocking an arrow. One of her two quivers remained full. At the start of her journey, Anna did not expect to kill so many people to remain alive.

Something zipped past her head, striking a thick oak behind her with a *crack*. Ahead, a man in black furs and boiled leather drew another arrow. Anna released hers, striking the shaft of his bow, spinning the man off balance. The crackling of icy snow came from all directions as Nathan drew his sword. Norman slid off Cole's back, igniting his hands. The flames reflected off the snow as his feet began to sink into it. Cole bleated as Anna urged him toward the archer ahead. She nocked another arrow and clenched her teeth. Heads appeared from the brush with swords raised amongst them.

A clang rang out. A roar of flames released screams into the chilling air. Another great flapping of wing felt close and concentrated. A faint yet booming voice followed. The command to *stop* reached her ears. Anna couldn't see the esant amongst the treetops. She released an arrow, striking down the archer, but as she readied another arrow her heart dropped to her stomach. There was a wall of black and gold around them. Her arrows numbered thirty. Norman was backed against Roland. The fight was at a standstill quicker than it had begun. She replaced her arrow amongst its remaining brethren.

Branches snapped and gave way, falling like a storm of jagged points as an esant landed before her. Its head was covered in a mask of iron shaped like a dragon's head. She had half expected a real dragon but breathed a sigh of relief.

"Halt your advance men. This is the woman we've been searching for," said the man astride the esant. "Lady Brighton," the figure gave her a slight bow. "I suggest you tell the rutoe to extinguish his fists."

The man upon the esant wore armor of black with a shine to it that captured the light. Gold ringlets made up the man's chain mail with the pommel of his long sword the sigil of house Kardan. The man's helmet made his deep commanding voice sound muffled. He removed it to reveal someone of advanced years, yet his closely trimmed beard and combed back hair held a blond to it amongst faint grays. Anna saw, but held her tongue about it, that the man's jaw rested at an odd angle.

"I'd—suggest he do so with haste," the man said. "For when I do favors for a friend, no lack of casualties is beyond my drive to see—things—through."

"What makes you believe I am Lady Anna Brighton?"

The man chuckled as he rested his helmet over the saddle horn of his esant."

"Because my friend said—you would be riding a storm bison with gray fur. And my dear, those poor loyal creatures tend not to live past their white coat these days."

Anna looked at Cole, reflecting for a moment upon the storm bison's of the Proving. Each was young, by what she remembered, pure white in their coat with their horns showing no sign of a change to silver.

"And is your friend the prime?" Anna grimaced, straightening her posture. "My life and those in my company have been at constant risk. Prime Luther wishes no competition for his sons."

The man raised an eyebrow then motioned to his men with a wave of his hand. A collective hiss filled the air as swords were sheathed. The man cleared his throat when Norman remained on guard. Anna nodded to Norman.

"You may already know this, dear girl, but campaign law demands no assassinations. As lord of house Kardan, I, Lord Martyn, would be a fool to deliver on such—treachery. I'm also not campaigning for I am old and without heirs to do so for me."

Anna released a tensed breath as the lord tried to ease her mind with a smile. It appeared difficult to manage, as if a smile wasn't something the lord did often. It left her with slight unease as he slipped a gold handkerchief from his gauntlet. He dabbed a thin stream of spittle from the corner of his lip.

"My companions and I head south to find a wizard," Anna said. "Who may I ask is the friend that sent you after me?"

Lord Martyn released his face from the strain of smiling. His eyes strained as he rested his gaze upon her.

"I was told not to reveal his identity," said Lord Martyn. "Although…, I assured my friend that you are welcome to reside at my—castle of Kardanhall."

Temptation rested its assuring hands on her shoulders. She needed food for Nathan and Norman, rest for Cole and Roland. Losing Norman's horse forced them to take only what food the saddlebags of both storm bison's could carry, and she hadn't seen much game the last few days.

"I have a clue to the one you speak of," she swallowed, stemming the tide of her building anger, "because he placed me in danger from the start."

The lord rested a hand on his helmet. It had narrow slits for eyes with the remainder of its metal in the shape of a dragon's long spiny tail. The mouth shield that went across his face had etched into it the snarling teeth of a dragon in silver. The leather straps to fasten it to his face were lined with gold thread.

151

"Come to my castle and warm yourselves at the—least," said Lord Martyn."

Anna looked at Nathan and Norman.

"I follow you, Anna," said Nathan.

Norman cleared his throat. Nathan rolled his eyes.

"You ain't technically campaigning green ears."

Anna turned back to the lord before Norman could utter a retort.

"Good," the lord said, straining as he smiled again. "Follow my men, and I shall have a feast ready before you can get—settled."

The lord aligned his teeth. His face braced slightly as he applied his helmet and fastened the mouth shield. Through the slits of his helmet the pain disappeared from his eyes. Anna didn't understand why the lord was in such pain. She turned Cole in the direction to which Lord Martyn's men went. The lord snapped his esants reins, launching the long gray feathered bird into the air. Norman mounted Cole behind her and whispered.

"Something plagues his lordship, Anna."

"I know," she whispered. "And I believe it has nothing to do with us."

* * *

Towering beyond the woods stood a castle built of a black stone not even Norman knew the origin of. Williamton, Natlendton and Cillnar were of a gray stone mined from the mountains of the south. The castle's stone had a sheen to it, and in the faint light of winter it was partially a blur. Anna rubbed her eye, but the castle remained hazy. It had guard towers along its thick outer wall. The castle spiraled up and up like a stairway to the heavens around its Keep. A gold dragon roared upon banners of black from every window.

The tall, studded doors before them opened. Hundreds of wing flaps buzzed overhead and into the castle. Anna took in the acre upon acre of trees lining either side of the dirt road. The dirt was muddy but free of snow with large puddles that narrowed their way at times. With a great thundering boom, the doors closed behind them, but Anna was calm somehow, as if she could trust the lord far off upon his esant. She wondered if, like her, the lord's speech had been formed by accident or had he angered Simdorn in some way. The goddess was fair to the faithful, she told herself, yet if so, why allow the dragon to burn her as it did?

"It will take us until nightfall to reach the castle, Anna," said Norman. "Lord Martyn could have a feast ready before we find the dining hall."

"I have to agree," she said, urging Cole to be faster. "There is less than two months to the tournament and I've only one town to support me."

"Put your words and such in step, and his lordship might support you," said Nathan.

Anna set loose a restrained breath, hoping Nathan was right. They came upon the crest of a hill as the sun sank behind the mountains protecting the rear of the castle like a malformed shield. The air grew colder. Snow slowly dotted the road until brown turned white, rendering the puddles near invisible as they found flat ground. The hill behind them had not been natural but of a smooth ramp with earth and roots holding it steady. Cole let out a low puff of clouds, telling her his nervousness had subsided. Her own remained. Not for the time they were losing, or for Lord Martyn and his plight, but for whom she believed waited for her.

"My grandfather is who Lord Martyn spoke of," she peered over her shoulder to Norman, "I know it."

He wrapped his arms around her, bringing her close. "I'll burn him if his words bring you harm."

Anna swallowed, shaking her head.

"I shall deal with him in my own way."

"But he is why you can no longer go home," Norman hissed. "He is why you are in danger."

"And yet without him no one, not even the council would know of the prime's plan."

Norman sighed. The castle was close now. Its doors opened, and immediately Lord Martyn's men entered. Their boots clanked against the wood of the draw bridge; its chain of an aged metal painted gold. Beyond the gates, Kardanhall's height seemed to go on forever. The ground before them was of mud and small stones, doused in straw. A stable to her left possessed no smell compared to what she was used to, standing two stories tall. Anna pulled upon Cole's reins, the storm bison groaned at how fast and hard she had done so.

"Anna. Why have we stopped?" said Norman. "Is there something that troubles you?"

Anna gaped, stroking Cole's muscled hump to calm him. The doors looming in the distance before them were lined with gold studs. Their wood possessed a shine to it, not of gold, but a finish that captured her attention.

"I have never seen such splendor," she murmured, barely noticing a stable boy offering to take Cole's reins. "It robs me of words."

"I possessed the same reaction, Lady Brighton."

Ahead at the top of a set of oak steps, Lady Evelyn Wayne stood. She descended them in a fine metal corset that hugged her slender frame. A fur collared cloak streamed from her back, trailing at great length. The dress about her waist was fringed with fur as well. She stopped at the bottom step before a half-moon of dark brick.

"My apologies for the choice in secrecy, Anna," she said, a soft, reassuring smile on her lips. "A mistress of the council must not leave the capital unless commanded."

Anna shook her head, rubbing away the amazement from her face, but deep within her heart, she wanted to explore the entirety of the castle's Keep. It stood out amongst the rest of the castle, a cylinder of brick, partially ringed in places by rows of catapults. She slid from Cole's back, and slowly handed his reins to the stable boy. Norman joined her, along with Nathan as the mistress of duels and debates looked upon them with admiration.

"I expected another in your place," said Anna. "Where?" She panned her vision around the courtyard, finding men about their business, pulling carts filled with hay. There was the distant *ting* of a blacksmith's hammer. "Where does Lord Martyn keep his esant?"

Lady Evelyn hovered at the edge of the bottom step for a moment, then stepped onto the muddy bricks. Her hand rested upon Anna's shoulder. A slight discomfort ran over her face until it regained the earlier poise.

"It's at the castle's rear side," she swallowed, eyeing her surroundings. "You've—more pressing matters. Now we shall join his lordship. I have much explaining to do."

Anna nodded. Lady Evelyn spun on her heels, striding ahead of them until there was an uneasiness in her steps.

Anna parted her lips to say something, finding the council woman's abruptness rude, but held her tongue.

"Somethin smells like horse piss with these high on the coin, lords and ladies," said Nathan.

"For once we are in agreement, Lord Barden," Norman stepped up beside Anna. His eyes narrowed, taking on an orange like the sun gracing the mountain side. "First, his lordship and now a woman we all believed to be a cunning warrior."

"I feel deep down we can trust them," said Anna. "But as the scripture of Simdorn says, Norman, 'The guilty always fall under the strain of time, and time is unyielding.'"

Chapter Sixteen

The Great Hall possessed six hearths in total with an immense banner of the Kardan sigil streaming across the ceiling like an actual dragon flying overhead. At the hall's center was a long, wide table with two cooked geese at its center, orbited by silver dishes of steamed potatoes, carrots and rolls the shape of coins and the size of a full purse. Anna sat beside Lord Martyn, who remained in his armor, and once his food was placed before him, reluctantly removed his helmet. An urge to ask what caused his pain came and went from Anna's mind as the lord slowly unstrapped his mouth shield.

Across from her sat Lady Evelyn, her earlier discomfort was absent, neatly cutting a small potato in two, then taking a small bite. Norman and Nathan sat at the far end of the table, requested by his lordship. Anna protested at first, but then Lord Martyn said.

"The fewer … ears hear what must be discussed … the better."

Lady Evelyn swallowed, dabbed her lips with a gold silk napkin. "Word reached the council of your acts in Natlendton. Everyone in Cillnar has been fed a line of snail leavings by Prime Luther about it."

Anna ignored her food, though its aroma lured her. Salted pork and stale bread had kept her full along with the others, but a castle-cooked meal could not be beaten.

"What does he say of it?"

The mistress of duels and debates rested her knife and fork down. There was a calmness in her eyes bordering on sleep that Anna felt from the heat splashing upon them from the hearths.

"He has declared you an agitator of the people," said Lady Evelyn. "Prime Luther has begun a country wide seizure of all bows. Only soldiers of Lampara may use them."

Anna gaped. The consequences of such an action were immense. She knew Lampariens could still defend themselves with a knife or sword, but a bow and arrow possessed a greater use beyond that of combat.

"You will have a greater … target upon your back, Lady Anna," said Lord Martyn, finishing cutting his food into the tiniest of bites. "Many favor and some don't the Lamparien armed forces. You will lose many to … that event in Natlendton."

"What if I spoke the truth of it?" Anna squeezed the armrests of her chair. Its soft leather back brought no comfort as she contemplated what to do next. "They must know the truth. I never wished to campaign, but with my choice of not doing so gone. I don't want anyone to need a reason to dislike me. They … already laugh at my…"

She slid back her chair, pressing her elbows to her knees.

Anna took hold of her face as anxiousness rode like a horse to the crest of her back. Creaking and footsteps filled her ears. Beyond the plate of steaming food, both lord and lady looked upon her with sympathy, yet there was an edge to it. As if they wanted her to summon the courage distant from her heart.

"What 'ave you two done?" said Nathan. "She's got loads of pressure on her, and you got to bring her mood down."

"Stress is the price for one wishing to be a primnoire," Lady Evelyn said, rising from her seat. "Lord Martyn says you seek a wizard in the south. May I ask did the people of Natlendton care that you were disfigured when you fought to save your friend?"

Anna looked up, removing her hood before wiping her eye of surfaced tears.

"No.

"I ... must say then, Lady Anna," said Lord Martyn, his handkerchief pressed to his chin. He drew it away, firming up his face. "That I took a blow from a horse in my youth.... My father didn't trust wizards, said a price came with their— magic. I went against his wishes after a physician was sent for. I did not want to be disfigured or reduced to lying in bed with broth to keep me ... alive. But I was selfish then, and my father never spoke to me again. The ... wizard warned me of this and punished me with eternal pain. I have grown to live with it."

"But you may have died under a physician's knife or have been bed ridden like you—"

Lord Martyn raised a hand, halting her words.

"My father died without ... a final word, a final act of love for me. I didn't allow him to be a father." Lord Martyn wiped spittle from his cheek, tossing the handkerchief aside. "I refused to allow him to do the best with what he had."

Anna looked about the room, but before her lips parted Nathan stepped forward.

"Your father had the wealth for a wizard. There's no bloody reason he couldn't have had one fix you."

"Once an ignorant lord's child, forever will you be an ignorant lord's child," said Lady Evelyn.

"I'm sorry, miss mud scares me." Nathan chuckled. "Some orderman you be."

Lady Evelyn's lips quivered then formed a firm straight line. She grabbed a knife, but Lord Martyn slammed his fist on the table, sending his plate skidding forward.

"She's right," he said. "And … despite my current wealth, none of it existed when I was struck by that horse."

Anna gasped, turned to Nathan and scowled.

"I'm sorry, Anna," said Nathan, storming off to the Great Hall's entrance. "I got to go before I get blood on someone."

Lord Martyn nodded to the men manning the doors. Anna watched her friend leave as she decided to deal with him later.

"What must I draw from your story, my lord?" said Anna, meeting Lord Martyn's eye. "You don't frighten children as I do."

Lord Martyn signaled for another handkerchief, slumping back into his chair. Lady Evelyn placed the knife beside her plate. The mistress of duels and debates narrowed her eyes. The candlelight barely reached them yet the look upon them left Anna unsettled.

"The point of his lordship's story was coping." Lady Evelyn

ate a small sliver of goose, dabbing her lips of juices. "You have gone how long without seeking a wizard?"

"Five years."

"And ...," Lord Martyn sat up, leaning close to her, "why in all that time did your grandfather does summon a wizard for you?"

Lord Martyn received his fresh handkerchief, and began to eat, chewing slowly as he did.

"He believed as your father did about wizards."

Norman cleared his throat. Anna turned to him, finding in all the trading of words that she had forgotten him.

"I think your deeds in Natlendton and Williamton," said Norman, "are proof your burns have no influence upon people."

"No influence?" Anna snapped. "You ... saw how that boy reacted, Norman. You saw how he fled from me."

"A child ... is new to this world," said Lord Martyn. "They are not meant to understand at first." The lord massaged his jaw, setting down his fork. "His elders will cheer ... you at the tournament."

"But," Anna sighed. "I want to feel whole again."

Lady Evelyn rose again, but this time amongst the dark and candle flames her eyes were soft.

"Time as you know is short. I," Lady Evelyn hesitated, then leaned in close, "shall send for a wizard."

Anna turned to Norman, every muscle begging her to leap into the air. But her eye went to the mistress of duels and debates, narrowing until thin like a knife's edge.

"All of you have spent this time convincing me to *cope* with my burns. To press on and campaign. Why make such an offer, Lady Wayne?"

"I want you steady in your feelings and focused for the tournament to come. You have my backing as our future primnoire."

***

The room Lord Martyn offered her was a fourth the size of a stable. Anna watched the chambermaid cast long slender shadows after leaving the fire she had built. The fire roared within the hearth whose depth could house a small family comfortably. She recalled the hearths of her grandfather's house which weren't nearly so huge despite his wealth. And no matter her constant anger for him, Anna did admire his passion for simplicity. Lord William never held feasts no matter the guest of high birth coming to town, preferring a small meal of meat and potatoes.

Anna sat on the bed, facing the dual doors of her room. Above them, two pale bears in a smooth, etched tile stood on all fours in opposing directions under a moon that captured the hearth's light. She rose, removing her quivers, bow and cloak. Joy rose in her heart as she reached to remove her hood. She had let it down for once. The knowledge of being complete, of her confidence no longer wavering because of a foolish mistake was almost too good to be true. Anna smiled. She would no longer be half blind.

There was a rap at the door. Anna reached for her hood but allowed her hands to fall to her sides. It would be over soon, and the hood no longer needed to be the shield she hid behind from the world. "Enter."

The doors opened to reveal Norman, followed closely behind by Lady Evelyn. And as the doors closed neither possessed a hint of emotion. Anna chewed her lip. The feeling as though life was about to begin anew faded.

"A cheefox has been sent out," said Lady Evelyn, easing into the chair beside the bed. Her arms shook as she did. "Most wizards have taken residence in Echnumbard."

Anna raised an eyebrow. Norman explained that Echnumbard was a rutoe sanctuary, where many went to learn control of their abilities.

"Prime Luther had all wizards banished to the south," Norman continued, "in the first years of his second term, after one left his niece with a stutter for joking about another girl's speech troubles."

A wave of regret crashed over Anna, tempting her to reach for her hood. It seemed all her grandfather said of wizards was true yet...

"I'm neither rude nor wish to become so in my pursuit to be whole again."

"True," said Lady Evelyn. "And my hope is by the time we receive an answer, and a wizard arrives at Kardanhall, no choice of yours will give a wizard cause to teach you a harsh lesson."

Anna's eye fell to the bear skin rug beneath her bare feet. She wished the mistress of duels and debates hadn't said that, for it seemed in her life when someone spoke of hope the opposite occurred. Peering up at her ladyship there was a slight twitch in her eyes.

"I will keep myself on the smooth path then," she said, searching for the right words, noticing the weakness the mistress tried to hide. "What troubles you, my lady? Nathan's words bothered you and I see pain in your movements."

Lady Evelyn weaved her fingers, resting them on her lap.

"My balance isn't what it used to be," she looked to Norman and then to Anna, feigning a smile. "I was told at my age the Quake was impossible, that such an illness came in older women of my mother's family. I can only hope that it stops with me."

Anna raised an eyebrow, though she hadn't meant to. "How can an illness end if within a family?" she asked, looking for anger on Lady Evelyn's face, but found only calm. "My tutor taught me that illness is—"

"An endless fight shared in bloodlines" Lady Evelyn finished for her. She placed her hand upon the chair's armrests and rose, both arms gave, but Norman caught her. "Thank you. Your friend, Lady Anna, would be a fine prime for you had he entered his name."

Norman eased the mistress of duels and debates to her feet. His eyes took on a bright orange as his lips grasped at words.

"I'm part of the council of affairs. Remember?" said Lady Evelyn, changing the subject from her illness. "We receive a list once the final calling has ended."

Anna licked her lips, curious now if an illness plagued her own family, daring to hope it wasn't like the one within Lady Evelyn, whom she admired.

"We've been working together since our journey began," said Norman. "Haven't we, Anna?"

"Yes," Anna said. "And I have learned much of what's been happening to Lampara thanks to him."

Norman smiled. His eyes went from their orange to a cherry red. Anna found herself wishing the rules of campaigning were different, that she had power to enter his name, but to do so would require her to be a man. She let out a low sigh, remembering what Norman told her, and if she did try to have him be a *prime at my side,* his name would already be on the mentioned list.

164

"If only the rules were different," Lady Evelyn grimaced, assuring Norman she was able to stand. "A woman of any class in this country can campaign, yet none possess the rights a man does." She moved closer to Anna and whispered. "Perhaps you can change that when you win."

Anna looked to her feet again, both within a forest of the bear fur. She found her confidence in a balancing act upon a rope. One end tied to a future where she must fight not just for Lamparien favor but for no chance of dictatorship. And the other end to a fear long upon her mind, one Anna hadn't been able to shake since coming of age. *Should I win, do I possess strength enough to govern alone?*

"I thank you for your faith in me, my lady." Anna hid her apprehension behind a small smile.

"You will have me at your side, Anna," Norman said, as if reading her mind. "I can make certain the coffers stay—"

"Everything will ultimately be on her shoulders." Lady Evelyn cut him off, her face stern yet there was a hint of sympathy in her eyes. "The council are both protectors and advisors to who governs the people, with power to vote out who rules if campaign law is broken. You will have to be chosen by Anna if she wins the tournament."

Anna frowned at this, finding herself daring to hope for her own success. She shook the thought away for now. Norman sighed; both his eyes faded from their cherry red to a dark dying orange.

"Has proof beyond what we've told you been found, Lady Evelyn," said Norman, "of campaign law being broken?"

The mistress of duels and debates moved slowly to the fire. She leaned upon the mantel as fire highlighted the sharp features of her face. "None. He rides with his sons to every city and town, using his name to gain them favor. He," Lady Evelyn turned to face them, the hearths light reaching around her like long gold fingers, "has been in power long enough to know how to hide and deny if needed."

"How many support his sons?" said Anna.

"Without wizards to read the minds of Lampariens, there's no telling. Perhaps the capital and Sponernar. Both are quite large."

"What of the town called Rockelton?" Anna knew the names of Lampara's towns and cities from her tutor. It was the country's lands beyond her grandfather's that were a mystery. "I've always wondered where it was."

Lady Evelyn's eyes brightened. A short thin smile crossed her red painted lips.

"You must have Simdorn on your side, Lady Brighton. You have only to step out onto your balcony. The town you seek lies at a distance behind Kardanhall."

"What will you do there?" said Norman.

Anna strolled to the door, realizing what was missing from the plan at the tip of her tongue.

"Where are you going?" Lady Evelyn said. "It's night now, and you are without your boots."

"I've traveled this far with two friends." Anna snatched up her boots from the rack left of the door. "I must find the other if I'm to win Rockelton."

***

Straw crunched as Anna entered the guest stables. Their high ceilings and smooth stonework felt unnatural, a mount in her mind needed a more earthy home. It sat within sight of Keep and the orchards stretched out for miles. Horse droppings, fresh straw, and a hint of oats from a loft high above filled her senses. A calm claimed her when within stables, like they were a place you could go where nothing mattered but the animals in your company.

Cracking and popping broke the pattern of snorting and hoof clopping. Soon the thick rafters grew cloudy and damp, Cole sniffed against the gate of his stall, dousing it. Above, moonlight lit the grays of his clouds through a skylight. Nathan sat afront Roland's stall as his mount lapped from a trough. The outlaw lord had abandoned his armor, his chin whiskers were longer too. His cloak was wet and his tunic a darker yellow than when she first met him.

"You here to lecture me for insultin' her delicacy?" said Nathan. "I'm not taken it back, nor do I care about his lordship's dribbling problem."

Anna sucked in a breath through her nose, half tempted to growl in anger at those words alone, but she kept reminding herself of the time.

"You've enough age on you to apologize when you're ready." She made a fist as every sense thrummed. "I will be heading for Rockelton to gain the favor of its people until the wizard comes."

Nathan looked up at her with bloodshot eyes. The flask he kept in his boot lay against his thigh, open and lip end in the straw.

"Good luck," Nathan hiccupped, "cus that town's full of tricksters and blockheads thinking they know magic."

Certainty escaped her as to what a trickster was as his refusal stung her feelings. Anna guessed he meant a thief and the people knowing magic sent her imagination churning. She watched as Nathan went for his flask, guessing with a hint of hope that maybe who she waited for lived in Rockelton.

"Will you come with me?" she asked, hiding every urge to smile with a stern face. "You have guided me this far. We may find a way to remove the guilt you still feel for me."

Nathan shook the flask, then tossed it aside.

"I'm willin' to take the chance then. I just got one request."

Anna smiled.

"Name it."

"When you win the tournament, kick that Wayne bitch off the council."

Chapter Seventeen

I t took until the sun was at its highest to reach
Rockelton. The town was tucked within the shadow
of the mountain, and unlike other towns Anna had been
to, no wall encircled it. Every home was of the same stone
as the mountain. By the distant crumbled roots reaching
out from the mountain's base, such stone had been mined
there. The roofs of each home and store were of dark wood,
explaining when they traveled to the town why a long stretch
of forest formed a wide, stump-littered road leading from
Kardanhall to the town itself.

Anna walked steadily, leading Cole by his reins, as did
Nathan with Roland. Norman strolled between them. There
was a calm about the accountant she found unnerving,
wishing she were able to feel the same even in such a pressing
time. He accepted her as she was regardless of the burns. And
he still honored her desire to be made whole once more. It
warmed her chest to have someone as faithful as Norman Tilt
at her side.

A tinging began at a distance coming from the smithy. The snow had all but stopped falling, resting heavily on roof tops. *Splash.* Beside the smithy under an awning a man scrubbed in an outdoor bath. A sign above the building the tub belonged to said, "*Baths, Three Coppers for a Soak.*" Far off among the homes beyond the bath house peaked a moon with a bell below it. Anna hadn't visited the house of Simdorn since before the fire of Williamton. Guilt swelled within her like a fire absent of control in a forest. Her reason for coming to Rockelton was to win its people in some way. But her faith was something she had kept close her whole life, yet recent events taxed it to almost no end.

Anna kept an eye on those roaming the streets. From what her grandfather had described a wizard to be, they were old with a face of mist, glowing eyes and wore black robes. A stream of men in robes came from a street to her left, but their robes were the gray of Simdorn's priests, their direction for the temple she had seen earlier.

"How do you plan on winning these folk over, Anna?" said Nathan. His mind seemed clearer after breaking his fast this morning. "They don't look like what I expected. Maybe the tricksters got bored, and left town."

"I haven't decided on it yet," she said, chewing her lip, "for before, a crisis or a fight won the support and approval of people."

"And you acted well," said Norman, smiling. "I will wager there are some in the capital that wish to see you govern."

Anna blushed, guessing he was right. The crackle of Roland's lightning-like breathing grew faint from her hearing. She turned to find Nathan had wandered off. She saw him and Roland below a tall vertical sign that read, *Wayne Trading.*

"Why have you stopped, Nathan?" she asked.

The lord raised his hand, pointing at a poster beside the entrance of the trading post. Anna gasped. Upon it was a rough portrait of Nathan. Below his image a ten and several zeroes.

"The prime is offering ten thousand gold nardans for his death," said Norman, reading the poster aloud. "I think you may want to leave with Roland for the safety of Kardanhall, Lord Barden."

"Norman is right," Anna rested a hand upon Nathan's arm. "I will find a wizard and discover a way to win Rockelton."

"I know there are eyes out for me, but I can't abandon you because some old bastard wants my head."

"Please, Nathan," Anna said, worry choking her words enough her throat needed to be cleared. "I have had so few friends in my life, and to lose you would be too much."

Nathan let out a breath that rustled his chin whiskers like a great wind on a stretch of trees.

"I hate to give you one more reason to be sad."

The former lord gathered Roland's reins, mounting the black storm bison as a chilling wind hissed across Anna's hood. She found her strength absent, wanting to wave him farewell, but when they had been parted for some time, it nearly cost him his life. Nathan rode off until there was no trace of Roland's lightning-charged breathing in the air.

"Let's see if a wizard resides in town," said Norman.

Anna sighed, turning from the sight of her friend nearing the edge of town.

"Let's."

They chose a road opposite, crammed with shops. Far to their left was a pub with a sign left of its entrance, etched

171

on a gnarled wood plank. *No Rutoe. No Dogs.* Anna huffed. Norman bit his inner lip then smirked.

"What's so funny, Norman?" Anna asked.

He returned to his human form with chestnut hair and blue eyes. As his skin matched the color of those inside the pub, his brow wrinkled. Anna hadn't noticed it before but when Norman changed form it pained him.

"I'm glad I kept to my studies and learned the *Trick of Skin*."

Trick of skin? Anna thought, as they entered the pub. She frowned slightly, curious if it was how the people of Williamton were able to accept him. It was another complex issue she wondered if she could change should she become primnoire.

"Me too," Anna said, a hint of worry in her tone. "I don't wish you to be excluded from this journey we're on at any point."

She took his hand gently in hers as they entered the pub. His hand was warm as always. Sparsely filled round tables were scattered amongst the room. The bar was shaped like an immense drum with one small section allowing the barkeep to leave it if needed. At the center of it was a vast support column ringed with shelves and stacked upon them bottles of wine and small kegs. Their labels were in Lamparien, but many were from countries Anna knew nothing of. She choked back a bit of bile from a foul scent rising out of a copper spittoon beside a table.

"Come on over and slip off those hoods, good lady," said the barkeep. "Have that lad of yours buy you some Brisolnut. I just got a few bottles this morning."

Anna rested her hands on the bar, splaying her fingers. Drinking wasn't something she normally did yet she wondered if it might earn the favor of those within the town. She held her breath, then answered.

"I haven't any coin, good sir. Do you know of any wizards in town?"

The barkeep ran his thumb and forefinger across his thick mustache.

"What if may I ask," he turned his head to the side, then flinched a little, "can a wizard do for you? Their services come with a price higher than the wines I sell."

Anna grimaced, bending her fingers like they were the hooked talons of an esant.

"You have been decent in saying nothing of them." Anna removed her hoods. The barkeep's eyes went wide then softened, his lips parting. His chin sunk deep into his chest. "I'm Anna Brighton. I wish to return my appearance to what it was and campaign to be your primnoire."

With a slight bow the barkeep met her eye, offering a small smile amongst his browning teeth.

"The Brighton's are why we have towns, my lady," said the barkeep. "I'd not have my family's pub or a place to do business without your ancestors. But I am sorry. The lord of this town doesn't allow wizards in Rockelton. And from what I know they have been banished to the south."

A deep throbbing anger ran through Anna. She would need to wait for the cheefox to deliver its message. And from what she remembered of learning Lampara's geography, a creature with even so great a speed may take days to reach the southern mountains.

"We'll be going then," she said, replacing her hoods over her head. "I will have to find a way to win Rockelton in the meantime."

173

She bid the barkeep good-bye with Norman trailing behind her. His human face lacked the deeper emotion of his true self, Anna thought, as his shoulders slumped.

"There may be a family requiring a good hunter, Anna." Norman said, eyeing her remaining arrows.

"You may be right, Norman," she said, running her thumb down the string of her bow. "My grandfather once suggested it and I…."

As they left the bar a brightly colored poster with three rings across its center caught their eye. Arrows raced through them, released from a handsome archer below. At the top in bold letters it read, WITNESS YOUR FUTURE PRIME. Below the archer in even bolder letters it read, PERFORM WONDERS WITH A BOW AND SOLVE YOUR DAILY WOES.

"I know what I shall do." Anna unslung her bow, testing the draw of its string. "This must be the man Nathan spoke of. I'll challenge him to an archery contest."

They left the pub briskly, Anna noting the archer would be in a place where crowds were massing. A lightning strike sent her nerves into a frenzy for a moment. Dark clouds were forming toward the direction of Kardanhall. It seemed strange for lightning to be so close and concentrated above the forest, but her mind was narrowed on finding the archer.

The gathering of townsfolk took little time to discover. A familiar thump reached Anna's ears, stirring up a resurgence of memory. Morning until noon she had heard such a sound after surviving the dragon. The swift sharp brush of fletching against her cheek became a way to find peace over time. It wasn't until after years of practice she was sharp enough in sight to knock a pot from a post with an arrow. Anna smiled as she and Norman halted short of the edge of a vast crowd.

Beyond the people of Rockelton upon a stage of dry stone, stood a man. She could make out his beard, sharp and pointed like a sword tip. His hair appeared short, jumbled with black curls. A target stood across the stage with a black dot at the center that emitted thin expanding red rings over a stretched white canvas. Atop the archer's head a helmet or more so a hat shined in the bright sunlight.

Three thumps came at once, each arrow from what Anna could tell had struck within one of each ring.

"He's quite skilled," said Norman. "Have you the arrows to spare for this?"

"The points will only need sharpening afterward, Norman," she said. "Targets aren't people or animals where damage can come to an arrow."

Norman chuckled. "We rutoe have our magic to hunt or fight, but I'd be pleased to learn to use a bow someday."

Anna kissed his cheek. "I will need to show you how when time grants it."

She handed him Cole's reins, finding more and more a deep connection with him. Wading through the crowd, her heart pounded like the hoof beats of a horse, but this time it wasn't from fear or nervousness. She found herself forgetting her manners as she pushed past, all her focus on the accountant behind her. They had been in classes together and spent time in her grandfather's study after he had done his accounting. Upon her eighteenth year, Norman became one of her best friends. Her heart grew heavy for a moment, finally understanding the look he'd given her before leaving to fight within the Proving.

Lightning clapped far behind her, disrupting the hopefulness she was beginning to feel. Anna gulped, momentarily losing sight of the archer, growing lost among people of greater height than herself. Another thump sounded louder than the previous, giving hint to being close to the stage. It came into full view with a set of aged wooden steps leading up to its deck that was covered in straw. Anna gaped. The archer stood upon a stool, his head and shoulders from a distance had convinced her he was a man of great height. She bit her tongue to stem the gathering of questions in her mind. The archer's boots were half the length of his legs. His doublet was belted tight to his waist, laced at the collar with gold cords.

"I've just demonstrated what skill I possess," the archer said, his voice deep and smooth. "As prime, I will do the same to our foes," He looked down upon Anna then grinned. "And I assure you my policies are as true as my aim."

Someone snickered beside her. Anna's gaze shot up to a man with a metal disk for a helmet. He was draped in a long coat of black leather and wore a breastplate bearing the badge of a silver horse shaded in black. She choked on a cloud of smoke released from his lips. The Orderman plucked his thin cigar from his mouth, giving her a wink as the archer raised a thick eyebrow at him.

"Does the Orderman among us doubt the word of a lord's son?" the archer shouted. "The word of myself, Arthur Manderlin?"

Around them the crowd gasped, backing away, and bowing. Many had a look of fear under a layer of respect as the Orderman tipped his helmet to the men and women closest to him.

The Orderman placed his cigar back between his teeth. "It takes more than fancy shooting to rule a country, your lordship." There was a hint of mockery in his tone Anna just barely caught. "And big talk that makes you sound richer than you are doesn't give me much confidence either."

Anna thought back to her own way of speaking. Her grandfather was amongst the wealthiest lords in Lampara. But from what the Orderman was inferring it seemed she wasn't the showman he believed Arthur Manderlin to be. The lord gave off the feel of a performer, and neither herself nor her grandfather ever acted in such a way.

"Hey, girl," said the Orderman. "Heard you been earning favor of late. Not so much with the prime of course."

"What does he mean, my lady?" said Arthur.

She took a deep breath, climbing the stage one step at a time until eye to eye with the archer upon his stool. "I'm Anna Brighton." Whispers wisped through the crowd as she bawled her fists, strangling the aged leather about her bow. "And I have come to challenge you."

Chapter Eighteen

The sky opened slowly to the blue of spring Nathan missed. Gray clouds faded to white as Rockleton grew distant and small. He ran a hand down his beard and smiled. He knew Anna possessed the skill to defend herself, and even the pretty boy, he admitted deep down, could hold his own. The rutoe helped save him from the chopping block with more guts than Nathan expected of a coin counter. *Guess I was wrong to want him banished like the rest of his kind.*

Snow circled every stump in Nathan's way like islands in a sea of white. Hints of grass broke through the white with the warmth of the day rising. Such a break in the winter was temporary as he hoped Prime Luther's existence in this world would be. He spat, chuckling as Roland's hooves crushed roots in their path. His men had sent a falcon off to put him in the old man's sights and paid for their treason. Now with Kardanhall, a towering dark blur in the distance he found himself feeling safe for once.

He reckoned it strange to see Rockelton wasn't the same as he remembered. Its streets were cleaner, the Wayne Trading sign replaced and pristine for once. He half expected his pocket picked. Wind raced across his chest, ruffing Roland's black well-trimmed fur. Nathan reckoned the town was like heaven compared to Natlendton from twenty years back. There was a mile or so left before reaching the castle and he wondered if Lord Ransom Wayne's wife planned on giving him grief for leaving Anna.

"That shaky highborn better have them skills ordermen got if she plans to chomp at my ear," he grumbled.

There was a faint fluttering on the wind, familiar to his ears, something he had heard twice in recent months. Nathan looked to his left. A glimpse of brown caught his eye racing over the trees. It rose higher within the seconds before he eased Roland to a stop. A crunching, then cracking, leapt at him from the right. Within the shadows, a row of armored men filled the tree line. He knew there had to be Lamparien soldiers patrolling Rockelton to keep its peace. How could they have known he was in town? Nathan's thoughts raced, slipping the vial of storm bison urine from a saddlebag. He popped the cork and leaned close to Roland's nose. The storm bison stomped in place; immense clouds burst forth from his nostrils as Nathan turned him back to town, sending his friend into a gallop. The clouds rose and gathered above, trailing them like an immense shadow.

Thunder boomed all at once as he strangled the hilt of his sword. Lightning struck within yards sending up bursts of snow and mud. The faint fluttering was a whisper the more lightning circled him. Roland moved like an unwavering guardsman, filling the air with noise as he released clouds from his nostrils. The soldiers gained but barely, their horses cowering from the lightning. Nathan gasped, finally in sight of the esant. Upon it, Lord Martyn drew his sword, the shine of his armor catching the lightning's bright flashes.

Nathan jerked Roland's reins left, realizing he'd be leading them to Anna if straight ahead was his plan. The soldiers followed as he entered the woods, trees rustled, and some split in two from the storm above. He eyed the sky, finding the drooling lord zipping back and forth like a fly over a corpse. Behind him the soldiers were closer now, the badges upon their breastplates, the silver horse of Lampara's prime shaded in black. To think he had once led the prime's men, been a semi-respectable lord with a place to put his feet up in the capital. Nathan spat, drawing his sword, ending his run from the soldiers as he circled a massive stump to face them.

"You won't be catchen' me kicken' and screamin' to that son of a bitch prime," said Nathan.

One soldier stopped ahead of the others, unclasping his mouth shield. "Who said he wants you alive?"

A lightning bolt struck behind Nathan, the flash blinding the soldiers for seconds, making his ears ring more incessantly. He rolled his shoulders and listened to the crackle of his stiff neck as he released a chuckle.

"Let's go then."

Nathan jabbed his foot into Roland's side, then aimed his sword like a lance at the lead soldier. The soldiers before him charged upon their white stallions, keeping their distance as the lightning struck at rapid points. Nathan swung, shearing off the head of a soldier as Roland bleated and bucked at the horses with his hooked black horns. A horse screamed as it was gored in the chest. Nathan drove his sword into the throat of a soldier, using his friend's storms as both a shield and sword to keep the others off his back. The noise was unbearable for he had always been at the head of Roland's lightning. He'd even used it once to break the heart of a woman he called his friend.

He hoped Anna was safe, proving herself to the people with that bow of hers. Nathan sliced the laces of a man's gauntlet, severing them, and cutting deep into his wrist. The man cried out as he tumbled from his horse. Nathan peered through the trees shaded by the dark clouds to Rockelton, counting his blessings for Anna's forgiveness. He charged forward, taking off a man's hand as the others chased him toward the clearing. Open space would give him a better crack at who remained.

And then like a flash the lord upon his esant struck, toppling Nathan, knocking Roland off balance. The black storm bison regained his footing, circling back to where Nathan had landed. But before Nathan was on his feet a sharp pain launched itself into his side. He cried out to see soldiers looming over him, eyes narrowed above the brim of their mouth shields. Nathan gripped for his sword, finding it nowhere, eyeing Rockelton again, wishing he had stayed with Anna.

Roland bleated and charged as the lord upon his esant pounced. The storm bison toppled over but snorted, rolling back on his feet.

"Leave him be you drooling twit."

Another sharp pain in his gut revealed a towering soldier in the Lamparien green and red. Nathan seized hold of the sword digging deeper into his stomach. He coughed, tasting blood. His eyes blurred with dizziness as his fingers grew weak. He felt a blade to his throat, and though he had never been one for religion, Nathan hoped Simdorn would protect Anna the best she could.

"Go ahead," he coughed. "Shaving me pretty when you're done."

The blade went deep across his throat. The fight with the sword deep within his stomach ended. Nathan looked up at the sky, catching the faint shift of the clouds, seeing for one last time the blue reminding him of spring.

Chapter Nineteen

The wind had changed direction with the lightning fading slowly from both sound and sight. Anna focused on Arthur, waiting on the edge of her breath for his acceptance of her challenge. He folded his arms. His bow was longer than he was tall and appeared as lopsided wings in his grip. The quiver at his back didn't possess red goose fletching like her own. They were of a silver swallow. It was a fine fletching, as was the bird by what Anna knew, yet it wasn't high priced since swallows were no longer rare like the red goose.

"You challenge me, Lady Brighton." Arthur chuckled. "Can you even hit the broadside of a deer with that tradesman bow?"

Anna looked down at her bow. Its shaft was dark brown, smooth, and sturdy. The string had been replaced, but the leather of its grip was worn and still possessed a craftsman's mark, one she'd never questioned her grandfather about.

"I'll show you my skill," she said.

Drawing an arrow swiftly from her quiver, Anna nocked it to her bow then drew, releasing and hitting the bottom of the target. A roar of laughter filled her ears like the buzz of bees from a disturbed hive. Arthur had to steady himself from falling off the stool as laughter leapt from his lips.

"So much spirit in you," he said, stifling his laughter. "You'll really frighten our enemies that way. Come everyone! I shall buy you all a fine brew."

The laughter faded around her as the people of Rockelton began to leave. Anna peered over to the Orderman. He dropped his cigar on the ground, stamped it out with his heel then tipped his helmet to her. Anna fumed, drawing three arrows and released. Three *thumps* halted Arthur at the edge of leaving the stage.

He turned back. "I don't believe it."

Anna let her arm drop. The arrows were in perfect alignment with Arthur's. Her confidence rose as he moved beside the target. The crowd returned too, each in awe of her placement.

"Challenge accepted, my lady," said Arthur, tipping his hat to her. "Remove your arrows and mine if you please. I've a challenge I'm sure to win at."

His last words robbed her briefly of confidence. A pang of uncertainty washed over her as she removed each arrow; the heads of his were rounded below the points. Her own arrows had a fine four-bladed point. Arthur snapped his fingers. Men raced from the ends of the stage, replacing the target with three tall plinths. Atop them were thin shafts with rings wide enough to act as bracelets. The crowd cleared the way behind the rings, opening things up to distant houses beyond a cobblestone street.

Moving beside Arthur as he mounted his stool once more, every nerve tensed her muscles. She pretended it was no different than hunting, that the rings were rabbits or pheasants, yet both were still larger targets than the rings. Anna handed him his arrows, placing her own back in her quiver, finding twenty arrows remained in it.

"After you, my lord," she said. "I suppose the challenge is to send an arrow through each of the ten rings?"

"Correct, my lady," said Arthur, grinning, each tooth a moon white. "But you will have to be swifter than the quick release you displayed earlier."

He drew an arrow, releasing it and then another in quick succession. The clack and hiss of each arrow shaft found Anna's ears before Arthur readied for the final ring. It rattled. Deflecting the arrow high into the air, sending the crowd scattering for cover.

"Damn," said Arthur. "A bit slow on that one."

Anna gulped. "Well shot. I barely noticed your hand to quiver."

Anna nocked and drew, releasing arrow after arrow. No sound of fletching brushing a ring came, but upon the final ring she sent the arrow an inch above it. The crowd clapped. Some young boys in the crowd ran to retrieve the arrows. She permitted herself to breathe for a moment, flexing her fingers over her bow's grip.

"It appears we are at a draw, my lady," said Arthur, with a strange look in his eyes. "We can't have that, can we?"

She shook her head, remaining still and emotionless at the awkward hitch in his smile. His eyes admire her yet not like her grandfather had after a good day's training, but in a way which left her wanting to hide. It sent her mind back to Ronald as she pursed her lips, stemming the rise of her disgust.

"No," she said, putting on a stern face despite her hoods hiding it. "Shall we go again? I think these rings are a challenge, but I wish to win Rockelton over with skill."

"Ha. Was your skill with a bow the only way you won the support the Orderman spoke of? If wizards weren't banished, I could have one show you the minds of Rockelton's people."

"The challenge isn't over," said Anna. "You've not won them. How could a wizard tell you that? They cheered for both our performances."

Arthur rubbed his eyes, the leather of his gloves riffling against his eyebrows.

"I've been in this town over a week. A fine wine from my family's vineyard in the north sits on the shelves of every pub."

Anna thought back to when the barkeep offered the wine he recently received. Keeping Nathan's money would have made campaigning easier. She'd need to work with what she possessed.

"I will out match you," she said, squeezing the grip of her bow, finding her strength. "And win them on merit in place of money and," she looked to find the Orderman had returned. He gave her a nod, lighting a fresh cigar, "not use big talk despite my grandfather's wealth."

Arthur looked her up and down again, cackling, showing the same strange look in his eyes that had left her uncomfortable earlier.

"Let's make things interesting," said Arthur. "I like you. Enough so to want you as primnoire at my side."

The crowd looked on with whispers on their lips. One she

caught speaking of why she wore her hoods, of not trusting someone that hid their face. Another wanted to see both her and Arthur join in governing Lampara. A third again spoke of not wanting her if she refused to allow others to look upon her face. Arthur kept his aged gray eyes focused on her. His tongue trapped between his teeth as if her answer would grant its release.

She had expected this to happen, to be wanted as primnoire at someone's side like Lady Evelyn said. But she wanted it to be with someone that didn't look upon her in a strange way. She readied to remove her hoods, wanting those whispering of them to cease. Anna hesitated, not wishing for Arthur to find an excuse to mock her despite his wish.

"If you can bring down a deer," Anna pointed beyond the town's limits. The dark clouds replaced by clouds of white, shading the woods below, "before I can then I may consider ending my challenge and … joining you."

Her final words were like a strike to the chest. It pained her to have said them, but hunting was her greatest strength. Some relief came in knowing Norman wasn't within earshot, believing he may get the wrong impression.

"I …," Arthur took tiny steps on his stool, the crowd cheering his name, shouting what great feast he could bring to the town. "I accept your challenge, my lady. And let it be what wins Rockelton."

***

They made their way out of town to the east. Anna took in the breeze, drawing in the scent of wet leaves, the staleness from nature lying dormant from the cold. Beside her, Arthur stepped delicately around mud puddles, keeping a sharp look out for roots. At a distance behind them the Orderman followed, volunteering to be the eyes of Rockelton, to see which of them killed a deer first. He had told Anna before entering the woods she needed to win this, for a man declaring a woman to be primnoire at his side was binding if she lost. Anna swallowed her nerves, making a face under her hoods like the consequences were porridge lacking cinnamon.

She turned back to the Orderman for a moment. His footsteps barely detectable amongst the frost and overgrowth. It was as if he were a ghost in some way. Her mind narrowed itself back to hunting, placing focus on smells, the direction of the wind, and on any clue of quarry. An animal's droppings lay at a distance between two baren bushes cloaked in snowflakes. Steam rose from them as did a scent she saw Arthur turn his nose up.

"I must confess. Lady Brighton," he whispered. "I rarely hunt. And when I do it is on horseback."

Anna faced the bushes again, daring a smile as she spotted faint tracks from where the droppings had been left. It was easy to understand his need for a horse, but for some reason she felt nothing from his words. They were pained to some degree, as if in a state of uncertainty. She knew comforting him was what Simdorn would do but the way he looked at her doused all feelings of sympathy.

"Keep close then, my lord," she said, listening for hoof thuds. "If you find any game first be prepared to fight for it."

Following the tracks beyond the bushes she kept her pace slow. Snow faintly crunched from her steps, overshadowed by the quick, erratic pace of his lordship's footwork. She peered over her shoulder and glared at him. He offered a faint smile, stepping lightly, creating a distance between them. His head cocked right, flashing a grin, disappearing into the overgrowth. Anna panned her vision across where he had gone, catching the sun's rays flashing off his hat.

Trudging through underbrush, Anna found herself at the advantage, knowing Lord Arthur's steel hat was a giveaway. The shine from it was sure to frighten a deer. A faint wet squashing led her to find the Orderman gone. She wondered if he saw the uncertainty in his lordship and decided on keeping track of him.

Branches snapped to her left, followed by a thudding familiar to Anna's ears. It was heading directly past her, hindering her vision with trees, and falling snow. Anna dashed close to the sound, catching the flick of a tail. There was a faint yelp as if someone had fallen. Following both it and what she knew was a deer, Anna readied an arrow, careful not to get caught up in bushes.

The thudding ceased with a head rising, ears pointing outward as the deer took in its surroundings. Anna couldn't see Arthur or the Orderman. She grinned, finding a tree thick about the trunk to hide beside. The deer's tail wagged, standing erect as if it were about to bolt, then settled. She had deciphered long ago hunting meant you needed to catch an animal in the calm. The deer was large and without antlers. Its thick winter fur matched the barren bushes. A faint glint caught the sun streaming down from an opening in the treetops. Through the light, a grin flashed across the Orderman's lips. He faded into a wall of twisted briars and low baring branches, trailed by his long black coat.

Drawing, the deer turned broad side as she anchored to her cheek. A voice rose from beyond the deer, startling it to take a step forward. The voice was more a laugh than words, sending Anna's nerves into an inferno. The deer shifted its head the sound, drawing back a step, its front shoulder trapped between light and shadow. Her arrow struck just before it, the arrow drawing blood like sap from a tree. The deer bolted toward the laughter, panting, blood dotting the ground. Anna raced to keep sight of the deer, spotting that her arrow had gone straight through.

Blood trailed thinly across snow, coating the bushes as the deer quickly outpaced her. Off to her blind side the hiss of low branches against fabric and metal. Anna took her focus from where the deer was going, noting where blood lay. Arthur emerged with a blunted arrow in one hand, the other a flask open, draining its contents. The lord eyed the blood and licked his lips.

"You are as well shaped as you are skilled with hunting, my lady."

The Orderman joined them, lighting a cigar with something Anna had never seen. A silver vial with a small button that made two tiny pieces of attached flint click together. She met his lordship's gaze once more and shook her head.

"You'd have won if your intention wasn't hunting me instead, my lord," said Anna, smirking at the disappointment forming over his face. "I will find my kill and then be done with the way you look upon me."

Arthur pressed the flask to his lips then tossed it in a bush. He unshouldered his blow, cracked an arrow to it, and loosed it. Her eye grew wide before a swift yank brought her upon her side. Anna peered over her shoulder as the arrow hissed overhead. *Thunk.* The arrow struck a tree a tree, its shaft rattled, scattering thin splinters. Arthur dropped to his knees and belted a hiccup.

"Are you mad and lustful?" Anna snapped. "You almost struck me."

She staggered to her feet, drawing her vision up to find a snarl on the Orderman's lips. His steel blue eyes narrowed on Lord Arthur.

"You may be right on both accounts, Lady Brighton," he said, searching for the flask before meeting her gaze. "My apologies for giving you a fright. Can you forgive my drunken jealousy?"

Anna turned from him, heading to track her kill.

"You lusted for me and nearly violated campaign law. I've no forgiveness for you."

She felt a strong grip on her wrist. The Orderman yanked her back, releasing a cloud of smoke from his lips.

"You won," he said. "I don't condone sore losers neither, but you got to be the better person."

"He disgusts me," Anna said, struggling to break free of the bodyguard's grip. "He looks upon women with what Simdorn calls *lust*."

She drew her chin to her chest before matching his fierce gaze.

"I think our goddess will agree someone *almost* ending life negates forgiveness." The Orderman sighed, smoke ran over his chin. "He wasn't in his right mind being drunk and all. Isn't part of being true to Simdorn pitying those in their moment of weakness? It don't make sense to me either, but *almost* isn't a thing with that goddess."

The orderman released her wrist.

"You're right," she said, shouldering her bow. "I have won. But with matters concerning my life I have no pity for men like Arthur. Now, I have a deer to track."

"You aren't the girl I fought," said the orderman. "You best fix what's broken in that head of yours."

She pressed her lips firmly together, every breath like pushing an immense stone.

"I have only one thing to repair," said Anna, "and that is my face."

Chapter Twenty

His heart pounded watching from a distance as Anna took to the stage. Resting a hand on Cole's fuzzy head he found the storm bison breathing heavily, digging his hooves deep into the shallow snow. Norman's sight was keen like all rutoe who wielded flames, the diamond shape of his eyes was narrower because of it. He saw Anna was unsettled by the man. Norman squinted, realizing the archer had been standing on a stool the whole time. He let out a breath, finding it calmed his nerves. The chilling air turned the rains of Cole's storm clouds to snow, dotting the exposed cobblestones.

Thump.

The crowd roared with laughter as Anna let her arm fall to her side. Norman couldn't see where her arrow had struck the target, but it mustn't have been where it should have been. He had no way of seeing Anna's reaction with her hoods, yet he felt her embarrassment. The crowd slowly parted from the stage with the man jumping off his stool. Norman's heart leapt as three arrows hit the target. He grinned, and with it, his chest felt lighter. A dryness overwhelmed his tongue. He slipped a hand into his pocket, fumbling with the small coin pouch in it. Norman shivered at a strong breeze, finding Lampara's winter growing in strength. So much so that the flames warming his blood weren't enough as he released the coin pouch. *It is not enough coin to have helped her campaign.*

Norman shook his head, returning attention to the stage to find the target had been removed. They were faint even for his own eyes, but ten rings upon plinths stood before both Anna and the archer. It was easy to tell the man's ego by his metal two-corner hat with its black pluming feather. Cole grunted, blasting swirling clouds back toward where lightning clapped in the distance. The storm over the trees leading back to Kardanhall faded and shifted. Norman turned back in time to see both Anna and the man leaving the stage. He thought of following them, but the dryness crusting his tongue grew worse.

"Shall we revisit the pub, Cole?"

The storm bison peered at him with his black eyes. He motioned with his massive head to where Anna had disappeared down a street. A man with something round and metal upon his head followed her.

"If that is who I believe," Norman felt a pinch of uncertainty in his chest, but he couldn't allow Cole to know it, "then Anna will be fine."

He mounted the storm bison, giving him a good scratch on the hump before flicking Cole's reins.

Norman rode back to the pub with only Cole's clouds filling the sky. The storm above the forest was gone and with it the sound of its lightning. He went down one street, and then

194

another passing the same line of priests in their gray robes from earlier. He had been too busy with accounting to learn of the practices of Simdorn while living in Williamton. And from what he learned in his travels with Anna none appealed to him. The priests merged into a side street, chanting as they did, in a language perhaps only the goddess's faithful knew.

Finally reaching the pub, Norman slid off Cole's back. His shoes landed with a click against the cobblestones. There was no place for a mount's reins to be tied, so he wrapped Cole's about a post steading the awning to the pub. Norman sighed as the reins whined from the knot he made. The sign about rutoe and dogs hung like a verbal guard against him and his kin.

He entered the pub half wishing he could shed his human disguise. It took most of his focus to keep up such a farce despite five solid years of practice in Williamton. Few rutoe learned such a skill. Until their recent banishment it was of no use. Norman made a fist. Lord William had forced both him and Anna to go on this journey. A journey he knew deep down his friend struggled to fully accept. Choosing a table by the door, clouds filled the windows beside it, trailed by snow as they drifted skyward. He ran his fingers across the table's smooth surface, its wood spotless unlike his recent adventures. He and Anna knew what was at stake, but when sharing a saddle with her, Anna confessed she wished for another way to stop Prime Luther beyond winning the coming tournament.

"What you'll be having, young sir?" said the barmaid, shuffling up to his table. "We got a wide selection, including Lord Arthur's family wine." She gestured to the bar with pencil in hand. "I hear it's the oldest vintage on account of how old his lordship's family is."

Norman licked his inner lip; it grew wet at the thought of such an old vintage. The wines of his kin possessed a grand taste with a vintage surpassing the founding of **Lampara.**

"I would like a glass of that," he said.

The barmaid smiled, scribbling on a scrap of parchment. She blushed like Anna did the first time they met.

"You're the first to sample it," she said, tucking the pencil behind her ear. "Be back in a snap."

Left alone, Norman cast his eyes to the rest of the pub, finding many people had taken tables close to the hearths. Each resembled a snug one-person hut made of small stones. Smoke sifted over the stones from openings on each side. The huts reminded him of the ones from the mountains around his home city. They housed rutoe youth too overwhelmed with emotion to contain their magics.

Running a hand over his chin, Norman shuddered for a second at the thought of being so alone. But unlike wizards, those secluded in the mountains weren't banished, and received food drops from crimsigil hawks monthly. Click went the glass on his table, and a dark purple splashed within its shallow bowl. Norman raised the glass to her, nodded, drawing in a slow, smooth sip.

The barmaid screamed, casting up her arms. The bottle crashed to the ground, wine seeping between the floorboards as Norman spat it out. The taste had been something between vinegar and pond water. He felt a ripple down his cheeks, a thrumming rattled his mind, heightening the barmaid's scream. His eyes burned, flashing red as his ears lengthened to their pointiness. Norman seethed, the roundness of teeth sharpened, nicking his tongue.

"You're a rutoe!" the barmaid screamed again. "Someone, help!"

Norman shot out of the chair as men from around the hearths swarmed toward him. He tripped over his fallen chair and released a torrent of flame from his fingertips against the ground. Righting himself, he burst through the door. Shouts pierced his ears for his imprisonment as he untied Cole's reins and climbed upon the storm bison's back. "Forgive me, old creature."

He jabbed his heel into Cole's side so hard the clouds amongst them combusted. With speed Norman never knew was possible in so old a beast Cole took off down the street. Yelps came from behind as men slipped on the snow. Others came from an alley on horses, slowly gaining, but both snow and clouds crashed upon them. Norman spat again, wiping his lips across his sleeve. Whoever this Lord Arthur was, he had swindled the barkeep. A snap went off in his mind that the man on his stool might be his lordship. Norman clenched his pointed teeth, passing the Wayne trading post. *Anna is with what Nathan titled a trickster,* he thought, squeezing the reins tight.

The edge of Rockelton was within a hair's- breadth as Cole's hooves pounded dirt. Behind them men were caught up in the snow as the sky itself joined in on the storm bison's winter releases. Norman gasped as a faint glimmer pierced the edge of the woods. His suspicion of who followed Anna earlier had been right. The Orderman was dressed differently though with a breastplate that sported the Lamparien horse in silver, shaded with black. Both he and Anna dragged a sizable doe, followed by who Norman guessed was the lord that brought the wine. The taste was gone from his mouth, but he still wished words with the lord.

Thundering hoofs filled his ears once he reached the woods. Anna looked up and smiled, rising to full height, waving. Her hand fell slowly once he dismounted.

"Why are you being pursued, Norman?" she said, taking him by the shoulders. "And why did you return to your rutoe self?"

"That," Norman swallowed, regaining his breath, "is from suffering the taste of Lord Arthur's wine."

His lordship waddled from amongst the trees with shoulders slumped. His bow loose amongst his fingers, churning through snow. The horses snorted and whinnied as the people of Rockelton reached them. Riding with the barkeep the barmaid dismounted first, bowing to Anna, the Orderman, and Lord Arthur.

"I saw your ladyship earlier, Lady Brighton," she said. Her auburn hair was dotted with snowflakes. She rose to full height, pointing at Norman. "Why do you travel with this rutoe?"

The faint despair on Anna's lips disappeared.

"He is my friend," Anna snapped. "I saw the sign outside the pub. What cause do you have to pursue him?"

"I discovered by its taste Lord Arthur's wine was foul," said Norman, eyeing his lordship and Anna. "I reacted poorly and thus exposed myself."

"I am insulted, Lady Brighton," said Lord Arthur. "I know I'm more a showman than a hunter, but I worked hard on bringing Rockelton my family's wine."

"That was no wine," Norman hissed. "If it were, the townsfolk would not have need to chase me."

His lordship shrugged, raising his hands up in surrendering.

"I cannot help if man and rutoe alike have weak palates."

Norman marched toward his lordship. His eyes burned with rage, rings of flame encircled his hands, hiding their green in yellow and orange. Anna pressed a hand to his chest, raising the other as the people of Rockelton gasped, then backed away. He felt a firm grip on his shoulder, peering over to the Orderman. A piercing gaze shot from the Orderman's steel blue eyes.

"His lordship's been through enough today," said the orderman. His words went to a whisper in rutoeis. His speech was swift and fluent with a hint of the eastern dialect in each word. He spoke of the lord nearly breaking campaign law, and of Simdorn and forgiveness. It made no sense to Norman but what the Lamparien bodyguard said next sent shock down his face. "Anna threw aside her beliefs."

Norman gasped, looking at Anna. *She has never allowed her feelings to trump her beliefs.* "This is most unlike you, Anna."

"I need not guess what he told you," she said. "I didn't appreciate the way his lordship looked at me, nor his jealousy." Anna turned to Lord Arthur, shoulders slumped. "Can you forgive my behavior?"

"I'm not ashamed of my desires," he chuckled, leering at the deer. "And now that I truly think about it my actions were justified. I had this town eating from my hand."

Both Norman and Anna stared at him, sharing their confusion. The townsfolk on foot and horseback looked at one another aghast. His lordship slowly grew, hair turning to short sharp quills. His nose narrowed to a point as the clothes upon his person morphed into a coat of chainmail. A long black kilt sewed itself into existence about his waist.

"The perfect guise to fool humans and have a country for

mi-self ruined by a green matchstick," said the Trickster.

Norman drew back from Anna, bounding his fist in flames. Anna cracked an arrow to her bow and drew back. The Orderman slipped a pair of long knives from his belt then spat out his thin cigar.

"Everyone, run!" Anna cried.

A piercing roar erupted from the Trickster's jaws. The people scattered, running for the town, clasping their ears. Norman winced, stumbling back, plugging his ears. Through the glow of his flames, the Trickster's needle point teeth captured the sun's light. A gray like that of early day raced over the skin of the once stunted lord.

"You'd have won over many within the mountain's shadow with those burns, girl," said the Trickster. "These humans are most sympathetic to deformed folk."

Norman heard the shuddering in Anna's breath as she aimed for the creature's throat. She stepped forward but each step was a shuffle, and misplaced. Norman sensed the creature's words had struck deep. He thrusted forward a fist, releasing a sphere of flames. The Trickster bent and twisted in an 's' shape. It pounded the ground as the tip of its quills fell, burning up before striking snow. Anna loosed an arrow, yanked down her hoods, nocking another. The burned half of her face stretched and tightened as she released again. The arrow bounced off the Trickster's head, releasing sparks. It yelped and scratched at its face, tangling fingers within its quills.

Norman lashed out with his flames, boiling a stretch of skin across his lordship's cheek.

"You bloody, green bastard!" Arthur yelped. "I'll kill you for that."

200

The Trickster's feet rooted to the dirt as his body stretched. He freed his fingers, splaying both hands as every finger grew and sharpened. He snatched Norman from his feet. Norman shook with ferocity, feeling blood rush to his ears. He reached forward, the air fleeing his lungs. A faint tear formed in her eye as she called his name. A glimmer shot across his line of vision as he could feel his strength leave him. His focus faltered and faded with the flames of his hands. Suddenly, he fell, hitting the ground with a thud.

"Norman," Anna said, running to his side. "Are you?"

"I'm well, Anna," he said, reclaiming his breath with the heave of his chest.

He glanced up as the trickster reared back. Blood black like ink rained upon the grass and snow. A blast of light blinded him for a moment. Norman shook it off, finding the Orderman straddling the back of Lord Arthur, plunging his long knives into the creature's sides as it clawed at him. The Trickster spun and seized the Orderman around the shoulders. Anna released an arrow. It struck true, piercing through and out the back of Lord Arthurs throat.

Norman steadied himself until afoot again. Leaping from the Trickster, the Orderman landed, churning up dirt. Repetitive thuds kicked up snow as the trickster shrunk, changing both skin color and clothing. The snowfall increased, slowly erasing the black of Lord Arthur's blood.

***

The stench from the lord's blood filled his nostrils. It wasn't potent enough to rob Norman of relief that it was over. What remained of his lordship lay face down in the snow. His blood was all but erased from sight by the persistence of winter.

Anna ran up to Cole taking in the storm bison's massive

head in her arms. Norman watched the creature welcome her, licking the burned side of her face. A faint *snick* of the Orderman's knives caught his attention. He stood watchful over the Trickster's body as if suspicious of its death not being permanent.

"I'm uncertain what to do," said Anna, parting from Cole, taking Norman's hand. "Rockelton will not trust me now, and all for our friendship."

He held her hand tight in his own, the heavy snowflakes pummeling the tangled locks of his hair. *If only all Lampara were like Anna,* he thought. That was one thing about Lord Brighton no one instilled better in others. The acceptance of everyone. He wished the lord of Williamton had spread that kind thinking to everyone, and with that, Norman found his anger for the lord less worth dwelling over.

"We shall have plenty to eat then," said Norman, smiling to stem the tide of her worry. "Nathan must have gained an appetite by the time he reached Kardanhall."

His words he felt were falling short. Anna's hand was warm and wet from the deer's blood. She let go, replacing her hoods over her head, facing Rockelton like a lone century. Norman took her hand in his again and pulled her close.

"It's only one town, Anna."

She met his eyes. Her own like green spheres deep within her hoods.

"It's not losing the town that troubles me," she said. "It's what Lord Arthur said. It reminded me of home, of a time when my hoods weren't needed."

Chapter Twenty-One

Anna took the return to Kardanhall at a slow pace. Her kill hung over Cole's back, tied tight with what remained of the rope from her saddlebags. The cold kept its stench at bay as Norman walked beside her. They thought of giving the deer to Rockelton regardless of recent events. Before she could mount the deer on the storm bison's back, the Orderman offered to help, and he told her in a hushed tone... "The people are gonna think your rutoe friend cursed it for chasing him." And before she could question how, he tipped his helmet and strolled back to town.

Anna eyed Rockleton, catching a brief flash of light from his helmet. She scratched her chin and returned focus to trip ahead. *Nathan would not like a servant of the prime as a part of our group,* she thought. Lady Evelyn was one too, except there was no intent in her to arrest Nathan, Anna felt. She worried with Nathan's attitude toward the council member that such a thing may change.

The falling snow had yet to cease its fury, pounding her

shoulders with wind and snowflakes. Cole's own snow tacked on more, making Anna wish it were spring or summer. Rain soothed her nerves, and when alone amongst the trees beyond Williamton, Cole's rains gave her an advantage on hunts by covering her scent.

Taking in a deep breath, Anna's thoughts turned back to the recent hunt. Her behavior felt justified with proof of his lordship being a trickster. She released a low breath. The orderman was right, and Simdorn's scripture contained lessons for her childish deed. *Words are noise-filled emotions capable of pain,* she thought. *Actions are blades with true intent to deal such pain.* She was relieved the trickster would no longer plague Lampara, yet her words were unnecessary.

She sighed at the towering sight of Kardanhall. It's strange blurring brickwork making it appear more distant than was true.

"I see some large black creature ahead, Anna," said Norman, pointing.

Anna shook her head, focusing on the creature's erratic pacing. The wind rushed against her cheeks, teasing her hoods like they were the open flaps of a tent. There was little sunlight to be seen but what pierced the gray clouds revealed the faint shine of the creature's hooked horns.

"It's Roland," Anna's heart went into a race. She leaned over her kill, squinted, then leaned back. "Why would he be out alone?"

Anna and Norman increased their pace, the wind dying down, allowing the snow to fall straight and orderly. She heard the faint crackle of Roland's lightning like breathing. A mustiness met her nostrils, telling her the bison had been among the elements a while. The black storm bison bleated and stomped. Three ravens scurried away and launched from within feet of his mass. Their movements uncovered a familiar…

"Anna." Norman cried. "It's…"

Dropping Cole's reins, she leapt to the ground, racing with all the strength she possessed. Her heart froze, with her emotions aiming to shatter it like a hammer to a block of ice.

"Nathan!" she screamed. "No."

Every muscle within her stiffened, the cold having no part in it as she collapsed. Tears filled her eye as she crawled, snow crunching. Anna rested a hand on Nathan's chest. What remained of his chin whiskers were but a stub. Her hand went to his cheek, slipping from it to the snow red with his blood. The ravens, in their greed, had pecked out her friend's eyes.

A faint rush of heat clasped her shoulder as words reached her ears. A lump formed in her throat, large, like a walnut. Rubbing the tears from her eye Norman's words grew clearer.

"This explains why the Orderman was in Rockelton," he said. "He was on the hunt for Nathan."

Anna glared up at him, forming her lips into a sneer.

"All Nathan wished was to make up for the dragon, for what he felt was his fault."

She took in where her friend lay. The snow eased its downfall as her eye caught sight of something long and brown woven amongst a cluster of tree branches. Rising, her heart pounding with anticipation and hope that what she saw wasn't a… *Feather.* It was the width of both her hands combined, resting high enough in the trees to be out of reach. She turned back to Nathan, finding a wide thin wound at his neck, black around the edges from the cold.

"An esant was here," she said, making a fist. "Lord Martyn attacked our friend."

Norman embraced her as Anna's chest heaved up and down. She ran a thumb along her bow string to ease her nerves. It was useless.

"I... I sent him away. I thought his lordship would protect him. This is my fault."

The warmth of Norman's arms gave her little comfort. He was without words for the first time, leaving Anna's thoughts to wander. Could they even return to Kardanhall with what they had found? Just like some villain in a book the lord would play off things with ignorance, she thought. Her grandfather told her once when she was twelve that books draw from the world we know. She swallowed, resting her head on Norman's shoulder.

"You possessed no knowledge of what could have happened, Anna," Norman said, kissing her brow. His long dark hair formed a forest in her hood. "Nathan did cross his lordship but not enough for blades to be drawn."

She kissed his cheek, parting from him, wiping her face of tears and the pain tormenting her.

"We shall leave my kill for the crows," Anna said. "Nathan deserves a proper burial under the instruction of a priest of Simdorn."

Norman cast his gaze on Nathan. The cold had preserved the former lord's final feelings with mouth agape and body twisted slightly in struggle.

"And what if Lord Martyn refuses to grant our friend proper burial?" Norman swallowed. His eyes faded to a weak, whitish red. "We cannot storm a castle with just us two."

Anna spun on her heels and went to untie her kill from Cole's back. It slid off the gray storm bison, striking the snow with a collective crunch.

"Help me with Nathan, Norman," she said. "We must bring him to the castle."

"You have a plan then?" he asked.

She guided Cole over to where her friend lay half buried in snow, some of it melted by Roland's lightning. Cole eased down for her as she stroked his side. They laid Nathan over Cole's back, snow falling from his limbs in large clumps, shattering against the ground. Anna possessed more strength than Norman, the accountant grunted and strained, clenching his teeth. Anna applied the ropes and cursed. Fingers shaking in grief, she'd accidentally made a knot. Tearing at the rope she fixed it and turned to march toward the castle.

"No matter what comes next," she said." If Martyn Kardan wants a fight, it will not end in his favor."

* * *

Passing across the draw bridge into Kardenhall, its moat was a solid sheet of ice doused in snow as it disappeared around the castle. Guards met them as they passed under an archway shaped at the point like a spade. Anna told them the truth, that her friend had been attacked, leaving out her suspicions.

"Where is the castle's high priest and temple of Simdorn?" she asked. "My friend must be properly buried."

The guards led her along Kardanhall's outer wall, their numbers increasing little by little for some reason. Anna looked at Norman. One of his hands squeezed Roland's reins while the other produced a faint glow. She took his wrist, feeling the heat through her glove. She mushed her lips together, but she needed to calm him. Her eye grew wide for a moment. For the first time, she was the calm one, and it felt unnatural.

Norman let loose a deep breath, whirling his hand. Its flame faded into the green of his skin, releasing steam.

At the end of the turn about Kardanhall's Keep stood a structure peaked with a bell tower. Her nerves tensed as the guards now numbered in the dozens, as if they were an armored audience at the beginnings of a dangerous event. Anna looped Cole's reins tightly about her hand and wrist. The storm bison remained calm, his clouds covering their tracks in fresh snow. Roland wasn't so at ease, matching the frustration on Norman's face, eyeing the soldiers about them. After what happened to Nathan, Anna guessed the rarest of storm bison's would never trust a man in armor again.

Two figures emerged from a door below a set of stairs to her left. The second stumbled forward after the first kicked him in the thigh. Anna focused, realizing the figure struggling to regain footing was bound at the wrists. *Evelyn.* she thought, seeing the mistress of duels and debates clamor to one knee. Snow darkened her dress and her long blond hair tumbled over her shoulders, shading her face from view.

"You've found the ... traitor's body, I see," said the figure pointing his sword to Lady Evelyn's back. "You are all under lordship arrest. Prime Luther was wise to make the rich commanders of Lamparien soldiers. The law of their own lands"

Lord Martyn's armor now bore the silver horse shaded in black of the prime. He wiped his cheek with a handkerchief stitched with gold. Spittle dripped on his family sigil that snaked its way up the horse's neck.

"You cannot arrest someone campaigning for the governance of Lampara," said Anna, containing her anger as she recalled what Norman taught her. "I would have to have killed another in the running or done damage to property in some way."

Whether she had done anything was irrelevant to how she felt. The dribbling lord had taken her friend's life, and for what reason she wished to know.

"I ... don't allow hunting on my lands without ...," Lord Martyn swallowed then wiped away more spittle, pressing his sword to the cords of Lady Evelyn's corset, "great need. Therefore, damage was done to property. A lord's granddaughter should ... know better." The lord coughed and wiped his chin again. "Your punishment commenced just before your arrival. There will be ... no wizard."

Anna clenched her teeth. *Does he know of the trickster too?* she thought. She bawl both hands into fists. It was all she could do to hold on to hope. *There must be another way. I must find a wizard.* She felt a deep wish to lash out, but held her ground, keeping an eye on Lord Martyn. He grinned through untouched by his age. Anna ignored it, curing herself for not guessing the woods beyond the castle were his, and as a hunter, knowing where one could hunt was vital. But it had not been an issue before on her grandfather's lands. To kill any creature on another's land and spill its blood was considered property damage.

"You're right," Anna said, eyeing Lady Evelyn shaking from cold and pain. "I ask you to take me while freeing the prime's mistress of duels and debates."

Lady Evelyn made it to one knee, but Lord Martyn drew

209

back his sword and kicked her legs out from under her. The mistress crashed against snow and mud, losing something silver and gold from about her neck. Anna took a step forward, but his lordship's blade pressed to Lady Evelyn's back again.

"Remain beside your green friend, Lady Brighton," said Lord Kardan. "You … will both be shackled before being sent to Cillnar. You've both pressed your … noses into business not your own."

Anna peered down at her friend; blood ran swiftly to Evelyn's lush lips from her nose. Her bow was strung across her chest. Anna tensed, losing the anger bound in her fists to block the urge to bring down his lordship with a swift shot. She was eager enough yet what might that mean for Norman she dared not imagine.

With a great stretching of her neck, Lady Evelyn seized the item beyond her nose with her lips and blew. Cole and Roland roared, then stomped, pulling free from their reins. The storm bison's charged after the men behind them, kicking about as a roar from far beyond the bend in the wall. A chill raced down Anna's spine. Lady Wayne blew again, sending up howls from cheefoxes locked in a kennel beyond the bend.

Anna was too familiar with the roar she'd just heard. A crash erupted. Thudding followed in the dozens of what Anna couldn't guess. The air grew colder, clasping at her throat like a vengeful phantom. Her breath formed, short thin, clouds. Another roar came with a collective crackling as if thousands of windows had been struck at once. She spun to face the noise. Far beyond Kardanhall's outer wall, the sun sank below the mountain. It was eclipsed by something fast and huge.

"What have you summoned?" Lord Martyn pressed his sword hard against Lady Wayne's neck. "Tell me!"

Evelyn gasped, dropping what Anna saw was some kind of whistle. It had a silver shaft, clasped over the center by a gold tongue. Over the tongue roared a multi-headed beast. Blood mixed with the blond of Evelyn's hair. "You'll see, my lord."

A great boom rattled the bricks of Kardanhall's thick outer wall. Anna's heart pounded so fast her ears rang, every breath grew short and hot. The crackling came again before four long claws of ice grabbed hold of the wall's battlements. Men drew their swords but soon dropped them as an immense head rose, great wings of ice and flesh retracted to a long slender body. Anna readied her bow, fumbling with the arrows in her quiver, caught between Evelyn and Norman upon the ground. Norman's hands flickered, flames swirled into being, then vanished. Her friend paled and curled into a shaking ball.

"I came here on a dragon of ice," said Lady Evelyn. "Relinquish your intention to arrest myself and Lady Brighton, Lord Martyn."

Lord Martyn clasped his sword with both hands and raised it.

"Call off the … creature! Or I shall feed it your—"

Anna loosed her arrow. His lordship cried out, dropping his sword, her arrow splitting and splintering the flesh of his hand.

"Kill the dragon and the traitors!" Lord Martyn roared, clutching his hand. "End them for your, Prime Luther."

"No," Anna said, readying another arrow.

The lord fled for the Keep, yanking free her arrow, wrapping his hand in his cloak. The dragon mounted the wall, cracking its brickwork, jabbing its head toward Lady Evelyn. Men thrusted at its belly. Ice coated their blades, falling in large flakes from the dragon's scales.

"Drop to the ground with your friend, Lady Anna," said Lady Evelyn.

Anna raised an eyebrow, then turned to the dragon. Its clenched pale fangs glowed blue, releasing mist. With a great roar the dragon spewed ice blue flame. Anna dropped and rolled beside Norman as the flames soared overhead. Lord Martyn screamed. His feet left the ground as the flames smashed him against the Keep. His scream faded fast as the air grew so cold Anna had to huddle against Norman. He shook, gasping at her touch. The heat she expected was a blistering, piercing cold. She wrapped herself around him and draped her cloak over them.

The dragon ceased its flames, roared, then devoured a man whole as the other guards cried for Lady Evelyn to show them mercy. With an immense swipe the dragon cleared the wall with its tail. Cries were long but faint amongst the wind as the dragon crawled on its belly to Lady Evelyn. Anna untied the laces around her neck, then covered Norman with her cloak. She raced toward the mistress of duels and debates, readying an arrow.

Lady Evelyn rose as Anna drew back her bow, aiming for the dragon's black heavy-lidded eye.

"Quiver your arrow, Anna," said the mistress, turning her back on the dragon. "You will only prolong my time bound at the wrists."

Lowering her bow, she kept the arrow nocked. Condensation lined its string as her breath quickened. Anna held her focus on the dragon as it released a tiny puff of mist from its long narrow nostrils. The ropes about Lady Evelyn's wrists froze, shattering as she yanked them apart. She took up the whistle again as men gathered in the hundreds with swords drawn. Anna spun bow at the ready to find them with long spears wrapped in cloth, dipped in flaming oil.

"Surrender," Anna said, eyeing Norman. His breath steady. The cloak was doing its duty. "Your lord is dead."

There was a hint of uncertainty in her words. She still found herself afraid of the dragon and wasn't sure of its loyalty to Lady Evelyn. She didn't wish to relive the past.

"We've got your storm bison's," said a guard amongst the others. "Send the dragon away and surrender now."

Anna craned her neck to the dragon as it curled up behind its mistress. A faint chill glowed over its teeth as it hissed. Cole meant more to her than most, but as the air remained so cold Norman was still at risk. Roland was without Nathan, captured with Cole. She swallowed her nervousness, barely able to keep it down, wanting, yet not sure how to end all of this.

"You will not harm them. If the council's mistress of duels and debates orders the dragon to destroy Kardanhall," She winced, bracing against the cold. The metal plates of her leathers tacked on a chilling burden to her skin, "She will bury you along with it."

Some men eyed her with unease, squinting through the constant winds between domed helmet and gold cloth wrapped tight to their faces. Clouds rose among them at a distance with a faint crackle and snap. Anna kept her eye trained, her bow slightly anchored. Her body shook more from the dragon's presence than the tension in her arms.

With great speed, the men parted and then aimed their

flamed-tipped spears. Cole and Roland were brought into view, huddled close. Her heart throbbed as the storm bison's pulled and twisted, bound by half a dozen ropes, each with men digging their boots deep to hold them steady. She allowed her arm to rest for a moment, knowing there was no use in drawing her bow. Lady Evelyn remained motionless before her dragon's head. It shaded her from the falling snow, draping the mistress in shadow.

"I… I will go."

There was no choice, Anna thought, none but to be brought before the prime and…

A roar erupted. Anna spun as the dragon rose on its hind legs. The air grew so unbearably cold she dropped her bow, collapsing beside Norman. Her body folded into a fetal position against him; all strength to remain awake fled like villagers from a flood.

Chapter Twenty-Two

The chill from her skin was replaced by the warmth of something Anna knew only briefly and in a less spacious room. Beside her, Norman slept softly, his clothes missing like her own. She climbed swiftly from the bed, wrapping herself in a cloak draped over a tall, leather bound chair beside the bed. They were back within Kardanhall yet why was she in bed with him, unclothed, her hair free from the string it had been in since Williamton?

She swallowed the confusion forming a storm in her mind. Before her Norman lay half exposed by her rush to be separated. They had lain with one another in Cillnar. Her heart was with him, but to awake in bed after the standoff amongst a dragon and the hostage storm bison's was jarring. Last she remembered she had been in a hurry, so Norman would suffer no more from the cold. The dragon's chill bit worse than any winter wind she had experienced on a hunt.

Beside the hearth, cloaked half in light and darkness, rested her green leathers upon a manikin. The sleeves hung like

215

the folded wings of a bird, casting thin shadows on the floor. Anna released a breath and covered Norman with the blankets. Her fingers found a faint chill remaining on his green skin as they graced his shoulder. *Sleep well.* She drew back his long dark hair, kissed his cheek, and dressed.

Finding her way to the Great Hall from the day previous was difficult. Lord Martyn's servants casted stern eyes upon her in passing and increased their pace. She thought, with the sun stretching its beams through every window, that Lady Evelyn would be having her midday meal. Thick oak columns supported the corridor; some appeared as if trees had been yanked free from the ground and turned upside down for roots clawed at the ceiling.

She reached a set of stairs leading down to familiar doors. Their brass handles shaped like Lord Martyn's sigil, its wood the same as the trees leading to Rockelton. Two men stood to either side, facing forward with arms folded at their backs. Anna pushed open a door and felt the heat from the Great Hall's hearths race across her face. Pushing the door open was as hard as trying to force Cole to bathe. The servants remained facing forward, one sneered at her, chuckling as strain ran down her face. She guessed the only reason they contained their anger for losing their lord was her title.

A tall sour looking man looked up from polishing the dining table.

"If you're looking for Lady Wayne," he said. His voice was faint for he was at the far end of the room, "find your way to the castle's temple."

Anna stopped at the end of the table. Her cloak enhanced the heat from the hearths, sending thick sweat droplets down her forehead.

"Can you lead me to it?" she asked. "I know little of Kardanhall."

The tall man rested the cloth and polish on the table, wiping his hands on a white apron about his waist. "It goes against my loyalty to my departed Lord Kardan, but I'd rather no more harm come to his lordship's home. Head out across the hall and follow the cold."

"How do I follow—"

"His lordship kept warm only rooms in use," said the servant. "By your dress I'd say you're a hunter. Figure it out."

She left the Great Hall, allowing the man to return to polishing, ignoring the slight riddle in his directions. It was plain those who served Lord Martyn weren't pleased by their lord's passing. His body had been fused to the brickwork of his castle's Keep last she saw of him. A powdery white mist rose from the dragon's mouth afterward.

Following the heat proved to be more difficult than expected. She found the kitchen, hints of onion and beef stew gave its location away. Anna pressed a hand to her cheek, the aroma both welcome and overpowering. She shook it off then pressed on for the temple. Anna returned to the main corridor, eyeing the Great Hall's distant doors before proceeding.

Her thoughts drifted back to her grandfather, glad once more for how simple his home was. The anger for him of these past months lessened its stranglehold on her heart. Anna saw great change was needed for Lampara. And the change need be more than who governed if from the capital. Though her grandfather's method of encouragement were still foul. She wished her mind were different, and that she had trusted in Lord William's faith in her abilities. She wished, too, that Norman would not have been a witness to the planning of Williamton's suffering. If this had all not come to pass perhaps Nathan... Her heart stopped. She thrust her hand into the pocket on her belt. Anna clasped the pale bear brooch, wishing her friend still lived. *Simdorn be with you, Nathan.*

The air grew colder as she made her way down a sloping corridor. A set of wide stairs spiraled downward and out of sight at its end. Lit lamps rattled from a strong breeze smelling faintly of mold. She rubbed her hands together recalling Nathan's complaints of the cold on their travels. Wiping away surfacing tears, she remembered Nathan spoke often of spring being his favorite year phase, that its blue skies and green trees brought him peace. She smiled, recalling his tale of one spring where Roland met another storm bison for the first time, of how he chased the two across a farmer's field amidst a lightning storm fierce enough to be heard beyond Lampara's borders.

Anna made it to the bottom of the steps, finding a door shaped like an upside-down fingernail. She opened it, bracing herself against a strong wind, shading her eyes from the light reflecting off the snow. Drawing her hoods tight against her cheeks she eyed the place where Lord Martyn's body lay fused to the Keep. His lordship was gone, a frozen crater remained, black at its center. A bell chimed ahead sending her senses into a race. She pressed forward through the cold, bracing for a second chime. A temple of Simdorn gave three chimes at mid-morning, two at midday, and three when night fell for the departed. Sorrow filled her chest wishing she had woken earlier, perturbed by even now being troubled at a bell's tintinnabulations.

Once within Simdorn's house mint incense greeted her senses. A wooden staircase led up to the bell tower on her right. Ahead at the end of the room, two windows brought the only daylight. One faced the north and the other welcomed light from the south, bathing an altar of granite in its glow. She hugged her chest, sending her eye to the floor. Her heart thundered as it met who lay before her. Slowly, she drew back her hoods, cupping her hands to form a crescent moon. Her faith demanded it so honor may grace Simdorn. And yet she wanted to curse the goddess for not protecting her friend, for not diverting the men sent to butcher him. She shook her head, nerves a buzz with frustration. Each step weighed her with a helplessness too late to feel. Anna buried her arms within her cloak, bounding her hands into fists. She passed pews of oak coated in a film of dust, their ends holding steadily lit candles of black wax.

Anna's senses, usually at ease within Simdorn's house, were on fire with her friend dead before her. A fire with such heat no dragon could match it. Nathan's wounds had been sewn shut with thick black thread. What remained of his thick chin whiskers shaved clean to the skin. Upon his eyes were two small smooth stones shaped like bears and painted white. Anna swallowed, grateful for whoever crafted them for Simdorn's guardians possessed the keen sight to find heaven.

A man rose from the last pew on her left. The figure's shadow cast itself over the flag resting upon Nathan like a blanket. Whomever it was reached out to rest a hand upon the sigil gracing the flag. The hand was long and slender, tested by the look of its flesh. Anna realized it wasn't a man but Lady Wayne.

"I'm glad you did not miss the midday chime," said Lady

Evelyn. Her hand fell from the sigil which was of a badger upon its hind legs. "You were keen on keeping close to your friend, so I commanded the servants to place you two together and build the fire to last."

Anna remained silent. Every thought trained on Nathan at rest with his hands folded across his chest. She breathed deep, feeling the flesh of her burns tighten then release.

"How long was I asleep?"

Lady Evelyn Wayne faced her with tears resting on her sharp cheekbones.

"Three days" Evelyn wiped clean her tears with the back of her hand. "There are men of Lord Martyn's guard that remain in a chilled coma from my dragon. You're one of few on record to have recovered in less than a month." She allowed a slight smile, resting both hands at her sides. "I knew Brighton's were of strong stock, but you are something else."

Anna's mind drifted back to the barn, of what she knew of rutoe from Norman. Anna shook off the impossibilities surfacing in her mind then cast her gaze on Simdorn's statue. The goddess stood barefoot on a plinth, wearing a breastplate of cremstone. She wore a bear's head helmet with her ageless face within its jaws. Long red locks streamed from the helmet, as did white robes down and about her body. Anna swallowed, trusting her faith had released her from the chilled coma. As to the barn, she tallied up to her friends under stress for her well-being.

"I wish to sit and mourn with you for Nathan," she said. "He will never see my face complete like he wanted."

Lady Wayne gestured for Anna to join her. They sat upon the pew in unison, neither moving to begin prayer.

"You have little time left," said Evelyn. "A month at most to return to the capital."

Anna looked to the north window, its light shifting slightly. The cold seeped through the temple's brickwork, telling her winter's months had only just begun.

"I still feel deep within Lampara will not want a burned woman to govern over them," Anna said, rubbing her hands together despite the fur woven within her gloves. "But from how our people live, how they treat storm bison's, someone must lead them to a kinder tomorrow."

Lady Evelyn snorted.

"There's the confidence I knew you possessed. I cannot say you will change anyone's minds on storm bison's, but your faith has made you wise enough to mend all else."

Anna tilted her head, leaning back.

"Prime Luther," Evelyn continued. "Has done more for his country's lords in twenty years than for the average Lamparien. He throws coin at every problem with no thought to the toll his taxes place on his people. You keep to Simdorn's ways, her use of kindness and concern for the many and not the few."

"So, you're saying my choices will gain our people's trust far better than if my face is complete?"

Evelyn nodded. "You have proven yourself skilled as a warrior. Use your mind as you have just done to win the people."

Staring down at her hands there seemed no reason to be complete anymore. Every thought visited her experiences of late. And though Rockelton may not support her there was still Natlendton and her home far to the east in the Greethumb region. *You were right, Grandfather.* she thought. *And I shall not let Williamton down.*

Anna gazed once again at Nathan. The midday sun reflected off his features, leaving little to be seen but his leather tunic that replaced his travel-stained garb and the flag up to his hands. She imagined his house sigil to be something much bolder than a badger.

"I will be risking my chances at the tournament," Anna met Evelyn's eye, "but I wish to find a wizard at the sanctuary Norman spoke of."

"I thought you realized your burns have no bearing," Lady Evelyn said.

Anna rose from the pew and offered her hand. "I won't be going for me."

Lady Evelyn faced Nathan then gasped as she met Anna's eye again.

"The dead must remain so, for they have earned peace," she whispered, quoting scripture. "You of all people know this is Simdorn's greatest law."

"Yes," Anna said, a sharpness in her tone. "But Nathan didn't earn such peace by death in battle, a family illness, or defending another. He was murdered."

The mistress of duels and debates narrowed her eyes, knitting her brow. Anna knew mentioning family illness wasn't wise, but having Evelyn's support meant the world. Evelyn took her hand, rising with a slight unsteadiness.

"You're right," she said. "Now. How do you plan on making it south and then to Cillnar in time?"

Anna bit her lower lip and exhaled from the nose. She knew only one solution.

"I must face my fear and ride a dragon."

* * *

Anna followed Evelyn at a brisk pace, the Keep towered beside them like an immense drum. It felt like a betrayal to travel without Cole for once, but her friend wasn't swift enough for the journey. She had visited him on the other side of Kardanhall where guest stables contained more straw and feed than Anna had ever seen. The storm bison greeted her in his usual way, and as always knew what was on her mind before the words breached her lips. She pulled tight her hoods over her face, for once doing so not out of fear of judgment. Only the cold bothered her now, knowing it would grow much worse. Cole's fur was warm when they parted. It had always been what saved her when caught in a snowstorm during hunts. At this moment she wished she could crawl underneath him and huddle against his belly.

Across the castle grounds massive bricks lay strewn. One was wedged in a window off on her right. Lady Evelyn moved with long, sturdy strides, as if her family sickness was held at bay by the cold. Looming ahead was a tower, punctured from within like a bird's egg. A foulness reached her nostrils, rotten and, more potent than any Anna had ever experienced. Around the tower's rear side, a cage reached from the top to the base like a set of ribs. Pressed between two bars hung limp the head of Lord Martyn's esant. Anna readied her bow, reached back for an arrow. A firm grip snatched her wrist.

"You cannot face your fear with intent to kill," said Evelyn. Her green eyes driven and focused. "Besides. Unless you possess strong enough magic, no arrow can pierce the chill protecting a crystalardan."

Shouldering her bow, its string was wet from her sweat with a slight film of ice over it. Evelyn had made it to the tower's entrance first, her long strides meshed with a purpose.

The entrance doors lie ripped from their hinges and coated in frost coated their wood. Anna pinched her nose, following Evelyn in, slowing her pace. Light filled the tower from above, the very top like broken teeth biting at the sky. Anna noticed the doors to each stall had been smashed in, coated in a film of frost, and doused in clumps of up turned straw. Thick beams of dark wood supported the circular formation of the tower. A ramp to her left climbed upward to more stalls.

"Look there," said Lady Evelyn, pointing to a half-moon shaped straight away. "The cold grows worse in that direction. I left my dragon out to stretch his wings. By my guess he grew hungry."

Anna cupped her hands, blowing into them. She rubbed her shoulders until some feeling returned to her fingers.

"What if he flew to Rockelton and caused harm?"

The mistress of duels and debates smiled.

"When you raise a dragon from a nestling, they tend not to wander off. The whistle," Evelyn slipped it from around her neck, holding it up by two fingers, "calls to them when not by their mistress's side."

Anna nodded as they went down the straight away, finding a more open section of the stables. Supporting it on either side, in gold, was the sigil of Lord Kardan's house upon squared columns of the same stone making up Kardanhall. She guessed this was where he kept and bred his finest steeds. Or used to. Blood streaked from every direction like the mouths of dried-up riverbeds. Sunlight streamed from diamond-paned windows along the way. Her heart pounded with each step until it felt as though the cold had frozen it still.

A long thin line of light ran from the tip of the dragon's icicle-spiked nostrils to the base of its tail. Its eyes rested upon Lady Evelyn as it lapped blood from its lips with its thick, black tongue. The dragon had gathered every bit of straw Lord Martyn's wealth provided to form a bed.

A gurgle rose through the dragon's throat. It belched a thin white mist as what blood its tongue hadn't collected fell, freezing before striking the ground. Anna gulped, stepping forward as her toes curled against her feet in retreat from the cold. She knew by facing the dragon would her fear disappear but fighting the elements while doing so made it harder.

"What name did you give him?" Anna asked. There was no answer. "I said. What…"

Lady Evelyn was gone. Anna faced the dragon once again, the chill ebbing from his body sending jolts of numbness down her burns. It was opposite the fire of years ago, but the same feeling occurred, that paralyzing feeling, a crushing pain in her chest. Anna raised her head, edging closer, shaking off those feelings. The dragon sat upon its hind legs, and grinded his teeth. He eyed Anna with slight suspicion, closing and opening his thick black eyelids.

"I cannot submit to my fear any longer." She stood tall, struggling, reaching for her hoods. "I have hidden my face, afraid of what people thought. Afraid to be more than what I believed I could be."

The dragon eased its long neck from on high. His head drew closer and closer until Anna could almost touch the bridge between his narrow nostrils. She strained for a moment then found the beginnings of her hoods. Drawing them back she felt as though her face may shatter if the dragon even touched her.

"I don't know if you can understand my words, but if you can, know that your speed is needed to bring my friend back."

"Touch him."

Anna remained still. Straw crunched as the dragon eased back, eyeing where the sound came from.

"A well-fed animal needs kindness," said Evelyn, resting a hand on Anna's shoulder. "You learned this with Cole."

A low deep hum ran across the dragon's lips as he trained his eyes upon her. Summoning all her strength, she reached and rested her hand just above the icicles stretching inward from the tip of his chin. Anna's eye widened slightly, finding his scales slick, an icy mist trickled from its lips.

"Now, just like your storm bison you have earned Thomas's trust," said Evelyn.

"Thomas?"

"My husband's father claimed my brother and I as his own children before his passing. He was a good friend of mine who died in the last war. He gave me Thomas. I know no other way to honor a man so kind."

Lady Wayne's words were heavy with pain. Anna let her hand drop, taking Evelyn into her arms. "Thank you. I could not have done this without your help."

"You just have," said Evelyn. "Now, let's bring your friend back."

Chapter Twenty-Three

᳐᳐᳐

Waking felt like harnessing his control over the fire his courage could produce. Men in rough spun tunics grabbed and shoved someone into a short alley. The alley constructed of two mills of matching faded brick and roofs layered with straw. Norman caught a flash from a bronze mouth shield below diamond shaped eyes of green. The quiet one pressed her parcels to her chest as Norman took a step from his father's side. Tears ran down and over the rutoe's mouth shield. She twisted and turned to free herself, knowing like Norman, she possessed no way to call out without burying herself alive. He peered up at his father, sucking in a breath, a burning churned in his chest like a fast-forming storm.

Norman felt his eyes burn, and soon flames erupted over his fists. He dashed for the men, one drawing a knife as the quiet one's eyes grew wide. Norman halted within the alley and in flash all he saw was...

A canopy blurred and black silks grew into focus. Norman

stretched, finding every muscle stiff like the aged spine of a neglected book. His skin surged with its familiar heat skin. He saw beyond the bed's edge the roaring flames of an immense hearth. He focused on the crackle and snap of its wood, centering himself to be in the now.

Rolling over, something crinkled under his weight. Norman reached, slipping a scroll from near his hip. He untied the black string about it then unfurled it.

Norman,

I have gone with Lady Wayne to the sanctuary you spoke of to find a wizard. I know less than a month remains to win the hearts of more Lampariens, and the tournament lies in Cillnar. My reason for the search is no longer for me but for the friend we have lost.

Norman smiled. "She finally sees her deeds are what truly matter."

You have been given control of Kardanhall under Lady Wayne's instruction.

Be careful, I don't know what hate the servants harbor for you. They hold a grudge against me, and I do not blame them in the least. I would advise one way of defense, and it goes against your nature. They hold great value for Kardanhall. Threaten it. And your safety will be certain. I hope.

Anna

Norman sat up brushing back his hair as he read the letter again. Upon reading the line concerning Nathan, his stomach lurched. Resurrection magic saw little success and great heartache. He planted his feet on the floor, hoping Lady Wayne possessed sense enough to discourage Anna from it. And yet he knew if Anna wanted something, there was no stopping her from obtaining it.

He slipped on his trousers, weaving its laces as another thought found him. Anna was right. Threatening arson was against his nature, even more so after what happened to Williamton. The loyalty was strong in Lord Martyn's men's eyes when they had returned to Kardanhall. At no time since reaching it, leaving for Rockelton, and then returning with haste did he trust them. He dressed, counting himself lucky for now as he stuffed Anna's note in his pocket.

Night filled every window with blackness as he headed down several corridors. Lanterns flickered to either side of black banners displaying Lord Kardan's sigil. Norman could feel the cold through his boots, reasoning a castle required little warmth if its lord no longer lived. He kept his eyes trained for servants, daring to hope that they would leave him be.

A roar came through the windows spaced evenly along the corridor. Glass rattled from some and shattered upon the ground. Norman looked up through a window to find stars. A great shape hid them for seconds and then appeared once more. Voices echoed down the hall before another roar shook loose a lantern. It clanged against the ground, cracking, rolling, fumbling the candle with it. Norman seized it, fixed its candle, and then followed the voices.

Stopping short of a corner, he peered around it to find familiar doors. Immense braziers lined the walls on either side, supported by the shafts of spears. The doors were thick, and towering made from a dark oak. Men stood at the ready to pull the gold rings across them. There was a tap on his shoulder. Norman leapt in place, dropping the lantern with a clang as he spun to find an old woman.

"This household will heed the instruction of Lady Wayne," said the old woman, "but should Prime Luther suspect something of you, the Brighton girl will lose another friend."

Norman met the old woman's eye, shifting his skin to the pinkish flesh of his disguise. His hair hissed up his face curling to become short and auburn. Straightening his collar he noticed a hint of gold in the folds of the old woman's dress, the weight of which the fabric seemed to hang. She patted her side, smiling, reaching, and raising the lantern. It highlighted her deep wrinkles which reached from her lips and eyes.

"I appreciate Lady Wayne's help," he said, wondering what business the Prime had here at Kardanhall. It dawned on him. "Is Prime Luther here for Anna?"

The old woman nodded. "And it appears you will have to break the news to him. You had best come up with a good story."

The old woman turned on her heels, heading for a dark passage in the distance. Her lantern's light faded with Norman's confidence. He should have ignited a hand, shown her he was in command, but his mind got the better of him. A great thrum rattled the walls, brushing the souls of his boots. Norman gulped, peering around the corner again as a pair of distant almond shaped eyes blinked. They glowed orange warped with red, large enough to swallow him with a blink. It wasn't the eyes that held his attention.

"Where's Lord Dribble?" Prime Luther stood in an 's' shape. His armor hung upon his aged person like flower petals in apprehension of their impending fall. His hat wasn't made of any metal as Norman expected, but a gold fabric, circled with long red oval gems. "He was supposed to give me the Brighton girl. Wasn't he, my boys?"

Norman froze as two hulking men, one in green-plated armor, and the other in red aligned with the prime. One possessed a chin thick enough to break down the door slowly closing behind him. His eyes seemed to have no firm direction, shaded by hair a golden red. The man nodded in sync with his brother, who was the same in all but his eyes and teeth. The second man's teeth were cracked and jagged as if he had taken a bit from the castle's dark brickwork. His eyes were wild and darting, as if someone was about to pounce on him.

"Well?" Prime Luther barked. "Where is he?"

The guards remained still, sweat running down their brows to the gold cloth across their mouths. Norman puffed up his chest and took a step out from around the corner. He clenched his stomach and released it. *For Anna.*

"I'm afraid, your prime-ship," Norman said, prancing out into view, spreading his arms wide. *The move worked well for Simon Sanderson.* "His lordship is out at the moment."

"And who might you be?" said one son, flashing his cracked teeth. "He's expecting the big man." The prime's son gestured to his father with a hand guarded by a jeweled gauntlet. It shook despite the sturdiness of his frame. "I want to make the burned girl my plaything."

Norman seethed through his teeth, feeling their points form. Prime Luther chuckled. His prime-ship took three great strides and then settled back into the hunch old man of before.

"Now, Unter," the prime said, eyes squinting through the

hall's brightness. "You can't sleep with one of your fellow.

Unter opened a small compartment on his gauntlet, plucked a tiny spoon from it and inhaled a blue powder through his nose. "Whatever." He coughed, the shaking ceased but a faint chatter raced from his teeth. "I bet she'd be a waste of a real man's time."

"That's a good boy," said Prime Luther, turning back to Norman. "What troubles you boy? Is your future prime too rough for you?"

"No, your prime-ship." Norman could feel his skin beginning to shift to its true form. He focused on the crackle of the braziers, the dance of their flames, imagining Anna placing a perfectly aimed arrow in Unter's throat. "Allow me to escort you to the Great Hall. Your journey must have been long and cold."

"Good man," said Prime Luther, gesturing to his sons. "Come along, boys. Perhaps the Lord Dribble's scrawny friend can put out a better spread than his master."

Upon entering the Great Hall, a spread, as the Prime called it, stretched the length of the table. Chairs with tall backs lined it, draped with half red and green banners with a shadow down the middle over a horse of silver. Norman's stomach grumbled as he stood at one end of the table. Servants received the Prime's cloak possessing pale moons along the trim. Two servants each received his sons trench coats that were of fine boiled leather, the collars ringed in a closely trimmed fur of black.

It appeared Lord Martyn had, in fact, wished to impress the Prime. Three turkeys cooked to a golden brown and ringed with a yellow sauce rested at the table's center. Bowls of roasted red potatoes orbited the turkeys, partnered with apples sliced in such a way Norman swore they resembled the Lamparien governing sigil. Prime Luther sat first, hovering over a plate displaying Lord Kardan's sigil.

"A fine spread, Lord…?"

"Norman Tilt. I am but a representative," said Norman, taking his seat after the boys did. "As for Lord Martyn, he is returning with Lady Anna Brighton as we speak."

"Good. Slide the potatoes over, Unter."

The prime's son looked up with a mouth full of meat hanging from his mouth like a disturbed bear. He grumbled, slurping the meat until his cheeks grew to twice their size. Norman stifled a bit of vomit in his throat. *Nathan was right,* he thought, slicing a potato then hesitating as he raised it to his lips. *Luther will most definitely be the brains behind that one and his brother should they win.*

With a rattle the silver platter slid down the table, scattering potatoes until the prime seized it by the decorative handle.

"I like potatoes, Norman," said the prime, loading his plate then stuffing his mouth. "I may make those idiots campaigning for my position be pelted by them."

Norman raised an eyebrow but swiftly hid his confusion as the prime eyed him for approval.

"I always said if you can put up with a pelting, you can face anything." The prime chuckled, narrowing his eyes upon his plate. "Even the complaints of the damn council."

"You ought 'ave 'em strung up and hacked to pieces, Father," said the crossed eyed son.

Norman dabbed his lips.

"Lampara needs the council. Does it not?"

Both sons trained their eyes on him. Norman kept his posture, eyeing them both with unease.

"We need the Wayne woman and her herd of ordermen like we need another rutoe uprising." Prime Luther stuffed a whole potato in his mouth. It opened a jar, the potato rolled off his tongue as he waved at his mouth. "Hot." He spat. "Those fools wanted peace with those southern snake riders."

"I have to agree with her, your prime-ship," said Norman. "I heard of your recent fight with them, and how you survived a quiet one's fierce attack."

"Fierce?" said Unter, spittle ran down his chin as he tossed a bone over his head. "You give those block-headed rats a lot of credit."

Norman released breath through his nose, trying as he could to allow the hearth's light to ease his nerves. Fear gripped his throat as he pieced together a response, but the abrupt energy Unter put into hating his people was too much.

"My apologies," he said, avoiding Unter's gaze. "I was taught to be respectful to all who reside within Lampara's borders."

Unter scoffed. "You sound like the Brighton girl's grandfather."

"Enough, Unter," Luther barked. "The young man can think what he wants for now."

"But Father—"

Prime Luther rose, slamming his fist on the table. The hulking boy fell silent, popping open the compartment on his gauntlet, then snorting three spoonfuls of the blue powder. He shook for several moments, the veins upon his neck bulged. Norman watched as he seized the turkey before him, raised it to his lips and gorged like a wolf on prey.

"Prama dust," said Prime Luther. "About the only good thing to come out of the south."

Norman shook his head to find his fingers straining for

relief over his chair's armrests. The hearths filling the Great Hall with heat no longer soothed him. Their crackle brought only noise in place of peace. His skin itched to shift from the flesh of human to rutoe. And yet if he allowed himself to be what he was, death was assured. Kardanhall would become unsafe for Anna once she returned.

"How are the potatoes ..., your prime-ship?" said Norman, trying to change the subject. "Are they to your liking?"

Prime Luther wiped his mouth with the back of his hand. "They're better than last time for certain. Anyway, to business. I await the Brighton girl and was told she would be here when I arrived."

Norman swallowed, loosening his grip on the armrests.

"Lady Anna is a skilled warrior and hunter. His lordship may have lost her in the woods."

"She has near the same amount of support as my sons," said the Prime. "I can't have that, not from some girl with no army to stop me I can't. My rule is ending, but when one of my sons wins it shall be rekindled."

"Will you rule through one of them?" Norman asked, fainting a chuckle. "Is that not against the law?"

"Father," said Unter. "You should wait a bit. This ain't Lord Martyn you be talking to."

"What? Oh, I'm done waiting for that slack jawed creatine." Prime Luther made his hands into fists, rising, he strolled to the nearest hearth. "You can keep a secret, can't you Norman Tilt?" He eyed Norman with a softness in his expression. "Anyway, it will be something like that once I remove a few barriers. The Brighton girl's parents were the first hurdle to fall, and she will be crushed along with those miserable—".

"Father." Unter barked. "That's too much. Wait a bit."

A flood of nerves overcame Norman as he watched the prime take a poker from the hearths rack and wave it as his son. He felt as Anna did but deprived of the warning her nerves provided her. Anna told him her parents were killed by robbers chasing them through the forests of the Greethumb. He rose to join the prime, but once close enough, he went stiff like a board. His feet rooted themselves in place as a red-hot poker hovered within inches of his face from the prime's grasp.

"The heat seems to not bother you, Norman Tilt," said Luther, turning the poker in his hand. "Unter's right. I'm not as sharp as I once was, but I'm sharp enough to notice your lack of perspiration."

Great heavy footsteps echoed behind. Norman turned in time to see a wall metal. He groaned as the towering prime's son grabbed his arms and pressed him toward the prime. Remaining in human form he clenched his teeth as the point of the poker neared his throat. His arms were growing numb the more Unter's squeezed.

"I assure, Prime Luther," he said. "I am human like yourself."

"You have no need to lie," said Prime Luther, eyeing Norman under thin white eyebrows. "The clouds seeping from the guest stables were clue enough, and the man your friend let escape told me of a rutoe with power over fire."

Norman gulped. "I'm not him. I swear—"

The prime pressed the steaming poker to Norman's cheek. Its heat was nothing, but the point sent his flesh to what it truly was and summoned a scream he had not the strength to bottle up. Finally, the poker withdrew as Prime Luther tossed it aside, rising to full height and grabbing Norman's collar.

"Tell me, rutoe of the ignited ones, where is Anna Brighton?" Prime Luther roared. "I shall have my son break your back if you resist again."

Norman heaved and wheezed; every breath retreated from his lip as he searched for a way free.

"She is long gone," he said, then ignited the tip of his finger, "as I shall be."

Releasing a spiral of flame it struck the hearth, engulfing the wood. Norman shut his eyes as a great flash of light and heat freed him of Unter. Prime Luther staggered back as Norman made for the doors. The other prime son raced to help his father when Norman halted before the doors. He couldn't open them alone, but time was short. He splayed his fingers over the door and released a torrent of flames. The door burned slow at first as the flames ate away at its thickness.

Shouts and racing footsteps reached his ears from the hall. He saw guards fleeing with their cloaks a flame. He felt himself yanked back.

"You nearly blinded me, you green welp," said the prime.

Norman gasped. He couldn't harm the Prime, but at this point being an outlaw was certain. The doors were crumbling, black and fragile. He yanked himself free of Prime Luther, then a jolt of pain raced to the roots of his scalp as the Prime seized his hair. Norman focused until the long dark locks of his true self slipped free, making his features human for a split second as he dove through the crumbled remains of the Great Hall's doors.

Making it to his feet, ash and charred debris fell from his shoulders as he dashed down the hall. Guards of both the prime and Kardanhall raised their swords. He recalled which way led to the main entrance, knowing a dragon remained before it, but Norman needed to warn Anna. He needed to find his way south, hoping Cole and Roland still lived. His heart rammed in his chest as he charged the soldiers. Until venturing from Williamton, fighting had never been something he imagined doing. Norman pictured his father, missing him, feeling pride swell in his belly for the battle he learned of in Cillnar was one his father might have fought in. He cast his flames at the feet of those coming at him, sending them racing for the walls. His father had returned south once Lord William's accountant had taken Norman in as an apprentice. It had broken Norman for a time to be without him, but when news came of a slow-burning uprising in the south, he knew only one rutoe with courage enough to start it.

Nearing the final stretch to Kardanhall's main entrance, no further resistance surfaced. Footsteps echoed behind him, silencing his rising curiosity as he let loose a breath. Again, another set of immense doors stood in his way, the low rumble of the dragon breathed through its cracks. Norman slipped behind a brazier, holding steady to one of the spears supporting it. The footsteps drew closer as he regained his breath. Two towering shadows raced past him with drawn swords. They vanished around a corner as Norman crept out from behind the brazier and aimed his hand.

"Go ahead."

A pang of fear rattled down his spine. Norman turned, allowing his hand to drop.

"You have far more courage than I expected for an accountant," said the prime, drawing a long dagger from a green scabbard at his hip. "Yes. I know much about you. Your father is in my prison."

"I don't believe you," said Norman, raising his hand to the doors. "You could have spoken with Lord William. He had Williamton burned to force his granddaughter to campaign."

Luther drew himself up, sticking out his lower lip as he folded his arms.

"I never would have expected such extreme a measure from a Brighton. I suppose the traitor spilled his guts about me, and it made campaigning all the more tempting."

"No," said Norman, shaking his head as he faced the Prime. "She wanted nothing to do with campaigning or you."

"Her actions say otherwise." Luther scoffed. "You may as well surrender where you stand."

Soldiers emerged from the distant hall, Norman last saw the old woman. Their torches grew in brightness joined by the clicking of spurs, like thousands of raindrops against a window. Guards of Kardanhall crowded beside the Prime with swords drawn, their mouths shielded by a gold cloth, wearing dome helmets and long heavy gold coats.

"Anna will win the tournament," said Norman, pressing his back to the doors.

"That may have been possible ten years previous," Luther said. A calm in his voice, "things have changed. I've made certain."

"No. She has greater potential than you know."

Greater than she knows, Norman thought, hearing the dragon beyond the doors. His focus trained on the men awaiting orders.

"Take him."

At once, like an immense wave, Norman was swallowed. His arms were yanked back. An icy metallic feeling snatched and bound them together. Norman focused, but failed to ignite his hands. The shackles negated his flames, yet he knew now how. Eyes narrowed with intent filled his vision then parted as swiftly as they had come. Norman leaned back and grimaced as the Prime appeared within inches of his face.

"We'll put him with his father," said the Prime, grinning beneath the brim of his hat. "Perhaps the wish of all fathers will come true, and Lunderuman will die before his own son does." He rested a hand gloved in red leather on Norman's cheek. "He has so little time left as is."

Chapter Twenty-Four

I t took much time to apply the dome saddle to Lady Evelyn's crystalardan without stable boys. The mistress of duels and debates gave Anna instruction, keeping the ice dragon calm with hand motions and the use of her whistle. Anna held firm to the edges of her seat, feeling the leather over wood. Near the length of her arms, windows long and thin lined the dome saddle's sides. The dragon's chill bothered only the souls of her feet as it flew south with them upon his back. Anna had never been within so small a place. She craved the openness of being upon Cole's back. She swallowed for what felt the hundredth time in a discreet attempt to hide her nervousness from Lady Evelyn.

She stretched her arms downward to their fullest extent, relieving the ache from climbing up and down the crystalardan to apply his saddle. Through the window beyond Lady Evelyn, day had turned to night. Her friend sat a head lower than her, holding firm, long, black ropes in place of leather reins. Relief washed over her chest, thankful for Evelyn offering to apply Thomas's bridal. Fear still resonated within her. And though she had moved past being within a dragon's presence, interacting in the same fashion she did with Cole would take time.

"We are near a day south," she said. "How will you guide Thomas when the day has long since gone?"

Lady Evelyn peered over her shoulder with a small smile on her lips.

"Thomas knows his way to where my father brought him from. South of Lampara is Breezenburg. A land of fire and ice few journey. I have been to rutoe lands before. And it shall be day by the time we reach their mountains."

Anna settled back into her seat, finding eagerness had placed her within a whisper's reach of Lady Wayne. The lady gave her an assuring nod, facing forward as she jerked Thomas's reins. With a great flap like the clap of thunder, he roared and sped faster. His wings rose and fell swiftly down in tune with his back. Anna fell forward, reaching to catch herself against Lady Evelyn's seat.

"My apologies, Anna," said Evelyn. "Man has yet to invent a way to secure oneself to a saddle, especially one fit for a dragon."

She crab-walked back into her seat as the walls about her felt as if they were closing in. Sweat ran down her brow. "I will manage." She wiped the droplets away, sighing to herself.

"Good. You will need such an attitude when we return to Cillnar."

"If we can in time," Anna said. "I have never seen a wizard and know only what my grandfather described. Do you know what they truly look like?"

Lady Evelyn placed Thomas's reins in one hand, turning so

she faced Anna entirely.

"No one does."

"How then shall we find one?" Anna gasped. "How have there been no accounts of them beside their deeds?"

Evelyn raised a hand to calm her as Anna's chest heaved. She felt the mistress of duels and debates place it on her knee, but it brought no comfort.

"I've heard they change form like the wind its direction." Evelyn heightened the pitch in her voice, giving Anna's knee a squeeze. Her grip was like that of her grandfather's, sturdy, and firm. "You will find one for your friend. I promise."

"How?" Anna yelled, throwing up her hands. "Nathan died because of me. He died because I thought he'd be going someplace safe."

Slap

Anna shook her head. The pain wasn't instant at first. She hadn't even seen the strike come. She groaned, letting her jaw hang slack.

"Did Lord William allow such hysterics?" asked Lady Evelyn, merging her lips into a thin, firm line. "I doubt it very much so."

Meeting the lady's gaze, the pain came not from her blind side as expected. Evelyn was truly an orderman. She fought with honor as Nathan said in their travels an orderman did.

"No," she said, rubbing her cheek. "He would flick my brow hard. He did so one time when his thumb was broken. It took many times for me to learn how to avoid such pain."

Lady Evelyn faced forward once more, taking Thomas's reins in both hands. She gave them another jerk, but this time, as his wings gave their thunderous clap, Anna refused to brace herself.

"You will learn to do so with me," said Evelyn. "Now. Focus on what you want and let us hope our search is swift.

* * *

The sun revealed its light through the saddle dome's window. It was their fifth day of travel as Thomas soared over the beginnings of what appeared to Anna like a whole other country. Mountains reached high up into the clouds while others formed canyons and valleys scattered with homes. She could just barely see them with snow topping their roofs. Lady Evelyn spoke true days earlier of it being day once they were south. Anna rested her hands upon her knees, rubbing them, guilt swelling within for being irrational at the journey's start. She rested a hand upon the mistress of duels and debates shoulder, sunlight highlighting the worn leather of her gloves.

"I cannot apologize enough for my behavior," she said. "My grandfather would be disappointed with me."

Evelyn rested her eyes on Anna's hand, then returned to guiding Thomas. The dragon parted the clouds with his roar, sending snow downward from the chill of his presence.

"I was disappointed," Lady Evelyn said, emotion trapping her words for a moment by the sadness in her voice, "but you remind me so much of my daughter that despite my orderman ways, I haven't the strength to remain so."

Anna gave Evelyn's shoulder a faint squeeze, then leaned close, and folded her arms across Lady Evelyn's chest. It heaved slightly as she rested a hand over Anna's. The firmness of five days previous was absent.

"I have not seen Emilia for nearly a year, Anna." Evelyn

swallowed deeply; tremors ran through her fingers. "She went out with her wife, seeking to campaign, telling me if I was only going to advise Prime Luther on what not to do, and not taking action when he did the opposite, then I was more guilty than him."

Anna removed herself from Lady Evelyn's shoulders, sitting back in her seat as her mind swirled. "The council has power to keep a prime from his declarations?"

"No," said Evelyn. "We can only enforce campaign law and remind the one who rules of what Lampara's long ingrained traditions demand. Of what Simdorn frowns upon. My daughter knows I must also be a protector of a prime. She believes assassination is worth risking all for an end to Luther's deeds."

"The orderman I fought within the Proving said his fellow guardsman contemplated assassination," Anna said. "It led instead to him placing his name in the final calling."

"I spoke with the man you mentioned after your duel. He is my eyes on our prime until we return to Cillnar."

Anna sighed.

"My faith in finding a wizard and returning in time is still uneasy."

Ahead through the window before them, a stretch of smooth rock emerged. It sat a top a narrow trail of stone leading to a higher mountain ringed layer upon layer in clouds. Immense braziers circled the stretch of smooth rock like a halo struggling to maintain its divine glow. Anna braced herself as they dropped lower with Thomas's long neck aligning straight as an arrow for what lay before him.

"I know you have many doubts, Anna," said Lady Evelyn. Her voice was low, calm unlike the nerves mounting in Anna's chest. "The one thing you haven't possessed doubt in is your faith. Use that. Use it as you would your bow on a hunt."

Deep regret thumped against her chest at the choice in Evelyn's words. She made her journey all about herself, barely hearing or paying notice to the struggles of those closest. Anna thought of Norman. His people were othered from Lampara. Made to appear as both enemies and someone not trusted to share the public with. Her thoughts narrowed to the woman before her, plagued by family illness and parted from a child fully grown.

The smooth stretch of rock drew closer. Tremors ran through Lady Evelyn's arms the lower Thomas went, but the dragon and dome saddle were steady. Anna felt unsure whether she should take control or allow her friend to land Thomas alone. The tremors grew worse sending Anna's nerves on full alert.

"You are ailing, Lady Evelyn," Anna said, maneuvering beside her. "Allow me to guide us down."

Ahead, their destination was absent of people, growing close enough to reveal each brazier upon brick pillars. Anna rested her hand on the rope. She coughed, choking for a split second, clutching her stomach.

"Do not do that again," Evelyn sneered, drawing back her fist, then threatening Anna with it. "I will not be made a passenger upon my own dragon."

Anna leaned back rubbing her stomach. From the corner of her eye, the stretch of smooth dark rock appeared directly below them as she felt Thomas touch down. Through the saddle dome's side windows, his wings retracted, crackling, and whipping like a thick sheet in strong wind. She turned back to the mistress of duals and debates, finding her quakes had ceased. The dragon clamored to a stop, stomping, and slowly settling upon his stomach. Lady Evelyn stood at half her height and dropped the ropes. She yanked two at the top corners of the window before her.

With a thud and crunch, Anna used the steps built above the window. Evelyn leapt over the steps upon Thomas's back, descending his side like it were a cliff face. Anna followed suit feeling breath returned. As she drew her hoods over her head, they felt more like a shield against the fire in Lady Evelyn's green eyes than a barrier against the cold.

"That is the second time you've been struck by me, Anna," Evelyn said, checking her gloves. "I trust and admire you. I know you shall rise to the tasks ahead. But I cannot be denied what independence remains for me." She spun on the heels of her boots and marched off. Evelyn cloaked herself with an ankle-length coat, its collar ringed with fur. "Let's be off. You have a friend to resurrect."

* * *

Overcoming the path from where they landed proved slick. Every instinct demanded of Anna to ignore her friend and guide her the remainder of their way. But her reflexes weren't a match for another strike, nor had they been for the previous two. Anna pulled her cloak close to her chest, snowflakes brushing the ends of her bow strung across her chest. Her quiver rattled with each step, making Anna wish she had searched for Kardanhall's armory to resupply. There remained only a dozen red goose feather arrows. She let out a low sigh, looked up, and halted abruptly.

"Why have we stopped?" she asked, finding the path now

wide enough for her to stand side by side with Lady Evelyn. "The sanctuary is still a good distance ahead."

"Listen." Evelyn whispered, the wind nipping at her bun, loosening hairs. "There is a matter of which I haven't told you."

Anna took each step with care, placing herself so the mistress of duels and debates was in full view of her working eye.

"What is it?"

"The Wayne's … have been smuggling nelka out of the South for some time."

Her jaw fell slack with both her hands finding the fur lining her cloak. The swift saber-toothed feline was held sacred amongst the rutoe, said to be near the size of carriage and hard to track.

"Must I go alone then?" said Anna. "Why did you not tell me this before?"

"Would you have been able to guide Thomas this far?" Evelyn checked the knives at her hip, buttoning her coat up to her neck. "You'd have used Cole and not faced your fear. Had I not given Thomas a stable full of potential meals your chances of finding him agreeable would be nonexistent."

Anna grabbed Evelyn's collar and shoved her. Lady Evelyn stumbled back. Tremors ran down her body as she stretched out one leg, then firmly planted the other. A blade hissed from her sleeve as her eyes narrowed.

"You didn't believe in me," Anna roared, slipping her bow free as she clapped an arrow against it. "All your words have been a lie." She drew back, aiming faster than she had ever done. "I should strike you down and find the wizard myself."

Lady Evelyn frowned, slipping the knife back up her sleeve.

"No," she said. "I always believed in you, Anna. Enough to take a great interest in you and abandon my duties on the council and as an orderman. Emilia was right. And now I am here to make certain Luther doesn't succeed."

Tension ran through her arms. The cold pierced every layer upon her person. Her eye narrowed to a slit but brought little focus against both wind and snow. She swallowed, licking her lips to hold strong against their dryness.

"I truly haven't faced my fear then," Anna said, feeling her arrow's fletching rub against her cheek, begging her to be released. "How much else do I not know?"

Lady Evelyn realigned her feet, dropping her hands to her sides. Anna eyed them for even a hint of something sharp but found them to be empty. "There is nothing else to tell, except that you are right. You must enter Echnumbard alone."

The arrow went without her permission. The string of her bow snapped to attention as her arm dropped, zapped of strength. She cried out as a gust of wind closed her hoods, blinding her. But there was no cry out of pain. No heavy thud against the uneven rock at her feet. Anna clasped her hoods, yanking them back.

"I'm grateful for this damn wind for once," Evelyn said, lowering her hand from her face. "Had there'd been none, and you an orderman, I would be gone from this world."

Held firmly in the mistress of duels and debates' hand was Anna's arrow. Anna shouldered her bow, searching for words and, finding none. She was doomed from the moment she entered the Proving long ago. The ordermen possessed speed and training beyond anything she could master. She shook her head, rubbed the stress from her face with a fist. Lady Evelyn held up the arrow to her fletching first. Snowflakes pounded its shaft dying the fletching from red to white.

"Thank you," Anna said, taking the arrow. "My guess is you will wait with Thomas until I return."

Anna placed the arrow back in her quiver. A slight smile formed on Evelyn's face. Evelyn brought the fur of her collar closer to her cheeks.

"I will," she said, breath steaming. "I noticed a set of stairs not far from where we landed. I'll wait wherever it leads." Evelyn rested a hand on Anna's shoulder. "Good luck."

Anna bit her lip, peering toward the path ahead. It was growing white from the snowfall. Farther ahead, the path appeared to have ended by the mist. The clouds had turned all around them gray and grim.

"And to you too, Lady Evelyn."

"We can put aside manners and ceremony, Anna." Lady Evelyn smiled. "You may call me Eve."

* * *

Snow crunched with every step feeling as though it may be her last. The path had narrowed enough to accept a cart one way. Ice made every step undependable. Anna felt her way with her feet, rolling the thought over and over of how any rutoe made their way to hone their abilities. The snow grew less intense once she reached a slight slope. She paused for a moment. It was faint yet what echoed to her ears sounded like Thomas. The constant wind kept her from knowing if his roar was out of anger or something else. With all her time with Cole, deciphering how a creature felt by its "voice," as she called it became second nature.

Anna found the slope ended as quickly as it began. Her curiosity about Thomas was gone with the snow's downfall. A towering image took shape and detail as the mist vanished slowly before her eye. Her breath fought to regain itself. Anna found a strange sense of calm; every nerve didn't buzz like it always did.

Two great pillars stood before her marked by symbols made of a red stone she had never seen. She could not bring an answer to how, but every symbol emptied her mind of worry somehow. The symbols upon the right column were a fist wreathed in flame like a tree set ablaze. Below it was another fist with one finger pressed to a pair of lips.

Upon the second pillar a man with flowing long hair evaded a shining red stone with great ease. Below him was shown a woman with one hand to her brow, and the other levitating a red orb inches above an outstretched hand. Anna passed between the columns, finding the cold absent from her muscles. Sweat cascaded down her back as she drew her hoods back and removed her gloves, tucking them in her belt. A hiss filled her ears. She looked around for a snake but reasoned that was impossible. Anna gasped.

Grass rose about her boots. The air grew warmer urging her to remove the cloak of nelka fur Emily had gifted her. She replaced her bow and quiver over her shoulders. She realized once in Echnumbard, not having the cloak may be wise. Refocusing ahead, trees rose, shading her from sunlight she hadn't seen since leaving the lands of Lampara. She moved toward the trees on her left, falling back when her feet found no purchase. *But how do the trees stand? A wizard?*

Anna regained her balance, keeping herself on the straight path of before. Chirping whispered in the distance joined by the slight ruffling of branches. Her mind felt clear like a sky absent of clouds. It was the first time she had experienced such a feeling since before feeling the dragon's flame. There was a tingling in her right eye. A tremor from the part of her lips sealed shut from her burns. No one stood ahead, behind or on either side of her, but Anna felt this had to be the work of a wizard.

She looked up, froze, and stepped back at a large shadow. It filled her vision yet at the same time the skin binding her eye shut loosened. She blinked, wincing. A screech left her lips as both eyes drew in the light. They both could open! They both could see! Resting a hand to her lips they parted and stretched, drawing in the air. Anna let out a laugh that shook her chest, tears met the corners of her lips. *Clank.* She leapt back, tremors ran down the soles of her boots. Chains rattled, fading into view only to grow blurry by a kick up of dust. Anna dropped to her knees uncertain even in the calm she still felt. She ran her fingers over every inch of her face. It was smooth and…

"I'm… I'm complete."

Chapter Twenty-Five

A great, unnerving roar reached Evelyn's ears. She felt her hand begin to shake, Thomas's roar slowly faded into the south's mountain openness. She raised her hand to eye level. Snatching an arrow out of the air was something she didn't believe possible in her current state. She weaved a finger through the hole in her glove and winced. She wondered if her friend roared out of hunger or impatience. Blood met the hole in her glove from the arrow's razor-sharp head. *Have I grown that slow?* she sighed, listening for her friend.

Leaving the glove on, she made her way back to Thomas. Her hope for Anna was strong. The girl had been through much since parting from Williamton. Evelyn smiled a small smile. After leaving the Brighton girl within one of the Proving's bathing rooms, it was difficult to imagine Anna campaigning. And yet, without Phillip's race with the cheefox Anna Brighton may have returned to Williamton or died by the blade of someone far more capable than Nathan Barden.

The snow was relenting. Evelyn wished the wind would follow its lead. She rubbed her shoulders and squinted. Thomas's immense serpentine outline grew larger and clearer with her quick pace. But there was no movement from the crystalardan, no chronic restlessness, she knew from her friend. There was no chill against her cheeks but what the high altitude provided.

Evelyn increased her pace, taking longer strides. She fought the tremors rattling her limbs as she pushed herself. There was no rise and fall of Thomas's back, no crackle as he'd shift his weight with each movement. Evelyn pursed her lips, rubbing away flakes from her wind burnt cheeks. Every sense readied itself. She knew no man with sword or bow stood a chance against a crystalardan. She caught from the corner of her vision the dome saddle far from where Thomas remained motionless. Its metal frame trembled from the wind. Burned and torn fabrics, furs, and wood hung from it as if savaged by a beast.

Unbuttoning her coat, she drew out a long knife for each hand. She ignored their weight. Pain wracked her body like rain against an unfurled sail. Evelyn screamed, pressing her knuckles to her brow. Thomas was black as the rock about his body. The blues and whites with each spike of solid ice was gone from him. His mass spanned near the width of where she landed earlier from tail to head. Her friend was one with the mountain top her feet touched upon. Tears invaded her cheeks, but Evelyn refused to fend them off, withdrawing her knuckles.

No footsteps filled her ears, nor the crackle and hiss expected from the flames of an ignited one. Evelyn's feelings begged her to drop to her knees like a hero in some story.

Like anyone may when they lose someone so loyal to them. She suddenly missed Thomas's chill, having grown used to it since he first hatched. Its persistence was...

Evelyn spun from where she stood, leaping as a high-pitched cry shook the ground. She collapsed on her side, dropping her knives. Crackling ran over what remained of Thomas, and then, he shattered before her eyes. An immense dust cloud overwhelmed her, choking every breath. The wind rushed over her, snatching away the dust. Evelyn grabbed her knives, slamming their points into the ground, rolling over to her stomach. A faint wish to surrender to her family illness pained her. A faint rattle met her ears as she stumbled to full height.

She outstretched her arms, jabbing them back at the sound of light thuds. Men wrapped in black bear furs and black silks slid under her arms. Evelyn thrust forward before either were upright. They coughed and choked. Their hands let loose the chain pressing hard against her back. Shackles topped their fists from either chain end making her wonder why kill Thomas only to capture her. She knelt, pulling free the scarves about either man's face. She huffed, eyeing her surroundings, narrowing her vision. The men before her bore the charcoal skin of the rutoe's swift clan.

A figure stood. The remnants of dust from her friend's body swirled past them on a current of strong wind.

"Do you aim to capture me, rutoe?" Evelyn raised a knife in alignment with his chest, blood white like milk dripped from its point. "You must know who I am."

The figure approached at a slow pace. Evelyn kept watch of his hands, his face, fighting the tremors her muscles demanded she succumb to. The rutoe had a mouth shield of steel held tight to his face by a leather strap. His garb was the same as the others dead behind her except for a strange breastplate of scales she'd only seen on the hide of inferno dawns. His shoulder guards were of a singular claw from the fire breathing creature, a dragon far larger than the one that damaged Anna's face.

"What have you done with Anna?" she demanded.

The rutoe narrowed his eyes, wrinkling the olive tone to his nose and brow. Evelyn felt a pang in her mind, tearing at her focus. A voice entered it, thick and swift in its accent. *"I know of such a person, but not her condition. Yes, I do know you, Wayne. I know of your family's dealings with nelka furs. The creature is sacred to rutoe, hard to keep safe and breed these days thanks to those wishing riches from their fur."*

"Am I to stand trial for my family's crimes against the clans? Or can I cut you down as I did those swift ones?"

The quiet one stopped within range of a knife throw. He gazed at the place where Thomas once rested. His silence hung on the wind. The pang within her mind faded, easing away her need to focus, to remain sane.

"Either way," Evelyn said, readying her knives. "I will strike you dead for Thomas."

The rutoe's brow wrinkled as a faint laugh seeped from under his mouth plate, shaking the ground beneath him. Evelyn firmed her footing, the quaking nothing compared to what she felt in her bones. The quiet one went silent and still. Heat pressed like a weight against her back. She narrowed her gaze and peered over her shoulder. Three ignited ones, each possessing green skin and red eyes. The diamond-shape of their eyes were lined with ash. A black cord bound their long flowing hair tight to their scalps. Amongst the constant wind Evelyn made out a large fist wreathed in flame upon their breastplates.

"You must be who killed my friend." She snarled. "I'll end you for that."

The ignited one in the middle stepped forward. His eyes flared like miniature suns.

"Our border scouts warned us of his coming," he said. His accent was lighter than the rutoe before her, though no less difficult to understand. "His chill ruined our crops and sabotaged our rebellion. His death was a necessary action."

Snick. The ignited one dropped to his knees, blood trailed swiftly down his breastplate. Those rutoe standing paces behind rushed toward her, their fists engulfed in flame. Evelyn dashed, slid, and ripped her knife from the rutoe's throat. Flames invaded her vision as she spun and thrust both her knives through their gut.

Evelyn met the quiet one's gaze, sneered, yanking free her knives. She heard the sizzle of ignited one blood fail to devour the steel of her knives. She bit her lip, eyeing what was left of her friend, part of his nostrils and jaws held their shape.

"I have taken my revenge," she said, pressing her lips into a hard line. "The Wayne's will fund your rebellion. Prime Luther has plans in action to create a dictatorship through his sons."

The quiet one held her gaze and then rested his eyes on those she killed. Her offer came knowing it would repair a mistake. Evelyn had been eager to help Anna, never considering the reach of Thomas's chilling atmosphere. She kept her weapons ready, the rutoe before her taking his time. His feelings were unreadable with the mouth shield, but his silence matched the volume of her own pain. Evelyn watched his attention shift, then narrow upon her.

The panging struck her mind again, loosening her grip on her knives. She went to one knee, slamming her knives into the rock.

"The rutoe demand two things before accepting your offer, Wayne," said the quiet one, his voice booming within her mind. *"Free our leader for us."*

Evelyn let out a growling scream. Spit flung from her mouth as she rose. The rutoe took a step back, reaching for his mouth shield. The mistress of duels and debates composed herself, rising to full height. All pain from the quiet one slipped away with her patience.

"And the second?"

The quiet one stepped forward, letting his hand drop to his side.

"Tell us how you came upon the last of the fifth clan."

Chapter Twenty-Six

⌒⟨♥⟩⌒

Anna kept her fingers splayed across her face. She saw no one ahead, only the faint wisps of her breath accompanied her. Releasing her face made her feel as if being complete would vanish before reaching the arch. Only once she was fully across the draw bridge did she dare to slow her pace. Pain no longer lingered from her wound, nor jabbed at her side when she'd twist or turn. Cobblestones met her footsteps as she came upon a darkened by a tunnel of sandy bricks. She remembered such a color from an illustration of Lampara's northern shore. Anna finally allowed her hands to drop, certain her old face would remain absent.

As her feet struck the cobblestones, she thought of Cole. Rubbing away the tears and sweat, she knew there was no certainty her friend lived. Or that Lord Kardan's servants kept to Eve's commands. Anna hoped Norman would heed her words and use his flames not just to protect Cole and Roland, but himself.

The longing for Norman was strong. She pressed a hand to her chest, missing his warmth and, the confidence she felt in his presence. He was the one Simdorn wished her to spend her future with, and she knew it. She sighed, wishing he had placed his name in for Prime. After all they had been through in recent weeks, he had proved to have the potential to lead. The same could be said for herself.

Brightness touched her eyes, forcing Anna to shade them both for once. Scaffolding netted around wood structures ahead. The sun was half in the clouds, graying some of what she witnessed. What structures were free of scaffolding possessed doors without ringed handles, windows without shutters to shield themselves against harshness of winter. Shoes lay beneath each door, shallow at the heel with a point rising like a hook at their toe. Tiny stones crackled under her feet before Anna stopped. The air was light and pure, as if the air down in Lampara had been corrupted somehow.

Voices off in the distance caught her attention. She used her right eye's peripheral vision. She smiled as for the first time in years she saw light in place of darkness. Anna balled her fists to stifle surging emotions. She needed to remember her purpose for traveling this far, for putting what was no longer a hindrance aside. *But how am I complete again?* She rested her hand on her bowstring. *Is this a trap set by someone who knows me?*

Three rutoe emerged from around a corner down the street. The street went for miles, ending with what she believed to be a temple, but not one of Simdorn's. Anna formed her lips into a hard line. The rutoe possessed long dark hair, one with skin the color of charcoal and eyes diamond-shaped showing a dark blue. He drew back, joined by his friends. Of the three, one was a girl of the ignited one clan. Her eyes went to a dark red and faint flames raced over her fingertips. Behind her stood a boy with eyes blacker than night, and skin pale like a full moon. They wore long flowing robes matching their skin.

"I come in search of a wizard," Anna said, offering herself with palms open, not wanting to frighten them further. "Can you tell me where one might be?"

The ignited one appeared near seventeen to the boy's eighteen. She pressed thumb to fingers, her flames vanishing once her thumb left her palm. The ignited one clasped the pale boy's hand. His eyes flashed a blazing orange. Anna froze. Swift as hornets, stones rose, surrounding her until there was no escape. They clicked against one another ever circling, increasing in numbers. His hand rose, teeth clenching as if what he did took great concentration.

"You leave," said the boy, bringing the ignited one close. She whispered something in his ear and shot Anna a fierce look. "Humans put families outside Echnumbard in the mountains long ago."

"Please. I'm here for my friend," Anna exclaimed. "My…" She didn't wish to use her grandfather's name, but if he gave opportunities to rutoe, these three may have heard of his generosity. "I'm Anna Brighton. Granddaughter to Lord William Brighton."

The stones drew closer, hindering her vision like smoke from an untamed fire. Anna squinted through them to find the rutoe had reduced their distance from her. The pale one spoke again, eyes glowing above the hard line formed from his lips.

"That human robbed the rutoe of its fifth clan," he said. "A great battle took them all in a village."

Thoughts crossed paths with memories. Anna remained still like the banner above the street. Its fabrics divided into colors she guessed represented the rutoe clans with the fifth being crimson. She thought back to the barn in Natlendton. And yet her skin was like most Lampariens, but her hair was neither auburn nor blond. She licked her lips, eyeing the three youths, their distrust solid and narrow like the tunnel behind her. The stories of how her parents died intertwined, one of a battle, and the other of them chased by robbers.

"I again wish only to find a wizard for my friend," she said, drawing back her hood slowly. A subtle gasp hissed from the ignited one. Anna released her hair from the string binding it behind her ears. "I have no knowledge of a battle involving my grandfather."

The stones dropped at once, filling the air like a sudden, brief downpour of rain. The ignited one looked at her, taking two steps forward, turning her head from side to side. Anna wasn't sure what to say. She half wished to say what her mind had puzzled together. That she believed she was a survivor of what her grandfather had done. Keeping her rising anger in check, the ignited one took Anna's hand in her own.

"We never seen fifth clan," she said. "Elders have. Yes. You look human yet have hair like ours."

"I thought the same." Anna nodded, then frowned. "But I have no magic like any of you. I possess only the skills I learned in life."

The ignited one ran a long slender finger down the string of Anna's bow.

"Skills are learned like control of magic. We are learning but you look like master of skills."

262

Anna blushed.

"I still wish I possessed magic like you three" she said, suddenly remembering how her cry of pain had shaken the barn's rafters. "You are gifted. It took years to be accurate, to learn how to hunt."

All three rutoe shook their heads. The ignited one released her hand, leaving it warm like the sun's heat on her neck. They conversed with one another. Anna noticed they each wore the low heel, hooked toe shoes she had seen earlier. They were black with faint grays from the dust lying across the stones. Finally, the rutoe possessing charcoal skin spoke, biting his lip at first.

"We thought like you once," he said, fumbling with his robes, "but not since Luther Prime sent us to the cold. Not since man with angry esant kill brave fifth clan and become story all rutoe must hear."

"And now you're in open rebellion against Luther," Anna said, summoning what lingered on her mind. "I do not believe all of the fifth clan are gone." She rested her hand on his shoulder. He flinched at first, but Anna assured him with a smile. "I am campaigning to replace Luther. And if what I believe is correct, William Brighton spared at least one of your fifth clan."

"Who?" all three rutoe said.

"Me."

* * *

The room was small. Well kept. But still not as spacious as what Anna had grown up used to. The pale skinned rutoe insisted earlier no shoes be worn in his father's house. She feared to tread on its smooth polished wood floors with her damp, worn socks. Her normal racing nerves were absent during the ordeal. New ones rose with slightly less intensity as she waited. She sat at a table on a stool which in the north passed for something a boy shined boots upon. Its cushion was a relief on her back, remaining so straightened and stiff in the dome saddle worked a terrible ache through it.

The ignited one, Grenuel, as she called herself, went to put out word for a wizard to join them. Anna cleared her throat, feeling her knees knock against the table.

"A friend sent a cheefox nearly two weeks ago to Echnumbard," she said, "but it was intercepted."

"It would not reach here," said the moon white boy. "Rutoe who rebel keep messages out of hands of traitors."

Anna bit back her frustration. Even if things had been different, that her wish to be whole remained, no wizard stood a chance of receiving her request.

"What can you tell me of the wizards who found refuge here?"

The two rutoe looked at one another. Their faces offered little in the way of comfort.

"You hear they banished south, right?" said Fradrul, biting his lip with red teeth. "Lamnic know truth."

She faced the moon white rutoe. His black eyes reminded her of Cole's. Deep emptiness opened in her stomach, wishing he were here.

"Four are here," he said. "They protect and train rutoe while priests join rebellion."

Anna's jaw dropped. She swiftly snapped it shut. Priests fighting was something she never thought possible, nor proper. Simdorn's priests kept to prayer, ritual, and council.

She swallowed as Lamnic summoned his words.

"Prime Luther offered what you call ... ultimatum," he said. "Join his army or banishment."

"And all of them chose banishment?" Anna asked.

Fradrul shook his head. Lamnic drew in his lips.

"Some join and others go back to where they came from." Lamnic whispered. "Where that is not even wizards of sanctuary know."

She sat up straight on her stool, reminding herself there wasn't a back to lean against, pondering what she had learned. "How could the four wizards residing in Echnumbard not know where they came from?"

The rutoe shrugged.

"I guess children who dream them to live grew self-loving when old," said Fradrul.

His words made no sense to her. Dreaming someone into existence wasn't possible.

"Is what I understand true?" she said. "Selflessness can create a wizard in your dreams?"

Fradrul nodded. Footsteps echoed faintly from the hall behind her. Anna faced forward catching only the sound of one person approaching. Though she wished to turn around she did not want to feel disappointment. A chill raced over her shoulder. Fingers short and soft gave a faint squeeze. She peered over her shoulder, shrieked, and spun off her stool. Her bottom slammed against the table's edge. A child of gray mist let his hand drop to his side. His eyes were placed too close to his nose, outlined in red, trapping their solid black with a faint glow. A smile journeyed with haste across the child's face.

"You must be the one, Grenuel couldn't silence herself

about."

"Yes … um," Anna said. "I'm Anna Brighton. Did … she tell you I'm here for my friend?"

The wizard nodded. His face spoke of him being eight at the oldest. She rose to full height finding he came up to her chest. He wore white robes with a sigil upon his breast. The robes shifted and crawled like mist across a bog. Anna kept her surprise behind a blank face, noticing the sigil was Nathan's.

"Grenuel says you believe yourself a survivor of Lord Brighton's raids," said the wizard.

Anna gulped, noticing that in some way the wizard's smaller features reflected Nathan's.

"I believe so. I didn't tell her, but my cries once shook the rafters of a barn. I was in pain."

The wizard stroked his child-like chin with thumb and forefinger. His eyes reflected her face, sending a shutter down her spine. He let his hand drop, meeting her eyes.

"How often did you use a mirror in your early youth

Anna raised an eyebrow.

"Mirrors are for the vain, Simdorn says," Anna said. "I never saw my reflection until after the dragon. I … was attacked at fifteen. My face burned and eye sealed shut. After seeing it for the first time I didn't wish to look upon myself again."

"And why do you suppose it took so long?"

"You ask questions for what reason I cannot guess!" Anna barked. Her skin grew hot and red. She felt he was delaying her. "I originally went in search of a wizard for myself, but this place has removed what tormented me, and more…"

Her face was red like an apple in the wizard's eyes. Anna raised both hands to find them red with her fingernails black as if dipped in ink.

"What's happening? Anna screamed.

The wizard smiled. He took her hand in his as she trembled.

"With the sanctuary's help," he said, calmly, "you are returning to what you once were, Anna."

"But how is this possible?"

Warm tears rolled down her cheeks, blurring her vision, turning the mist making up the wizard into a fog. She cleared her vision with a swipe of her hand.

"Gems in columns you pass heal wounds and reveal true self," said Grenuel, resting a hand on Anna's shoulder. "I came here with bruises upon my cheeks, fear of mother's fist finding me again."

"Fradual and Lamnic came here after joining the rebellion, blaming their wounds upon lack of strength, and of courage," said the wizard, peering up at them. "Their wounds are healed but their courage still wavers when put to the test."

A tingling forced Anna's eyes shut. They burned for a moment, pain fading as swift as it had come. She opened them to find in the reflection of the wizard's eye they were yellow. A bright red flared within her pupils.

"Leave me alone!" she screamed.

Anna shook herself free. She dashed down the hall. The ends of her bow scraped the walls for a brief second as she rounded a corner. There was no one following her, no one to come and slow the surge of emotions striking her all at once with the strength of a smithy's hammer to hot iron. The floor grew murky, its smooth brown wood a blur. She looked ahead to find her vision was clear.

Dropping to her knees the emotions compounded, as if all the nerves and heightened senses of old had returned. Anna pressed her knuckles against the floor, hearing the rattle of her arrows as her arms shook and slowly caved.

"You were lied to, Anna."

She turned to face the wizard. His face possessed more definition, faint stubble grew from the end of his chin. His robes remained white, but the sigil on his chest was now a badger within a diamond.

"How have you aged?" Anna said, swallowing the pain in her voice. "How did I not hear you following me?"

"Let's stay on point, Anna." The wizard shook his head. "You were lied to. William Brighton found pity in his heart and raised you, but now you're seeing who you really are."

Anna found herself tempted. Tempted to hide within her hood like she had done for so long. There were no footsteps from down the hall, and for this she was glad. Anna drew up her hood.

"Why hide now?" said the wizard, taking her gently by the wrists. "You must have been doing so for some time by my guess. It's written in your movements."

She drew back her hood with both hands firm against its fabric. Every finger shook, sweat ran down her knuckles as the wizard eased down on one knee.

"You're right," said Anna. "And I stopped hiding long before coming here."

"Good." The wizard smiled. "Now! Who is the friend you wish to help?"

Anna dropped her hands to her lap, focusing on them for a moment.

"Nathan," she said, finding the wizard's lips trembling, his eyes on the verge of tears. "Nathan Barden."

* * *

They left the house finding the streets busy. Dust rose with the traffic of foot work. Anna found herself in the strange position of being the calm one again. She held the wizard's hand, refusing to tense at its clamminess. He kept his other across his lips, uncovering them when a question surfaced. He led the way some, but by the shock of hearing about Nathan's passing no exact destination came of it.

Passing an alley ending in a shear wall of jagged rock, five dummies of straw and burlap hung on posts. Five ignited ones aligned with them, reaching with fingers splayed. Flames roared at swift narrow streams, setting the dummies ablaze. One rutoe sneezed. A blast larger than Cole erupted from his palm, scorching the rock face. Anna gaped, stopping herself as the wizard stormed toward the youthful ignited one. She listened, guessing by his gestures that discipline was being served yet she understood not a word. *If I am a rutoe, then why can I not understand their language?* she thought, narrowing gaze, finding it harder with both eye not as they once were. *Grandfa- William Brighton mustn't have thought knowing it necessary.*

She cleared her throat and relaxed her gaze as the wizard rejoined her. His posture was upright, though he came only up to her shoulder. A slow procession of what the wizard said were quiet ones passed them, their faces buried in books. They wore robes of an olive color with copper in place of steel mouth shields. Anna decided against reminding the wizard of her purpose here. The pain in his eyes showed glimpses of a younger Nathan. Memories by her guess of her friend chasing a storm bison through a field. She kept her face emotionless, sucking back breath before her emotions caved in.

"So, you have come to resurrect Nathan and think I can do it?" he said. "I will admit my connection with him has begun anew in recent months. My hope was dragged from the confines of my mind thanks to it."

"Did… Did you feel it when he died?"

The wizard drifted to a stop, mist swirling and ebbing from the fringe of his robes. He returned his focus to the ignited ones. They had replaced the previous dummies with new ones.

"No." the wizard's voice cracked. "Our connection is through deeds of selflessness. After Nathan reached manhood, our ability to feel emotion, physical pain, ended."

"Are you able to bring our friend back to life?" Anna said. "I feel with what you know now, and the power I am told a wizard possesses, that such a miracle is possible."

He looked up into her eyes. Anna felt her heart take off at a sprint as the wizard with the face of her friend stared in silence. The memories she had seen in his big eyes were gone, replaced by blackness given light only by the red outlining them.

"I would need to leave Echnumbard," he said, stroking his chin. He turned to face the ignited ones again then folded his arms. "I will consult the other wizards." He faced her once more. "You need to understand, Anna. I love Nathan. I miss him. But my place here is of great importance."

Anna weaved her fingers, finding his point in the young rutoes training and the guidance needed for the three she met earlier. Her eyes widened.

"You also risk trouble with Prime Luther," she said, unweaving her fingers, binding them into fists. "The monster banished you like he did the rutoe."

"Oh, ha." the wizard chuckled. "That old man cannot stop me if he doesn't hear of my deeds. My guess is you missed the tiny print. Our services to Lampariens are banned. Oh, how word of mouth and decrees on paper color things."

Messing up her face, she resisted the temptation to thump herself on the forehead.

"Consult the other wizards then," she said. "I wish my friend back and must return to my … other friend. The Tournament of Primes is less than a week away."

The wizard held up his hands, raising an eyebrow. "I will be but a moment."

He melted like snow heaped upon a fire, vanishing into the tiny stones with a hiss. Anna thought back to Eve and Thomas. She hoped they were well. The last time she had left a friend and mount behind they had gone missing. She wondered if Norman and Cole were well. If Norman had taken her advice and purposefully threatened Lord Martyn's servants with Kardanhall's destruction. *Eve shall be fine like Norman,* she thought, *especially Eve.* Anna felt like the mistress of duels and debates could conquer any challenge. There were her quakes to deal with but from her perspective Eve was too stubborn to allow it to hold her back.

The ignited one's training kept at a steady pace as she waited. Anna noticed beyond the smoke and scorch marks blackening the ground, a door off to the left revealed arms of straw and burlap. A rush thrusted back her hair, nearly knocking her off balance. Anna planted her feet, outstretching her arms, hearing the flutter of her arrows' fletching. Turning back the street intersecting at the square where she had met Grenuel and the others, two pairs of dark blue eyes flashed then vanished. Robes the color of charcoal trailed like thin streams of fabric from who passed her. *So that is Lamnic's power. Speed.*

A chill ran across her boots, sending her body into a shiver and her teeth chattered. Anna faced up the street in time to find a pillar of white formed up to her chest. It shaped into sleeves with many wrinkles. A head emerged from the heavy hood between rolling shoulders. The wizard's eyes flashed a dark red as his face faded into focus.

"Let's be off, Anna," he said. "Time is not on our side, and you have a mad man to stop."

Chapter Twenty-Seven

⁓ঌ৩৩৩⁓

Prime Luther made no move to harm Cole or Roland, and for this Norman was grateful. He tugged against the metal of his shackles. They appeared like ordinary metal, yet he could not summon his flames. The tingle within his eyes remained dull and faint in the small mirror across from him. His stomach churned from the up and down of the dragon's back. Bile lined his tongue urging up vomit, but he took a big gulp. His quarters were at the rear of the largest saddle dome he had ever seen. The dragon itself possessed barely enough room to stand within the grounds of Kardanhall.

A chamber pot sat tethered in a corner beside the door. Norman could hear the breathing of who guarded him beyond it, as if the man were snoring while awake.

His thoughts were more on Anna than all else. He was unsure if Echnumbard had changed since his father began the rebellion against Prime Luther. Had it gone from a place of learning to control one's clan gift and home of healing to something more? He knew his friend possessed the strength to deal with change. The letter still in his pocket proved it.

Planting his feet upon the floor the rug sifted against his shoes. Their soles were worn, despite sharing Cole's saddle with Anna during their travels. What he missed most on those many miles with her were the things they shared. Conversation built upon what he knew of his people. A comforting feeling fluttered within his belly for her greatest passion, hunting. She spoke of tricks she'd learned and those of her own design to trap game. He smiled. Her burns didn't trouble her in those conversations, and now, they no longer troubled her entirely. He sighed, eyeing his surroundings. A click, turn, and thud broke Norman's focus.

"Hello. Oh!"

A woman entered with a tray in her hands. Her skin was an olive tone, and her hair was bound back tight against her scalp with a ribbon. Pressed firmly across her mouth was a mouth shield of iron. Norman pretended not to notice the lock constricting the shield's straps to her head. He cast his gaze down to the floor and clenched, his pointed teeth. Prime Luther had given this quiet one a skirt to wear, but nothing to cover her chest. Her feet made little noise, barren of any shoes.

She set the tray upon a table across from him, turned and bowed. She made for the door taking a swift hold of its handle.

"Wait," Norman said. "Speak with me. Tell me what you know, and we may be able to overcome Luther's men."

The quiet one looked upon him over her shoulder. Her eyes were dull, nearly lifeless. Norman focused on her mind speech, unable for some reason to believe he had said such words. It came in a whisper, swift and panicked. He ignored the pang rattling his mind.

"Will you need any other service," she said. *"Prime Luther speaks of you joining your father, but that I am to accommodate your wishes. He says you are a political prisoner."*

Norman edged himself to the wall at his back as the woman turned to face him. His chest fluttered as she knelt before him, eyes to the floor, casting her hands wide as if offering herself.

"No," he said, scooting to the bed's edge. "I don't want contact of that kind. I wish to free us both, end Luther, and find my father."

"That will remain impossible," she said, folding her arms across her chest. *"He has wizards and traitors to the clans as part of his orderman."*

Norman eyed the door, wincing at the continued contact with the girl. The guard remained oblivious. He wondered for a moment what he would do if she left upset. Her eyes were focused on the sharp edge along her mouth shield. The quiet one's nose twitched above it as if ready to shed tears.

"Luther has terrible plans for Lampara," he said, rising, bringing the girl to her feet. "I need your help in stopping them." Norman raised her chin. Her eyes met his own. "Can you find the keys for these shackles?"

The quiet one took his hand in hers, examining them closely. Norman exhaled as she severed their connection. She made for the door in two great strides, knocked, and left with the guard eyeing her like a vulture. He smiled at Norman, displaying teeth yellowed and caked with blackness in places.

"What 'appened?" he said, chuckling. "You get too 'appy too quick."

"Just close the damn door." said Norman, a slight queasiness overwhelmed him.

With a slam, Norman was alone again, the need to vomit gone as he realized how bad the guard's breath had been. He sat at the table, the chair whining from his weight. His mind went to the short chain linking his wrists. The shackles were cold like the porridge as he ate. He pressed his teeth to his tongue, withdrawing a long, black hair.

Not knowing if it was night or day he listened for a change of guard. The man Norman become an accountant apprentice under was also a guard of Williamton. A change of guard required a short briefing of one's post. So far with the minutes passing he heard only the sound of the guard's breathing and the infrequent roar of the dragon.

He rested his porridge spoon beside the bowl. The tin goblet of wine did little to ease the porridge down. Norman searched the room for some other way to remove his shackles. There was nothing sharp to pick the lock like the stake Anna used from her hair for Simdorn's priests. He took hold of his spoon. Its bowl and tip were coated in gray and too wide for what he needed. The handle was round at the end.

"You back for more short squirts?"

Norman heard from beyond the door.

"What you? Get out of mi head!"

Thump.

The door opened. The guard lay across the doorway, shaking and groaning. Tears ran from the corners of his eyes as he tried to raise his head, fumbling with the sword in his belt. Over him the quiet one clenched her fists. Her chest heaved as her eyes focused on the guard's.

"Come quick," she said, her voice swift and breathless in his

mind. *"I've never done this before."*

"And I have never escaped from anywhere," said Norman, rising swiftly from the table. "Hold him."

"His ... keys ... are on his person." The quiet one took hold of the railing against the wall. *"What are you doing?"*

Norman grabbed the guard by the arms and pulled. His back strained with each muscle begging him to stop. "I will look odd roaming the halls with you as I am."

With a great heave Norman made it within his room. He snatched the keys from the guard's belt, freed his wrists, and began undressing the man. Norman held his breath. The guard coughed up great plumes of what he could only guess was cheese gone foul.

"This is no time for pleasures," said the quiet one.

Norman removed his clothes, applying the guard's trousers, tunic, and boots before heaving on his green plated armor. "That isn't my plan."

The dome helmet was snug, and the red mouth shield reeked, but Norman had no choice. He altered his skin to a human, then closed the door. The quiet one dropped to her knees, her breath heavy and muffled. Norman took her by the hand, helping her up,

"Let's go."

She eyed him strangely as he handed her his old tunic.

"You are odd," she said, slipping it on. *"Is that why the Prime keeps you alive?"*

"No," Norman said. "And he won't be keeping anyone much longer once I am done with him."

* * *

The hall was lit by wall sconces with their flames trapped inside small glass globes. A faint his came from them. Norman shrugged off a build-up of thoughts. There was no time to wonder about how Luther had spent Lampara's coin. If Anna won the tournament in less than a weeks' time he'd demand what coin was wasted earned back.

He motioned to the quiet one for conversation, his footsteps slow but deliberate. Norman winced as her voice pierced through to his mind.

"Should we not hurry for Prime Luther," she said. *"Inferno dawns are far swifter than a crystalandan."*

"I don't wish to churn up suspicion." Norman stopped them at a corner. Voices met his ears as he peered around it. Two ordermen left a room, closing the door with smiles swiftly covered by mouth shields. "And with the guard you released, we've little time before we are caught."

She shrank back from him. Her eyes strained as if connecting with him was growing more difficult. *"I apologize. Our actions. My actions. Are something I never dared to dream of."*

Norman shuddered, not daring to imagine how long she had been a servant, been forced to give 'pleasures,' as she called them to strangers. He offered his hand as she folded her arms, crouching, her eyes fixed on it as if being offered poison.

"I promise you," he said, swallowing, pushing past the strain their connection placed on him. "You will live through this."

The quiet one took a half a step forward. She sighed, rising to full height. *"I trust you."* She took his hand.

Norman exhaled as their connection ended. Every hall appeared the same, sconces topped in globes, walls lined with a brass railing at waist height. Anna had told him during their travels when the woods were quiet, she would let Cole graze. She'd walk for some time and listened for an animal to snap a twig or snort in reaction to a smell. But he wasn't in the woods where an animal could slip up. He steadied himself with every turn they made, having to compromise every few minutes with the rise and fall of the dome saddle.

He wished that he hadn't made such a promise to the quiet one. There was no certainty of keeping it with ordermen patrolling the halls. At the hall's end, double doors thick and lined with gold studs with two large wall sconces bracketed on either side came into focus. The closer Norman came the wider the hall became, lined with spade shaped shields displaying the prime sigil of a silver horse shaded in black. Norman caught hints of green from the corners of his eyes.

"Why have you left your post?" said a guard emerging from the left. "I was to swap with you within the hour."

Another guard appeared from Norman's right, lunged, and grabbed the quiet one. She pulled, stumbling to the ground as her hands slipped through the cuffs of Norman's tunic.

"She wasn't placed in our prime's service to look decent," said the guard, righting her up on her feet and then pressing her face against the wall. "By order of the primnoire herself."

"I don't know how she got clothing," said Norman, using the worst grammar he knew.

A quake ran under his feet, unsettling him, but the ordermen kept their balance. They wore disk helmets and arrowhead-shaped shoulder plates like Phillip. Unlike him they wore green breastplates fastened with gold buckles and polished leather straps. There were no stars on their boots, and both kept their mouth shields firmly across their faces.

"Rip this rag from her flesh you whelp," the orderman

sniffed. "Did you finally clean those teeth of yours?"

"Yes …, I was sick of you blockheads harping on me," said Norman, taking hold, feeling his tunic through the guard's gloves. "I've come for a word with his prime-ship."

"For what reason you rotten toothed wanker?" said the orderman pressing the girl harder. "You best rip those rags off quick before another quake slips out from under her mouth shield."

Norman took a handful of his tunic, narrowing his vision to be more convincing. She peered up at him, her face compressed between a black leather glove and the wall's hard finished wood. Her eyes pleaded. They spoke of the promise he had made, the dignity he had given her being taken back faster than she possessed time to cherish it.

I am truly sorry.

The tunic ripped first at her shoulders sending a swift breath from her nostrils. Norman realized she must have been clenching her teeth under the mouth shield. No quake sent his hands clambering for support. He knew refusing to continue was not an option. There was no sudden, harsh blip within his mind, no plea sent that she wished for him to hear. Raising his other hand, the quiet one's back rose and fell in quick successions. Norman puffed up his chest and ripped until only the sleeves held the tunic like a ragged sail to a ship's mast.

"My guess is your reason for needing to see our prime is this girl?" asked the orderman, watching him go. He raised a finger. "You can stop. Anymore and there will be no evidence of her crime."

There was no fatigue in letting his hands drop, but his heart was tired. Pained by what he had done to someone of his own kind. They shared not the same skin color, or magic, but they were, above all else, rutoe. And, in this moment, Norman felt being human was the worst he had just been. *This isn't the rutoe way.* He thought, remembering Anna. *She would be ashamed of me.*

"I'll take her by mi-self, mates," said Norman.

Norman snatched the girl by her arms, rushing her to the doors. His hand shook as he raised it to knock.

"You know such matters require an orderman present for interrupting his prime-ship," said the orderman that had kept the girl from escaping. "It seems you not only forget the rules but also your place."

"And even a low-level stooge as dull as you can remember both," said the other orderman.

Something sharp pressed at Norman's back. At first it felt like a muscle misbehaving, but soon he had his hands raised in surrender. The quiet one pressed his tunic to her chest, her face shrouded in the depths of her long black hair. Its ribbon lay adrift against her hair, rendered loose by the earlier struggle.

"I knew you weren't the one I was to replace from minute one," the orderman said. "Can you guess why, Norman Tilt?"

Tingling ran through his skin as curled chestnut hair lengthened, making the helmet feel like a vice upon his head. Norman's eyes flashed a sharp piercing scarlet as heat surfaced to his fingertips. The knife moved to his side, weaving under the cords that bound his breastplate to his person.

"Because that ugly sow is the cook. No one armed upon this dragon isn't either an orderman or the prime himself."

"You've been fooled, mate," said the other orderman. He

opened both doors one at a time. "I'll take Enemilu to Unter. They both have business tonight."

The quiet one stood erect, dropping the torn tunic at his feet. She flashed her long eyelashes, piercing into his mind at such a speed he nearly fell upon the orderman's knife.

"You kept your promise, Norman," she said, reaching into Norman's mind once more. *"Keep such happy a thought close when you die."*

Pulling swiftly from his side the orderman's knife pressed to Norman's back once more. He clenched his teeth, resisting the urge to shake free the man's hand at his neck. They moved into Prime Luther's chambers with a speed Norman didn't know he could manage. He gasped, falling to his knees. A dais rose before him. He peered up at a throne carved of the same dark wood as the trees between Rockelton and Kardanhall. A slight shiver ran over him, fading fast with the build-up of his magic. The shackles of earlier had kept them dull and faint within the core of his very being.

"You're far more cunning than most accountants," said a voice. "I didn't expect you to refuse a woman before a lengthy prison sentence. Any woman could surpass the Brighton girl you were following around."

From where the breeze came stood Luther in long robes of red silk. Upon his head sat not the hat of before, but a wide gold band. A sigil not of a prime but of a beast Norman had never seen either in the mountains of the south nor in his travels with Anna. It roared above Luther's brow to a full moon made from a white gem. Around the band Norman knew to be a crown, four paws tipped with claws of silver.

"Keep your eyes to the ground!" Luther barked.

A sharp pinch forced Norman's hands to his face. His

fingers dug into his skin as ordermen emerged from the darkness. Sconce globes came to light, leaving a dimness in the air. Taking up a position next to Luther upon his throne was an orderman of great height. His olive skin was darker than any quiet one Norman had ever seen. Luther raised a hand weighed by thick gold rings. Norman let out a gasp, spiraling into a coughing fit.

"Why?" Norman said, quelling his coughing. "Why put me through all this?"

"Because you string bean of slime," Luther twirled his index finger. "I need a good story to tell your father before one of my sons has him executed. A future dictator needs something big to set his reign in motion."

The cold went from a breeze to a torrent of chill as a door slid open. Prime Luther pulled the robes close to his face. "I would feed you to my dragon, but the last time I tried that my dear wife fell to her end."

Two ordermen seized him under the arms, dragging Norman to the door. The cold sent his teeth into a chatter. He balled his fingers into fists, striking both men in the gut, flames raced over them. Norman yanked himself free and stumbled to one knee. He screamed. Tumbling over, his back met his heel as he stretched out his fists. Norman tried to rise, to ignite his fists once more, but the quiet one had him.

"I ... will not give up," Norman said through his teeth. "I'll fight you as my father did."

Prime Luther crept down from the dais, rubbing his hands together. The quiet one narrowed his eyes, forcing Norman to bite his lip. Blood ran down his chin as Luther slammed his boot into Norman's chest. Norman felt his heel slip and slide across the guard's armor.

"Temper those flames, boy," said Luther, reaching out his hands. "I paid good money for all this."

"You have made many poor." Norman gripped the floor finding no purchase. "You have made them hate all rutoe."

"I will not argue politics with you." Luther pressed harder, eyeing the ordermen rolling upon the ground. Their flame licked bodies shook and twisted. "I have much in my way still, and while my sons' rule, I will clear the weeds from the grounds of my country."

It was no use. The quiet one kept him from using his flames. Prime Luther had him in so compromising a position he could hear his ankle crunching. He eyed the old man, feeling the blood on his chin meet his neck.

"But only one son can win both the people and the tournament," Norman rasped. "Just one of your dull-witted children can govern."

Prime Luther let up on Norman's chest. His eyes flared before placing two and two together. Luther smiled. "So be it, rebel's bastard."

Norman's eyes widened. He threw his gaze outside. Daylight touched his brow, highlighting the immense leathery wing of the dragon. It kept the forests and fields out of sight. A horn sounded, long and deep.

"You would see a son die and use the other as a vassal?" Norman said, meeting the prime's weathered eyes. "Is the life of your sons worth so little to you?"

"Throw him out." Prime Luther removed himself to the throne upon the dais. "I will not be set upon by conflicting emotions."

The quiet one ceased his pressure on Norman's mind. Their eyes met as the orderman raised him to his feet.

"You cannot go along with this," Norman whispered. "No rutoe would allow anyone to put their wants over a child."

No pain raced through Norman's mind, yet by the Orderman's eyes, by his deep but subtle breaths, the quiet one showed guilt.

"Throw him out! Damn you!" Luther growled. "I don't intend to freeze before reaching home."

With a great heave the orderman threw Norman out. Norman tumbled and slid toward the dragon's rolling shoulder. Thoughts of igniting his flames came and went, knowing such heat might bring him within inches of the dragon's jaws. Norman gripped and clawed, finding the clouds below growing closer and closer.

Something glistened in the sunlight, round and controlled somehow. Its color nearly matched the dragon's scales for a moment. Norman spotted something thin and brown streaming from it. The disk-like shape swung behind him. Deep down he knew it was strange but there was only one guess to what it was. Norman kicked off the dragon's shoulder, turned and hugged the disk with everything he had. There was a quick dip, but slowly he rose, doing so for a long while.

Once finally upon the dragon's shoulder Norman lay flat on his back. His chest heaved as the disk slid from his grasp. A figure placed the disk on his head, helping Norman up.

"You sure are brave for a green fella that counts coppers."

"Phillip."

Chapter Twenty-Eight

nna fumbled with her thoughts, running her fingers down the length of her bow's string. Her mind was more on Eve and Thomas than the direction the wizard led her. She drew the hood over her face, preparing for the cold and the truth to come. There was no certainty the wizard could read her thoughts, no sign of such a power. Lady Evelyn was an enemy of the rutoe, and by the wizard's attention to their lessons, he may not find the mistress of duels and debates a friend. Their steps didn't pass through the tunnel of before, leaving Anna to wonder how she would manage the cold to come. Her cloak remained in the warm lush place from yesterday, the place which removed what ailed her. Anna found familiar flexibility with the wound at her side gone.

Instead, they used a door off to the tunnel's right, bringing a mustiness to her nose once it was closed. Each step was cut in such a way her feet barely had room for a complete step. The wizard drifted down, making no sound, leaving a brief residue of mist. His eyes brightened until their path no longer needed the lit sconces guiding their way. The sconces went out all at once. Anna froze, teetering a heel on the upper step while firmly holding balance with the other. A half minute passed before the wizard stopped at a landing and looked up at her. A slight smile crossed his childlike face.

"We have little time, Anna," he said, drifting up to her like a cloud meeting another. "We cannot travel by whatever means you used with the storm upon the mountains."

"How do you know there is one?" Anna asked. "Or how I traveled?

"Being we are high above the rest of Lampara, a storm reaches us first every day. It will then either spare the lands north and below or hammer them like there is no tomorrow."

She descended a few steps, using the wizard's eyes to guide her, realizing he had ignored her second question.

"I must tell you something … now since our journey will not begin where I wished it would."

The light from the wizard's eyes faced toward the landing, returning caution to Anna's movements.

"I left a friend behind before entering Echnumbard," she said, trying to use what light reflected off the walls to ease her fear of tripping. "Her name is Lady Evelyn Wayne."

"Ah. So, that is what caused your break in speech earlier?" the wizard said, facing her once they found a second landing. "I learned of the orderman and her dragon when consulting the other wizards."

Anna gaped. "How do you? She means no harm to the—"

"Calm yourself, Anna." The wizard raised his hand in a fan motion. "She pays for both her and her family's crimes against the clans now, and soon with more than just words."

"You must not harm her," Anna said, taking hold of the wizard's shoulders. Her hands phased through like a traveler wading his way through fog. "She is my friend. I … never would have made it this far without her."

"I said nothing of harm," he said, taking her by the wrists. "She funds the rebellion with Wayne coin." the wizard sighed. "I can see the enchantments cleared much of what troubled you and returned you to true form, but your worrisome nature remains."

Anna shook her head. His grip was cold, stronger than expected for someone with hands so small.

"I thank you again … for all of it," Anna said. "What crime did she commit on her own?"

The wizard released her, turning to face a long narrow tunnel. Its walls were rough, uneven, and cracked in places. No unlit sconces hung on either wall, but a faint white light crept around a corner to the right. He kept at a steady pace, and soon, the lights of his eyes faded to their normal glow. Anna let out a breath, glad for no more stairs.

"It wasn't so much her doing, more regret for not remembering the power of a friend's abilities."

"Thomas?" said Anna. "What has his cold done?"

"Let's put away the subject for now, Anna."

"No," Anna snapped. "I wish to know. I have experienced plenty in a short time. I have even conquered my fear of dragons with Eve's aid."

He looked up at her, blinked, sending a thin gray line along the red of his eyes.

"The dragon's cold laid waste to crops," he sighed. "Crops meant for both family and soldier alike. He… he had to be destroyed."

The light met her chin, outlining the wrinkles of her hood. Words clamored to her lips but swiftly slipped back down her tongue, choking her somehow. Anna found killing Thomas an impossibility for anyone wanting to. To be in his presence chewed through every layer she wore without leaving a mark, chilling her to the bone.

"How?" she said. "Eve told me great magic is needed."

"And it was used," said the wizard, folding his arms. His sleeves hung like curtains of snow falling in winter. "Now! Let's make our way."

"Wait," Anna gaped. "Answer me this, was killing Thomas necessary?"

The wizard frowned, resting his hand on the sigil on his chest.

"I wish I possessed an answer for you," the wizard sighed. "Perhaps when this is over the rutoe will make up for their harsh decision. For the moment we must travel to Kardanhall and resurrect our friend."

Anna raised an eyebrow at the wizard. Her mood was grim and sad for Thomas, wishing the wizard wasn't so fixed on pressing forward.

"I made no mention of Kardanhall."

"You can thank, Lady Wayne," he said, turning and leading her further. "Once I told her of you, she mentioned that grim place."

Anna pulled her hood forward, shading her eyes against the sun. Comfort flowed through despite the chill taking hold of her limbs. Wind rattled her remaining arrows, reminding her more may be needed.

* * *

Upon the earlier smooth stretch of rock where she had last seen Eve, an enormous serpent sat. It breathed easy against the cold, coiled up in many long, round layers. Folded upon every layer were feathered wings of orange and white. A fuzz covered its coils matching the wings, fluttering with the constant shift of winds. Anna kept her distance at first, hand to her bow string, wondering where the dome saddle for such a creature may fit. Or if it was just as unpredictable as the serpents of Lampara's Greethumb region. It was certainly far larger, with a wide hood streaming from the base of its head. She swallowed, finding only one part of the serpent not unsettling. Its teeth were like a dog's, pointed at the canines, but not piercing like a regular snake's fangs.

"Up on the saddle you go," said the wizard.

The serpent uncoiled itself. Its wings whooshed across the ground as it stretched. On its back, close to the head, was a dome saddle hidden easily by the serpent's great girth. Anna scaled its side, the creature unfazed by her need to use its fur for steadiness.

"What's its name?" she said, peering over her shoulder.

The wizard looked up at her, eyes reflecting sunlight.

"Colbwing," he said, chuckling. "And since we seem to have passed it, my name is Brian."

Anna made it beside the dome saddle. It was silver and worn in places. She could hear a faint flapping as if air passed through a hole somewhere.

"Brian?"

"Nathan Barden wasn't the most creative with—"

"No," Anna said, opening the saddle door. "I quite like it.'"

Backing up, she lowered the door of the dome saddle to find chains. They were rusted, hanging over the back of both seats. Brian drifted inward first, taking the front seat. There were no reins or bridal upon the serpent's head, yet after she closed the door she saw, through the window, long thin whiskers streaming behind its diamond shaped nostrils. Brian took hold of them as they slithered through holes below the window.

"Secure yourself," said Brian. "Riding cobraswifts are far less safe than a horse or storm bison."

Feeling the chains against her back, both eyes widened for a second. *It comes together now.* Eve had told her humans hadn't found a way, but it appeared the rutoe were wiser. She removed her bow and quiver, then with some effort she slipped the chains over her head. They rattled against her hood until she secured them about her waist. The wizard nodded, gripped hard the corbaswift's whiskers, and flicked them. A rush pressed Anna's back to the seat. There was a crack like an immense whip behind her. Clamping her hands over her ears, the wizard was unfazed by it.

With a blink they were amongst the clouds. Anna gulped, breathing fiercely, unable to take in the smoothness of being air born. It wasn't this way on an esant nor from her recent experience on a dragon. Her heart sank with the loss of Thomas. From how Eve spoke, her tone so delicate, the dragon was almost a part of the mistress of duels and debates. Anna hoped to see her again, but for now focus needed to be placed on Nathan, and then, the tournament.

* * *

A tremor ran down her spine. It felt strong enough to rattle the chains about her waist. They were north within a day, but it wasn't the corbaswift's speed that made her wish her hood were a cave to hide within. Remnants of an immense fire wound its smoke around the vast castle of Kardanhall. Its source was the one place she had seen destroyed by fire before. Except it was only by her dedication to Simdorn that it tore at her insides. Anna drew her hood back. Her hair matted by sweat, clinging to her face as she suppressed tears. She knew deep down that not even Lord Kardan's servants would set fire to the house of the goddess. They even knew the punishment for such a sin. *Suicide,* she thought. *No. Someone came when I was gone.*

"Where did you leave Nathan when coming south, Anna?"

"I…," The thought struck Anna harder than any blow ever forced upon her. "We thought he was safe."

"Safe where?" Brian demanded. He leapt up from his seat, grabbing her by the shoulders as his lips trembled. "Tell me!"

"The temple."

Brian collapsed into her arms. Beyond him there appeared only gloom, and within her own thoughts a journey she felt been wasted. She wished she had just buried her friend out amongst the open sky. And when spring came its clear blue would be upon where she laid him to rest. Anna let out a faint gasp. *Cole. Roland.* Whoever burned down the temple must have noticed Cole's clouds drifting from the stables. She reached for Colbwing's whiskers but then hesitated.

A faint flash met her eye as Colbwing glided on the winds, awaiting somehow for Brian to guide him further. "I will bring us down," she whispered.

Brian looked up, focusing upon her through his tears. "What? Why? We came north for nothing. My friend is gone, and I knew deep down my magics would have found a way to revive him."

Anna slipped off the chains, seizing Colbwing's whiskers as she pressed her knees to the floor. For Brian, she decided to investigate the fire first, hoping the storm bison's hadn't been taken in what was no question an attack.

"Our time is better served getting you to the capital," said Brian, tugging her sleeve. "I loved Nathan but even he knew when time was short in a crisis."

"I understand," said Anna, whipping the serpent's whiskers. "But deep within me I know something can be gained from us learning more."

A sudden realization claimed her mind for a moment, this was the first time she had flown any creature. Not even her... Lord William had ever permitted her to fly his esant, Sharp Beak by herself. But with Brian consumed in grief doing her best was imperative. Anna flicked Colbwing's whiskers in the same fashion Eve had Thomas's reins. She raised them upward slightly, the serpent dipping toward Kardanhall. The castle's dark brick work a blur even at this distance. She firmed up her grip, feeling the serpent circle around the temple's collapsed bell tower. Straight on ahead she pulled up a hint, sending a great roaring hiss into the valley formed between the outer wall and the Keep. An immediate thud, then whoosh against the dirt shifted her balance. Anna faintly heard the crunching of snow. She eased up the tension, coming to within feet of the bend continuing around the Keep.

"We're alive." Brian let out a clenched breath. "You landed Colbwing without trouble."

Anna peered over her shoulder, finding him lighter in spirits. His childlike face had an immense smile on it, and the red lining of his reflective eyes was a bright pink.

"Let's go."

She armed herself then made for what she saw earlier. A long deep trench of snow stretched a distance from the tip of Colbwing's tail. Dirt and snow built up against the smooth surface of his coils. His bright fur met the sunlight, making the snow appear as if it were reflecting the dance of flames. Toward the temple, a shell of its once aged, glimmered a spear head. Its long wood shaft pounded into the dirt. Anna's eyes narrowed. Her heart pounded against her chest; an unease sank her stance. It was still so incredible, to finally have both her eyes. Fluttering and rattling at the spear's head, a scroll was tied.

"Whoever did this meant it as a warning." said Brian, catching up to her. "Let's find out who we're dealing with."

Untying the scroll from the spear, its paper smelled of smoke. Despite the cold, Anna found the parchment warmed somehow by the temple's fire. She unfurled it, catching sight of lingering flames on the seal of both windows to either side of the temple's entrance. *The fire ended recently.* She began to read with an unease bubbling in her belly.

Lady Anna Brighton,

I have your rutoe. By the rules set under campaign law, I cannot slow your arrival to the Tournament of the Primes. But since only two days remain, a late campaigner can be disqualified. And with the surprise coming your way such tardiness is...

Anna bolted upright like a startled deer, feeling the chill of Brian's presence against her back. From amongst the shadows, below the outer wall, men in plated armor emerged.

Upon their breastplates, the sigil of a prime except it was within the jaws of a beast she had never seen. A beast with a thick mane around its head. Its eyes were like red hot coals. Anna dropped the scroll, readied her bow, and peered over shoulder.

"I don't have enough arrows for them all," she said, drawing and aiming for the closest man. "Can you fight?"

"I can," said Brian, biting his lip, "but not in this form. Can you get us back to Colbwing?"

Every man came at them at once, forcing Anna to release quickly. The arrow soared overhead of a man coming from her right. She nocked another arrow as she guided Brian swiftly back to the serpent. She realized, drawing back, that both eyes had been open. She had been so used to being half blind, so one with her bow, that such a great change placed her aim off balance.

Clamping her right eye shut, the balance returned for a moment. One man fell to her aim, but now eight arrows remained. Her pulse quickened. The men advanced on them as the Colbwing roared and hissed. She swallowed her hesitation, nocking, and drawing, releasing, and reaching, touching fewer and fewer arrows.

"Can he not defend himself," Anna said, wincing at the bite of her bow string. "He could easily clear them all away."

Brian peered up at her, lips trembling. Anna could see the frustration on her face from the reflection in his eyes.

"Colbwing is like a horse," said Brian. "He cannot fight unless trained or possessed."

"Possessed?"

"Yes," said Brian, firming his tone, removing the fear on his face. "Now get me to him."

295

Anna reached back to find four arrows remaining. They circled the inside of her quiver as they ran, teasing her with feelings of desperation. As she grabbed another arrow, she wondered why the men with their arrowhead shaped helmets didn't attack at greater speed. They didn't close their formation tight like a fist. It was as if they knew she possessed no chance of winning, no chance of escape. Several drew swords as steam slipped swiftly from under their mouth shields. She hid her worry behind a stern face. Her hood grew in weight as snow cascaded upon Kardanhall in heavy, swift flakes.

Uncertainty crossed her mind at what Brian meant by possession, such a word never meaning more to her than what was owned by another. Every thought refocused on the men closing in on them. With a final reach she fumbled with her last arrow, tensing her fingers around its fletching. A soldier swiped high from her right. Anna ducked, holding firm to the arrow as a slice and crack met her ears. Anna lunged, piercing his exposed cheek with her final arrow. He stumbled toward the temple gripping his face.

She looked up from her action, freezing in place. She felt her throat close for a moment. Her chest heaved with pain to find her bow had been cut in two.

"Run" Anna hid her heartbreak, grabbing the wizard's wrist. "There are too many."

Brian saw what remained of her bow, speeding out of her grip with haste. Anna felt him slip from her grip, as the soldiers chased her hurried footsteps. She shook her head wishing for time to mourn her trusted weapon. The soldiers increased their pace, raising their swords.

Anna dodged an avalanche of swipes, rocking on her heels.

"Go! Possess Colbwing before aaah…" The soldiers grabbed her arms and legs.

She felt herself raised, every breath forced from her lips. And with great force, they slammed her against the ground. Snow crackled like glass under her weight as her head glanced off a stone. Her head thrummed with agony, opening a jar her lips, heavy snowflakes filled them, choking her. Anna rolled over, head spinning and crawled upon her belly. A swift encompassing shadow rose. The soldiers' swords poised all at once.

And then with a roar greater than any she had ever heard the sharp shadows of soldiers' swords fell limp. Feet shuffled across snow, kicking up dirt, clicking small stones against muddied boots. Anna found herself alone. One man removed his mouth shield, eyeing the others as Colbwing blotted out the sun, rearing to strike. Colbwing's eyes glowed. His long whiskers bolted back in jagged lines.

"Flee," said a deep thunderous voice from the serpent's mouth. The soldiers charged. Colbwing swirled, striking the ground with his mouth agape. He gobbled up man after man, blocking Anna from harm as he crushed those not in range of his immense jaws.

Rising to her feet, only one soldier absent from the fight was within feet of the temple. His sword was gone. One hand clasped where her arrow remained lodged as he crawled backward. Anna approached him slowly, questions crossing her mind until his arm gave way. The coppery scent of his wound met her nostrils. The cries of his fellow soldier were all but gone. Flames crackled and danced upon the temple, keeping the castle from complete silence.

"Why attack us?" Anna said, towering before the man.

"Answer. And I may help you."

"We were supposed to off Lady Brighton," he said, slipping a knife from his boot. He swiped at her, sneering. "Stay back rutoe!"

"Does she look like the one you speak of?" Brian asked, his voice thundering with eyes narrowed.

Anna found her jaw had dropped. She closed it, eyeing the soldier. He crawled away, made to stand, and then collapsed.

"She supposed to 'ave a burned face." He rolled over to face Anna again. Blood rand down his face, the hand holding the knife shook as he eyeballed Brian. "We thought the girl was her since she trespassed on Lord Kardan's grounds."

Seeing where the wizard was heading with things, Anna focused on the soldier, finding him quivering but not from the cold.

"I know of who you seek, and she is no rutoe," said Anna, edging close to him. He jabbed at her. Anna kicked his wrist, freeing the knife. "I have no intent to harm you."

She swiftly pressed a knee to his chest, laid her hand flat to his face, and pulled the arrow free. The man screamed and groaned, pressing his hand to his punctured eye.

"Go now and see your family."

"That bloody well hurt," said the soldier. His chest heaved as he peered over his shoulder to Simdorn's temple. "Thanks, I guess. There ain't no going home after what I've done."

She took the man's hand and pulled him to his feet. The small metal plates upon his gauntlet were ice cold, dotted with blood.

"Beg the goddess for forgiveness," she said, softly. "Tell her you will build another temple greater in size."

He met her eye, a tear on his cheek.

"Thank you," he said, "for sparing me. I'll make good on your words."

Chapter Twenty-Nine

The deep emptiness remained. Evelyn kept it locked within as she stood with the rutoe clan commanders, facing their unforgiving eyes over mouth shields and clenched pointed teeth. The journey to Cillnar had been quick, faster than any she experienced upon Thomas.

She bawled her fingers into fists, averting them from the knives hidden on her person. *I killed their kin,* she thought, crossing her fists behind her back to appear neutral. *Will they take revenge after their leader is rescued?* It would take nothing, not even the span of minutes to cut the throats of those in her company. But there were her servants to consider, their eyes fixated on her guests' armor and minds on their mistress's decision to break the law. She had ordered them to serve the rutoe wine and avert their eyes. Evelyn couldn't deny it, the commanders were the strangest folk to ever visit Wayne tower. That and with the rutoe who murdered her friend dead, acting against his superiors was an unnecessary ending of lives.

Upon the table before her was a map of the capital. The commanders had marked points of entry for their forces, ones they explained in broken English had been discovered months previous. She leaned against the smooth polished wood of the table, scanning the map and thrumming her fingers. It was one of her father's maps, browned by decades and faded in quadrants. To the commanders there was only one entrance to the city. She traced point to point with her gaze the tunnel exits she'd discovered as a child. Ones neither her father, the city guard, or any orderman beyond herself knew about.

"You have a plan in place," said Evelyn. "And once Anna wins the tournament in two days, we can take the capital if Luther decides not to accept the results."

The commander of the ignited clan stepped forward, finishing his wine, and setting his crystal goblet on the table.

"We can be, how you say, 'certain' she will arrive on time with the wizard doing the flying. I ... uh, am still uneasy with the last of our fifth clan being raised by the man who crushed our first rebellion and killed her clan. Are you telling true she is friend to rutoe?"

A faint sharp pang struck Evelyn's mind. Doing so the commander, but he pressed his lips together as she released a breath through flared nostrils.

"Does being friend with our captured leader's son," said the quiet one commander among them, *"not prove this?"*

"I agree," said Evelyn, eyeing them both, digging her fingernails into the table. "I have seen the care she has for the boy in her actions and words."

"I will trust in that for the time being," said the ignited commander, resting a hand to the flaming fist of his breastplate.

"I worry for the leader's son. You left him at strange castle with the blacnavinstin's servants."

With a guess such a word must have been a rutoe's way of calling someone a bastard. She remembered the lord's sword at her back, the force of his kick on her legs. The quakes had been too much then for her orderman training to have much effect, even though Martyn Kardan wasn't a young man anymore.

"He took on Lamparien soldiers to save Anna," she said, refusing to wince. "I think we had best push past this issue of trust."

The quiet one commander severed the connection. Evelyn released a faint gasp as the commander was pushed aside by the ignited one. He slammed his fist on the table rattling his goblet forward until it eclipsed the Proving.

"You do not get to earn trust of rutoe by tales you did not witness."

Evelyn raised an eyebrow. There was no reason to lie, nor for her to have been in Natlendton to make her words true. She knew the rutoe by their clan abilities, way of travel, and care for nelka. But it was apparent their ways of trust were far more complicated.

"Then what now?" she said, folding her arms. "Do you wish to gather your soldiers and leave after coming this far?"

He glared with eyes bright red, steam rising from them slowly.

"No."

Stepping forward the commander of the swift clan rested his goblet over the palace. Its location not far from the Proving on the map. And by what Evelyn thought was sheer coincidence where his soldiers had set up camp in the woods north.

"No. There is no turning back for rutoe," he said. "My friend knows words pass differently with humans."

The commander firmed his thick lips into a hard line. His dark blue eyes were soft, calmer than Evelyn saw in his fellow leaders.

"We are in agreement then?" she said.

Rising to full height the ignited one unclenched his teeth.

"You best hope she wins, Wayne," he said.

For a moment the room grew unbearably hot, the immense hearth behind her devouring the logs swiftly.

"Or what?" she said, molding her face until without emotion. "Will you take revenge for the rutoe I've killed? Will you burn down my husband's home with me in it? I know Anna is more than capable of defeating a few spoiled lords and ladies."

A hiss loud enough to make her ears ring came from the hearth. The logs were gone, robbing its fire of fuel.

"Fine," said the ignited commander. His eyes faded to a soft red. "Now let us focus on freeing our leader."

"Very well."

She drew another map out from under the one of Cillnar. And as Evelyn explained the layout of Nar-ton prison, a need to not shake her head at the commander came and went. *Men are the same no matter where they come from,* she thought, pointing to where the council had gone to meet Norman's father. *Willing to show their might to threaten those they do not trust.*

* * *

Evelyn leaned heavily on the balustrade, focused on Proving separated from her home by hundreds of houses below. It was far colder than the previous evening. The plan was already in motion for the commanders to send agents to rescue their leader. She had offered her own skill with a blade, and familiarity with the capital, but rutoe ways were old. Women served only three purposes in a clan, none allowing wives and daughters to become fighters or an orderman like herself. Rising to full height, the removal of her breastplate and gauntlets made managing her family illness easier.

"I wonder what they would think of Emilia, of her wife, being willing to lead," she sighed.

Creak.

Evelyn kept facing forward. Her ears twitched under her long blond locks. Letting free the thin knife tucked up her tight sleeve, faint breaths broke the silence behind her. The room possessed only moonlight and starlight, streaming over the balcony to aid her vision. She didn't require light to make out where the intruder was. And whoever it was must know whose home they trespassed within. Every tower within Cillnar was made indistinguishable from the other. The prime and long passed primnoire didn't wish for their brilliance to be outdone.

"Cross onto the balcony intruder," said Evelyn. "You won't be given a second invitation."

Her nostrils drew in the smell. *Misnem?* Every muscle felt limp like the grand curtain meant to separate the room from the balcony. The tips of her fingers held firm the short knife, finding it real, certain, unlike her feelings. A boot clicked against smooth stonework. It broke the rule set by her daughter long ago, one even the servants obeyed. *Even I obey it still.* She felt the coolness against the flesh of her feet. They were growing numb from the cold, but her long thick night robes kept any loss feeling from becoming absolute.

"I know who you are. Though I find it difficult to believe my senses."

The footsteps came once more, slow, but deliberate in measure.

"I didn't believe you would remember the misnem," said a voice Evelyn had almost forgotten. "I wear it for her, you know."

"And I always found a good wash better than the laziness of perfumes."

Evelyn turned slowly on her heels, finding Emelia hooded and cloaked. Her eyes were incapable of believing what she saw. The words she had said back in the Proving came true. Even in the way her daughter carried herself, she reminded the mistress of duels and debates of Anna Brighton.

"What have you come home for?" said Evelyn, carefully measuring her words, not wanting her daughter to find reason to be upset with her. "I must tell you that I have changed my position and am trying to stop Prime Luther."

Emelia stepped forward into the moonlight, drawing back her hood and letting loose her long blond hair.

"Finally, you see the old man for who he truly is," said Emilia.

"Yes."

"I come here for rest. Nina will be joining me shortly."

"How much support have you gained in your travels?" Evelyn asked.

Emelia raised an eyebrow. "So now, you are for me campaigning?"

"I was never against it," Evelyn said. "I was uncertain of going against the prime, of what you discovered to be true."

"Father was more than willing to fund my campaign. Are not couples of the council supposed to be in full agreement?"

The conversation was coming to a boil by Evelyn's guess. She needed to bring down the rising anger she saw in her daughter's eyes. She looked so much like a leader. Emilia kept her chin at proper height, her eyes fixed upon Evelyn's. A true leader kept focus on the conversation at hand. *I don't know why it never occurred to me before*, Evelyn thought.

"Our prime has become more powerful with the rutoe willing to betray their own kind." said Evelyn. "I did not want to risk your life and that of our family's by placing coin on the subject."

Emelia smirked.

"That is why I put my faith in the people. They kept me hidden in case our prime saw me as a threat to his dimwitted sons."

For this, Evelyn found herself both grateful and guilty. She had not had much faith in Lampara's citizens, knowing how much had changed in recent years. She cast her gaze at the ground, guilt compounding like a wave towards a shore.

"I am here to support you now, but also someone who I believe will lead us to a better tomorrow."

"And who may I ask is this man?" Emilia asked, fumbling with the string of her bow across her chest.

"It is no man but a woman." Evelyn played with the idea of telling her daughter about Anna. She was uncertain if revealing such information was necessary. *Emelia was always the jealous type.* "The woman is from a family long since absent from politics." She sighed. "Her name is Anna Brighton."

"Anna Brighton?" said Emelia. "I hear she is without half a face. How will someone of such deformity lead?"

"I have taught you better than that. Appearance has nothing to do with strength and leadership. From what I have heard of late she has grown in popularity."

The door opened to Emelia's chambers. Nina stepped through to find an awkwardness about the room. She nodded and closed the door. Evelyn thought the girl was wise for keeping out at a time like this.

"Place your backing behind this half-burned girl, Mother."

There was an edge in Emilia's voice that Evelyn sensed may strike soon. *End battles of emotion with greater speed than those with a blade.* Her master once said. *For death of the heart is far worse than any man can invent.* Evelyn had felt close to death when she last saw her daughter. It pained her far more than the quakes of which left her unbalanced. Tremors rolled upon her as she took a step forward. Her balance bent her in a fast motion, bringing the ground within inches. Evelyn coughed at a sudden pulse from her chest. The room felt more stable as she was guided to full height.

"I've not yet experienced the first signs of quakes," said Emilia. "But at no time with my anger will I ever allow you to fall, Mother. If you will back us both then there is no reason for us to remain at odds."

The emotion in her daughter's voice was clear and kind. Her hopes went from her belly to her heart in a flash at the thought of no longer being parted from her only child. She embraced Emelia with all the strength she possessed.

"And you shall have it." She leaned back, still uneasy in balance, finding the emerald in Emilia's eyes. "Now. I must tell you about the siege."

Emilia gasped. "Siege?"

Chapter Thirty

━━━⟨෧෨ඁ⟩━━━

A cold sweat broke upon Norman's brow. The heat flowing through his veins felt like the ice chilling the soles of his feet. There was a deep wish to leave, to flee within the depths of his mind. Norman gazed up at the prison while his skin trick ability fluctuated with his feelings. The prison towered over the homes of Cillnar, tucked into a corner of the capital sparse of life. Fog encircled it, disguising its true height. Its bear statues black with marble sheen. Their coloring displayed the prisoner's lack of respect for Lamparien law. Unlike the Proving, these statues stood on their hind legs with their backs to the city, as if to keep something terrible inside. Ravens fled from a window high above the entrance with scrolls tied tight to their ankles. Below the window and between two cracked columns stood guards in armor pitted and rusted. Norman thought if either man moved their armor may crumble off.

Beside him stood Phillip, a tall man, wearing a long heavy trench coat. He released a gray cloud of smoke from his lips.

His thin cigar at half the length from when they left the palace. A ring of fur about Phillip's collar made his disk helmet appear like a lid over a tall black kettle. Norman firmed up his face and focused on keeping his flesh that of a human's. His hair ruffled despite the lack of wind, battling to return to its long dark thickness.

"Are you ready for what's coming, Tilt?"

"Yes," Norman said with a stutter. "My… My father is within that place, and I must free him."

"Good," said the Orderman, dropping his cigar on the ground and squashing its glowing tip. "'Because I won't be holding your hand. This place has more than guards they say.'"

Norman gulped, bending his fingers into fists to push down his nervousness. Flames ignited over his knuckles for a moment as he reminded himself of Anna's courage. *I must be like her with my fears,* He extinguished his flames, shaking off his worry. Norman gave the Orderman a nod, following Phillip toward the entrance. His pace was far greater than Norman could match. He didn't wish to appear as if he were running, yet with the snow's depth such movement was inevitable. Once they made it to the entrance both guards crossed their spears, halting Phillip whose fingertips had met the door before either noticed.

"Do you have papers to permit entrance?" said one guard.

"And papers to see a prisoner of our prime?" said the second guard.

"You're both cute." Phillip smirked, narrowing his eyes. "Ordermen don't require papers."

The guards eye one another, one biting his before raising his chin as if to reassure his point. His dome helmet was well over his brow and his mouth shield was caked with snot across the rim like the other guard's. Norman noted the light film of frost over their evergreen breastplates. He thought Phillip walking up and demanding entrance arrogant. There was no way such an act could work but he had seen along their journey citizens seeking refuge from the Orderman's presence. Making their way from the palace had been both easy and nerve wracking. Norman forced himself earlier to take on a slightly different form. He abandoned his curls for close cropped hair. His face remained the same Anna had grown to know, adjusting his chin slightly to match Phillip's. He clenched his jaw. Even two minor changes sent sweat down his brow.

"They do when a tournament of primes is upon us," said the first guard, signaling his partner. The other guard strolled toward a bell within a hollow left of the doors. "We've got a few campaigners in here, and my guess is you're someone they know pretending to be an orderman."

Norman stepped forward, parting his lips, but Phillip glared at him over his shoulder. The steel blue of his eyes made Norman's boiling blood feel as if it had frosted over. The Orderman sighed deeply. He eyed Phillip's hands, knowing they would be far too swift for him to notice… Both guards dropped to their knees, heads jerking back, throats split horizontally, opening slowly like waking eyes.

"Was that your doing?" said Norman. "How can a human move like that?"

"You'd be surprised," said Phillip. His knives hissed swiftly from his sleeves. "But this time it wasn't me doing the cutting."

Gazing down from where the guards knelt footprints lie. Light snow fell. The tracks lead down a distant alley.

Norman heard and saw snow tumble from the overhang of a condemned shop. A faint trail of red droplets followed the tracks.

"We ain't alone, Tilt."

Phillip raised a finger to his lips, returning it to the hilt of his knife. Norman heard footsteps coming from the left of the ally. Four figures in black drifted from the shadows. At the fingertips of the one leading them, long thin blades dripped blood.

"I suggest you drop the disguise, Tilt," said the Orderman, "cus we gonna need that fire of yours."

Norman released air from his nostrils as his skin tingled and shifted. Flames outlined his fists, but then he realized who they were up against. *Rutoe. I should speak with them before it is too late.*

"We come to free my father, Huldinarf," he said in rutoise. "He is leader of the rebellion against Prime Luther."

The leading rutoe raised his blade-tipped fingers. The others stopped many paces short of the alley's end. She halted within a spear's throw of Norman and Phillip. The rutoe slipped off a black cobraswift helmet. What Norman perceived by the figure's physic to be a woman was a man of extreme slender build. He had sharp dark blue eyes, and charcoal skin displaying a faint white scar down the brow, the eye missing from its socket, and continuing to the chin. He held the helmet at his hip. His hair was drawn back and tied.

"You are who he calls, Sheckaldurn?" he said.

Phillip snickered. "Your father calls you horse droppings?"

Norman's green skin darkened. His cheeks burned with embarrassment. Rutoe possessed no list of common names.

Leaders, priests, farmers, whomever throughout the generations were called the first thing they pointed to as an infant. Norman's family once worked in the fields of a farmer at Lampara's most northern region. He ground his teeth, remembering the plow horse defecating not far from where his mother watched him play.

"Let the subject die," said Norman.

"If live through this," Phillip chuckled. "I might."

The swift one sneered at the Orderman then placed his focus back on Norman.

"We must be quick," he said. "Our forces await the rescue of your father, Sheckaldurn."

"Let's be off then," Norman said. He eyed Phillip, but his eyes couldn't instill the fear the Orderman possessed. "What did you mean about this place having more than just guards?"

"Touch the doors," Phillip said, pointing a knife at them, keeping his focus on the swift one.

Norman maneuvered past the guards. Their faces buried deep in the snow, blood pooling from their throats in long wide arcs. He extinguished a flame-ringed hand, reaching for the door's immense rusted ring. A jolt rushed through his arm, lifting him from his feet. Norman gasped, flying backwards. A grunt let out behind him as he felt a sudden stop. His head cracked against something thin and sharp.

"That's what I meant, Tilt," said Phillip, placing Norman back on his feet. "I knew coming along was a good idea."

"What keeps me out?" Norman said, rubbing his head.

"Being rutoe."

"This is a wizard's work," said the swift one, casting his hand over the door. Wincing. "Must we trust in another human to achieve our freedom from the mountains?"

"I don't much care for that tone of yours," said Phillip, gripping his long knives tight. "You got that skin changing thing. Use it if you don't want to be trusting more humans."

Phillip raised his chin, clenching his teeth. The swift one's blades dug into the skin above the Orderman's throat. Norman snatched her wrist. "He just gave us the key to freeing my father."

The swift one peered at him, a flicker of blue lightning in his eyes.

"We shouldn't have to change our appearance for anyone." He withdrew his blades, placing his helmet back on. "Or anything. Such magic is forbidden."

Norman felt taken aback for a moment. Uncertainty flooded his chest as he looked up at the prison. His father had gone from a farm hand to the leader of a rebellion. Taking risks. Placing him in the care of Samuel, who had taught Norman much. Before leaving the south, learning the trick of the skin meant survival to him. His father told him rutoe used it to keep humans from acting rash, from the need of a rutoe to use his magics in defense of hatred.

"I must go alone," he said, rubbing his head once again, finding no blood. "I will free my father so our banishment may end."

He moved to within an arm's length of the doors. Norman shut his eyes, drawing all focus away from his flames, picturing the man he guised himself as before. His chin tingled until pointed and strong like the Orderman's. His hairs hissed up his cheeks, shortening and fading into chestnut. It felt as though a fan of feathers caressed the back of his neck. Both ears rounded off as his eyes glazed for a moment, churning to the color of a mountain spring. Gasps rose from the rutoe in his company. Whispers reached his ears of how his skin was so light and red at the cheeks.

"I'm going with you like we planned," said Phillip.

Norman smiled. A thought crossed his mind, robbing him of focus.

"Will this disguise fool a wizard's magic?"

"You've only one way to find out." The Orderman rolled his shoulders, cracking his neck with both blades at the ready. "After you."

Norman grabbed hold of the handle. Lifting it, he felt a surge of power flow up his arm. He clenched his teeth, fighting the urge to let loose his natural form. Pushing with all his might, Norman felt the door give way, hissing against cracked brick work. Phillip pushed the other door with ease, gripping both knives in his left hand. A rush of dampness and mold teased Norman's senses as the door slowly opened. The hall before them was long and filled with doors to either side. A spiraling metal staircase led up to where he had seen the ravens take flight.

He released a pent-up breath feeling his hair lengthen and burning behind his eyes return. The rutoe leader entered followed by the other, finding no resistance from the wizard's magic. The jarring power dissipated from Norman's limbs as his skin phased to its natural green. He looked on ahead feeling the hairs upon skin stand on end. An ice-blue surge of light raced over the walls, over the floor and across the ceiling. A crackling boom sounded at the hall's end, fading to nothing.

Clattering and rattle answered. Out of the darkness beyond the hall's end, guards approached at great speed. They wielded swords and were armor equally pitted plating to the soldiers who had protected the entrance. Norman ignited his hands, charging at them, thinking of his father as he released a heavy beam of flames. Phillip sprinted, lunged, piercing the throat of a guard. The Orderman spun and shoved his knife up into the jaw of a man swinging his sword in heavy downward motion.

Those among the swift one's group released flames, losing lanterns from their places, and bashing guards across the face. The swift one ran at an arc Norman was unable to fully see until eleven men collapsed to their knees. Men toward the rear of the falling guards fled for the grand staircase ahead.

"We must separate from one another," said the swift one.

"Doing that won't end well for any of us," said Phillip, yanking his knife from the back of a man he had killed. "That room above the entrance must have something we need to find your father, Tilt."

Norman focused on the stairs. They were wide, parting at the top in two directions. He felt deep down there was little time to search among documents for his father's location.

"We shall separate," he said, chewing his lip. "Those guards will return with more of their own. It's a risk, but we must press on."

Phillip shook his head, readying his knives. "You don't know this place. Hell, I don't know it."

Shouts echoed down to their level, followed by heavy foot falls with equal measure. Norman ignored Phillip's concern, dashing for the stairs. For a moment, there was no one following him, then all at once, the Orderman and those of the swift one's group were at his back. He took the stairs bracing against a powerful rotting scent. Phillip bolted past him, thrusting a sharp glare at Norman from under his disk helmet. Norman threw his focus upon freeing his father. His brow knitted as they reached the next level. It seemed the stairs reached and spiraled off in two directions for every floor to come.

"You're letting emotions cloud that accountant logic of yours," Phillip hissed. "I asked the fast rutoe to take out the guards. Leave us to do the searching."

Norman raised an eyebrow, deep down agreeing to such a strategy. There was too much eagerness within his heart. And he knew, from what Anna said regarding hunting, a rush to find what you seek led only to trouble.

"You're right," said Norman, the click of more footsteps reached his ears. "We shall return to the room you mentioned."

Phillip tapped his knife to the edge of his helmet in a salute. They raced to the bottom level pausing in mid-step before another orderman. He was tall with olive skin, eyes burning a dark green. Norman knew him from Prime Luther's saddle dome.

"Have you come to aid us?" Norman asked, peering over his shoulder to find guards at his back. "Or have you come to..."

A piercing sent both him and Phillip to their knees as the quiet one connected with their minds. The guards raced down the steps, shackles in hand, and then there was a hiss. A hiss like metal across flesh.

"Drop flat," said the orderman within Norman's mind. His mouth shield clanged against the ground.

Norman dropped on his belly beside Phillip. A great cry forced his hands to his ears. He saw the shackles drop but couldn't hear them as dozens of feet rose at once. A collective thrum sent a cloud of dust over him. Norman coughed, peering up the stairs to find its center obliterated. There was a great gaping void, strewn with bodies, leading to a hole large enough to consume a dragon.

He rose to his feet as the quiet one picked up his mouth shield and applied it. A long knife with brown leather woven over the hilt slipped out from the sleeve of his trench coat. Norman ignited his fist, confusion sending a warm sweat droplet down his brow.

"Douse those fire starters, Sheckaldurn," said Phillip, raising his knife to the brim of his disk helmet, saluting the other orderman. Laughing.

"I said drop it," Norman barked, letting his flames go out.

The orderman before them clamped shut his green eyes, clasping his hand across his mouth in what Norman believed was a quiet one's version of a fit of laughter.

"OK, kid," said Phillip, composing himself. "Let's see where they're keeping your dad."

* * *

At all corners cages were piled to the ceiling. White and black dung lie clumped upon the bars with squawking ravens pecking at corn in small bowls. Norman found himself wanting another assault upon his senses from the quiet one rather than the constant caws and feather ruffling around him. He searched amongst paper stacks, knowing just like Lord William's financial records, the most recent entries would be on light colored parchment. The search felt like time being consumed in a slow fashion. There was no organization. No alphabetical order to the prisoner names.

"I can't find anything in this mess," he said, removing an ink bottle from atop a stack of papers. "Nothing but names I don't—"

Beyond him a narrow hall lead to more pillars of clutter. There were shelves chock-full of books molded and disheveled. But what drew his eye from searching was faint breathing. The ordermen in his company readied their knives, setting down handfuls of lists. Norman crept toward the hall, heart pounding, slowly maneuvering along a wall of cages. Caws assaulted his ears, muffling the sound. Amongst the room's confusion, a foot appeared, wrapped in rags. Hands reached out with a cawing, irritated raven as a man sprinted for the window ahead.

The ordermen raced to stop him. Norman saw a message tightly bound to the raven's ankle. The man huffed and puffed, just feet from releasing the bird. Norman dashed to grab him, tripping over a stack of leather-bound ledgers. He gasped, releasing a torrent of flames. The flames set the man's back ablaze. The man screamed, dropping the raven, tumbling against a wall of cages. Every cage ignited as the man tossed and turned. Cries of pain let out at once from the ravens as they squirmed and smashed their way between the bars.

The raven, no longer in man's grasp, hopped its way to the window. But before it could reach the window a knife pinned it to the ground. The knife was the length of Norman's hand, cutting through the base of the raven's neck, lined with blood. Phillip tipped his hat to him, heading to retrieve the knife. The flames grew and climbed up the walls, silencing the remaining ravens. Norman scoured the room but still found no list with his father's name.

"Come on, Tilt," said Phillip, grabbing him by the shoulders.

319

"We'll be dead if we don't up and run."

"But" said Norman, grabbing for more papers. Cages collapsed and tumbled upon valleys of ledgers, "I won't find my father without—"

"We gotta go, kid."

Norman's arms went numb, soon followed by his legs. His eyelids felt heavy as his fingers clawed for more names. The room went dark as he found himself mumbling with spittle oozing from his lips.

A moment later, Norman found himself within the hall he started from. A cool breeze sifted its way under the doors to the prison. Its chill nipped his cheek as the scent of smoke filled his nostrils. The quiet one opened the doors slightly releasing smoke wove its way down the spiraling staircase from the room above.

"I had to do it, Tilt," said Phillip, down on one knee beside him. "You had a look in your eye like you didn't mind dying, and that wouldn't help no body. Not even your—"

"Father."

Norman sat up so fast that his head spun. There was a flooding pain in his temple as he found his father standing before him. Behind were the rutoe of earlier, their faces concealed within their cobraswift helmets. His father stood with hair long enough to cover his chest. His eyes were a faded red, and his skin possessed scars deep and frightening. Norman stood with slight unease as his father looked upon him. Hanging limp upon his father's person were gray trousers and a tunic with sleeves cut off above the elbows.

"It has been," Norman embraced him, "too long."

"It truly has, Norman,"

The strength his father once possessed was faint. Norman

could see Prime Luther had fed his father poorly, thinness had shrunken the muscles formed from his days of farming and rebellion. His father's thinness almost matched his own.

"Now, Norman," his father said. "Let's kill that bastard Luther."

They marched forth from the prison to find the street bustling. Lampariens' with golden blonde hair and those of a dark auburn streamed from both shops and homes in the direction of the Proving. A screeching-like blade against blade made Norman wince. He spun to find the swift one raising his hand, scraping the blades upon his fingers once again. A scream rang out, and soon, a top of the distant city walls flames erupted. The humans heading for the tournament scattered as swift ones appeared in a blink within alley ways.

"We got to head for Evelyn's place," said Phillip, dashing west. "Bring your father, Tilt."

"Come father," said Norman, grabbing his father's arm. "The Wayne's can be trusted."

His father yanked his arm back, eyeing the rutoe behind him.

"The Wayne's have profited from nelka furs," he said. "You know how important nelka are to rutoe."

"Listen," Phillip said, sheathing his knives. "I helped your son save you. That counts for something."

The weathered form that was his father swirled his fingers into fists, flames consuming them.

"Do think after all Prime Luther has done, all Lampara's humans have done, that I will trust you?"

The swift one clasped the rebel leader's shoulder.

"I have no love for the Wayne's, General Huldinarf," he said.

Primnoire

His voice metallic through the cobraswift helmet. "But Evelyn Wayne now funds our rebellion for she has wronged us and is paying back that wrong in full."

Norman sighed. The street was clear of all humans except Phillip. Upon the city walls faint cries rang out and flames lit and vanished. His father flashed his pointed teeth at Phillip. His anger simmered, the flames over his hands vanished amongst the scars and blisters across his fingers.

"That is not enough my son."

"There is something else Father," said Norman. "Someone that will help us win. She means much to me."

"And who is this girl that she will make me trust a Wayne?"

Norman met the burning crimson in his father's eyes. His chest thundered with conflict. There had been so many signs both recent and in the past. But in the past uncertainty kept him from summoning the courage to be proven right.

"Her name is Anna," he said. "And she is the last of the fifth clan."

Chapter Thirty-One

It was never hard to find him. He always gave himself away, which was both his biggest fault and his best quality. Cole's clouds were almost invisible in the darkness, slowly replacing day. Anna knew she possessed only a night and a day to reach Cillnar. But knowing that her first and best friend was alive meant more than all else. She dropped to her knees and embraced Cole's immense furry head. The lantern light reflected off his silver hooked horns. A change in her appearance mattered not to the storm bison, as if he recognized her no matter the burns or… It came to her. Anna rose to her feet, finding an unsteadiness in her stance. She had been so happy to see her friend again, and finding relief in the wake of losing Nathan, that…

"I cannot return to Cillnar as I am."

She led Cole and Roland out of the stables. Kardanhall loomed like an abandoned ruin, no light filled its windows, and with night almost upon it the castle resembled more a mountain than anything else. At a distance, Brian stood with arms folded, a slight smile on his face, but the way in which he looked at her reminded Anna how short they were on time.

"I'm glad you have reunited with your friend," he said, the smile upon his lips fading fast. "If only I could have done the same with Nathan."

Silence fell on them both, the truth of failing to return north in time left her heart heavy with grief. And yet she believed the former lord was in a better place, free from Prime Luther ever troubling him again.

"I cannot return to the capital as I am," she said. The thought of returning to her burnt self felt both insane and unwanted in her mind. "Lampara's people do not know me as I am now, and we have no time to find another dra—"

"The effects of Echnumbard's gift cannot be reversed by my magics either," said Brian, looking upon his childlike hands. "I do have one solution, but it would be hard to accomplish."

Brian's eyes lit the ground with their brightness. The light revealed an indentation covered in a light layer of snow. Anna scanned the grounds around them, finding the courtyard of Kardanhall had been trampled by something large. She thought of it being another crystalardan like Thomas, except what she realized were tracks that possessed far more depth than a dragon of his size.

"Someone else was here," Anna said, diverging her focus from her current predicament, "and rode an inferno dawn far larger than the dragon who left me half blind."

The thought of becoming so again squeezed at her chest like a hand a ripe fruit. She did miss having swift and easy use of her bow, but that was gone with her burns. Her bow was shoulder across her chest, bound with every cord she had from her belt.

"My thoughts are more on our current problem."

"But this will explain why Norman has not…" Anna clasped her lips, drawing her hand away, it felt as if she had forgotten him entirely. "Luther has Norman."

"We must focus on getting to Cillnar then," said Brian, reaching into his robes, drawing out a small black book. The wizard flipped through its pages at unusual speed. "Your friend is in danger, and you have a tournament to win. Ah, here it is."

"Is what you've discovered will return my face to what Lampariens recognize? I wish not to burn myself."

Anna dropped the reins within her hands, moving away from the storm bison's. As she found the writing in a language she didn't understand. Brian peered up at her with an uncertain smile.

"You're familiar with a rutoe's *Trick of Skin?*" Brian asked, resting a finger on a page. "It may help us, but it affects rutoe of the fifth clan differently than others of your race."

Anna swallowed, knowing what pain it put Norman through despite his attempts at hiding it. With her though, it would only be her face, maybe even her hands. And yet she had only been her true rutoe self for a short time. She worried it may be too difficult, or return the senses that drove her mad, except with double the ferocity.

"I will do it," she said, embracing Cole for a moment, soothing his nerves with hand strokes across his head. "What does such magic do to a rutoe like me?"

"You will be at risk of death in place of pain. You must be strong to take such risk," said Brian, eyeing his book once more. He sighed. "It requires complete focus, Anna. Are you certain?"

Anna sighed, removing her hood. To be the hunter she was before, giving her all into this *Trick of Skin* was necessary. Brian instructed her to close her eyes, to picture the face she wished to mirror. But Anna had only seen what she looked like once. The memory of her face was distant and difficult to focus her thoughts upon.

"Wait," she said, opening one eye. "Will I have control enough to become a rutoe again?"

Brian frowned, resting his hand within one of her own.

"You won't," he said, meeting her eye with a faint smile that shattered his worry. "This is why the *Trick of Skin* is forbidden amongst all rutoe. The risks and costs are too high."

She closed her eye, releasing a shuddering breath. Brian was far too truthful with her. Anna pressed her lips tight, focusing upon the darkness of her eyelids. The memory of her face was still faint. What was most familiar came to her. The feeling of complete darkness in her right eye, how heavy it had always felt. A crawling ran over it. The cold night air touched her cheeks, reminding her how soothing such a feeling used to be. The crawling ran down the surface of her cheeks, warping away at the right side. Then Anna recalled how limited her speech was with half her lips trapped by their fused skin. Five long years hiding and hating herself for wanting to impress others, for being disfigured, crept back into her subconscious. *No. I no longer care if others find faults in me.* There were people who accepted her. Norman. Eve. And Nathan.

Soon the right side of her face felt heavy and twisted. She parted her lips, feeling the tug. Brian released her hand, his instructions continuing. The pain ran across her face the longer she focused. Thoughts blurred. The pressures of what lay ahead assaulted her emotions as the fully formed burns fluctuated. She had only to focus on making her crimson rutoe flesh the pinkish white of a human. And then all at once balance left her, concentration abandoned her, all breath Anna possessed came out in a shrill scream.

* * *

The stars were at their brightest, telling Anna the night was at its midpoint. She had learned to tell such things from Lord William himself. His aged fingers pointed as he spoke of how Lampara stood still while the stars drifted from place to place, giving their siblings a different perspective of life below. She looked to the woods ahead, and then with surprise she could barely contain Cole. They were on the move at a speed the old storm had never reached before Nathan's attack on Williamton.

She felt something cold and metallic about her waist. Anna sat up straight finding she had been slumped over for what may have been hours by the pain in her back. Peering behind darkness filled her vision with only the light of moon and stars to give her eye... She rested her hand to her face, flinched, feeling relief hit her all at once. Anna tried to open her mouth to speak, yet just like before half of her lips were sealed by skin. Her right eye pressed against its lid, making Anna miss the full sight she briefly possessed.

She peered down at Cole, finding despite his speed, despite his heavy panting no clouds released from his nostrils. By the moon's faint light his silver horns were now a shining black. She touched his massive hump, finding it white like snow.

"I'm relieved you survived," said Brian.

Anna shrieked, leaning forward to find a large smile on the storm bison's thick black lips.

"Once you fainted, I panicked but found life still within you. You truly possess a strong will. I never met any within the clans who survived the *Trick of Skin*. I used Colbwing's seat chain to keep you atop your friend."

She ran her fingers over the chain, finding upon her shoulders a cloak with fur about the collar. Anna pulled it tight across her chest. The familiar feelings of her old face no longer as troublesome as they had been before. Her senses were on full alert once more, increasing both her worry and awareness. A smile crossed her lips as she took hold of Cole's saddle horn. Its aged wood smooth of splinters.

"How far have we to Cillnar?" said Anna, clenching her fingers, half missing her rutoe self. No. She had accepted her burned human face. "Nathan … guided me throughout our travels."

He guided Norman too, she thought. Brian raised Cole's head to her, the light reflecting off the storm bison's marble-shaped eyes.

"With my help, Cole will reach the capital by midday tomorrow," said Brian, returning his focus to the woods ahead. "He is old. Older than us both. My magic will keep all strain at bay. He will need to be left somewhere safe for a long rest."

"Let's move swiftly then. Cole deserves rest for his friendship."

"Agreed," Brian sent Cole west then north, trampling roots in his wake, "I sense something on your mind, Anna. Are you regretting your decision?"

"I was for a moment," she said, finally touching her face. "But I long ago accepted myself, accepted my appearance."

She licked her lips, not hesitating, her tongue no longer feeling the thick flesh from before. The wind ran across her face and into her hood, its chill returned her focus to what lay ahead. A throbbing worry surfaced in her throat for not just the tournament but for Norman. If Rockelton was any clue to the prime's distaste for rutoe, then her friend… Her love, if she dared say it, needed her help.

"Perhaps someday I shall miss being what I truly am," said Anna, holding fast to the saddle horn. "But Norman needs me and means more to me than what lies ahead."

"I understand your feelings for him," Brian said, huffing through Cole's massive jaws. "But worrying for him will make no difference if a prime's son wins the tournament."

Anna stiffened her chin knowing he was right, but Norman had shown her loyalty, friendship, and above all love. Something she believed for so long would come only from the man she now knew wasn't her own blood.

"I shall need to be at my sharpest then," she said. "I don't wish to let my people down."

* * *

Cillnar was grim. Beyond the hill Anna stood on, winter had made the days dreary and gray. In the distance, Cole lay on his side shaded by low branches of pine. His clouds drifted through the branches like smoke from a campfire. It pinched at her chest as the cold did her cheeks to leave the storm bison behind again. Anna had always felt at her best as both a hunter and woman with him at her side. There was some small comfort though in that Brian had decided to stay and watch over him. It seemed fair after separating from Cole.

He had since returned to the gray fur giant she loved like a brother.

She faced the capital once more, moving at pace with the snowfall. The sense of danger ahead was reaching a limit as she passed the sign concerning weapons. Anna sighed, feeling naked with her bow and quivers of no use. She dreaded the thought of being given a weapon she wasn't used to. Lord William had taught her at a young age the use of many weapons, but a bow was what she excelled at most.

After several hundred paces her legs felt taxed by the deep snow. She offered her hands at her side, telling the city guards she was unarmed and that she was here for the tournament. The immense thick doors thundered as they opened, sending a shiver of dread down her spine. There was still a city to navigate. If Brian hadn't left Roland at Kardanhall relief may have been possible. And yet there was no logic in it, a second mount meant a slower pace, the possibility of being too late for the tournament. *I will return for him some day.*

"Oi, mi-lady."

Anna halted short of passing the cheefox shop.

"Yes," she said, pivoting to face a man bundled in furs before the shop. "I'm sorry, sir. I have no coin for a…"

Ronald. She gasped. He approached at a slow pace, a slight limp in his step. She held back frustration, pressing her lips into a hard line. At the Proving, she had struck him in the side, ending their duel. Men were needed to carry him off.

"I'm sorry, Ronald."

"You best be," he said, halting to catch his breath. "I 'aven't left the capital since our first going about. Thank our ginger goddess the people 'ere love me."

Meshing her fingers into fists, it was the only thing to do

without breaking into a rant. The goddess being acknowledged so casually ground at her mind like a stone against beer hops.

"I didn't wish to leave you in such a state," said Anna, every feeling thrumming. "What business do you have with me?"

Ronald stared for a moment. Anna hadn't noticed it upon the grassy field of the Proving, but his left eye was a milky white. Its pupil a solid black. She thought it blind but there was enough focus in it to say otherwise at the time. He licked his lips, resting a hand to his chest.

"Oh, just to increase me chances."

With swift action he was upon her, knife in hand, her heart pounding against her chest. Ronald punched her across the cheek. Anna spat, kneeing him in the crotch. They rolled in the snow as a crowd gathered. Cheers came from the direction of the cheefox shop for Ronald as those behind her called for him to leave Anna be. The knife hissed through her hood, catching in the thick fabric, ripping it away.

Anna snatched his wrist, pressing her thumb deep. Ronald ground his teeth; spittle dripped upon Anna's cheek as he cried out. The knife fell from his grasp. She reached over grabbing it, spinning it, and with a swift thrust. Blood fell to her chest, thudding against the leathers and metal of her tunic. Anna pushed Ronald off, grunting, untangling his arms from her own.

Cheers rose as she eased to a sitting position. Anna peered over at Ronald as she found her breath. She drew her hand away, finding it stained red. Anna climbed to her feet and massaged her jaw. The crowd seemed divided about her victory as the snow gradually ceased its downfall. There were no calls for her arrest even as she saw six men on horseback approach from an alley. They wore evergreen plated armor with chain mail dyed red underneath. Upon their heads were arrowhead-shaped helmets of metal and below their noses green mouth shields.

"She was attacked," said a woman from behind Anna.

People echoed the woman's words as the armored men drew closer. Anna felt the wind bite at her sealed eye, teasing at the skin holding half her mouth hostage. Her hood flapped open and shut in quick successions where torn.

"You must be the last of the campaigners," said a soldier, a scar split his left eyebrow in two. "It's clear you finished the fight. The tournament begins on the morrow. You may share my horse, or we can summon a carriage to bring you to the Proving."

Anna focused on Ronald for a moment. Lampara had truly changed. Through all Lord William's lessons, facing justice was stressed most. The spectators around her remained divided with some claiming she smuggled the knife within her cloak.

"I will walk," she said. "Time isn't against me at present, and I must find a sense of Cillnar if I am to lead someday."

Silence fell amongst the crowd. Her nerves eased as she drew her gaze from Ronald's lifeless body. She pulled her cloak tight about her person. Snow crackled and the wind howled with each footstep. Anna watched their eyes upon her, pondering as she always did what thoughts ran through the minds of others. After rounding a corner where once a man told of Lord Arthur's achievements, voices rose, breaking the dominance of winter's silence. Were those who witnessed the struggle against Ronald in favor of her now, she wondered.

Anna focused on the directions Nathan had spoken of long

ago. The soreness in her legs grew worse as she avoided icy patches. She blotted out the final realization that laws meant nothing in Cillnar. In Williamton crime was infrequent but handled as it should be. Understanding this, Anna slowed her pace for more time to think. Tension rested its hands on her shoulders, squeezing them, whispering of how it might someday be her duty to restore order. If she won, that is.

Chapter Thirty-Two

Tying off the final cord there was nothing left to do but wait. Norman took in Lady Evelyn's thinking room, unable to imagine a place like it. It possessed smooth polished tile floors and tall, smooth wood columns, topped with the face of Simdorn herself. The hearth was large enough to live within, stocked with wood, the crackling louder than heavy rain against a roof. Across from him the quiet one stood still like a statue, receiving orders from his father who paced back and forth. Norman's nerves felt as raw as they had ever been. Every thought was either on Anna or the rutoe closing in upon the palace. The armor upon his person felt useless despite the bold burning fist upon its breastplate. His father had him wear it should Luther's men find them.

"Be at ease, Norman Tilt," said Lady Evelyn. "You're safe within my husband's house."

She rose from a tall leather-bound chair beside the hearth. Each inch she rose met unbalanced resistance from her quakes. The mistress of duels and debates released a long shuddering breath, clenching her teeth as she regained composure.

"I forfeited my thoughts of being safe once I managed to save Williamton."

"What truly troubles you then?" Lady Evelyn moved slowly to a column where a servant's bell hung. She strained, leaning hard against the column's smooth wood. "Is it the siege about to commence or our—"

Norman dashed to her side. Phillip rose from another chair, catching her at the same point Norman did. They guided her to a chair, the Orderman nudging the table before the hearth away with his foot. The mistress of duels and debates panted as if reaching a final step to a long staircase.

"It's Anna, isn't it?" she said.

"Yes, my lady."

Lady Evelyn Wayne leaned back in the chair, straining to stay up straight.

"I think we both know, Tilt, that girl is just fine," said Phillip, removing his disk helmet and setting it on the table. "If Anna can walk away from a fight with me, then she can get north in time."

"Neither of you were meant to die either way," said Lady Evelyn, finally slumping where she sat. "You're too set on winning, Brother."

Norman's jaw dropped. Phillip smirked as he rose to his feet, shrugging before drawing a long thin cigar from a pouch on his belt. He took his eyes away from the Orderman, casting them on his father. Lady Wayne's servants had given him a shave and haircut. General Huldinarf whispered into the quiet one's ear. A flicker spun across the olive-skinned orderman's eyes. He had been a spy, from what Norman learned. Meant to follow orders to the letter to avoid doubt from the prime.

"I wish I was with her," said Norman, an emptiness forming in his belly. "I care for her deeply and feel useless up in this tower."

He felt Evelyn's hand on his cheek. It was unsteady, warm, but slipping fast. Norman held her hand in both of his. A deep wish for a way to heal her surged. He knew only that family illness was in the blood. Unlike sickness caused by the cold of winter, or the ingestion of poison, it couldn't be stopped except by the end of a family line.

"You're a good man, Norman," she said, as warm tears ran down her cheeks. "I feel my time is near. I'm unfortunately expected at the tournament. The prime will not care what state I am in, in fact, he would enjoy me like this."

Norman thought for a moment, finding her grip almost gone. What raced through his mind sounded risky, and his father needed him should the attack upon the palace fail.

"I will take your place."

Phillip raised an eyebrow. His cigar fell limp from his lips, clicking and rolling across the table.

"You want to do what?"

Rising to full height, Norman rested Lady Evelyn's hand in her lap. His father parted from the quiet one, expressionless for a moment.

"This can work to our advantage," his father said. "The palace resists both wizard and rutoe, but the prime hasn't surfaced to face them. Norman. Doing this will place you close to Luther."

Fear clasped his throat at the sudden realization of what

his father's next words might be. He'd be able to end rutoe banishment in an instant. Norman met his father's eye, a smile forming on the general's thin face. "The law will see me executed by the order of who wins the tournament," Norman said. "If Anna wins, then the duty will be hers."

"That is a chance you must take," said Lady Evelyn. "Either way you will be ridding Lampara of a potential dictator."

"And thus," his father said. "Freeing your people."

Chapter Thirty-Three

⚜

By the time Anna reached the Proving, every one of her senses were on fire. Her head thrummed and her ears rang despite how far the explosions were. Dashing toward the bridge, city folk criss-crossed before it upon horse and on foot. Some pounded on shop doors for refuge while others hid in the carriages lining the street. Anna stopped at the crest of the bridge to catch her breath. The day was near its end as she deciphered that the capital was under attack. Yet with all the time it had taken to reach the Proving, no one outside the city guard appeared armed or dangerous.

She increased her pace once more, noticing the waters below the bridge were solid ice. Ahead soldiers protected the arena, and esants were perched upon the arena's rim, mounted by armored soldiers. Between the fallen a familiar face bundled in furs summoned a smile from her worry as he drew back her hood. Simon Sanderson sat at a table with quill, ink, and parchment. He looked up from scribbling out a name, sighed, and then rose.

"The last to arrive again, Lady Brighton," he said, rotating the parchment to face her. "And without your handsome friend and that storm bison I see."

Anna ignored his second comment, dipping a quill and then signing beside where her name already existed in fine lettering.

"The journey had its share of complications," she said.

"Pity," Simon pursed his lips, rolling up the parchment after pocketing the quill and ink. "My hope was to introduce myself too, what was your friend's name?"

"Norman. Norman Tilt.

"Tilt," said Simon. His voice sounded overly intrigued when saying it. "Follow me, Lady Anna. Tilt? Such a commoner name for someone lacking the features to match it."

Anna decided against asking what Simon meant. She wanted to go in search of Norman, despite the tournament requiring her attention. Anna had never seen the inside of Williamton's prison. It was vast, tucked into a corner beyond the neighborhoods. Swallowing her assumptions, she held onto hope he was still alive. The corridor was lit with more braziers than last time she was here. There was no longer a compulsion to hide her burns.

"I'm told you were attacked," said Simon, unbuttoning his fur collar. "I didn't much like that street slug to begin with."

"I had little choice," said Anna, hiding her lack of surprise at Simon's tone. "It does trouble me that despite being a campaigner I wasn't arrested."

"Arrested?" Simon chuckled, leading her up the stairs they used for the champion's platform. "Had you been the aggressor an arrest would be deemed appropriate. No. Justice isn't gone entirely from Lampara no matter what strange rumors says of our Prime."

Anna raised an eyebrow; suspicion invaded her mind like a rodent in a pantry. Simon turned back to her, unable to peer over his shoulder with the storm bison fur of his coat constricting his neck. "Hope isn't gone from this country yet, my lady."

"I know it isn't, my lord," she said. "I've come to end the strange doings and much more."

The lord smiled.

"I put my faith in you, Anna. You have grown from a shy woman with no wish to help others to someone that understands."

After several flights of stairs, the night sky greeted them, hindered by lit braziers. The arena was full near beyond capacity with tents and ornate pavilions of rich color. The snow began its descent again, and in greater waves of flakes. Anna could faintly hear the explosions of earlier dying down, as if the night and encroaching storm signaled what Lord William called a temporary truce.

"The tournament will begin at morning's first light, my lady," said Simon, a final distant boom made the lord jump in place. "You need not worry about the rutoe within the city. They think Prime Luther is within their grasp, but he's here. And anyway, the rutoe shall be beaten back to the mountains by dragons like they were long ago."

Simon Sanderson cast his hand to the ornate viewing box across the arena. Long rich fabric enclosed the openness it possessed before with a section to its front set with an arrangement of several chairs.

"I shall find an inn to stay the night," said Anna, drawing over her hood. The hole at its side flapped open and closed like lips. Anna ignored it. "Goodnight, Simon."

She made for the stairs, snow crunching underfoot as the dampness met her nose again.

"Slow your pace, my lady," Simon called from over her shoulder. "You already have a place here."

Anna returned to the platform. "What do you mean? I was late as you said."

Simon waved her over the railing, pointing at a large yet modest-looking tent right of the prime's box. She gasped. Above its entrance, illuminated by roaring braziers, hung a banner. Upon it an eight-pointed silver star over a field of red.

* * *

Her mind was in a storm. The immense granite steps under her feet were slick with ice. Wind tousled the tent flaps before her, giving thin glimpses of light. Simon had offered to announce her, but she knew Lord William was an informal man. She could see him through the parting flaps, asleep on several stacked cushions, a lit brazier to either end. He had declared her to no longer be part of the Brighton family. She knew this was true more than by his words, but she still cared for him.

Anna slipped inside, brushing cool snowflakes from her shoulders. Rage was all she felt the last time she had seen him. She had every right to feel that way forever. He was the reason she no longer had parents. A clan. There was still much she didn't know about what she had lost. It made her question at this moment if she had truly lost anything.

Removing her cloak, it was wet and heavy in her hands.

Anna set it aside before slipping her gloves off. Lord Brighton may have taken her past away, but he had raised her from a babe. The lord taught her all he knew under the sigil of the guiding home star. He did the one thing most important in her eye. Lord William Brighton loved her.

"Grandfather," she said, the word both bitter and comforting. "I have come to do what you believed I could."

His thick gray eyebrows twitched. The blanket upon his person rose and fell like a frustrated ocean. Anna remained still, at a distance, the incline of the arena placing her several heads shorter than where her ... grandfather stirred from sleep.

"Anna," he said, releasing a short yawn. "I never expected you to change your mind. I regret all that I've said, all of what I did."

She scaled the small wood steps in front of the cushions, every thought wishing to double back to the anger she had once felt. "I fled from you with so much anger in me. It took ... time, but I overcame my fears."

"Good," said Lord William, opening his arms to embrace her. "I have missed you, sweet girl."

His arms were warm, filled with the same strength she remembered. Anna felt her arms raised to return his kindness but like in all Simdorn's teachings no secrets should be kept between kin. She rested her hands upon his chest, looking deep into his eyes, finding only welcome.

"I missed you too, Grandfather," she said, hesitation snatching at her breath. "I have learned where I come from, and what I am."

The old lord parted from her, descending the wood steps until within an inch of leaving. His head sank into his chest.

"It leaves me with boundless relief then to not have woken with a knife at my throat, or an arrow…" Lord William turned slowly. From his expression he had noticed her bow and quiver were missing. "I made certain your identity remained a secret up until the dragon. I don't know how its fire could alter your appearance outside of burning you."

"Perhaps, I shall learn the truth someday, but" Her stomach loosened its tightness, "my potential past isn't as important as the life you gave me."

"I can see not knowing still troubles you."

"A little," she said, in a whisper. "But I owe so much to you, and not just the life I had. There is a…"

"I can guess of who you speak, sweet girl," said Lord William, placing his hands behind his back. "I think at this time and place we must return your focus to winning the tournament."

"Then I must tell you what I have learned."

Lord William stiffened his chin, strolling toward her. His feet hissed across the bear rug.

"I hope my worst fears haven't come true."

Anna sighed. Her eyes went to the ground for a moment, the wood burning within the braziers smelled of kory. It was something that always calmed her grandfather to a peaceful slumber.

"If one of Luther's sons win the tournament, he will rule through that son as a dictator."

Her grandfather folded his arms for a moment, seeming more bent than usual by it. The wind howled outside, teasing his tent's fabric.

"There must be more to his plan," he said, moving to a small table and pouring wine from a decanter. "We've both met those boys. They are beyond what men of education would call dull. Luther would have no trouble manipulating them. However, that still leaves the council in his way."

"The council knows of his plans."

"How?"

"Eve. I mean Lady Evelyn Wayne."

Cough. Lord William choked, spitting his wine.

"You put your trust in a protector of the prime himself?" He wiped his mouth, slamming his glass on the table. The glass cracked in his grip. "She will tell him what you know of his plan if she hasn't already." He raised an eyebrow, wiping his mouth clean again. "How do you know of his plan?"

Her words caught in her throat for a moment. "I'd rather not say. What is important is we can trust Lady Evelyn. She aided me in learning where I come from."

"I will trust in that then," Lord William said, allowing himself to smile. "Now! It's time we prepare you for the first event, and I know just where to find you a new bow."

* * *

The wind was calm. Calm like herself, which seemed strange as the sun's light met the lip of the Proving. She stood upon its grassy center, the net from last time gone. Tents and pavilions were open, shading viewers from the light fall of snow. Anna felt whole, except for once it didn't mean her face. The wood of her new bow was smooth, its build light, the rest possessed a new device that kept the arrow steady in quick actions. Her grandfather had even purchased arrows of red goose fletching.

A bow placed her in control. The control she felt was most powerful when on hunts. The targets before her and the twenty campaigners upon the field were small, their three rings red, black, and gray. The parchment containing the targets was set against a narrow bale of straw. But what made Anna less relaxed, even feeling the control she had, were the people upon the field around her. They numbered four heads deep, some with children upon their shoulders.

"To prove you care for the lives of your fellow Lampariens," Prime Luther said, speaking through a cone of smooth dark wood. A gold mouthpiece pressed to his lips. "You must fire every arrow in your quiver. Should you miss, the cost will be greater than execution."

Anna refused to look directly upon the prime. Even after ten years, something about him robbed her of the warmth in her blood.

"You must be Anna Brighton," said a voice, light, yet direct in word placement. "My mother told me to wish you luck."

The voice came from her blind side. Anna found it belonged to a girl younger than her with long shoulder length blond locks. Her face possessed high cheekbones and eyes an emerald green. But amongst all that was familiar the sigil upon the fine leathers the woman wore sparked her memory.

"You're Emilia?"

"At your service, my lady," said Emilia, bowing deep. Her bow was of dark wood. From the leather holding tight against her muscles the bows draw strength must have been high. "Or should I say in Lampara's service at this current event."

Prime Luther called from his cone. "Refusal to prove yourselves in this fashion will end in banishment. Show you care for your people. Remain and don't miss."

"He's a mad one," said Emilia, nocking an arrow.

Grass shuffled and snow crunched. Anna readied an arrow,

while five campaigners, three women and two men dropped their bows. Beside them, both towering in muscle and wrapped in furs were the prime's sons. Unter glared at her, elbowing his brother.

"Are you staying, Lady Ugly?" Unter chuckled. His brother whispered in his ear. "My less handsome brother says you'd be better off going for half a coin at a poke and tickle than here."

Strength fled from her fingers. Anna closed her eye as she felt herself wishing to be far away. Her throat went dry, the cold jabbed at her face like a thousand hornet stings. The crowd joined in with Unter's laughter, and soon, all she could feel was shame. *I overcame this,* she thought, *I no longer cared what others think.* Her teeth slammed shut. Her bow fell from her hand.

"Ignore them," said Emilia. "Here. You'll need this to do it." She handed the bow to Anna.

Anna rose to full height, hands shaking, the laughter remaining within her ears like a lone leaf on a tree during the year's harvest phase. *I've come this far.*

"Thank you," Anna took her bow. "Strike true, Emilia."

The gong's great vibration rang throughout the Proving, rattling her senses.

"Last to empty their quiver is a sleepy nutsnatcher." Emilia said.

Poom. Anna gasped. Emilia let her bow arm drop. "You're looking sleepy, Brighton."

Anna nocked and released in quick succession. She kept her eye on the target, and the target alone. Gasps reached out from those behind the targets. A series of cracks told her arrows had soared over the crowd to be blunted against the arena's walls. Faint thuds combined with rushed footwork made Anna guess her opponents were thinning in number. She dared not remove focus. Her arrow count had started at forty, now it was at thirty-five. A giggle graced her ears but again Anna kept focused.

A scream came. It was deep and guttural, followed with pleas for mercy. "Don't execute me, your primness." said one of the campaigners. He fled for the exit, grabbed by the arms once within it. A most unmanly scream trailed a faint slice and clunk.

Anna gulped. The crowd cheered her name, and soon, it was obvious. At her fingertips twenty arrows remained. The target before her possessed no center now. She aimed for the next ring, placing each arrow within a partner.

"And there my people," Prime Luther called out once more. "Is our first-round winner. It's … Emilia Wayne. Wonderful."

Anna let her arm drop, its strength all but gone as the crowd cheered. She peered to where Prime Luther sat. Rising from her seat, Eve waved to Emilia, sneering slightly at Luther. The mistress of duels and debates seemed shorter. Anna blamed it on distance.

"You're swift with that thing," said Emilia.

"Not swift in comparison to you, Lady Wayne."

Emilia shouldered her bow then waved at her mother.

"You need not hide your disappointment," she said. "We have two rounds left, and I hear the old man up there made them to please those two idiots he split seed for."

Both brothers left the arena in a rage. Lampariens in their way parted like frightened birds in an open field as two loud cracks and hard thuds revealed the brothers had split their bows in two. Anna smirked. Neither of them had missed but their arrows were erratically placed.

"I can guess my disappointment isn't so great as theirs," Anna said.

Emilia chuckled. "Now you're learning, Lady Anna. Mother said you lack one thing. Confidence. It appears you've found it."

"Yes," Anna said, heading to retrieve her arrows. "I have."

Chapter Thirty-Four

T he sun was at its highest, although within the Proving such heat expected from the time of day was barely noticeable. Those beside Norman shivered in richly made cloaks, lined with nelka furs of fine quality. Norman strained to keep himself disguised as the mistress of duels and debates. No matter the cold, sweat would not be an issue as he maintained Lady Wayne's elegant features. He let free a small smile. This time Prime Luther would be fooled. Kardanhall's hearths hadn't bothered him. The hearths hadn't lured out a drop of sweat, and thus, without him knowing, Luther had seen past his *Trick of Skin*.

Norman adjusted his posture to keep the long knife in place. Its position rested within a silk holster in his coat. He gently raised his hand to signal the gong-man high above the champion's platform. It puzzled him how Lady Evelyn moved swiftly in what she wore, and for that matter with more than just the one knife he possessed. The gong sent vibrations throughout the Proving. Below the prime's box, immense doors parted, releasing clouds that blotted out the sun in moments. Faint bleating below reminded Norman of only one thing. *Storm Bisons.*

The grassy field rose from among the clouds, long black posts secured an immense net around it, blurring for a moment those upon the field. He let out a faint shudder, understanding the suffering Anna described long ago. Norman didn't know if Cole and Roland remained alive in Kardanhall, but if they did, it was better than here.

"Pardon my concern," said the councilman next to him. "Are you well, Lady Wayne?"

Norman shook his head, finding focus once more. "Whatever do you mean?"

"There was red in your…," The councilman paused with his mouth agape. "Oh, it must have been the sun reflecting off your eyes. My apologies."

"None is needed," said Norman, folding his hands upon his lap. It felt cumbersome to possess long slender fingers, yet he granted himself credit. His father said Norman would be the first rutoe ever to push the *Trick of skin* to greater limits. "I'm excited to see my daughter once again."

The councilman smiled, tugging at his long pointy beard. "When will it be done?"

Norman peered at him over the furs of his high collar, thankful the real Lady Wayne had his blond hair done up with a long pin. "Once Lady Brighton wins, my lord."

Something shattered behind them. Norman turned to find Prime Luther raging at a boy holding a silver tray to his chest like a shield. Wine seeped from shattered remains of a decanter.

"You best hope she does," the councilman whispered.

"We've had this planned for months. Your aim must be at its best. You seem less plagued by your family illness, Lady Wayne."

Returning his eyes to the Proving, Norman heard the boy weeping as ordermen dragged him away.

"I'm managing it better," he said. "Your care is appreciated."

Norman rose. His balance went astray with the thick raised heel of his boots. Bringing himself to match the height of Lady Evelyn had nearly crippled him. He rested both hands on the balustrade. Lying across it was a banner displaying the prime's silver horse shaded in black. Norman shrunk back a bit at an immense shadow. Great leather wings snapped, echoing the arena like a lightning strike. And then the immense shadow landed within the arena with a boom, shaking the arena and rattling Norman to the bone. Heavy lidded almond eyes met his and flashed orange. Scales black as pitch covered the dragon before him as smoke trailed from its nostrils.

Calling out to either Anna or Emilia would end it all. Telling them to move with caution or warn them in any way meant imprisonment or worse. *I wish skin changes came with a change of voice.* he thought, peering over his shoulder at the council in their seats. The council had recently been made aware of him. All they knew was what the real mistress of duels and debates told them.

Norman watched as the twelve to survive the tournament's first round surrounded the dragon. Anna appeared out of place unlike the others, swinging a long spear tip with five sharp prongs. He could sense it was heavy, shaped like a bear's paw, the spear shaft pale and thick. Norman wished his friend had been granted a choice of weapon, but the prime made tournament rules.

The dragon released a torrent of flames at five fleeing campaigners. Their bodies melted against the netting, turning its chains red hot. Anna and Emilia thrusted at the dragon's fat dragging belly. The creature spun and rose on its hind legs, wiping clean in a single swipe another eight campaigners with its tail. Both sons of Luther thrusted their spears into the dragon's chest. It cried out, grabbing for and missing Unter. His brother braced and was knocked across the Proving. He crashed upon the snow, skidding to a halt below the champion's platform.

Norman bit down hard on his lip, tasting blood, skin shifting. Off on the far end of the viewing box Luther pressed himself to the balustrade. His eyes upon Unter dragging his brother away. Norman refocused on his friends, reshaping his face to Evelyn's, comforted in the thought that his words had done good. *Luther does worry for them. He doesn't wish to lose...*

"Unter," Prime Luther shouted. "Finish that blasted dragon. Your brother will keep until later."

A tear ran down Luther's cheek as he said it. Norman watched the Prime pound his fists, searching for his speech cone. Norman refocused on the downed brother to find his immense back heaved. His head shifted in the snow.

"Go, boy," Luther cried, finding his speech cone. "Kill it before you're both eaten."

Norman breathed a sigh of relief. It caught in his throat as he saw Anna and Emilia missing. He scanned the field for them, his vision hindered by the net. Blood streamed from the dragon where their spears had last been, and then he saw them. Heard the crowd cheer their names as the dragon charged at Unter. The prime's son readied his spear as both Anna and Emilia emerged from the chaos, thrusting their spears into the dragon's neck.

With unease, Norman went back to his seat with a hand on his chest. He gasped as his feet tangled in Lady Evelyn's dress, witnessing the dragon cry out and fall silent. Someone with thick, coarse fingers caught him under the arms. Soon, Norman found himself beside the councilman, being asked if he, or in this moment she, were well.

"I am," he said. "I am just grateful for this round to be over."

"Your gonna need to show us that gratitude at dusk, Sister," a voice whispered.

Norman kept his eyes straight, recognizing the crisp voice, the smell of cigar on the breath of who spoke. "I will, Phillip. I…"

And with the same familiar swiftness the orderman was gone.

Chapter Thirty-Five

A nna's cloak smelled of smoke, bits of it had streaks of grass stains from rolling out of the dragon's way. Anna sent it to be cleaned, thinking back to her first cloak resurfaced her fear of fire. That fear was gone for good unlike her strength which clung to her muscles like snow on a low hanging branch. Steam slowly rose from the bath. Its heat and depth removed the ache from the tournament's first two challenges. The bathing room was the exact one she used when trying to remove herself from campaigning. This time benches aligned with every side of the bath, stacked with towels and bathing soaps.

"Nina would enjoy this," said Emilia, sinking deep enough only her face was above the surface. "We've been cramming ourselves into copper tubs at inns and taverns for a year."

Anna kept to the corner of the bath, a lathered washcloth in hand. Emilia was quite beautiful. She was far more adventurous than any woman Anna had ever met. And to have found the one you will love eternal was quite brave. *Have*

I found love eternal with Norman? Anna wanted to believe so, but she was uncertain if the prime had allowed him to live.

"Do you need help with your back?"

"What?" said Anna. "No. I need no help with washing."

"You have no reason to be shy." Emilia rose from the water. It was well below her breasts once she was at full height. She pushed her hair behind her shoulders. "I promise I won't do more than wash. Simdorn says when one is married treat…"

"… a friend as a friend, and your love as your love." Anna finished, smiling as she offered the washcloth. "Take it. You're correct in that I am shy."

Emilia began washing Anna's back. Bubbles surfaced around her chest as her friend plunged the rag beneath the water, gently wiping her lower back.

"My guess is you hunt like myself," said Emilia, tossing the soggy rag on the bath's edge. It plopped and flapped against it, sliding back into the water. "Dammit. I best stick with a bow."

"I do hunt," said Anna, moving to retrieve the rag. "It's all I wanted in life. Now, I must stop the prime's sons from winning. If they do," she bit her lip, "I don't know if I should reveal any more."

Emilia climbed the short steps out of the bath, choosing a towel from the bench before her. "I know his plan, Anna. I envy your freedom to be out in the wild, hunting instead of entertaining those of your class. I'm the daughter of a councilwoman and have even had to mingle with the prime's spawn. Both are dull and river mouthed."

"River mouthed?"

"You may have another phrase for it in the Greethumb region," Emilia said, drying off and applying her leathers.

They were like Anna's except their plating was thicker. "Anyway, both told me the whole plan. I have no idea what the old man will do about the council."

Anna saw what Emilia meant, hoisting herself from the bath, and letting her feet dangle in the water as she dried off. "My grandfather shared a concern like your own. My thoughts lead to assassination, but your mother is an orderman like Phillip."

A faint bell tolling caught both of their attention. Anna dressed swiftly, struggling with her boots.

"We'll have to ponder what remains of the old man's plan another time," said Emilia.

The daughter of the mistress of duels and debates yanked open the door. Anna grabbed her shoulders as Unter charged past the door, cracking his shoulder off the lantern beside it. The lantern clanged, cracking against the brickwork, rolling like a burning wheel into the room. Anna poked her head out as Emilia rescued the sconce from the bath steps.

"I swear to Simdorn," said Anna, "that I heard him cursing his father. Weeping even."

Anna and Emilia went down the hall, following the devastation left by the prime's son. The woman Anna had given her cloak to was being tended to. Blood made a thin red stream from the woman's brow. A small cart filled with straw for campaigners to use in the privy was tossed over and cracked.

"His brother died by my guess," said Emilia, ignoring her wet hair as it clung to her cheeks. "I had a brother once, but our family illness caused my mother to…"

Anna rested her hand in Emilia's. "I have not seen your mother since last I was in the south. How does she fare?"

Emilia held her hand tight, forcing Anna to slow her pace.

Their eyes met, making Anna wish what she saw in Emilia's untrue. Words fled from her mind. Her every nerve felt as if they may ignite with pain. She took Emilia into her arms, hearing the girl's tear drops tap and run down the surface of her leathers. Anna slammed shut her eye, burying her face in Emilia's chest. Another bell tolled, echoing throughout the halls, but this time she didn't allow it to trouble her.

"Wait!" Anna looked up at Emilia, rubbing the snot from her nose. "How can your mother be gone from us if she…?"

"Is at the tournament?" Emilia gasped. She took off at a sprint.

"Wait!" Anna yelled, drawing closer to Emilia. "We cannot go learn who the imposter is now."

"I'm aware," Emilia snapped. "If I have learned a thing from my mother, it's that those who *believe* they're clever always slip up."

"And what shall we do until the imposter does?"

Emilia stopped short of a long narrow hall. Light from the arena reached down it, joined by a faint chilling breeze that nipped at Anna's wet cheeks. She knew what awaited them upon the Proving. It pained her to say the words out loud. All Lampara depended on it and Anna was uncertain she could step out there and face it.

"We fight," said Emilia. "And whoever lives will reveal the truth."

* * *

The nets and posts were gone. Immense braziers large enough for a single man to rest his hut upon, burning bright enough to render the crowd hard to see. Day was gone from the sky, yet Anna knew the time of day wasn't right. She guessed a wizard was involved. But what unsettled her most was Emilia being her opponent. To add even greater danger, Unter too was someone she had to fight. Anna focused on her hands for a moment, her back against the wall, braziers to either side, summoning courage from every part of her.

Across the Proving, Anna met where Unter's eyes led, finding Prime Luther standing at the balcony, hands planted upon the balustrade. To Anna's right she found Emilia for the first time nervous. Her fingers flexed against the arena's brickwork. Her stance made Anna believe the daughter of the mistress of duels and debates may take off for the exit across the way.

Anna peered back at the prime's box. Eve raised a hand from where she sat. The gong went off sending vibrations strong enough to raddle the braziers. She bawled her fists, taking off at sprint for Unter, but the hulking man paid her no mind. He charged like a furious storm bison for his father. The prime's son pounded his wine cask sized fists against one another, seizing the banner hanging from the prime's box. It stretched and tore, so he yanked it, and ripped it in two.

A hard rush hit her side. Anna coughed. She collapsed on her back against the grass. Emilia straddled her, raising a fist.

"I'm sorry," she huffed, her long locks a mess. "I saw it in you from the start." Emilia punched Anna in the face. "You can fight." She cocked her fist back. "You can even ride from what … my mother says."

Anna grabbed her fist, and then yanked, throwing Emilia off balance. She heard a crunch, felt the pressure come faster than her grandfather's esant. Blood seeped from her nose. Anna choked, spitting a glob of blood. Anna focused her good eye, but like lightning Emilia broke free, and struck her square in that eye.

"Please!" Anna cried, seeing only Emilia's outline. "Stop!"

"You know I cannot," Emilia said, striking Anna's sealed eye. "You would do the same. You don't know what I've lost."

Raising and crossing her arms, Anna bent up, blocking each blow, grabbing hold of Emilia's wrists. Anna pushed with all her might, shaking as she grounded her teeth. She tensed her grip against the anger Emilia possessed.

"You're right," Anna said, seething, "about all but one thing. I can govern. I can bring the lessons Simdorn taught us both back to—"

Emilia withdrew her arms, rounded them, then struck at the beginnings of Anna's shoulders. Anna felt her arms drop. She screamed through her teeth to raise them. She found herself falling back, the cheers from beyond rattling her ears. Unter calling for his father to come and face him. A faint voice, familiar in depth, called her name. She watched Emilia cock her fist back, crushing her hopes within it. It was over, but…

Screeeech!

The sound exploded from her lips as Anna cried out her grandfather's name. Emilia flew back, hands clasping her ears. And within an instant the girl who bested her with a bow struck the prime's box. A crack rang out, rendering all within the Proving to silence.

Chapter Thirty-Six

I t didn't matter. Norman felt his skin shift. His hair blackened. Every part of him felt the impact he witnessed. Anna lay at a distance upon her back, calling Emilia's name, twisting, and turning to be upright. He heard the girl he had met long ago fall, but her body found no dirt. No grass doused with snow. Norman stood with Luther against the balustrade, peering over to find Emilia in Unter's arms. There was emotion upon the broken-toothed face of the prime's son. One Norman never expected of a man raised by...

"You!" said Luther, snatching Norman by the collar. "So, Wayne finally met her end. Begin my end game."

Dozens of footsteps filled his ears as he watched Unter bring Emilia to Anna. Norman's eyes flared bright red, feeling Luther scour his coat, then drew the long knife from it. Prime Luther struck Norman across the cheek with the pommel of the knife. The crowd across the Proving seeing Luther accost Norman hissed and demand he be arrested. Ordermen flooded the viewing box as the enchantment above broke off, casting sunlight against the metal of a dozen disk helmets.

"You won't win," said Norman, wincing at the pain in cheek as he ignited both hands. "I will not allow—"

Prime Luther pressed the long knife to Norman's throat, its blade drawing blood. He heard Phillip calling out, trading knife strikes until his fellow ordermen forced him into the hall.

"I have already won you, green rat," Luther chuckled, turning his vision to Unter. "Stop your foolish heroics, Unter. Your dictator commands it."

Over his shoulder, the council protested, falling silent at the hiss of knives being drawn. Norman peered back to find the council in the grip of a dozen ordermen, all of whom possessed the features of quiet ones.

"Do you not know what this man has done to our—"

"They know, Norman Tilt," said Luther, pressing the knife's tip under Norman's jaw. "And they don't give a damn. I've given every rutoe and wizard under my employ their greatest desires."

"Let them go, Father," Unter roared, stomping toward them. "Your son is dead. My brother is … dead."

Luther sneered. His grip loosened. The tip of the knife sent another trickle of blood down Norman's throat.

"You, stupid boy." The prime pushed Norman off. An orderman seized Norman under the arms, drawing him into the shadows as Luther cast his hands up. "It will all be mine once the council is gone. And when I die, you'll get it. And the people will have no choice but to obey."

"Now's your moment to light 'em up, Tilt." Phillip whispered.

Norman felt himself released, taking courage from the words the man he was thought dead. Flames roared from his fists. An ear-piercing scream rang out as a black outline of Luther twisted and turned within the flames. The crowd fled for the nooks along the Proving, disappearing into its immensity. Norman released a gasp, extinguishing his flames. Before him lay a heap of blackened robes and bones.

The quiet ones looked amongst themselves, withdrawing their knives. Amongst those of the council the one with his long white pointed beard adjusted himself. He eyed Norman for a moment and then shrugged.

"You're not one for subtlety," he said, "are you?"

"I used to be," said Norman. "I was an accountant. We are not ones for theatrics."

"Well, you will have no time for practice. Two campaigners remain and one of them will be executing you."

Chapter Thirty-Seven

Her strength had returned. Anna rolled over, enveloped within Unter's shadow. Emilia's chest rose and fell in quick succession as Anna climbed to her knees. The Proving was empty except for those within the prime's box. Footsteps crunched and hissed upon the snowy grass behind her. A pain constricted her stomach to see Emilia twisted and weeping. The daughter of the mistress of duels and debates looked upon her with eyes overrun by pain.

"I... I don't know what that was, Anna." Emilia clenched her teeth as blood ran from the corners of her lips, "but this isn't over. You still got that one."

Unter faced them. His cracked, broken teeth on display as he wiped his barrel sized fist across his eyes.

"I've got no interest in governing. My mum's gone. My brother too. And my father was the only brains I had."

Anna felt a hand to her shoulder. She peered over it to find her grandfather. His eyes were lowered, and his presence brought her some comfort. She rested her hand upon his, all her focus upon Emilia.

"I must put my friend first before I accept your forfeiting, Unter."

Emilia coughed, releasing a raspy laugh. "You have won, Brighton. Bury me with my mother."

"No," Anna cried. "I am not too late this time. Not as I was for Nathan."

"Anna," Lord William said. "What can you do to stop death?"

"I know a wizard, Grandfather. Go and retrieve your—"

"Shut that mouth of yours, Anna," Emilia cried. "Just tell my wife I fought for her, and … that I love her. Tell her I couldn't go on living knowing how cruel I was to…"

A shuddering last breath left the girl Anna had known for so brief a time. Anna wrapped her arms tight about her stomach. It felt as though all she had done was for nothing. She knew Emilia's very being would find her mother's. To die in such a way ensured it. Anna didn't wipe her eye of tears, wanting to live with them for the moment. She rose to full height and gasped at who approached. Norman wore women's clothing, and it became obvious he had used his *Trick of Skin* to impersonate Eve.

"I shall honor Emilia's wish," Anna said, facing her grandfather. "I never listened to your lessons of history, or the politics of our country. What do I do now?"

Lord William sighed. A faint smile crossed his lips for a moment. Perhaps, Anna thought, it was pride for her finally embracing the potential inside of her.

"There will be a ceremony like that of a coronation, except with a medallion," he said, "but that will not be more taxing than your next duty."

"And what duty must I perform?"

"You must… You must execute Norman."

* * *

The sword was heavy in her hands. Heavier than the sword she last held to dual Phillip. Norman's neck was thin enough he could slip free of the pale bear guardian's jaws with ease. She had no wish to stop him. No wish to do what was expected of her. Simdorn's law felt like a dagger to her gut. And if she refused to execute her friend, there would be many questions about her competency as a primnoire. The council would have to vote to see who favored her continued governance of Lampara. If all voted against her, another year of campaigning would be required. And with her true self now in the open the council could only keep the country from civil war between rutoe and human for so long

Her palms were slick with sweat. The Blade of Final Finishes, as the council called it, matched her in height. Its long hilt was of brown leather, worn and rough in her hands. Those within her presence to make certain she followed through were the council and rutoe commanders. Peace had been struck the day she became primnoire, and by her own orders the banishment that had lasted ten long years for both rutoe and wizard alike was ended with a pen stroke.

One of the commanders in the finest armor was Norman's father. General Huldinarf had pleaded his son's case before her once she arose a primnoire at dawn this morning. She listened with tears in her eye, begging Simdorn within her mind for another way, but like every time before, all she heard were the lessons from scripture, and the ones her grandfather had taught her.

"I Anna Brighton, am of sworn duty to bring justice for my predecessor, Prime Luther Brollerfin."

Norman turned his head slowly. His eyes flashed a light red as his lips trembled.

"I love you."

Her grip increased upon the sword's hilt. All of it felt as though she were back at the Proving, still ashamed of her burns. The crowd's presence heightened the nervousness in her chest. Executions were made private for a crime of such magnitude, with the bells to announce when all was done. And for this, Anna found gratitude, but still, the task was no easier.

"I love you, Norman." Anna dropped the sword. "I will accept what fate gives me because of it."

"You know what this will mean," said Norman. "You will be—"

"I am a hunter, Norman." Anna pulled Norman to his feet. She yanked from around her neck Eve's whistle, blew, and within seconds the wall behind her came crashing down. A roaring hiss exploded from the falling rubble as both commanders and council fled. "I think I shall handle banishment well."

She waved his father forward. They climbed Colbwing as his saddle dome opened. The serpent's eyes glowed as the serpent said, "Are you sure of this, Anna?"

"Brian," she said. "I have never been more certain in my whole life."

About the Author

Andrew Johnston is a high fantasy writer from southwestern Pennsylvania. He developed a passion for writing after reading the first A Song of Ice and Fire book and hasn't stopped writing since. He enjoys studying history and reviewing books for his fellow creatives when not writing. Primnoire is his debut novel.

Milton Keynes UK
Ingram Content Group UK Ltd.
UKHW010845280324
440101UK00001B/19

9 798869 193698